EARNING HER TRUST

BRAXTON ARCADE BOOK ONE

ADORE IAN

WARNING: Adore's books contain too much smut, ridiculous plots and are written for a twenty-first century audience. This book contains a strong female lead with a fainting problem and a creepy stalker, a hot alpha male, and lots and lots of sexy times.

To everyone who never learned the difference between the vulva and vagina.

PART I

PLAYER SELECT

FEMME FATALE
or
PANTY-READING FORTUNE TELLER

1
_____

Damian

I hate everything about this club. It smells awful, the music sucks, and the laser light show is trying to give me a seizure. I would've left hours ago had it not been for Marrin Braxton—who's currently grinding her ass all over some random bro on the dance floor. She's wearing a short black dress and the leather jacket I like best on the floor of my apartment.

But this isn't my apartment.

So I take another sip of beer and act like I don't care.

It's my friend Vicky's birthday and she decided she wanted to spend the evening dancing until some ungodly hour to some ungodly music. So here I am, holding up the bar with my best dudes Jayce and Hayden—who both look about as over this place as I am.

At least I'm not suffering alone.

I glance at Marrin just in time to see Mr. Frat House Douchebag run his hands up her bare thighs. Fighting the urge to break each and every one of his fingers, I remind my inner alpha male that Marrin is not my girlfriend and I am not her boyfriend.

I also remind myself that no one in our group of friends knows we've been sleeping together.

Vicky would freak if she knew. When she started dating Jayce, she announced to his friends that hers were off limits. I'm no stranger to this rule. Hayden and I have been friends with Vicky since high school, and after I ruined one of her friendships with a casual hookup, she set the boundary. I've respected it ever since.

Well, until recently.

My eyes slide back to Marrin. She taps our friend Devon's shoulder and hitches a thumb at the douchebag with his hands all over her. Devon nods then swings her around so fast the dude pawing at her nearly falls over. An effective cockblock if I ever saw one. I make a mental note to buy Devon a beer.

Mr. Frat House Douchebag takes the hint and moseys along to find someone else to grope.

Bye, asshole.

Marrin goes back to dancing with Tiana and Vicky, and I sure as shit can't complain about the view now. She's a fantastic dancer. I pull out my phone and shoot her a text.

Damian: *How come you never dance that way for me?*

About a month ago, I ran into Marrin at the arcade bar where she works. We'd hung out in groups but never really had the opportunity to talk. We'd had a great conversation and the night ended in my bed. It was only when she'd refused to sleep over that I'd realized she lived in my apartment building. She'd just signed a lease for a place right down the hall. Apparently, I'd been "*elbows deep in some redhead*" and hadn't noticed her moving in. Her words, not mine.

Of course I hadn't tried to deny it. I need no help with the ladies. I'm handsome, rich, and gifted with the kind of soulful eyes every person, pet, and vegetable dreams of getting lost in. Not a brag, just the truth. A truth that's made its way around campus and built me a nice reputation.

A reputation that was perfect until the night Marrin Braxton found her way into my bed and then refused to stay over.

I know for a fact I'm a fantastic lover—again, not a brag, just the truth. And it's exactly what I'd been thinking a month ago when Marrin climbed out of my bed.

"*Stay,*" I'd said.

She'd looked at me as if to say, *How cute*, before heading to the door.

I'd never chased a woman before, but damn if she hadn't become the first. I'd jumped out of bed like a Golden Retriever after its owner and followed her into the living room where I then offered to make her breakfast in the morning. I straight up tried to bribe her back into my bed with waffles and omelets. Who does that?

Me, apparently.

Until that moment, no woman had ever denied me the pleasure of making her breakfast the next morning or seeing her home. That just didn't happen.

Women who stay the night in my bed know they're in for three things: multiple orgasms, no strings attached, and the best morning after ever.

Apparently, Marrin hadn't gotten the memo, because while I'd stood there buck naked in my own living room, waxing poetic about waffles and omelets (like some street vendor peddling my wares), she'd looked over her shoulder and said, "*That's so sweet. Maybe another time.*"

Then she'd left.

And I'd had no idea whether to be offended or impressed.

The music in the club switches to some new techno horror. Marrin pulls her phone out, looks at the screen, then stuffs it back into her pocket.

Did she just ignore my text?

This woman is going to drive me insane.

When Marrin had refused to stay the night that first time, I'd gone over to her apartment the next morning and made her breakfast. Stupid, maybe, but I have a reputation to uphold. We'd had a nice morning that had led to my face between her legs and ended with me dumbfounded when she'd gotten dressed and left for work.

She'd just walked out.

Even had the audacity to tell me to lock the door on my way out.

In less than nine hours, the same woman had walked away from me—*twice.*

It was as if she'd declared war.

The next weekend, we'd run into one another at a party I'd gone to with Jayce and Hayden. I'd honestly tried to stay away from her because Vicky was there with Jayce, and Marrin is technically one of her friends. I'd kept our conversation casual and made a point to be polite to the other women who'd been talking to me.

Marrin hadn't even batted an eyelash.

But almost as soon as Jayce and Vicky had left the party, I'd once again found myself dick deep in Marrin's skirt. We'd barely made it to my Jeep before I was inside her.

Fucked. I was well and truly fucked. I couldn't get enough of this woman.

We'd exchanged numbers that night and had agreed we'd only see one another for sex—good, kinky sex—an arrangement that'd been working nicely for me until tonight, when I'd looked up to see some douchebag pawing at her. The dress she'd chosen to wear, and the ample amount of cleavage bursting through the plunging neckline, aren't exactly helping. I've been sporting a quarter chub since I walked in.

I pull out my phone and send another text.

Damian: *You're killin' me, baby. Grindin' that sweet ass all over your girlfriends. How about you follow me outside and grind that ass on me?*

I don't normally talk like this. Actually, Marrin is the only person I talk to like this. She made it clear that if we were going to start sleeping together, she wanted certain things from our encounters—or *scenes* as she calls them. Specifically: me being dominant, demanding, and bossy. Her words, not mine.

Marrin checks her phone, rolls her eyes.

Marrin: *In your dreams. Too many witnesses. Why don't you entertain the blonde eyeing you at the bar?*
Damian: *Not interested. I only got eyes for you, babe.*
Marrin: *Ha! Well you're not the only one.*
Damian: *I wanted to kick that guy's ass.*
Marrin: *Why?*

I don't know why. We aren't dating. I have no claim to her. *Because that douchebag was pawing at you like some animal,* I want to text. *Because he shouldn't have had his hands on you in the first place. Because I was jealous.* I take another sip of beer and go with:

Damian: *He was sloppy. An embarrassment to guys everywhere. If those had been my hands, you'd be beggin' me to take you outside. Your panties would be soaked.*
Marrin: *How do you know I'm even wearing panties?*

My dick twitches and I have to turn around and face the bar before the whole club sees the tent I'm pitching.

Jayce knocks back the last of his beer. "Another round boys?"

"Always," Hayden and I reply.

While Jayce orders more beer, I turn to Hayden, desperate to think of anything but the possibility that Marrin is bare beneath her short dress. "Not to be a dick, but who've you been texting all night?" From the moment we walked in, Hayden has been on and off his phone.

He fidgets and both Jayce and I turn our full attention to him.

He sighs, defeated. "Who do you think?"

Hayden is the stereotypical southern gentleman. He grew up on a farm (in what I'd consider to be the middle of nowhere), he studies sports medicine, and his views on dating are painfully mid-century. Meaning he pays for dinner, gets the door, and there's no kissing on the first date. Then there's Jayce. He grew up traveling the world with his parents, he studies art, and his views on dating are firmly grounded in the twenty-first century. Meaning his date can buy him dinner, get his door, and kiss him on the first date.

"Jesus, dude," Jayce says. "You've been after this Sasha girl all semester."

I hold up a finger. "Correction. He's been acting like her lap dog all semester. Not the same thing."

Jayce agrees, clinking his beer glass with mine.

My phone vibrates in my pocket.

"I have not," Hayden grumbles.

Jayce says, "Have you made a move yet?"

"Of course."

I make a sound like a game show buzzer for a wrong answer. "You carry her books and organize her study notes. Not moves, dude. Have you even asked if she's seeing anyone?"

His white skin flushes with embarrassment. "Pffft —*yeah*. Of course I have."

A total lie.

"Have what?" Vicky says, shoving between us and throwing her arms around Jayce. I straighten and casually look for Marrin—but I don't have to. She squeezes between Vicky and I, rubbing her tits along my arm as if she's just *innocently* trying to get the bartender's attention. Damn if my dick doesn't grow three sizes.

Remembering my phone, I pull it out and glance at the screen.

Marrin: *Unzip your left jacket pocket.*

I obey the text then pivot toward Marrin so we're pressed together from thigh to chest and—*holy shit*—I've never been so glad to be in a crowded club in all my life. The view of her tits is amazing. They're soft, round, and just begging for me to let them out of that restrictive red push-up bra, which I can totally see from my vantage point. Her white skin glistens with a sheen of sweat that catches the many laser lights, reflecting the colors like glitter.

She looks down the bar and the top of her high ponytail brushes my mouth. It smells like citrus and I know she's rubbing it in my face on purpose because she knows how much I love her hair. It's that trendy silver-white all the girls are doing. It's soft and long and shiny, like liquid starlight...

Jesus. I'm drooling over a woman's hair. What the fuck's wrong with me?

"Can I get a bottled water?" Marrin shouts. I press my stiff cock against her hip and don't miss the bob of her throat or the too-deep breath she takes trying to calm herself.

Fuck. Yes.

The bartender returns with her water but before she can pay, I tell him to put it on my tab. I lean in close and whisper, "Left pocket's open, babe."

Heat glosses her eyes and she smirks, taking the most inappropriate sip of water I've ever seen in my life.

"Down, Damian," a slightly inebriated Vicky shouts from behind Marrin. "You're not allowed to be this close to my friends."

I put my hands up. "Only buying the lady a water."

Vicky's eyes narrow. "If you said something inappropriate to her, I'll kick your ass."

She probably couldn't kick my ass, but I'm not willing to find out. She's like a scary Shirley Temple—all golden, curly, and angelic, until you piss her off and discover she's got a mouth like a hardened criminal.

"It's fine," Marrin sighs. "I've heard worse from better." She gives me a disinterested once over then links arms with Vicky. "I have to pee."

They walk away.

Hayden leans in. "Brutal."

I try not to bristle. "Please, she only looked at me like

that because she knows she can't have me. Vicky's rule, remember? I'm sure it applies to the girls as much as it does us."

"That rule doesn't apply to me, dude. Vicky only acts like it does so it won't hurt your feelings."

I turn to Jayce.

"Don't look at me," he says. "You're the one who fucked his way through her friends in high school and never called them back."

"It was one friend," I protest. "*One*. And I made it clear it was just a hookup. Not my fault the girl caught feelings."

"Whatever the reason," Jayce says, "you don't want to get involved with Marrin."

I frown. "Why?"

Hayden leans in. "I heard she put a guy in the hospital last year."

Whoa, what?

Jayce nods just as the laser lights above us shift, tinting his dark brown skin in an eerie shade of yellow. "I don't know exactly, but I think her family is kind of weird. She and Vicky were roommates freshman year. Vicky said one day she walked into their dorm and Marrin's cousin was there. You know Alice Braxton—hot blonde who owns the bar?" Hayden and I both nod. "She'd packed up Marrin's things and told Vicky that Mar had some family stuff to take care of and wouldn't be back or something. I don't know."

"What do you mean you don't know?" I say, trying not to seem too curious.

"I mean, I don't know. When she came back the following semester, she had a waiver to live off campus. And there was this one time..."

I stare at him. Then flourish my hand. "*There was this one time...*"

"I don't know, dude," Jayce says. "She moves a lot. One time Vicky asked me to help move her into a new apartment in the middle of the night. It was weird."

I know that look. The one Jayce is giving me—he's hiding something. But before I can ask what, Vicky and Marrin return.

Vicky throws her arms around Jayce and the two start making out. Marrin brushes against me just as I tell them, "Get a room." A request they both answer by flipping me off.

I look for Mar and find her dancing with Tiana. My phone vibrates.

Marrin: *Left pocket.*

I move my hand to my jacket pocket and find it zipped. Clamping down on my excitement, I discreetly unzip it, slipping my hand inside. *Jesus H. Christ.* My fingertips brush silky, lacy fabric.

Marrin's panties.

They're still warm.

All the blood in my body rushes to my dick, and once again, I have to turn around and face the bar to hide the evidence. She must've taken them off in the bathroom. They're folded into a tiny square, and as I run my fingers over the fabric—*holy shit*—I find a damp spot.

Clenching my jaw, I rip my hand away, trying to think of anything but the fact that Marrin's wet panties are in my pocket. That Marrin's *bare* pussy is just one wardrobe malfunction away.

Drowning puppies. Pat Sajak. Vomit. Jayce and Vicky making out—

That does the trick.

"Are you all right?" Vicky asks, finally disconnecting from Jayce's mouth like Neo waking up in *The Matrix*.

"Peachy." I glare at Marrin.

Damian: *Look at me.*

She checks her phone and looks up. I make a show of sniffing the fingers of my left hand. Her lips part and she stares at me for entirely too long.

I smirk in a way that lets her know I'm ready for a scene.

Damian: *You want me, babe. Quit torturing us both.*
Damian: *I've been hard for you all night. And now I know that pretty pussy is drippin' for me, I gotta get it in my mouth.*
Marrin: *Where, Sir?*
Damian: *Second floor. Last bathroom. I'll leave first.*

She nods from across the dance floor, and I can see the lust addling her senses. Jesus, she isn't wearing underwear. Maybe I should've let her go first so I could follow her up the stairs?

My cock twitches. Bad idea.

I close my tab, say goodbye, then make up some excuse about having to piss and how the bathrooms on the second floor are the cleanest and least crowded (which is true).

I take the stairs two at a time then make my way to the far end of the building where the bathroom the club reserves for VIPs and guest DJs is located. It's a one-stall deal with mood lighting, a large marble countertop and a floor-length mirror. It's completely empty when I walk in. I wash my hands (because I want to give Marrin an orgasm not an infection) and pull out her panties. They're red silk.

Of course they are.

I bring them to my nose and inhale deeply. Fuck, they smell good. Like something sweet, the tang of sweat, and whatever detergent she uses to wash her clothes.

The door pushes open and I give myself one second to devour the sight of Marrin before I pounce.

I shove her panties into my pocket, and in two strides, I have her pinned against the door, legs around my waist. She locks us in as I force my tongue past her lips, taking her mouth. God, she tastes better than anything I've ever had in my life. Like Christmas morning, a snow day in school, New Year's Eve. It's visceral and all consuming.

Her skin is smooth and slightly sweaty as I run my hands over her thighs, pushing up her dress to grip her generous backside. "This ass has been driving me crazy all night."

She responds by slipping her tongue into my mouth, and I retaliate by sliding my fingers between her legs. I brush along her opening, finding it drenched and throbbing.

"Please, Sir," she gasps, biting my lip incredibly hard.

Regardless of where we're playing on the dom/sub spectrum, I love it when she calls me Sir. So I reward her by sinking a fingertip into her core then circling the rim. Her head tilts back and she moves on me as best she can. We do this for a bit then in one swift motion, I drop her legs to the floor, grab the shoulders of her dress—bra straps included—and pull both down to her waist.

Surprise, arousal, and protest flash across her face as her breasts spill into the room.

I bend down and suck a perfect, swollen nipple into my mouth, pinching the opposite one hard, then pulling.

"Oh God," she moans, trying to free her arms of the

straps and sleeves trapping them at her sides. She wriggles out of her jacket, but I grip her wrists, pinning them to her sides before she can be free of her sleeves.

I don't move.

Just brazenly watch her bare breasts rise and fall in front of me. She's completely at my mercy.

I force a knee between her legs and claim her mouth. My kiss is brutal and objectifying and owning—just how I know she likes it.

She whimpers and rubs herself against me, desperate for my attention. I know she needs more. Know she's lost to her lust and drunk off my touch. This is how I like Marrin best: pliable, compliant, and wanting.

So I give her the Damian she likes best.

"You don't get to have your hands," I say into her mouth, grinding myself against her. "You've had enough fun torturing me tonight." She bites my lip *hard*. I growl, pinning her harder with my body. "Do you think I liked watching you grind your ass on some other guy? Think I liked it when you stuffed your soaking wet panties into my pocket? Did you think I wouldn't come to get what's mine?" I thrust a proprietary finger into her pussy and she groans so loud I'm surprised no one bangs on the door in response.

"Oh God, keep talking."

I chuckle darkly.

"This," I curl my finger and rub it over the spot that drives her crazy, "is mine."

Her whole body shivers and she nods, meeting my eyes as if to say, *Yes, this is yours.*

I pull back and kneel before her.

"Oh fuck," she breathes, watching through heavy eyelids as I lift the hem of her dress and press my nose into her curls. I inhale deeply.

"I've been thinking about this wet little pussy all night. If I don't get it in my mouth, I'm gonna go crazy."

I order her to hold up the hem of her dress. She obeys. I lick once then spread her flesh with my thumbs, getting a good look at her engorged clit before sucking it into my mouth.

She gasps—the song of the instrument I'm playing.

I suck her soft, swollen clit like it's the tip of a chocolate covered strawberry. It's smooth and velvety, and when I gently pull it through my teeth, Marrin's knees buckle so badly she nearly falls onto my face.

That's it, baby. Feel good for me.

I suck and kiss and massage that aching bundle of nerves until she goes off like a rocket. She curses, grinding on me as she comes into my mouth. I lick her clean, careful not to penetrate her, then stand. As I do, I pick her up, hooking her knees over my elbows. She's boneless and limp in my arms, but when I press her into the door, grinding my cock against her center, she comes alive again.

She shimmies her arms free of her dress and reaches between us to unzip my pants. A warm hand wraps my cock as she pulls me out and strokes.

Now it's my turn to moan.

"Back pocket, baby," I rasp. She reaches around, grabbing the condom I keep in my wallet. She rolls it on and lines us up.

I take over, pushing into her.

"*Fuck*," I exhale into her neck. "This pussy is hungry for me."

It's true. My cock is above average in size, usually I have to use lube to make sure my partners are comfortable during sex. But right now, Marrin is so turned on, I slide right in without having to worry about hurting her. Not that she'd mind if I did hurt her because, as I've learned, she's sort of into that.

But I'm not an asshole, so I ask if she's comfortable and if she needs anything. To which she responds, "Just fuck me."

One order of 'just fuck me' coming right up.

I thrust to hilt then slide out before thrusting deep again. "God this pussy is tight, Mar."

She groans into my mouth and starts sucking on my tongue. I don't know what it is, but being inside her in two places does wicked things to my inner alpha male and he comes out in full force, compelling me to take what she's offering.

I push off the door, stepping into the room. "Sit back," I command. She obeys, hands locked behind my neck. I lean back too and start pumping into her, watching her tits bounce with the movement.

"I've been thinking about you all day, Sir," she moans, silver-white hair swinging behind her.

"Yeah? What'd you think about?" I slow my thrusts.

"You. Your big cock. This." She wiggles her hips, trying to get me to speed up.

"Did you touch yourself?"

She nods and I almost come right then.

"How many times, Mar? How many times did you stroke this sweet little pussy thinking about my big cock?" I brace her against the door and hook one of her legs up on my shoulder so I can bring a hand between her legs. I brush my thumb over her clit, still thrusting into her entirely too slowly.

"Oh God," she moans. "Twice. Damian. Twice." She grinds into my thumb. I take it away.

I'm not sure why, but I say, "I didn't like seeing that guy's hands all over you. I don't want you sleeping with other guys. I won't fuck other women." I punctuate the words with the hard thrusts we're both dying for while simultaneously pinching her clit. She cries out in want and frustration, but somewhere in the haze of her pleasure, I see my words strike home. See her understand this isn't part of the scene.

"You're not my boyfriend," she breathes. "But we can be exclusive until one of us gets bored."

Fuck, yeah.

I give her what she wants—I fuck her hard, fast and to the hilt. Her inner muscles clench, contracting around my cock. I bite the inside of one of her breasts, leaving a mark.

She gasps. "So good."

My own pleasure builds and builds.

"Oh fuck, I'm gonna come." She's staring at the floor length mirror beside us—watching me take her. For a moment, I watch too. Watch her bouncing breasts, my thrusting hips, her hand rubbing her clit.

I grip her chin. "Eyes on me, Mar. I wanna see the face you make when you come for me." Heat floods her eyes and slicks her pussy. I groan.

She likes me like this. In control. Bossy. She told me the first time we had sex that she got off on being dominated in the bedroom, on feeling owned, used. It's her kink and it's why we make good fuck buddies. I like being in control in the bedroom. (That's been my kink ever since I accidentally stumbled upon a late night porn channel when I was eleven years old.) But it also gives me confidence, makes me feel powerful, respected.

Shocker, right? Why would a guy like me need a confidence boost?

You know what they say, if you have to advertise...

I'm still gripping her chin when I demand, "Say my name when you come. I wanna hear it."

"Yes, Sir."

Her moans fill the room, my senses. I'm not gonna last. Not as her inner muscles start clamping down on my cock.

"Come for me, Marrin. Right now."

She does.

Spasming and writhing and half screaming as pleasure sweeps her away. The feel of her body squeezing around me, milking my cock—*oh fuck oh fuck oh fuck*—is my undoing. I come hard and hot and thickly inside her, thrusting to new depths and groaning her name as I fuck to completion.

When it's over, I set her down on the counter and close my lips over hers sweetly. We're both breathless and spent, but I'm smiling like an idiot. I want nothing more than to take her home and tuck her into my bed. But I know she'll never go for that. So I steal what affection I can while she's pliant and delirious, basking in the remnants of her orgasm.

Then I slip out of her.

Once the connection is broken, that's it. We clean ourselves up, she makes sure to pee then asks for her panties back.

She shimmies into them and I deposit the memory into my spank bank for a rainy day.

I pause at the door. "I meant what I said. I won't sleep with other women if you don't sleep with other guys."

She glares. "I meant what I said, too. Just because we're exclusively sleeping together doesn't make you my boyfriend."

"Fine."

"Fine."

I open the door and we go our separate ways.

Until we reach the parking lot of our apartment complex.

Where we both happen to be getting out of our vehicles at the same time.

I key in the building code and hold open the door for her. We pass the security guard in the lobby and share the elevator. When the door slides open on our floor, she goes left and I go right.

I watch her slip into her apartment alone, waiting until I hear the slide of locks before entering my own.

I have no idea why I feel so possessive, so protective over her.

The feeling follows me all the way to the bathroom where I strip down and jump into the shower. I hate that I'm washing her off me, but I stink like bad techno club.

I soap up thinking about what Jayce said. Thinking about why Mar would move in the middle of the night, and why she might choose to live in this particular complex. It's one of the most expensive in the area and has very few university students living in it. It mostly houses young professionals who commute into the city each day.

It's also one of the safest.

I climb into bed and decide I'll just have to find out who Marrin Braxton really is.

And that starts with earning her trust.

2

Damian

By the third knock, I'm ninety-five percent sure she's not going to answer.

I knock again anyway.

There's a scrape of sliding locks then Marrin hauls open her apartment door wearing an oversized T-shirt and looking about ready to murder me.

"Damian Wane, it's eight o'clock on a Saturday morning. Why the hell are you banging on my door?"

I smile, holding up a grocery bag. "I brought breakfast."

"I'm sleeping."

"You look pretty awake to me." She opens her mouth, but I add, "You also look pretty hungry and wouldn't it be nice if the handsome man you're *exclusively* sleeping with made you breakfast?"

"You don't have to buy me, Damian. I already agreed to only smash you."

I frown. "This isn't about buying you, it's about taking care of you."

"I don't need or want you to take care of me." But she

steps aside.

She follows me into her kitchen where I set down the grocery bag. I face her, leaning against the oven. "You didn't seem to have a problem with me taking care of you last night."

She narrows her whiskey-gold eyes but a lovely, distracting blush blooms over her chest and neck.

I turn back to the stove. "That's what I thought."

I make myself at home in her kitchen. She disappears onto her bedroom, which I note has a lock on it, returning a moment later wearing pajama pants. She slumps into a barstool across the counter from me.

"Why are you awake this early?" she says.

"I have to work."

"You have a job?" she says incredulously.

"Of course I have a job, don't you?"

"Yeah, but aren't you rich? I mean you *can* afford to live here." She motions to the building.

"*You* live here." I hand her a cup of coffee. "And you still have a job."

"Because I'm not rich. I have several jobs so I can make rent on time."

I crack a few eggs and pour them into a frying pan. "Why not just live someplace cheaper?" I don't miss the wary look that flashes across her face.

She covers it up with a shrug. "I like it here."

"What about this place do you like?" I ask as casually as possible. What I really want to know is why she moves around so much, but something about the way Jayce brought it up last night makes me think it's not something I should ask.

Another shrug. "It's fancy."

"Ah, so you're a woman who likes fancy things."

"Not really."

Not really, indeed.

Her apartment is nice, but it lacks any real personal touches. There's a couch and a rug and a TV, but that's it. No pictures on the walls, no posters, no funny refrigerator magnets. It's not minimalist. It's just... empty.

"I can tell." I flip the first omelet, feeling her watching me.

"What do you *really* want to know, Damian?"

"You. Your likes, dislikes. Friend stuff."

"Are we friends?"

I give her a bedroom smile. "With benefits." I wink.

She snorts into her coffee.

I don't press for any more information. Clearly, she's private. The last thing I want to do is scare her off. We spend the rest of the morning eating and talking about classes and TV shows. A quarter till ten, I get up and leave for work.

Technically, I have a job. That wasn't a lie. The thing is, I don't get paid. I volunteer, helping teach a self-defense class.

At the campus rec, I change in the locker room then head to the small gymnasium where we hold class. Holly is already there setting up the mats.

Holly is a master's student at the university but started teaching self-defense on campus her freshman year. She's kind of my hero. She's a strong Black woman with a mountain of dark curls atop her head, and a fierce love of all things self-defense.

"Mornin', Hollywood," I say, calling her by her nickname. I help her with the mat she's laying down. "What's up?"

"Not a lot. You get my email about Jessica?"

"Yeah. Honestly, I'm not surprised. She had all the signs."

The women who show up for the self-defense class range from workout enthusiasts to victims of muggings and assaults. As instructors, we get training on how to identify behaviors and deal with people who've been assaulted. The last thing we want to do is retraumatize someone. After helping teach this class a few years, I've gotten good at spotting the warning signs.

Regardless of whether or not a student shows any outward indicators of anxiety or discomfort, we treat everyone with the same respect and mindfulness. Everything we do as instructors starts with a conversation about boundaries before we touch a student and that conversation continues throughout our contact with them.

Consent is a big part of this course. Holly designed it that way. We spend a chunk of each class roleplaying consent in various situations because, as Holly says, "*We need to stop thinking about consent as a one time yes-or-no agreement that happens before sexual activity. Consent is an ongoing, active conversation that applies anywhere at any time.*"

It can also change at any time and relies on all parties to be aware of themselves and others. Holly's a big believer in roleplaying consent and so am I. Two people can have two wildly different ideas about what it means, and if they're not on the same page, it can have devastating, life-altering consequences.

"I'm going to pair her with me and Jada today," Holly says. Jada Marks is the Chief of Campus Police and the official sponsor of Holly's program. "If she wants to try anything with you or Vinny, I'm gonna suggest letting Vinny work with her first."

"Roger that."

Vinny is the other student instructor. He's built long and lean, so he's less physically intimidating than I am. He's also funny as hell and that helps put people at ease.

The students start trickling in, and by the time we get the room set up, class is ready to start.

We split into groups and go over everything we learned last week. Then Holly starts talking about new material.

"Today we're learning about chokeholds," Holly says. "There are different ways an assailant can put you in a chokehold—all of which we'll go over. But one of the most important things to remember is to tuck your chin. Tucking your chin to your chest before anyone can get an arm around your neck will protect your airway and help buy you time to get away."

She goes on a bit more before asking me to help demonstrate. We verbally establish consent then I come up behind her and wrap an arm around her neck.

"When I don't tuck my chin," Holly says, "Damian has a lot more control over the situation doesn't he?"

The students nod and agree.

"I'm also a lot more prone to panicking because I can't breathe. I can still get out of the chokehold if my chin isn't tucked, but every little thing we can do to prevent ourselves from panicking is going to help."

We spend the rest of class going over different holds, and when we're done for the day, I stay behind and spar with Holly. By the end of an hour I'm sweaty and gross and in desperate need of a shower. I'm also in desperate need of Marrin.

Marrin

At five o'clock on Sunday night, I head into work.

I'm a bartender at my cousin Alice's bar, the Braxton Arcade. It's a vintage arcade bar dedicated to all things nerd.

The bar top is a collage of carefully pieced together comic book clippings set with epoxy to give it a smooth, glossy finish. The display case behind the bar holds everything from Gundam figurines to a signed copy of the first *Pretty Deadly* comic book, to an actual piece of Hal from Stanley Kubrick's *2001: A Space Odyssey*. Displayed along the walls are rare Mondo prints and cult classic movie posters. My favorite is a replica of an original poster from the film *Double Indemnity*. It's probably my favorite film, not just because Barbara Stanwyck is a goddess, but her character, Phyllis Dietrichson, is a badass femme fatale who knew her only way out of a shit marriage was to manipulate the hapless Walter Neff. She played the cards the patriarchy dealt her. Can't fault a girl for that.

The film also helped inspire our newest themed night: Film Noir Thursday.

Themed nights are big at the bar and none during the school year is more well-attended than Sunday night when we play *The Walking Dead* on the projector. It's a popular event in this college town.

Tonight I'm working with Elle and Conor. Conor's carding at the door and Elle's at the bar with me.

Elle is short with dark eyes and long dark hair. She's a good bartender who tends to keep to herself, but there's something about her, like she's always watching or alert. Like a rabbit maybe.

If Elle is a cute woodland creature, then Conor is a scary-as-hell junkyard dog. His physical prowess does the talking for him. He's large, corded with muscle and has a few well-placed tattoos inked across his bronze skin. On any given night, he's sporting an array of bruises on his face. I'm not stupid enough to ask how he gets them. Unlike Elle and I, Conor is not a student. He's a few years older and works full time for Alice wherever she needs him.

For a few hours, everything goes smoothly. Then at about half past eight, over two hundred pounds of blond-haired blue-eyed trouble walks in. Jake. He's tall, muscled and tattooed.

Jake grew up in the same inner-city neighborhood as me, but unlike me, he never made it out. He dropped out of high school and started working construction. He's good at what he does, but he runs with a rough crowd. He's been in and out of trouble for years, and as much as I hate to admit it, he's kind of a friend. We dated in high school, and although he's now as sleazy as they come, he wasn't back then. I suppose he was technically my first love.

He takes a seat at the bar. "Hello ladies."

Elle's deep gold skin heats with a thread of irritation. She frowns at me as if to say, *Are you going to get rid of him or should I?*

"I got it," I whisper, switching sides of the bar with her. "Hey, Jake. You want the usual?" I reach for a bottle of whiskey.

"You always knew me better than anyone." He eyes me up and down and I fight the urge to projectile vomit.

I never wear super revealing clothing to work, but I do try to look sexy. It brings in tips. Tonight I have on high-waisted jeans paired with a black tank that's cropped to reveal a few inches of midriff. And of course, I'm wearing a push-up bra.

I pour Jake a double and set it on the bar. He smells like booze and cheap cigarettes.

"Keep it open?" I ask, taking his credit card.

Please say no.

"Yes." And from the way he slurs and the flush staining his white cheeks, I can already tell he's drunk.

Fan-fucking-tastic.

I hate when he comes in here to get drunk—or more drunk in this case. He usually gets obstinate, usually leers at the female customers, and I always feel as if it's somehow *my* responsibility to make sure he gets home okay. I know I don't owe him anything. We haven't been *friend* friends in years. But still...

He was the only one who came to help me that night two years ago. The only one in that shit neighborhood who'd cared that I was screaming—

I don't want to think about it. Don't want to think about why I feel like I owe him.

Lucky for me, the bar begins to fill with locals and students coming in to watch *The Walking Dead*, and we get so busy I can't think about anything other than bartending.

I mix a soda and vodka, not bothering to look up at the next customer before asking for their order.

"I don't know, what's good?" purrs a familiar voice.

I hand over the mixed drink then look up to see Damian. He's smiling in that charming way of his, and my stomach does a backflip. Why? Because that smile is now reserved for me. And I know that makes no sense because I don't want a boyfriend. The absolute last thing I need is a boyfriend complicating my already complicated life. But damn if the idea of a little normalcy doesn't give me butterflies.

Ugh. Marrin. Stop. You can take care of yourself. You've been doing it for years.

I catch myself, remembering where I am. All my friends

are standing right behind Damian, and Jake is perched five feet down the bar.

I school my features and take his credit card. "What are you in the mood for?"

Vicky shoves past him. "Because Dame is buying, I'll have whatever beer on tap doesn't objectify women in their advertising. Jayce, Dame, and Hayden will have the darkest beer you've got on tap, and Tiana will take the usual."

I glance at Damian, who motions that it's okay to put the drinks on his tab.

"Top shelf?" I ask Tiana before reaching for the nicest bottle of tequila.

She dips her chin, her brown skin absorbing the pink glow from a neon sign near the bar. "That's me. And in a wine glass, please."

I chuckle. Tiana has always been too fancy for our friend group. Sometimes I have no idea how we'd managed to convince her we were worthy of her time. She's supermodel pretty and her family is loaded. Her mom's a notable attorney and her dad's probably going to be our next governor. They're rich and connected.

The exact opposite of my family.

Fifteen minutes after I serve my friends, Elle turns on the projector and the show starts. A few people play games, but almost everyone sits at the high tables down the middle of the room or at the bar to watch. Elle and I take the opportunity to relax and clean up a bit. I'm restocking beer glasses when my phone buzzes. It's charging on the counter behind the bar near the register.

Turning my back on the room, I pick it up and check the message.

Damian: *To your left.*

As casually as possible, I slide my eyes to the left edge of the bar top where there aren't any stools because it'd potentially cut off access to the fire exit. Damian's standing there, a panty-dropping smile on his face. He's wearing an expensive-looking jacket over a simple white V-neck that reveals the hint of a tattoo. The evidence of summer sun lingers on him like wet after rain. His dark hair is an utter mess around his face—just the way I like it.

I try not to look *too* eager as I pad over and lean my elbows on the bar, pushing up my cleavage.

"Hello, Sir," I say, in a voice too low to be overheard.

"Hello, *Red*."

"Red?"

He sips his beer, eyes settling on my cleavage. Something hungry passes through them. My core tightens. His eyes are so light their color depends on what he's wearing. Sometimes they're blue, sometimes they're hazel, and sometimes they're brown. It all depends.

"I've decided," he says, slowly dragging his eyes to mine, "that if you're going to call me Sir, then I'm going to call you Red."

"Oh?"

"Mhmm."

"And why is that?"

He gives a low chuckle. "I think you know why."

My body heats, remembering the look in his eyes when he found my red panties in his pocket, the way he took me against the door after.

He swallows thickly, as if remembering the exact same thing. "When do y—"

"Not here," I whisper, motioning to the crowded room with a tilt of my head. He pulls out his phone. A second later, mine buzzes behind me.

Damian: *When do you get off?*
Marrin: *Whenever you're ready to help me. Or after we close at 2 A.M.*

He chuckles.

Damian: *Get your mind out of the gutter. And 2? It's a school night :(*
Marrin: *You're the one staring at my tits. And bars close at 2 around here. I don't make the rules.*

I walk back over, idly wiping down the bar in front of him. "I suppose it's convenient that we live in the same building," he says.

"Why?"

"So I can lend a hand when you"—he leans in—"*get off.*"

Liquid heat pools in my core, and I know he can tell because he sips his beer with a stupid, satisfied look on his face.

Two people can play this game.

I lean forward, pushing my breasts together and commanding his space like an SUV in a compact parking spot, ready to tell him exactly what I want him to do with those hands—

"Braxton," Jake barks. "Put your stripper tits away and get me another drink. This ain't your city job." He says it loud enough for nearly everyone in the quiet bar to hear. A few customers shush him and several turn to see who he's talking to.

Embarrassment and anger flood my body and I swear my blood begins to boil in my veins. Taking a deep breath and not daring a look at Damian, I prowl over to Jake. I snatch his empty glass as Elle waves off Conor, who's started walking over.

"One more outburst and you're out. You know the rules," I say as low and vicious as possible, not wanting to make a scene.

He chuckles. "More whiskey."

I turn my back to grab the whiskey and dare to glance at Damian. His eyes are alert, assessing as they flicker between Jake and me—as if he's already sized up Jake and knows exactly where he'll strike to bring him down. I shake my head once, warning him to stay out of it.

"Ah-ha," Jake says. "Now I get it." He points a finger between Damian and me. "You two are fuckin'."

I don't look at Damian. Not when that's what Jake wants, and not when all our friends are around.

I snort derisively and set his whiskey on the bar. He can have this one then I'm calling him a cab.

"Jake," I say, letting out some of the inner-city accent I try so hard to hide. "You and I both know I don't date."

He sips his drink. "That's right. Miss college girl is too good to date any of us, but not good enough for any of them."

I swallow hard. His *us* refers to my old neighborhood and *them* refers to my new university friends. Where I come from isn't a secret, but it's not something I advertise either.

"Don't forget," he continues, "I still remember what that sweet ass tastes like. When these rich bitches realize you ain't good enough for them, I'll take you back. I still remember how you like—"

"*Jake,*" I snarl.

I'm halfway to signaling Conor to escort Jake outside when his voice grows low and somber. "The old man's been asking about you."

Everything stops.

I blink.

And blink again as his words hit my ears, my brain. They register and it's as if my brain has to reboot from a power outage.

"Anniversary is coming up," he slurs. His eyes dip to where my hand has unknowingly pressed against my lower stomach. I feel hot. Too hot. Don't want to think about the screaming now echoing in my head or why the sweat on my hands feels like blood—

"Leave her alone."

I snap to the present, realizing Damian has just spoken and that he's now standing next to Jake.

Shit.

Jake laughs, sizing Damian up. "Looky here. Pretty Boy's got some balls."

Behind them, Jayce, Vicky, Tiana, and Hayden all stand up and start heading over.

"Thanks for noticing," Damian says sarcastically, fingers beneath his chin. "I am quite pretty, aren't I? But enough about me. Why don't you leave her alone, man? Clearly you're making her uncomfortable."

Jake knocks back his drink. "He's got spunk, too."

"*Enough,*" I hiss, signaling Conor. "You're done."

He ignores me and stands—practically chest-to-chest with Damian. And unless Damian has some unique fighting skills, he's about to get his ass kicked. Jake's got a few inches and about fifty pounds of muscle on him.

I remove the glasses from the bar as Conor comes over. His eyes flicker to Elle, who I'm faintly aware is standing behind me, trembling hand fisted in my shirt.

"Damian," I warn. "Touch him and I'll throw you out, too."

He looks affronted but I ignore it. He isn't my boyfriend, and I don't need him fighting my battles. If he wants to trade punches with Jake for being a jackass, fine by me. But not at my work while I'm in charge. The last thing I want is to explain to Alice why I had to call the cops.

"Jake, I'm calling you a cab." I grab the retro bar phone and dial the driving service we use. They're fast, trustworthy, and they don't ask questions. Alice pays a retainer to use the company for her businesses. I'm not sure why she has a driving service on payroll and I'm not about to ask. All I know is we're to use it sparingly and to prevent situations that could involve cops.

Elle closes out Jake's tab and hands me his card. I round the bar as Conor grabs Jake's arm to steady him. He's drunker than I'd thought.

"Vicky," he slurs as Conor steers him to the door.

"Jake," she replies.

Outside, Conor sits Jake on a bench by the curb. I tuck his credit card inside his wallet then hand him a bottled water.

"You were always too good for us," he murmurs to me.

I don't have an answer for that. So I just stand there until the cab pulls up. When it does, I tip the driver and make sure he has the correct address, then they're gone.

I stand on the curb with Conor, rubbing the back of my neck. I have no idea how much damage control I might have to do with my friends, but the thought stresses me out. I feel anxious, jittery.

My eyes fall on an old red truck parked across the street and it feels like all the blood in my body drains to my feet. Conor must notice because he says, "It belongs to one of our regulars. Guy named Kevin."

I take a deep breath and realize the make, model, and

license plate are wrong. It's not the red truck I thought it was.

God, what's wrong with you, Marrin? Since when are you so paranoid?

"Want me to call Alice?" Conor says. It is, after all, Alice's bar, and anytime we use the cab service, we notify her. Only I'm pretty sure that's not what Conor meant. He'd no doubt heard what Jake said.

Conor has worked for Alice for years. He's a trusted bouncer and bodyguard at her club in the city. He was also my bodyguard for a few months after everything happened freshman year. He knows more about me than I'd care to admit.

"No, I'll tell her. Tomorrow... maybe."

"I'm telling her the next time I see her, so figure it out."

Sighing, I walk back inside.

With a pleasant look plastered to my face, I round the bar. Vicky's already running interference and I could kiss her. I hear her explaining in a roundabout way how Jake knows her name. She says they met at the Braxton one evening—which, truthfully, isn't a lie. It's just not exactly the truth.

Vicky has met a drunk Jake at the Braxton many times. But the reason he remembers her name is because he's met her sober. It was only once but the situation had been dire enough that he remembers her. It was the fall semester of our freshman year of college—

And that's about as much as I want to think about it.

What I'd rather think about is Damian Wane. He's sitting on a stool next to Vicky, brooding. I'm not sure what to do. Emotions are not my thing. Conversations *about* emotions are even less my thing.

So I open a bottle of his favorite beer and set it on the

bar. "Thanks for not pounding Jake even though he deserved it."

He accepts my offering with a smile that doesn't reach his eyes. "Your wish is my command."

I realize then that Damian isn't brooding over what Jake said to him, he's brooding over what Jake said to me.

I clean up behind the bar then move around the room collecting empties and trash. When I get back, Damian still has that look on his face.

Ugh. Why are guys so complicated?

Fine. I'll admit it was hot as hell that Damian got all alpha male on Jake ready to defend my honor. Just thinking about it has my lady bits tingling. A part of me desperately craves that kind of devotion. I want someone I can rely on, someone I can trust to keep me safe, who will always put me first.

The problem is Jake is a jackass. He'd love nothing more than to ruin everything I've built by publicly spilling details about my past in an effort to remind me that he and I are the same breed of white trash, from the same neighborhood, and just because I got into a good school doesn't mean I'm better than him. And I don't feel better than him—or anyone. But I've worked my ass off to get where I am and I won't let him, or anyone, ruin what I've built.

So, yeah, I fear losing control over the persona I've crafted for myself. Hell, I fear losing control over everything. It's why I think I like to be dominated in the bedroom. It's the one place I can let go and allow someone else to take care of me. But out here in the real world? Hell. No. If anyone knew how weak and pathetic I really am, what kind of family I come from...

Marrin: *My mind is in the gutter again. Will you be*

awake when I'm off?
Damian: *Depends*
Marrin: *On?*
Damian: *What'd that guy mean when he said this isn't your city job?*
Marrin: *If you play your cards right, maybe I'll tell you.*

My other job involves shifts at an exclusive members-only club Alice owns called the 13th Floor. It's located about forty-five minutes away in the city. I suppose it's *technically* a burlesque strip club but it also incorporates interactive erotic performances. The best way I can describe it is to say it's Cirque du Soleil meets the Crazy Horse in Paris meets Lust, the erotic dinner party place in New York. It's edgy, titillating, and exclusive. It caters to sex kinks and fetishes on the upper floors, which is why I usually only waitress in the main lounge. If I do work upstairs, I'm usually performing. I rarely strip, but if I do, I never show more than I would at the beach in the summer.

Performance wise, if it involves dancing, I do it all. And while I love aerial silk dancing, pole dancing is my forté. That shit is hard work and should honestly be an Olympic sport.

Jake is not a member, nor could he afford to be. All he knows is it's a fancy club for high rollers and that I waitress there. But he's an ass, so I wouldn't put it past him to twist the story.

I smile internally, thinking of how blown Damian's mind would be if I showed him my skills on the pole. But he doesn't need to know. At least not right now because he's wearing a face that says he wants to ask more questions, and because right now all I can think about is how anxious and on edge I am—and how badly I want to get lost in him.

3

Damian

I'm still brooding over what happened when Marrin knocks on my door. It's 2:47 A.M. and she looks as though she's just jumped out of the shower. Her hair is damp and she's wearing a slender robe with what might be thigh-high stockings.

"May I come in?" she asks.

Hell yes.

I step aside and no sooner is the door closed than she's on me—crushing her body and mouth against mine.

"Mar—"

"Don't," she says, wrapping a hand around my cock and stroking me through my thin pajama bottoms.

I'm instantly steel in her hand.

"Shit, baby." My eyes close. I'm pretty sure she intends to fuck me in this doorway and I'm one hundred percent sure I'm going to let her. But after a second, my damn conscience overrules my dick and I pull her hand away. "Mar, I don't care where you come from."

She freezes, and I swear I can see the wall she's erected between us.

Shit.

I have absolutely no idea why I'd felt the need to say that.

She blinks, and for a second, I think she's going to leave. But then she says, "I don't care what you think and I didn't come here to talk." She drops her robe, revealing thigh-high stockings held up by a black, high-waisted garter skirt.

Good. Fucking. God.

She's not wearing a bra.

Her bare breasts just appear before my eyes like a magic wish from a genie. All the blood that should be fueling my brain rushes to my cock. I'm so hard it hurts.

She pulls my pants down and my dick springs free. She kneels and licks me from base to tip, and then stares up at me as she takes me into her mouth.

I brace my hands on the wall and almost come at the sight of her. Marrin on her knees before me, sucking my cock like her life depends on it—and maybe it does. Because the way she's staring up at me tells me she hasn't just come here for sex. She came to escape something. She runs her teeth gently up my length and—*holy shit*—that's fine with me. She can use me to escape her problems. I'm happy to do that actually.

I keep my eyes on her as she devours me like a popsicle melting in a midsummer sun. She squeezes my balls—*fuuuck*—I'm pretty sure I'm in love with this woman. Pretty sure I'd do anything for her.

"Please, Sir," she begs, a wary edge in her eyes.

And I realize what she needs, the part I've forgotten to play.

Marrin

"Touch one of those titties for me, Red. Let me see you roll that pretty pink nipple in your fingers."

I'm liquid at his command. I obey, and almost immediately, my anxiety leaves me.

I moan, spreading my knees a bit wider and sucking him harder. His cock is velvety and firm and salty at the tip. He reaches down and pulls my damp hair into a ponytail in his fist, controlling the rhythm as I suck him off. Lust-fogged eyes consume me as I touch myself for him.

Abruptly Damian pulls me up and pushes me against the door. He doesn't come any closer. Just stands there surveying me. He rubs his jaw with a hand, his tongue running along the inside of his bottom lip, considering. As if he can't decide where to gorge himself first. I feel the same.

But I'm aching to be touched, fucked. So I say, "Please, Sir."

He grabs my swollen nipples, pinching hard. My eyes roll back as sharp, exquisite pleasure spreads like lightning from my breasts to my core. I moan.

Damian yanks me off the wall by the nipples. Pain and pleasure mix in me, coiling tighter and tighter. As if he can tell, he releases my nipples only to take two greedy handfuls of my breasts. I whimper, biting my bottom lip as he works my flesh.

My body is on fire. Every commanding, possessive touch goes straight to my pussy—*and the bitch is hungry.* If I'm not already dripping, I'm about to be. I rub my thighs together, feeling my swollen clit protruding from my outer lips.

Noticing, Damian pulls me forward by the breasts, close

enough to let me feel his hot breath on my face but too far away for me to kiss him. I still try.

Drunk off his touch, I lean forward, desperate for his mouth, for any part of him to be inside any part of me.

His smirk aims to torture. "Sorry, Red. Your pleasure belongs to me. Keep your legs apart. I want that sweet little clit swollen and aching for me."

Oh. My. God.

He releases me and I almost cry at the lost contact. But then he throws me over his shoulder like a rag doll, smacking my ass hard enough that I don't know whether I yelp from pain or pleasure. Probably both. He carries me into his room like a Neanderthal might an unsuspecting female to his cave, stolen from her group for the sole purpose of keeping him well fucked for the winter.

Why does that idea turn me on so much?

Damian throws me down on his king-size bed and grabs my ankles, spreading my legs for his viewing pleasure. Liquid heat gathers in my core at the selfishness, the dominance. At the fact he left his pants on the floor by the door and is utterly naked and hard before me. I drink in the sight. He's tattoos and muscles and pure, unadulterated man.

He groans eyeing my red lacy thong. "You're killin' me, Red."

He begins stroking himself, and for a moment, I think he's going to stand there until he comes all over me.

He hasn't done that. *Yet.*

Instead he moves to the nightstand and grabs a sleeve of condoms. I track him the whole time, eyes flickering between his massive cock and his mouth. He saunters back to the end of the bed, watching me. He knows I'm having a hard time focusing as he climbs onto the bed to kneel over me.

My breath is erratic, anticipation eating me alive from the inside out.

He bends my knees toward the ceiling and slowly unfastens the garters. They snap free and he glides large, calloused hands down my thighs to my knees then back toward my hips, pushing the garter skirt up until my lacy red thong is in full view.

"Jesus H. Christ, baby," he groans. "This pussy is drippin' for me." He runs a finger along the damp fabric between my legs.

I fist the sheets at my sides. "Oh fuck, Sir. Please —*please*."

He sits back. "Take the thong off, Red. I want to see this pussy bare for my eyes and my eyes only."

The command does wicked things to my body and I obey, lifting my hips and raising my legs straight into the air. He hisses in a breath at my flexibility and I make a show of sliding off the thong, enjoying every second of torture I see in his hungry gaze. I dangle the red lace from between two toes, waving it in surrender.

I sweep it across his face once, twice—

He rips the thong from me with his mouth then balls it up in a hand. "I should shove these in your mouth, Red." My eyes glaze. He chuckles. "But I think you'd like that too much." I think he's right. He jerks his chin to the condoms. "Roll one on me."

I practically jump off the bed to appease him. I rip open a wrapper—

"Pussy where I can see it," Damian demands.

Heat, like lava, flows to my lady parts, and I adjust my position so I'm sitting up, legs spread wide so that my wet, needy pussy is in full view.

I roll on the condom.

His length is obscene.

Damian wastes no time hauling me up to claim my mouth—hard and passionately. He dips a hand between my legs, and for a moment, my body is so excited he's finally touching me I can't tell where exactly he *is* touching me. Every nerve like a live wire sparking in a thunderstorm.

His fingers circle my entrance. "So wet for me."

I moan between kisses.

He teases me. Moving my wetness in wider and wider circles, then in smaller and smaller ones. The heel of his hand presses my clit but not enough. I need more.

I rock into him.

He smiles into my mouth, mocking me.

"Tell me what you want," he commands.

"You," I breathe.

His hand between my legs vanishes and suddenly my head is being yanked back by the hair. Not hard (we're not that hardcore) but enough to get my attention and send a jolt of pleasure straight through me. "That's not how you address me, Red."

God, I'm wound up so tight a stiff breeze could set me off. "I'm sorry, Sir. I want you, Sir."

"Better." His fingers resume their teasing, but he doesn't release my hair. "Be more *specific*."

"Inside me, Sir."

"Where exactly?"

The fingers that were between my legs push into my mouth, and I wrap my lips around them, tasting myself. "My pussy."

Damian replaces the fingers in my mouth with a brutal kiss—one he punctuates by thrusting those fingers into my aching core.

I'm so wet we both hear it. Every slip and slide. It feels so good I forget how to kiss. Forget we *are* kissing.

He pulls away. "Elbows and knees."

I move so fast, he chuckles—but stops when I arch my back and press my greedy pussy against his cock. He inhales a curse.

Hot hands grip my hips, and we groan as his blunt head forces my body to yield to his intrusion. He's thick and hot and hard as granite as he presses into me. The feel, the pressure of him, is exquisite.

The whole world narrows to his cock.

"You okay, baby? You need anything?" he asks, sliding out a few inches then pressing in deeper.

I shake my head, unable to remember what words are or how to use them.

He leans down and kisses my spine. "Let me know if it hurts."

I nod, growing wetter at his concern and knowing I shouldn't.

Damian has one of the biggest penises I've ever encountered in the wild. The first time I saw it, I flat out told him I wasn't having sex with him. There *is* such a thing as too big and he's right on the border. He'd spent the next ten minutes explaining to me that he buys special condoms, always has top-shelf lubricant on hand, and that he's learned how to ready a woman for his penetration. I was still skeptical by the end of the sales pitch, but I was also horny and desperate. And, as I'm learning, horny and desperate tend to win over logical thought.

Like I said, my pussy's a hungry bitch.

I exhale a curse when Damian finally sinks himself to hilt. I relish the feel of his hips pressing against my ass, his balls brushing my clit. He stays there a moment, enjoying the sensation before pulling back and sinking deep again. I turn my head to watch through the mirrored doors of his closet. I love the sight of a man's hips when he's thrusting into a woman.

Even better when I'm the woman.

He pushes and pulls me over his length while continuing to thrust with his hips. The sensation is maddening. He quickens the pace and I fall forward, moaning into the mattress. But Damian fists my hair and forces me to look at him over a shoulder as he fucks me deeply.

"You like that, Red?"

I nod, wishing the position allowed for him to bury his tongue in my mouth, too. His lips are perfection and the way his mouth hangs open looks so good it should be illegal.

He begins kneading one of my ass cheeks with his free hand when something dark and covetous flashes in his eyes.

Damian

I'm thinking about how much I want to kiss Marrin when all at once, what Jake the Jackass said comes back to me. I'm not bothered that Marrin slept with him. I've slept with plenty of women—some of whom were, and still are, jackasses. What bothers me is that he'd talked about her sexual preferences as if he were going to use it against her by telling a bar full of people.

Then I remember she'd told me to back off—*which she had every right to do.*

But Jake had been acting like a grade-A douchebag, and I would've stood up for any of my friends like that. I don't tolerate douchebag very well.

"Marrin," I say, watching her in the mirror. I grab her

arms, pulling them back like the reins on a horse. Her torso lifts into the air and her beautiful, soft tits bounce with each thrust I gift her. I pull out. "I didn't like the way that Jake guy spoke to you." I thrust in hard and deep enough to elicit a moan from her lips.

I pull out painfully slowly, staring at her in the mirror.

"I didn't like what he said"—a hard thrust back in, a slow pull out—"I didn't like the way he looked at you"—another hard thrust and slow retreat—"and I wanted to kick his ass for ever thinking he could have you."

Sure, it's a shitty way to broach a conversation she doesn't want to have, but right now I think I'm pretty fucking clever for framing it in a way that will only turn her on more. She likes to be dominated, and I'm rewarded when her pussy tightens around me. I decide to push further. Pun intended.

I haul her up so her back is pressed to my chest. I palm her soft breasts—and fuck if her pussy doesn't clamp down even harder on my cock. Jesus, she's so close to coming.

I position her so her hands are braced on the headboard. I kiss and nip her shoulders and back, hands roaming her body like the gift it is. She's completely at my mercy. I fucking love it.

I pinch one of her nipples and her clit at the same time. She nearly screams, bucking.

"Do *not* come, Red."

"Please," she begs. "Oh fuck—please, Sir. I'm so close."

I release her nipple and grip her hip to stop her from moving. "Do not come. I'm serious. This pussy is mine, Marrin." She nods vigorously, looking down at my fingers between her legs. "You're too good for Jake." Again she nods, white-knuckling the headboard. "Understand?"

"Yes," she gasps.

"Yes, what?"

"Sir. Yes, Sir. I'm too good for him."

"And?" I release her clit and start moving my fingers in slow circles.

She moans, head falling back, silver-white hair tickling my hips. "My pussy is yours, Damian. Oh fuck."

Marrin

"You're mine," Damian declares, then he fucks me to completion, rubbing commanding circles into my clit.

Pleasure explodes through me as I take all of him to hilt over and over. I can do nothing but hold on as my orgasm tramples me like a stampede. I'm powerless beneath his touch, beneath the onslaught of my own pleasure.

Damian comes a second later. Grunting and fucking.

When it's over, I sag against the headboard.

He lays me down beside him, his arms envelop me tightly, and I'm too exhausted to pull away.

Once I've recovered, I gather my things to leave. He asks me to stay, knowing I'll give the same answer I always do. When I refuse, he walks me to the door and watches me until I disappear into my apartment.

I look at him through the peephole while I slide the locks. It's not until I get to the third one that he finally retreats into his apartment.

I empty my bladder and clean myself up.

As I'm climbing into bed, I get a text.

Damian: *For what it's worth, you are good enough.*

4

Marrin

"What's eating you?" Priya says, walking into the dance studio at the 13th Floor.

I didn't have class this morning, so I figured I'd get in early and work on a routine I'm choreographing for the new Femme Fatale show we're developing for the club. It combines two of my favorite things: film noir and dance. I'm a film studies major, and I'd love to one day apply that knowledge as an artistic director for dance productions or something. I'm lucky Alice owns this club and that the current artistic director is letting me help out to gain experience.

The number I'm working on for the show features seven dancers who start in chairs and end up on the pole. I want it to look sharp and deadly, but buttery and smooth at the right moments to project a false sense of security. The best femme fatales are masters of this art. Constructed through the male gaze, they seem to project an unattainable ideal that draws in the male lead, then they turn. Or more accurately, the man realizes he's allowed his emotions (and his penis) to cloud his judgment.

"Nothing," I lie.

Priya starts warming up at the pole nearest me. She's average height with long dark hair and killer curves. She catches my eyes in the mirrored wall in front of us. "It's eight A.M. and you've been in here for more than two hours. Spill, bitch."

"Kiley rat me out?" Kiley's the head of security. Nothing happens in this building he doesn't know about.

"Of course. He caught me on my way in and asked if I'd check on you. You going to tell me what's up?"

"Nothing's up." I flip off the closest security camera and hope Kiley's watching.

She chuckles. "That'll teach him."

Priya bartends at the Arcade a few nights a week, but her main job is working here at the 13th Floor. She's one of the headliners and she brings in a shitload of money. She's queen of the burlesque striptease, but she also caters to the members who are into dom/sub kinks on the upper levels.

The main floor of the club is located on the thirteenth floor of a high rise in the city—hence the name. But the whole club is five floors total.

Currently, we're on the fourteenth floor where the dance studio, costume shop, offices and kitchens are located. It's basically the club's backstage and it's for employees only.

Priya adjusts her purple bralette, the color perfectly complements her pale brown skin. "So you're not in here wearing yourself out because of Mr. One Direction?"

I snort at the name Priya gave Damian the first night he came to the bar and started flirting with me. It's true, though. He does look like a taller, more muscular Zayn.

"He asked me to be exclusive." I say it as if it's not the

single most terrifying and exciting thing to happen to me in years.

"*Get out*," she squeals. "Aren't you excited? That boy is cute and clearly into you."

I shrug.

She does a back stretch with the pole and I get the distinct impression she's angling her cleavage to the security camera. "What aren't you telling me?"

I spill. I tell her about the scene Jake made at the bar and how the night ended with me in Damian's bed. I tell her about the text he sent (that I have no idea how to respond to) and that he came to my door early Monday morning and that I didn't answer.

Yeah, I'm an asshole.

"Let me get this straight. Your hot-as-sin fuck buddy asked you to be exclusive and you said yes. And you're stressing about it because you're worried he'll get the wrong impression and want to be your boyfriend...?"

I groan. "No. Yes—I don't know."

She faces me. "This isn't about him getting the wrong impression, this is about you not wanting to let anyone in. You really like this boy, don't you?"

I let my silence answer for me.

"What are you scared of? That he'll find out you grew up in a shitty neighborhood in a shitty home? That you're smarter than Einstein and got a full ride to one of the best universities on the east coast? That you're a fantastic dancer who can work a pole better than anyone on this side of the Mississippi?"

I laugh at that last one.

"Help me out, Mar. You're a catch and one tough bitch. Any man who can't handle your background is a soft prick and not worth your time."

I sigh because she's right.

"What did you tell him when he saw your scars?"

I straighten, a hand going to my lower stomach. "He hasn't. I always keep them covered."

She whistles out a breath as she twirls around the pole. "Damn, girl. You are a serious control freak."

"I know," I whine. "What do I do?"

"Talk to him, get to know him better. Just because he grew up in a mansion doesn't mean his life has been perfect. Maybe he can relate."

I slide to the floor. "And I broach the conversation how, exactly? Hey, Damian. FYI some asshole tried to kill me a few Thanksgivings ago, but don't worry, she's in prison and I have a restraining order against her psycho boyfriend who sometimes stalks me from his red truck." I give Priya a level look.

"Well, when you put it like that it sounds—"

"Trashy?"

"I was going to say like a soap opera." When I groan, she adds, "My advice is get to know him better. Don't invite him to Christmas dinner or anything, but do more with him than just sex. Knowing more about him will give you a better sense for how he might react to your story." She spins around the pole, dropping to the floor in the splits. "And relax. Right now it's just sex. And you trust him enough to safely give you that, so let him. And build from there."

She makes a valid point. I know things about Damian, but I don't know Damian. I know he's rich, has a killer body, and is skilled in both the bedroom and the kitchen. I know he threw a huge dorm party freshman year and the cops were called. Rumor has it, he threw the party because his dad died, but that's probably not the whole story. Point is, I don't know enough about him to safely say whether or not he'd judge me if he knew what happened to me.

So maybe I should try to get to know him...

I spend the rest of the morning working out in the studio before I have to leave for class.

It's Film Noir Thursday at the Braxton Arcade, and tonight we're showing *Double Indemnity* on the projector. I'm working the bar with Elle and it's slow. Weeknights usually are.

I lose myself in the film, in the way Phyllis draws Neff into her orbit. She's shiny, beautiful and dangerous. She reels him in like a fish on a hook. They're not in love, they're in lust. And in the end, it doesn't work out between them because it can't. She's using him to get what she wants.

Right or wrong, I've always admired Phyllis. But I don't want to be like her. Not when it comes to Damian anyway. Whatever's between us may have started in mutual lust, but it's different now. Changed.

Fuck if I know.

I'm so engrossed in the film, I don't notice the phone ringing. Luckily, Elle does.

"Braxton Arcade, how can I help you?" There's a pause. "Hello?" She hangs up. "That's annoying."

I turn. "Who was it?"

"A butt dial."

The phone we use is as much a piece of memorabilia as the items in the display case behind the bar. It's classy and retro and lacks caller ID.

I check the time. "Why don't you take your fifteen? I'll watch the bar, seeing as we're so busy."

She grabs her purse and heads out front, sitting at one of the tables. I don't miss the way Conor's eyes follow her. Nor do I miss that the people whose IDs he just checked are Damian and Hayden.

I brace myself as Hayden heads to the quarter machine and Damian heads toward me. I still haven't responded to his text, and because I never expected him to show up, I have no preplanned excuse if he asks why.

He leans against the bar and my stomach does an annoying flip.

"Thought I'd find you here," he says cheekily.

"It is where I work. Can I get you a drink?"

"Are you avoiding me?"

I glance at Hayden, who's trying to feed a wrinkled dollar into the quarter machine by the door. No one else is within earshot. The other customers are either playing games or watching the movie. "No."

"So you weren't in your apartment the other morning when I came over?"

I look away. "Do you want something to drink or not?"

"You *were* home," he says. "Why didn't you answer the door?"

At the confusion on his face, I snap. "Because I'm not obligated to let you in, Damian. I don't want you in my space all the time. Once in a while is fine, but not every time we have sex. It's weird and annoying."

Hurt and embarrassment sober his face. "Wow, okay. I overstepped. My bad." He turns to leave, but Hayden comes up.

"Hey, Mar," he says. "Can I get a—"

The phone rings.

"Hold on," I grumble, pivoting to answer. "Braxton Arcade. How can I help you?" I look at Hayden and point to the tap handle of our darkest beer. He gives a thumbs up, and I grab a glass. "Hello?" I hear nothing but rustling on the receiver. I hang up. "Update your phone, asshole."

"Butt dial?" Hayden asks as I slide him a beer.

"Yeah. This is the twenty-first century, they don't make phones susceptible to ass dials anymore. Jesus, get a new phone. It's fucking annoying." I check my anger because— let's be real—a butt dial is not why I'm angry. I take a deep breath. "You want anything, Damian?"

He doesn't look at me. Just shakes his head, pretending to be busy with his phone. He and Hayden move toward the pinball machines and I feel like a total asshole.

I don't know why I got so mad. I'm just weird about my privacy. I like Damian and the last thing I want to do is actively scare him away—not when details of my life will likely do that for me.

I grab my phone.

Marrin: *Sorry I got mad.*
Marrin: *I didn't answer my door cuz this whole thing freaks me out a bit. I'm trying.*

I set my phone down and go about my work, checking inventory and restocking things. Every now and then I look over at Damian. He and Hayden have moved on from pinball and are engaged in a heated two-player *Tetris* battle. It's nearly a half hour later when I look up and see Damian standing at the bar. It's just us. Elle is talking to Conor at the door.

"Why does it freak you out?" he asks.

I work my jaw as if I'm annoyed and not terrified. He wants to have this conversation now? Face to face? I glance at my phone. I could text him...

Sighing, I push off the back counter and stand across the bar from him. "Full honesty?"

He nods.

"This is the closest I've come to a real relationship in years. I don't know how to trust people and I'm not in the habit of trying. But for some reason I can't figure out..." I cross my arms and hope I don't regret this. "I find myself wanting to trust you. And I swear to God, if you ever repeat that or bring it up again, I'll hurt you."

He grins. "Apology accepted."

I huff, relaxing a bit.

"Would you believe me if I told you I haven't been interested in dating anyone until you?"

"No."

He taps the bar with a finger. "It's true."

"Why?" I blurt.

Hesitation clouds his eyes, like he's about to confess something serious. But he doesn't.

A charming smile masks his face. "I could ask you the same thing."

I consider telling him. Considering getting it all out in the open now so he can walk away from me before this goes too far. Before he learns the truth about where I come from and about the kind of woman I really am from someone else. And before I give him the ability to break my heart. Because that's where this ends. In heartache.

But the idea is fleeting and gone before it can take root. So I say, "You could, but you won't."

"And why is that?"

"Because you don't want to scare me away." I swallow hard.

His brows pinch. "That's an answer I have to earn, isn't it?"

I only stare.

He studies me so long I feel naked. "There's something between us, Mar. I know you can feel it. I'd like to see where this goes and I think you would, too." I'm a statue. Staring and listening. "But this will go nowhere if you don't talk to me. I need you to tell me when I'm pushing too much and not get mad. I don't know where your boundaries are and I need you to help me find them."

"Okay." The word a shadow of a whisper.

Damian smiles with every part of his body and I'm powerless to stop the corners of my own mouth from curling. I feel like a damn schoolgirl with a crush. It's public and embarrassing.

He taps the counter. "Think I'll take that beer now."

I roll my eyes and pour him a drink.

"And just so we're clear," he says, "this doesn't make you my girlfriend."

He's mocking me and it does funny things to my insides. He heads back to Hayden and I spend the next few hours trying not to glance over at him every chance I get.

5

Damian

It's been a week since Mar and I talked at the bar. We haven't had a chance to hang out in private, but I've made every excuse possible to drag my friends to the Braxton Arcade.

It's ten o'clock on Friday night and there's a line out the door. I'm standing with Jayce, Vicky, Tiana and Hayden. It's mid-October and about forty degrees outside. I'm freezing my ass off and just about to ask Vicky to stop complaining about the temperature when Priya walks out front for a smoke break.

She's wearing a black bustier bodysuit with dark jeans and stilettos. She's pulling on a leather jacket when she looks up and spots me. Her gaze flits to my friends, and I get the impression she knows about Mar and me.

She points a red nail in my direction. "Damian, right?"

I smile. "Yeah. You're Priya?"

"You remembered." She winks and lights her cigarette.

"I never forget a pretty face."

A large man watching the door comes over. And when I

say large, I mean action hero size. The dude is huge. Like he could go a few rounds with The Rock and win.

"Everything all right?" He's looking at me, but talking to Priya.

She rolls her eyes. "Why are you here again, Kiley? Oh, right, to piss me off."

Next to me, Jayce chokes.

Kiley doesn't seem to notice. "Someone's gotta protect the boss's investment." He smiles and I'm not sure if he's talking about the bar or Priya. She takes another drag and blows smoke in his face. "You should stay away from that shit, it's not good for you."

"Funny, I told you the same thing about me, yet here you stand." She smothers her smoke with a shoe. They stare at each other for a moment too long, then Priya walks away— toward us. "Come on, follow me."

We jump out of line and follow her to the door where she gets us past a disgruntled-looking Conor.

The place is crowded, the bar especially, but I don't miss the way Priya taps Marrin's hip and whispers into her ear. Mar's eyes find mine and we share a brief, secret moment. I can tell she's fighting to keep a smile off her face, and my inner alpha male practically roars in satisfaction.

Down, boy.

Tiana and I get drinks while the others get quarters. We find a spot between two women sitting at the bar and decide I have a better shot of wedging my way through.

"Excuse me, ladies." They look up like they want to be annoyed by my intrusion, but when I smile, they fluster and blush. "I'll only be a second."

"Take your time," one of them says, raking her eyes over me.

Mar comes over and takes my credit card. "Hey. What do you want?"

My eyes dip to her outfit. She's wearing a skintight pair of high-waisted black leather shorts with a long-sleeved top cropped to reveal several inches of midriff. "Nothing I can say in public."

Her eyes flare as if to say, *Not here, idiot.*

One of the women I'm standing between sighs, disappointed.

I order drinks for my friends, passing what I can back to Tiana to hold. When Mar hands over the last drink, I say, "When's your next break?"

She motions to the crowded bar. "No idea. I haven't even had time to order dinner."

I gather the drinks and follow Tiana. She finds our friends standing by a half-empty table near the middle of the room. We spend the next few minutes looking for arcade games not in use. There aren't any, so we opt to get in line for a four-player game called *Gauntlet.*

While we wait, I whip out my phone and take the opportunity to be a gentleman.

The Braxton only serves drinks, so they don't mind if customers bring in outside food. I check the time and text Devon. He works at a burger place a few blocks away and he's planning to meet us when he's off. I ask if he'll bring us a sample platter of sliders. Nothing fancy, just beef and veggie burgers with the toppings on the side. He texts back a "yes" and I give him my credit card info.

Two spots open up for *Gauntlet* and I'm not sure how long Tiana and I play. Eventually Devon shows up and I let him take my spot. I leave to find the food he brought sitting on our table. It's separated into three to-go boxes. I mix the items so one box has a little bit of everything.

"Tell me I can eat some of that," Vicky says, stopping at the table to drink her beer.

"Of course." I turn to leave, a box in hand.

"Where are you going with that?"

To lie or tell the truth...

"It wouldn't be nice if I didn't offer *all* my friends some."

Her eyes flick to the bar, her mouth falls open. "Oh my God. Damian. Priya is, like, five years older than you. Not to mention that big scary dude at the door who's totally into her."

I shrug like a cartoon character and walk away without a word. I round the far side of the bar where there aren't any stools. It's not as crowded as it was, but Elle, Marrin, and Priya are still hustling.

Setting the box down on the bar, I wait to catch Marrin's eye. When she sees me, she holds up a finger letting me know she'll be over in a second.

I watch her work.

She moves like a well-oiled machine. Listening and looking at customers while her hands grab bottles and fill glasses on pure instinct. She crouches to the floor, reaching into the back of the near empty shelf where they keep clean glasses. Her shorts are so tight I'm surprised they don't split down the middle.

Marrin's got a great ass. It's high, tight, and thick with muscle. Her whole body is kind of like that. She's built like a dancer. And maybe she is. I've seen her dance at clubs and parties before and she's definitely got rhythm.

She finishes the order and moves over to me. "Another beer?"

"Sure." I push the box forward. "You said you hadn't eaten, so I got you dinner."

She blinks, stunned. And I wonder if anyone has ever done this for her before.

"There's enough for you to share with your coworkers, so don't worry about it looking suspicious." She rolls her lips together fighting a smile then gets me a beer. "Also Vicky thinks I'm bringing this up here for Priya—which is a testament to how much she trusts me to stay away from her friends. If she only knew."

Marrin tilts her head back and laughs. I'm pretty sure it's the most amazing sound I've ever heard.

She opens the box. "Are these from that place Devon works?"

"Yep."

"Bless you. You have no idea how starved I am." She stuffs one of the sliders into her mouth and sighs.

"Mar," Priya calls over the noise. "Why don't you take your fifteen—*are those mini burgers?*" Mar pivots to show the box. Priya rushes over and wastes no time taking a bite of one. "All I need now is a foot massage," she says through a mouthful of food.

Marrin grabs her wrist, "*Right?*"

I sip my beer, enjoying my victory. Whoever said the way to a man's heart is through his stomach clearly never tried feeding women. Marrin eats two more burgers before taking her break. We head to the table we've commandeered in the middle of the room and she helps herself to more food.

"We should play something," Marrin says, fidgeting. "So, like, no one gets suspicious."

"Sure you're not just looking for an excuse to spend time with me?"

She rolls her eyes, but I detect a slight curl to her mouth.

I follow her across the room to a two-player game called *Realm Quest* that's hidden in the back corner. She inserts coins for both of us and the player select screen pops up. I've never heard of this game so I have no idea what character to choose. I scroll through fae, dragons, and evil shadow looking things before selecting a Prince Charming type character with high magic stats. Marrin chooses a witch and the game begins.

Right off the bat, she hits me with a blast of power and Charming's life points plummet.

"No fair," I say, blindly hitting buttons. "I've never played this game."

"Want me to go easy on you?"

"Never." I try a few combinations and manage to block her next attack. "FYI. If you'd like a foot massage, I can make that happen."

"Don't play with me, Wane. Are you serious?" Her witch attempts to behead Charming.

"As a heart attack. I never joke about massaging a woman."

She barks a laugh then blasts Charming to smithereens.

We play five more rounds (I lose each one) before Marrin has to go back to work. The high score screen pops up and I'm not surprised to see her initials at the top.

Could she get any sexier?

Marrin knocks on my door at 2:45 A.M. She's fresh from the shower, wearing pajamas with a robe thrown on top. She laughs when she sees the coffee table. I've laid out several bottles of lotion, and as a joke, a travel-sized bottle of baby oil.

We sit at opposite ends of the couch, and I pat my thigh for her feet. She leans back and places them in my lap.

"Does the lady have a preferred lotion brand?"

"Whichever one you don't jack off with. I don't want my feet covered in your juices."

I grab the closest bottle. "You'll be pleased to know I prefer to masturbate in the shower."

"Oh good. A lotion-free zone—" She moans when I drag my thumb along the arch of her foot. Her eyes close and she settles in. "God that feels good."

Unsurprisingly, the sound of her moaning makes my dick hard.

Sorry, buddy. It's not about you tonight.

I stuff a pillow on my lap and she smiles like she knows exactly why it's necessary.

"Seeing as I told you something about me," I say, "it seems only fair you do the same."

"Do you want me to tell you where I prefer to masturbate, Damian?"

"Do you *want* to tell me?" I punctuate the sentence by massaging a line up the side of her shin. I'm rewarded with another moan.

"I prefer my bed."

"Do you just use your hands?"

A smile curls her mouth. "Yes, Damian. Just my hands. I've thought about buying a vibrator, but it just doesn't interest me that much. How about you?"

"Just my hands... I bought a pocket vagina once, though."

"And?"

"Nothing compares to the real thing. I consider it a waste of money."

"Why'd you buy it?"

I look away as a thread of anxiety slithers up my spine. For the first time in years, I think about the anxiety meds I keep for emergencies in my nightstand. "Once upon a time, I... um, wasn't sure if intimacy with other people was something I wanted." I feel it the moment her eyes open.

"Did you think you were asexual or something?"

"No. I just..." *Thought I was dirty. Was terrified of letting someone else touch me. Didn't want to be taken advantage of again.* I choke on the truth.

"You don't have to tell me." Her voice is soft but strong. There's no judgment, just quiet understanding.

I shrug, gaining control of myself. "I had a bad experience."

She nods, looking away. "I've had a few of those."

It's the most she's ever offered me. I'm not sure if I should push, or let it go. If I push, she may want something in return, and I'm not sure I'm ready for her to know about the worst experience of my life.

"True or False?" I declare. "Rumor has it, you put a guy in the hospital last semester."

She flinches like I hurt her. Eyes wide, face pale. Clearly, that was the wrong question.

"Did I hit a boundary?"

She licks her lips like her mouth has gone dry. She nods.

"Too personal?"

She nods again and it's not lost on me that she's fine telling me the intimate details of how she touches herself, but a story about something that happened in public is off limits.

I pivot. "Have you ever waxed your lady parts?"

Her tension eases. "Of course. Have you?"

"Seeing as I don't have lady parts the answer is no. I have shaved myself bald once or twice, but ultimately decided it wasn't for me. I prefer things well groomed but with hair."

"I appreciate that about you. I feel the same." She closes

her eyes. "I've had a few full Brazilian waxes before, but I prefer to keep hot wax out of my labia. Give me a deep bikini wax any day but go no further."

I move to her other foot.

"Do you have an opinion on vulva hair?" she asks.

This sounds like a trick question. "Am I allowed to?"

"Of course. But just because you prefer something doesn't mean I'm going to do it for you."

I massage up her calf. She moans. "I like how you groom. I think a bald vulva is fun every now and then, but I prefer hair on my women. This one time—"

Her eyes pop open. "Ooh, I love a good sex-gone-awry story."

"Well get ready. When I was in high school, I started babysitting for some of my neighbors. The kids were mostly old enough to take care of themselves, but sometimes I'd have to change a diaper or whatever. A few months after I started, I was at this house party, hooking up with this girl. One thing led to another and we started undressing. When I saw she was totally bare, I went completely soft—"

"No way."

"Yes, way. Like a wet noodle, I shit you not. All I could think was how her vulva looked like it belonged to a child and it freaked me out."

"What did you do?" Marrin chuckles.

"What do you mean '*what did I do?*' I went down on her then got the fuck out of there."

"Didn't she notice? She had to have noticed."

Now I'm laughing. "I told her the night was all about her and when it was over, I made up an excuse and bolted. I almost couldn't go down on her. I seriously thought I might have a panic attack. I was so freaked out."

"Oh my God. That's awful."

"It was." We're not laughing anymore, but she's clearly still enjoying my misery. "How about you? Have any embarrassing sex stories?"

Her brow furrows. "Not that I can think of right now. I have a period horror story. Not sure if you're one of those guys who'd prefer to believe vaginas don't bleed."

I deadpan. "You realize I'm majoring in biology because my plan in life is to be an OB-GYN."

"You're lying."

"Why would I lie about that?" Her mouth opens and closes like a fish. "Why do you think I spend so much time with my face between your legs?"

She launches a pillow at me.

I laugh. "Period story. Give it to me. I'm ready."

"Okay. So when I got my period, I didn't have anyone around to ask about what to expect and how to manage it. All I had to go on was that shitty talk they give in health class. And trust me when I say, they don't teach you about pads and tampons and ibuprofen or anything useful. So freshman year of high school, I get my period and think a tampon will last all day."

"Uh-oh."

"Yeah, uh-oh is right. Third bell, I'm sitting in study hall and I can feel it leaking. I ask to go to the bathroom and my stupid male teacher looks at my planner—we had to get planners signed to leave the classroom and get through checkpoints in the hallways and stuff—and sees that I'd gone to the bathroom in second period. So he refuses to let me go."

"That's fucked up."

"I know. I swear male teachers need special training on how to deal with female students. So anyway, I sit back down and my friend Jeannie leans over and tells me there's blood on my pants. I freak out. I mean *freak* out. I'm on the verge of tears when my other friend... Jake," she says.

"Jackass from the bar?"

"That's the one. Anyway, he asks what's wrong. Long story short, Jake gives me his sweatshirt to tie around my waist, then makes a scene so Jeannie and I can sneak out of the classroom and go to the bathroom. It was horrible."

"I bet. What'd Jake do to distract the teacher?"

"He threw a chair through the window."

"Oh shit."

"Yeah. Got a week's worth of suspension." She yawns. "He wasn't always an asshole... I'm sorry he called you names and stuff. I should've kicked him out right then and there. I just..." She shakes her head.

"It's complicated. I get it. And don't sweat it. You think those are the worst things I've been called? I've heard worse from members of my own family, okay?" Her brows pinch. "My dad was a rich white man from a rich white family and he married a woman whose grandparents immigrated from the Middle East. Thanksgiving was always a nightmare in my house. I used to hide upstairs with my brother—he looks way more mixed race than I do."

She cocks her head. "Is that ever strange?"

I shrug. "Only when people don't believe me. I get it though. I look just like my dad. Most people, white people, can't tell from looking at me until I point it out. No offense."

"None taken. But for the record, I've always seen you clearly." Her eyes travel over my face. "There's a hint of taupe always present in your skin tone and something about your browline and nose maybe."

I smile because she has a good eye. "All from my mom. Only thing you forgot was my hair. My father was blond."

She sits up, tucking her feet beneath her. "Can I ask you a question?"

"Shoot."

"Vicky told me once it was you who threw that dorm party freshman year that the cops had to break up."

"Guilty as charged. And before you ask, yes, I threw it because my dad died." I wait for a follow up question that never comes.

"Must've been a huge asshole if you threw a party."

I smile. "The biggest."

6

Damian

The next two weeks are filled with midterm exams. I only see Marrin in passing, sometimes in our building and sometimes on campus.

I've texted her a few times and I know she's busy, but every time I check my phone and see she hasn't texted me, I get a little pang of disappointment. Which is stupid because I'm not her boyfriend.

"I need a beer," I say, slipping my phone back into my pocket.

Hayden sighs. "You don't *need* a beer, you just *want* a beer."

I glare at him from the space between my eyebrows and the top of my sunglasses. We're sitting on a low stone fence outside the English department where Jayce is taking his last exam.

"Say that to me again."

"Jesus, who got your knickers in a knot?"

Marrin.

"First, who says 'knickers' anymore? Second, I've been studying my ass off for two weeks straight. I'm about to start bleeding out my eyes. I just want to get a beer with my boys. Besides, Vicky and them are going to that new cowboy bar. Perfect excuse for a guys' night."

He glances at his feet. A telltale sign he's hiding something.

I wipe a hand down my jaw. "You didn't."

He makes a face as if to say, *Well...*

"Vicky invited that Sasha girl you've been crushing on, didn't she? And you're going as her lap dog."

"I'm not her—"

"Unbelievable." I stand to pace. The sun is starting to set and the temperature is dropping. "Un-fucking-believable."

"What's unbelievable?"

I whirl around to face Jayce, who's just emerged from the big brick building in front of us. "Hayden. Sasha got invited to Vicky's little ladies' night at that new cowboy bar, and he's going because she's going."

Jayce glances at Hayden. "What's wrong with an old-fashioned cowboy bar?"

I freeze. "Mother of fuck. Please don't tell me you're going?"

"Where Vicky goes, I follow."

"You're both pathetic, you know that? Whipped and pathetic." We start walking toward the parking lot.

"Just come with us," Hayden says. "It'll be fun."

"No. Vicky in cowboy boots with spurs?" I point at Jayce. "You know they're real, right? Real spurs. That do *real* damage." Lifting the hem of my shirt, I twist so he can see the scar on my lower back. "Evidence."

"As I recall it," Hayden drawls. "You were drunk off your

ass, going through her closet, where you tripped—of your own accord—and fell into the spurs."

I round on Hayden, who's standing on my right. "We can play the blame game all day. Doesn't change the fact that those shoes are a danger to the community. I refuse to be around them when they're strapped to the feet of a drunk girl." I turn to Jayce. "Sorry."

"Come on," Jayce pleads, "it'll be fun. Everyone will be there. *Marrin* will be there." He wags his eyebrows.

I don't dignify that with a response. I just keep on walking. One foot in front of the other, my Jeep in sight. Yep, I'm just gonna keep on walking, keep on ignoring.

"Cat got your tongue, Dame?" Hayden chides.

"What I do with my tongue is none of your business, sweetheart." I lower my sunglasses and wink.

"But is it Marrin's business?" he muses to Jayce.

I shut my mouth because I walked right into that one.

"That's not a no," Jayce says, fist bumping Hayden before stopping at his car.

I take a few more steps before swiveling and walking backward toward my Jeep. "Have fun losing your dignity falling off mechanical bulls like a bunch of rednecks. No offense to your people Hayden."

"My parents are farmers, not cattle ranchers."

I look at Jayce. Jayce looks at me. We both look at Hayden. "Same thing," we say.

Hayden shakes his head, grumbling.

Jayce says, "We'll tell Marrin you said hello."

"Fuck you very much." I flip him off before turning my back.

"Come on, Dame," Hayden yells. "We all saw you ready to go a round with that Jake dude."

I stop. My Jeep is so close I can almost taste it. I pull out my phone. I'm not surprised when I see zero new texts, I haven't felt it vibrate. I put it back in my pocket and turn around.

"I fuckin' knew it," Jayce roars, slapping the trunk of his car.

"How long?" Hayden says, equally satisfied.

I smile. "A gentleman never tells." But I walk back to my friends. "How long have you suspected?"

"Since that night with Jake," Hayden says.

Jayce adds, "You confirm it every time you drag us to the Braxton."

Oops.

"Does Vicky suspect?" I ask.

Jayce shakes his head. "Not that she's mentioned to me. She was sure as shit pissed that one night, though. What'd that Jake guy say to get you all riled?"

"I don't remember," I lie.

"So you coming tonight?" Hayden asks.

"Are you both going to keep this little discussion to yourselves?"

They both agree. I nod.

Marrin

I've never been in more pain in my life. Well, okay, that's not true. But this is a close second.

I'm curled up on the couch in my apartment in the jeans and T-shirt I'd intended to wear to some cowboy bar Vicky convinced me to be seen at. But there's no way in hell that's happening now.

"*Fuuuck,*" I half cry as another cramp spasms across my abdomen.

I grab my purse and pull out the IUD aftercare instruction paper the doctor gave me. Cramping is normal and they recommend a heating pad and a few different kinds of pain meds. Listed under "Warning Signs" it says to contact your doctor if severe cramping occurs. I'm pretty sure my suffering doesn't qualify. I'm just a baby when it comes to any kind of stomach pain. It brings back bad memories that make the pain seem worse.

This is the one downside to living alone, there's no one around when I need help. Right now, I wish I had a roommate to run and get me some pain meds. I've looked through all my drawers and cabinets. I've got nothing. I've been on the pill so long, I barely get a period anymore. I can't even remember the last time I had cramps bad enough to require pain meds—so I have none.

I stuff the aftercare instructions back into my purse and glance at the clock. It's a quarter past eleven. Everyone I could call to bring me meds is either at work or out with Vicky. And I don't know any of my neighbors.

Except Damian.

I never responded to his last few texts. I'm not avoiding him, I've just been so busy with exams that I haven't had time to answer before I forget. I've also been so stressed and busy that sex is the last thing on my mind.

Yet you still made that doctors appointment today, didn't you?

Another cramp rolls through me and I swear my uterus is trying to escape.

Fuck. This.

It's kind of Damian's fault anyway, and I'm in so much pain that I don't care if I embarrass myself. I reach for my phone and pray my sexiest neighbor is sitting at home on a Friday night.

Damian

I've been at this shitty bar for less than thirty minutes and already I want to hurl myself through a window. The music is shitty, the atmosphere is shitty, and Marrin texted Vicky earlier to say she wasn't coming. Shitty.

Worse, there are plenty of ladies hitting on me. I'm just not interested in even pretending to entertain their attention. The little dude in my pants isn't either—surprising, because usually he has a pretty stiff opinion. Pun intended.

I finish my beer and say goodbye to my friends. I'd rather be sitting at home alone than stay a minute longer.

I'm unlocking the door to my Jeep when my phone buzzes. I climb in and can't stop the smile that spreads across my face when I see who it is.

Marrin: *Random: are you home? If yes, do you have any pain meds?*
Marrin: *I'm not picky. I'll take anything.*
Marrin: *Off brand, expired, your aunt's dog's pain pills —anything.*
Damian: *I'm fresh out of aunt Ethel's poodle's Vicodin, but I'm at the store now & I'll grab whatever you want. My treat ;)*
Marrin: *~swoon~ my hero. I'll take whatever ibuprofen is cheapest.*
Damian: *See you in 15.*

I pull out of the parking lot and head to the nearest drug

store. Thirteen minutes later I'm knocking on Marrin's door with a six-pack of beer, a bag of chocolate, and a bottle of top shelf ibuprofen.

I hear the locks slide then the door opens.

My expression drops.

Marrin's hunched over as if she's shielding her body and mascara is pooled around her eyes like she's been crying. She's wearing only a T-shirt, which she's holding down in front because it's barely long enough to cover her underwear.

"Are you all right?" My eyes go straight to her exposed skin, scanning for bruises and defensive wounds. I don't see any—*thank God*—but I check her ankles, wrists and inner thighs one more time just to be sure.

She shakes her head, noticing. "I'm fine. How much do I owe you?"

I realize then that she's not going to let me in, and I'm not okay with that because clearly something is wrong here.

I fish out the bottle of meds from one of the bags and hold it out. "You don't owe me anything."

"Yes, I do. How mu—"

She doubles over, biting her lip and gripping the door-frame like it's the only thing keeping her on her feet. Tears pool in the corners of her eyes, and her knees bend so far forward I'm not sure her grip on the door will keep her standing.

I don't think, just move.

Losing the bags, I grab her shoulder to steady her and push into her apartment. I wrap an arm around her back and bend to scoop her into my arms.

"*Please don't.*" The pain in her voice stops me dead. I freeze, one arm still around her back. "That'll make it worse. Give me a second."

"Can you walk?"

She nods.

I steady her and carefully guide her to the couch. A pair of jeans is heaped on the floor as if she'd kicked them off while lying down. I help her sit then run back to get the bags. I move to the kitchen and come back to the living room, handing her two pills and a glass of water.

She takes both, downing the water completely. "Thank you." Her whole body visibly relaxes.

"You're welcome. Do you want more water? I also brought beer."

Her stomach growls. "More water would be great."

I take the empty glass. "You shouldn't take ibuprofen on an empty stomach. You'll get an ulcer." I give her a cocky smile when she frowns at me, then move into the kitchen. "What do you want to eat?"

I'm not surprised when I open her fridge and see it's as empty as any college student's would be after exams.

"I'm fine," Marrin says.

I close the fridge and look at her over the counter. Her face is wrinkled in pain and she's leaning in a weird position as if she'd tried to lay down, but got stuck because it hurt.

"You're not fine." I round the counter with more water and the bag of snack size Kit Kat bars I picked up at the store. The pain on her face breaks into a genuine smile when I offer her one. She starts laughing but winces, grabbing her stomach.

I sit down next to her, careful not to shake the cushions too much.

She notices. "I'm not on my period, Damian. But ten outta ten for effort."

"I try. You should've seen me in the feminine hygiene

aisle at the drugstore. I couldn't decide if you were a tampon girl or a pad girl."

Marrin looks at me the same way I imagine she looks at puppies and piglets—like I'm utterly adorable.

"For the record," I add, "I was going to go with tampons before they kicked me out for loitering."

We laugh.

"Ouch, no more jokes. It hurts."

"My bad." I unwrap a Kit Kat and hold it in front of her mouth. She raises an eyebrow, glancing from me to the chocolate.

I smirk.

She grabs the candy and stuffs it into her mouth then pulls her knees to her chest and leans back into the couch. I unwrap a Kit Kat for myself and she taps my arm, holding out her palm. I shake my head and surrender the chocolate.

"What do you want for dinner?" I take out my phone and pull up the closest restaurants that deliver.

"I'll find something."

I look over and see her head resting back, eyes closed. I also see that, once again, she's wearing red panties... Goosebumps pebble her skin.

I stand. "I checked your fridge, Mar, it's empty. How do you feel about Chinese food?"

"Ooh, I feel really good about vegetable fried rice and orange chicken."

"Done," I say.

I open a thin door on the other side of the kitchen and am pleased to find that it is, in fact, the linen closet. We live in the same building but our apartments are laid out differently. Hers is a one bedroom with concrete floors, a high ceiling and big industrial windows lining the brick wall opposite the kitchen.

I know the door near the windows leads to her bedroom because I've seen her disappear into it. Other than the bath-room door, and the front door, this was one of two possible choices. The other must be the pantry.

Just like her kitchen and living room, her linen closet is a joke. There are a few odd cleaning supplies and what might be an extra pair of sheets, but no blanket. I imagine there must be a blanket on her bed, but she's private. In the few times I've been over, I've gotten the impression that she doesn't want me near her room. It's a boundary.

"Be right back," I announce.

I'm out the door before she can ask where I'm going. I run to my apartment and return a second later with a big fluffy blanket. I wave it out, ignoring the puzzled look on her face, and drape it over her legs. Then I sit down and order food.

I lean back, crossing my ankles on her coffee table. She glances behind us at the door. I don't have to see her face to know she's just realized that when I came back in, I left my shoes and jacket by the door.

Smooth, if I do say so myself.

"What are you doing?" she asks.

I lace my hands behind my head and give her an inno-cent look. *Working my way into your heart and earning your trust. Showing you there is more between us than sex. Making you mine.* I go with, "Waiting for dinner to show up...?"

She narrows her eyes.

I add, "With my friend who doesn't feel well and who won't tell me what's wrong because she's too stubborn to ask for help. A friend who I'm also exclusively sleeping with."

"And who is not your girlfriend."

Semantics.

"A friend who desperately wants me to be her boyfriend but I'm just not there yet."

She chuffs and turns to the TV. It's paused on some old black and white movie. "I *did* ask for ibuprofen."

"Yeah, and had you not nearly collapsed in the doorway, you'd have shut it on me and likely never made it to the kitchen to get the water needed to take it. Nor would you have had dinner."

She works her jaw in silence, and I know I've won.

"What are we watching?" I ask.

"*I'm* watching *Cat People*."

"Really? To the guy who just bought you dinner?"

She sits up, eyes flaring. "You're not paying for—"

She clutches her stomach, grinding her teeth.

Instinctively I reach out to comfort her, but catch myself. "What do you need?" I have no idea what's wrong with her, so I have no idea how to help.

When the pain subsides she sits back, knees still tucked into her chest. She pulls my blanket around her and my inner alpha male swells with possessive pride.

Fucking Neanderthal.

"A heating pad," she declares, staring at the ceiling. "A heating pad would be nice."

I stand. "Where is it?"

"I don't have one." She rolls her head to me. "Sit down. I'm fine."

I sigh, pulling my keys from my pocket. "I wonder some-times how you've survived this long without me." Three seconds later, I'm pulling a heating pad from beneath my bed.

On my way back to her apartment, I get a call that the delivery person is downstairs. I run to the lobby and pay for our food. I return to her with everything she needs. *Myself*

79

included. Damn if the alpha male in me doesn't want to bang his chest like King Kong.

Down, boy.

I get everything we need to eat and set it out on the coffee table. I even plug in the heating pad and hand it to her. She lays it on her lower abdomen and groans, her whole body relaxing as she soaks in the heat.

"So what's this *Cat People* movie about?" I ask, sitting down.

The couch cushions are stiff but not uncomfortable. I wonder if it's because the couch is brand new or if it's just never been used. I notice that she seems to sink into the cushions on her side better. Maybe she's one of those people who has a specific spot where they always sit—like Sheldon on *The Big Bang Theory*.

But as I look around at how empty and impersonal her apartment is, I wonder if she just never has anyone over. Never lets anyone in...

"It's a noir film from 1942," Marrin says, swallowing a mouthful of orange chicken. "On a really surface level, it's about this lady, Irena, who thinks she's descended from ancient Serbian cat people who shift forms when they feel threatened or sexually aroused. The idea sort of haunts her the entire film. She marries this guy, Oliver, but it doesn't work out because she's paralysed by the idea that she might be a cat person. It sort of prevents her from living her life. Oliver also falls in love with his coworker, Alice Moore, and Irena gets jealous. There's a lot more going on about suppression of female sexuality and stuff, but yeah. By the end of the film, a few people get stalked and murdered. It's pretty good."

"Timeout." I point at the TV with a chopstick. "Are you saying a house cat goes on a killing spree?"

"No," she chuckles. "I didn't explain that well. It's a big panther, but you mostly just see its shadow."

"So is Irena a cat person?"

"You'll just have to watch and find out." She starts the film from the beginning and we settle in to watch.

By the end, Marrin and I are nestled into our respective ends of her couch. She's curled up on her side, fast asleep. I'm lounging in the opposite corner, legs tucked under the end of the blanket she's wrapped in. It's nearly one A.M. when I check my phone.

Carefully, I get up and turn off the TV. It's dark so I use the light on my phone to see. I clean up, and before I leave, I set the ibuprofen bottle next to a full glass of water on the coffee table. I grab her keys from the counter and pen a quick note letting her know I have them. Then I slip out, quietly locking her apartment door behind me.

A part of me wanted to pick her up and tuck her into bed, but I didn't want to freak her out. And again, I get the impression her bedroom is off limits. I mean there *is* a lock on the door.

In the two-ish months we've been sleeping together, I've been in her apartment enough times to count on one hand. Until recently, we've always ended up at my place. She's never once asked me to come over, and I've never once asked if I can. I do prefer to bring women to my apartment where I can control everything from the evening's entertainment to the breakfast menu, but it is kind of strange that she never invites me over.

I was honestly shocked when she didn't kick me out tonight after we ate dinner. A fact that has part of me dancing with excitement.

Something about Marrin makes me want to be the guy she asks to come over. To be the guy she lets in. Call me a romantic, but I knew within five minutes of talking to her that first night we slept together that there was more than sex between us. I think she knows it, too.

She's just ignoring it.

Lucky for her, I'm not. She and I are endgame. I want her to be mine. Tonight was one of many small victories I've planned to slowly break down her defenses until she finally lets me in all the way.

7

Marrin

The deadbolt slides and I jolt upright, eyes going straight to the door. The only light is from the streetlights outside. It's not much, but it's enough to let me see that the sound was from the deadbolt locking, not unlocking. I sag with relief.

Wait, who the fuck has my keys?

I get up, flipping on every light, and peer through the peephole. I see Damian entering his apartment, my keys in his hand.

I set the rest of the door locks and turn, ready to grab my phone and demand my keys, when a note on the counter catches my eye. It's from Damian. He says he has my keys because he didn't want to wake me up or leave with just having set the simple twist lock on the doorknob. He promises to return them tomorrow morning when he comes over to make me breakfast.

I snort. But whether at his arrogant assumption or because I actually want to have breakfast with him—I have no idea.

I ready for bed and walk to my room, stopping to pick up Damian's blanket and heating pad. Both smell like him. Not that I'm smelling them or anything. Because I'm not.

Liar.

I stare at the glass of water next to the ibuprofen.

I leave his blanket on the couch.

In my bedroom, I lock the door, plug in the heating pad and climb into bed.

I lay there for two solid minutes before getting up.

I grab the water, the ibuprofen, and the blanket from the living room and return to my bed. I have no idea what I'm doing or why. I don't need anyone to take care of me. I'm fine on my own.

But you want someone to take care of you, don't you?

Letting Damian in will only end in heartache. I'm Irena and he's Oliver. If I let him in, I'll destroy us both.

I wake up the next morning to knocking on my door. I try not to jump out of bed and fail. I check my appearance and brush my teeth. The pounding grows louder, and I mentally clip the wings of the butterflies flitting around in my stomach like birds around a Disney princess.

I look through the peephole then open the door. I have two deadbolts that open with a key from the outside that are both attached to separate, reinforced strike plates. I have a chain, an industrial slide lock, the shitty twist lock standard on most doorknobs, and a door wedge. Alice's husband, Gavin, installed most of it when I moved in. I briefly wonder if Damian has noticed.

I pull open the door and step aside.

He cocks his head, working his chiseled jaw, which he hasn't yet shaved today. Goddamn he's sexy.

"What?" I say.

He shrugs, crossing the threshold. "Nothing. Simply noticing that you're not putting up a fight about letting me in."

I shut the door and nonchalantly slide onto a barstool. Damian checks the oven before turning it on. "It's easier to just let you in. You're like an alley cat in heat, yowling at my door."

He bursts out laughing.

"What? I don't want you waking the neighbors."

"First, you've clearly been watching too many films like *Cat People*. Second, you're the one who shows up at *my* door whenever she has an itch that needs scratching."

Now I'm laughing, feigning offense. "Excuse me? This coming from mister '*how about you grind that sweet ass on me in the bathroom*' is rich."

His muscles flex. "I did not say that—"

"Wanna bet?"

"—and you're the one who stuffed her *wet* panties into my pocket. If that's not a yowling cat, then I don't know what is."

I'm off the stool in a second, pulling up the texts from Vicky's birthday on my phone. "We both know my panties were sweaty not wet. And don't act like Vlad the Impaler didn't immediately rise from the dead when you put your hand in your pocket. Half the club saw it."

I hold my phone in his face. He ignores it, grabbing my wrist instead and pulling me toward him so that our chests touch. "I think I know the difference between pussy sweat and glossy need, babe."

"Hmm. Do you though?"

85

Mischief glints in his eyes. Before I can pull away, he opens the oven door and swings me around so that my back is to it. It's still preheating, but blistering air pumps out.

Or maybe it's just Damian.

He forces my legs open and backs me up so that I'm straddling the corner of the hot oven door.

"Don't. Move," he commands in his Sir voice. He holds me tightly to him with a hand around my waist, the other braced on the fridge.

"What are you doing?"

I get my answer when he leans forward, tilting me into the oven's heat. I wrap my arms around his neck as I'm pushed off balance. He's the only thing keeping me from falling and getting a serious burn.

Heat billows out of the oven, soaking into my pajama pants and causing my skin to prickle with sweat. Not to mention Damian's body is like a furnace.

I should be terrified.

I should be screaming.

But I'm not.

I hold onto him as I feel the first bit of sweat spread across the crease of my ass. Son of a bitch. I know where this is going. A few minutes later, he tilts us back to safety and closes the oven door.

He slides a hand down my back, over my butt and between my legs. Making sure my panties soak up the sweat now speckled there. His middle finger slides around to my clit then dips into my center before his hand retreats the way it came.

He straightens and steps back, crossing his arms. "Take off your panties, Red."

"No," I challenge.

"Wasn't a question. Take 'em off or I'll do it for you."

If I wasn't wet before, I sure as shit am now.

I consider my options. I could go into the bathroom and take them off, which technically isn't breaking the rules because he didn't set any. Or I could take them off right here in the kitchen. My pajama shirt is long enough to be a night-gown, so not only will it cover my stomach, it will also prevent him from seeing anything good.

I go with the second option. I step out of my pajama pants. Then, with my eyes on Damian's, I reach beneath my top and pull down my panties. My *red* panties.

Restraint gutters in his eyes, but he reins himself in. He holds out a hand and I pass him my underwear. He turns them inside out, displaying dark fabric damp from sweat and dark fabric glistening from my wetness.

He pinches the perspiration. "Sweat," he says. He does the same to the other spot and his fingers come away sticky and glossy. "*Need.*"

I cross my arms. "So what, you're like a panty-reading fortune teller?"

"Yep. Wanna know your fortune?" He steps up to me and runs a finger between my legs, over my folds. My breath hitches and I have to grip his bicep to stay vertical. I'm fully turned on and ready to go. He pulls a now-glossy finger from me, and sucks it into his mouth, humming in satisfaction of his cheap victory.

I snatch back my panties and put them on.

"You're really not on your period?" he asks honestly.

"Worst panty-psychic ever." I pick up my pants. "Why would I lie about being on my period?"

"Then what's wrong with you?"

I slide onto a barstool. There is no way I'm telling him I got an IUD. For about a thousand reasons.

Before Damian and I had sex, we'd had a brief conversation where we'd established that I was on birth control and that he wore condoms regardless. We'd also discussed the last time we'd both been checked for STDs and STIs. For the record, we'd both recently been given a clean bill of health and neither of us had any partners between the time of our check up and sleeping with one another. The beauty of college: you can literally walk into campus health and get tested any time of day.

If I tell him I got an IUD, he's going to ask if I lied about being on birth control. When I tell him I didn't lie, that I switched because the IUD makes more sense for preventing pregnancy, he's going to know I got it so we can have unprotected sex.

I've never had sex without both birth control and a condom. I'm too much of a control freak—a fact of which Damian is aware. The minute he realizes I'm considering sex with him without a condom, he's going to read into it and think I trust him and that he's more to me than just a fuck buddy and *blah blah blah.*

Nope. Sorry. He doesn't need to know I switched. At least not right now.

"Nothing's wrong with me. Just normal, random cramps."

He clearly wants to ask more questions but the oven dings, letting us know it's preheated.

Saved by the bell.

8

Marrin

After Damian leaves for work, I head to the 13th Floor. I spend the better part of the day teaching the choreography for my numbers in the Femme Fatale show.

In no time at all, the dancers have the timing and moves perfect. I can't wait until we can rehearse on the main stage and I can start setting up the lighting. I have a few ideas, but nothing's concrete until I can see it with my own eyes.

When I get back to my apartment, I jump into the shower. It's Saturday, so I have to work, but I'm hoping it won't be too busy because it's fall break and a lot of students go out of town for the weekend. There is also a freak wind-storm about to roll through that the news won't shut up about. I doubt many people will be out in it.

I get to the Braxton a little before five and see that I'm working with Elle.

"Not heading home for break?" I say.

"No. My family lives on the west coast. It's too expensive to fly home for a weekend."

I don't know Elle that well, but in the time I've known

her, I've gotten the impression she's not close with her family. She never talks about them. She also works as many hours as she can and when it's slow, she pulls out a book to study or read.

"No offense," I say, "but you dress like you have money."

"My dad's side of the family does. I stayed with them in South Korea for a bit and wanted for nothing. But when I got back to the States..."

"They cut you off?" When she looks uncomfortable, I add, "You don't have to tell me. I'm just being nosy."

She shrugs. "I sort of cut myself off. I don't want them paying for me. Their money comes with too many caveats and I'm fine on my own."

"I hear that." I look through the empty arcade to the windstorm now raging outside. A garbage can flies down the street and the lights flicker. "I got a scholarship to study here. It pretty much pays for everything except the cost of living, insurance and"—Elle says the next word at the same time I do—"*books*."

We both smile.

"I don't understand why they're so expensive," Elle says. "And the fact they're only good for sixteen weeks."

"Ugh. Tell me about it. Is this your only job?"

She barks a sarcastic laugh. "I wish. I bartend at a hotel near campus. The owner is an absolute ass, but a lot of alumni and parents stay there when they visit, and they tip really well."

"Too good to quit?"

She nods.

"If you like working for Alice, you should ask her about getting a waitressing job at the 13th Floor."

"Thanks," Elle says. "Maybe I will."

The lights flicker, then go out. They come back on a

second later and the arcade games gutter back to life. The only two patrons in the place lose their progress and decide to call it a night. Thank God they already paid because waiting on the wi-fi to restart so I can use the register is a pain in the ass.

My phone vibrates on the counter next to me.

Damian: *Does the Braxton have power?*
Marrin: *Currently. But it's in and out. You?*

The wi-fi connects and I start closing out as much as I can. It's only seven o'clock, but the wind is blowing so hard I swear I can hear the building groan. I'd rather have as much of the closing procedures done as possible. Just in case.

Damian: *Complex lost it about 10 minutes ago. It hasn't come back on.*

I finish counting the money and receipts when there's a loud popping noise outside and every light on the block goes out.

It's eerie listening to the hum of power recede. As if it's a living thing that might never return.

We wait in silence for it to come back on.

It doesn't.

Elle turns on the flashlight on her phone. "I guess this means we're off early."

"Guess so."

Even with the emergency lights by the exits on it's still hard to see. Conor locks the front door and comes to the bar to help us close. We empty the garbage and sweep the floors. Elle tapes a sign to the door stating we closed early because of the weather.

"I think we're good to go," Conor says. He looms in the dark—a wall of solid muscle.

We head to the back. I set the alarm and Conor opens the door. Or tries to. The wind is blowing against it so hard, he has to lean his weight into it to get it open. He manages fine, and Elle and I slip out. The door shuts with a loud bang, and I turn to my car as Elle turns down the alley.

"You're not walking in this weather," Conor says, voice so deep it's more like a growl.

Elle's hair whips around her face and she desperately tries to tuck it into the hood of her jacket. "The dorms are closed for break. I'm staying at a friend's house a few blocks away. I'll be fine."

It's dark with the power out. Too dark to be walking alone.

A sheet of metal caught on the wind slams into the ground right in front of us, chunks of asphalt go flying.

"Shit," I yelp, jumping at the same time as Elle. "You're not walking. Let one of us drive you."

Another gust roars down the alley and we all turn our backs to it.

The wind is frigid and icy and strong enough to sweep us off our feet if we're not careful. The little bit of rain on the wind slicks the ground just enough that I feel myself sliding forward. I grab onto Conor just as he grabs Elle's shoulder. She's at least a head shorter than me, and while she's gifted with killer curves I'd die to have, there's no way she has more traction that I do.

The next blast of wind sends her sliding, and Conor's hold on her shoulder is the only thing keeping her upright.

"This is insane," I yell over the wind.

Elle turns, grabbing both Conor and me. Her hood flies

off, loosing long dark hair into the night. "I'll take that ride now."

As a group, we walk to our cars. I ask them to text me when they're home safe, saying if I don't hear from them within the hour I'm calling 9-1-1. Conor takes Elle, and I drive down dark, deserted streets until I get to my apartment complex.

Emergency lights illuminate the lobby. The security guard stands next to a small box of flashlights.

"Generators are keeping the security systems up and running," she says. "The emergency lights are keeping the hallways lit, but you're going to need a flashlight once you walk into your apartment."

I take one and say thanks before heading up the stairs.

Once inside my apartment, I turn on the flashlight and set it down pointed at the ceiling. I rummage under the sink and pull out a box of matches and an old-school hurricane lamp I bought at a garage sale. It does a good job illuminating the place—plus it looks cool. I pull my phone from my purse to check the time.

Damian: *I'm sitting in the dark bored af.*
Damian: *Just kidding. I found a glow stick.*
Damian: *Is the power still on at the arcade? I'm trying to order a pizza from that place on the corner.*

I get a twinge of excitement thinking about Damian sitting at home texting me.

I put on comfortable clothes, grab my purse and the hurricane lamp, and head down the hall. Damian answers on the second knock.

His expression changes like a kaleidoscope, going from intrigued to excited, sliding into confusion before finally melting into disappointment. "Damn. If you're here, that means the power's out at the Braxton, which means it's also out at the good pizza place." He steps back, letting me in.

"Sorry to disappoint. No pizza for you." I've never shown up at his apartment without permission and usually with the promise of sex. Showing up to hang out is... new. I move into his living room where a random glow stick sits on the coffee table next to the saddest excuse for a candle I've ever seen. "Wow, you weren't lying when you said you were sitting in the dark."

"Nope."

I set the hurricane lamp on the table and sit next to him on the couch. He's only wearing a thin pair or pajama pants, which means his abs, chest, arms, and tattoos are on full display. The swirling, black lines of ink look stark in the dim light. They crawl over his shoulders and chest like the first bit of ivy in spring.

His skin is luminous in the low light. It's not white or brown, but somewhere in between. Naturally tan might be the right phrase—but it's cool not warm, that undercurrent of taupe running through it even in the places never seen by the sun.

And I would know because I've seen those places. All of them. My eyes follow the trench between his abs lower and lower and—

Quit staring, you creepazoid.

I snap my mouth shut and focus on his face.

His eyebrow dances up.

Busted.

Full honesty, I did come over here just to hang out. But one look at Damian in his half-naked glory and my lady parts have made other plans.

"How many pizza places have you called?" I ask, attempting to salvage my dignity.

"Three. None answered."

"Darn."

"I know."

"What should we *do* to pass the time?"

Goddamnit, Marrin. You hussy.

Unmistakable heat flares in his eyes, but he makes no move to come closer. Instead he does the opposite, leaning away from me back into his corner of the couch, arms and legs propped wide in invitation. The cocky stare he gives me makes my core clench and my breasts tighten. I settle into my corner of the couch because two can play this game.

I rub my foot over the top of his thigh.

He hisses in a breath when it dips between his legs— then surprises me when he grabs his phone. "Before we start anything, we should get food."

He calls three pizza places before one answers. I'm shamelessly rubbing my foot along his erection.

"Hi, I'd like to order a pizza for delivery? Yeah, no problem." He looks at me. "They put me on hold."

I slide forward, running my hands up his thick, muscled thighs. I hook my fingers on the waistband of his pajama pants and pull.

"What are you doing?" Damian purrs. His eyes are wide with lust and mischief.

I slip a hand beneath his briefs and stroke his bare erection. "Passing the time," I say innocently.

I pull out his cock and his head tilts back on a silent groan. I lower myself between his legs, my tongue running along his length. He's smooth and hard beneath my touch. A kick of satisfaction jolts me when I notice his breathing has become shallow and breathy. I kiss the tip of him then suck him into my mouth.

"Oh fu—" He bolts into a sitting position as if he's been struck by lightning. "Yeah, hi, I'd like to place a delivery. Order. An order for delivery."

I smile around his cock.

He caresses my cheek, as if to say, *Hold on a sec.*

Not gonna happen.

I grip his shaft and suck him deep into my mouth. He falls back on the cushions, fist to his mouth.

"Uh, cheese. A cheese pizza. Please."

I bob hard and fast, using my hand to work the length of him that won't fit in my mouth. I pull back momentarily to swirl my tongue around his head then sink back over him.

"Toppings? Uh, what toppings do we want?"

His hand tightens on my hair and it takes me a second to realize he's talking to me. I look up at him, his dick still in my mouth. Desire and worry war on his face. But his eyelids are heavy and I know desire is winning.

"Toppings, babe. What do you w-want?"

I release him with a pop, but continue stroking him. "The Wane sausage"—I swirl salty pre-cum with my thumb —"and the special sauce." I suck my thumb into my mouth, tasting him.

His eyes roll to the ceiling, he mouths, *Fuck.*

"Just cheese, please."

I smile wickedly and take him in my mouth again.

I hear the person ask him what size, to which I answer, "Eight and a half to nine inches." They ask how he'll pay, I say, "With my mouth." They ask for the address, I whisper, "The corner of *About To* and *Come.*"

I punctuate my last answer with a squeeze of his balls and Damian says, "Okay, thanks, gotta go, bye." He hangs up the phone, grabs my head and starts to come. His hips thrust off the couch as he fucks my mouth, pushing and pulling my head where he needs to feel good. I take everything he gives me.

When it's over, he's limp and sated.

He pulls me to him so that my head rests on his shoulder.

"That was very good and very bad, Red." At the use of the nickname, I know what's coming. My body goes tight and loose in all the right places. "I ought to punish you."

Yes, please.

My panties are uncomfortably wet.

He strokes my cheek with a knuckle while his other hand draws lazy circles down my back. Fingertips trace along the band of my yoga pants but go no farther.

I push my hips into that hand. He gives me a wry smile, tracing my mouth with a thumb. "You don't know how beautiful you look with my cock in your mouth."

I love it when he talks dirty.

The hand on my pants moves down to lazily knead my ass. "I imagine I must look similar to you when your clit is in my mouth." The thumb tracing my mouth presses against my bottom teeth. "When my lips are glossy with your need." It glides over my teeth beneath my lips. "When I fuck you with my tongue." His other hand slides to my center. I push into it as he traces devastatingly slow circles over my core.

We stare at one another.

"Are you wet, Red?"

"*Yes.*" I'm not sure if I spoke aloud or not.

Damian's hand leaves my face for my breasts and I realize I'm grinding myself on his thigh, finding whatever friction I can.

His hand moves beneath the neckline of my tank top

and under my bra cup. It's too dim for him to see what he's doing. He's guided by touch alone.

He finds my nipple and lightly circles it with a finger. My breath catches, I'm nothing but feeling, anticipation ratcheting up inside me.

I close my eyes and lay my forehead on his chest. Still my body rocks over his thigh, on the hand still between my legs.

"Does that feel good?"

I nod. "Yes."

He pinches my areola and I moan so loud I should be embarrassed. "Your nipple is very swollen," he says in the same low, gravel-rough voice. "Is this for me, Marrin?"

"Yes."

"Kiss me."

I'm powerless to disobey. My lips find his and I open for his tongue, needing to feel him inside me.

Then I'm completely lost in him, us. I have no concept of the real world, I forget who I am, who we are outside this moment. Outside our kissing. Our bodies. His tongue in my mouth. His hands on my skin.

I'm faintly aware I'm now straddling his lap, my tank top bunched at my waist, my bra on the floor. I'm grinding myself into his hips desperate for attention. His erection grows, but he makes no move to give it to me.

Hands snake up my torso to twist and tease my breasts. I gasp and pant into his mouth. A hand dips beneath my panties and slips right into my core. I shiver at the sudden intrusion, arching up, breaking our kiss. My nails dig into his bare shoulders, and I look down to see him staring at my tits. His eyes dip lower to watch where he's now inside me.

I must have whimpered or begged because Damian's

eyes snap to me. "Fuck yourself on me, Red. I want to feel you come in my hand."

A fresh wave of need floods out of me and into his palm. His lips part in awe. He adds another finger and curls them, putting pressure exactly where I need it. My head tilts back, my hips rock over him.

"So beautiful," Damian murmurs.

Seconds later, my core tightens, my body spasms and pleasure crashes through me like a freight train.

When I come down, I notice three things. The first is that I came with my forehead pressed to Damian's. The second is that I'm now kissing him with a kind of desperation I've never allowed myself to feel, let alone *show*. The third is that Damian is kissing me with that same desperation. Like lovers separated by war. Like kissing and touching is our only language. Like he's finally found me and will never let me go.

I tell myself to stop.

Tell myself to pull away.

Tell myself this is how you get your heart broken.

It's only when I feel his hand glide right over my scars, leaving my pants, that I really snap back to reality.

I jump up, tripping over my purse and spilling the contents everywhere.

"Shit." I put my back to him, pull up my tank top, then crouch down, pretending to be very focused on shoving everything back into my purse.

Anxiety crawls over me like centipedes across a corpse. I ignore it. Ignore the voice in my head telling me the scars are proof I'm white trash and that Damian will never want me once he knows.

"Mar?"

I'm not sure I can turn around—scared of what I might see on his face, what he might've felt on my stomach.

Calm down. He didn't feel the scars.

I force myself to relax. When Damian slipped his hand in and out of my pants, the angle had been weird. He'd had to keep his palm pressed to my pants and there's no way he could've felt my scars with the back of his hand.

Plus it's dark as a cave in here.

When I think I have everything back in my purse, I get up and turn around.

Damian's standing inches from me.

His gaze too keen.

Too knowing.

His phone rings.

We both startle.

He answers and I gather that our pizza is downstairs. He hangs up and grabs a shirt and a pair of shoes. He pauses on the way to the door.

"You okay?" His fingertips drag up my bare arm, sending goosebumps over my skin.

"Of course," I say, shoving my money in his pocket.

He frowns. "You don't have to pay—"

"Either you take my money now and let me buy you dinner or I hide my money somewhere in this apartment and you find out I bought you dinner later."

His face wrinkles. I can tell he still wants to ask about my freak out but decides against it.

Instead he frowns theatrically. "For thousands of years, men have been providing food for their women. I consider myself a feminist, but I'm feeling a little emasculated right about now."

I laugh so hard it's a miracle I don't piss myself. "Okay. First of all, so much is wrong with what you just said I don't even know where to start. Second, I just sucked you off and came in your hand, and you're going to let something like me paying for dinner—*to even the score for the dinners you've bought me*—make you feel like less of a man? Clearly, I've underestimated the patriarchy's fragile ego."

"What can I say, I want to give you nice things."

"Oh my God." I shove him toward the door. "Get out of here."

He laughs all the way down the hall.

9

_____

Damian

"Who are you supposed to be?" I say to Jayce as he climbs into the backseat of my Jeep.

"Clark Kent."

Hayden and I exchange a confused look. "How the hell is anyone supposed to get that?"

Jayce unbuttons his shirt, revealing the Superman logo beneath. Hayden and I give a collective, "*Oh.*"

It's Halloween and we're all heading to the Braxton Arcade's costume party. It's ten o'clock and I'm driving.

Hayden says, "You should probably leave your shirt unbuttoned or no one is gonna get your costume."

"Why? Because I'm Black?" Jayce says, clearly messing with Hayden.

"No. Because without the logo you just look like a businessman."

"Or Lester Holt," I add. They both laugh. A second later, Vicky and Tiana climb into the backseat. "Let me guess," I say, glancing at their costumes "Beyoncé and Lois Lane?"

"Duh," Vicky says. "And who are you supposed to be?"

She grips the back of my seat and practically climbs into the front to get a good look at me. I turn, showing her my outfit. She shakes her head. "I got nothing."

"You're Rick Deckard," Tiana says. "From *Blade Runner,* right?"

"Finally," I say, fist bumping Tiana. "I knew you'd get it."

"It's only one of the best neo noir films of all time."

"Wasn't Ryan Gosling in that?" Vicky asks.

I sigh. "Vick, if you weren't one of my best friends, I'd kick you out of my car right now."

"For not getting some random movie reference? Since when are you so pretentious?"

When we get to the Braxton, I park on the street. We skip the epic waiting line, because Marrin got us on a list, and walk right up to the door where Conor lets us in.

Every year the Braxton has a costume contest, and people get serious. There are awesome outfits everywhere and people are running around trying to get pictures of one another. It's chaos. Eventually, I make it to the bar where Marrin takes one look at me before her lips pucker into a lovely expression of bemused annoyance.

About two weeks ago, I covertly asked Priya what Marrin had planned to wear on Halloween. She'd kindly told me that Marrin planned to go as Rachael from *Blade Runner*, Deckard's love interest. Priya even went as far as to tell me where I could find a costume.

Marrin's wearing a black pencil skirt and suit jacket with severe shoulder pads and a glittering collar. Her retro hairstyle is spot on and her makeup is smoky eyed and red lipped. She's even wearing fake red nails.

She rests a fist on a hip. "Who told you?" she accuses.

I give her a bedroom smile. "How do you know it's not a surprising coincidence?"

"Because nothing with you ever is."

"Babe, I'm full of surprises."

She snorts and comes in close. "Well you better be full of excuses because someone's going to notice we're dressed to match and then come the questions."

"Already thought of an excuse."

"Oh?"

Tell them you're my girlfriend.

"Yes," I drawl. "The couples costume contest—"

"No way."

"You haven't even heard what I'm about to suggest."

"Don't need to. I'm not entering the contest."

Priya's head pops up behind Mar's shoulder. "Hello, detective Deckard. Retired any humans by mistake lately?"

Marrin's jaw drops. "It was *you.*"

Priya smiles, tossing dark hair over a bare shoulder. "I have no idea what you're talking about." She walks away, her pale brown skin sparkling in the light reflecting off her costume's sequins. She's dressed as a very convincing Dita Von Teese.

"Dang," I say. "She could be a real burlesque dancer."

"You've no idea," Marrin mutters. "What's your backup plan, detective?"

"We lie. If anyone asks, we say we've both wanted to do *Blade Runner* and knew if we did it alone, no one would get it."

Begrudgingly, she agrees to use the excuse.

I spend the rest of the night mingling, dancing and playing games. It's just past midnight when I find the bar again.

I pop onto a stool and order another beer. Marrin passes it to me just as a cute woman dressed as a mermaid stumbles up to the bar. She grabs my arm to steady herself before sliding into the seat next to me.

"Sorry," she giggles.

"No worries." I sip my beer. "You all right?"

She smiles. "I'm a mermaid."

"I can see that." She's wearing a shiny shell bustier and leggings patterned with metallic fish scales.

"What are you? Some kind of sexy nerd?"

I'm uniquely aware that Marrin is mere feet away and that the Little Mermaid over here is still holding my arm. Politely, I remove her hand and set it on the bar. "I'm Harrison Ford from *Blade Runner*."

Mermaid squeals, "I've seen that movie." She grabs my shoulder. "Damn, this jacket is legit. Where'd you get it?"

"Internet."

"Holy shit, how much was it?"

I shrug, moving out of her hold. "Not much. Got it used on eBay."

"I'm Chelsea, by the way." She sits back.

"Damian."

"Nice to meet you."

"Same."

"Can I get you something to drink?" Marrin asks.

While Chelsea orders, I try to catch Mar's eye to let her know this is totally innocent and one sided, but she doesn't look at me.

Sweat prickles the back of my neck.

Am I nervous?

Chelsea gets her drink and turns to me. "Are you here alone?"

"With friends. You?"

"Sort of. I came with a guy I've been seeing, but he's now

sucking face with some hot redhead dressed as a Playboy Bunny."

I have no clue how to respond to that, so I go with, "That sucks."

"The worst part is I can't even be mad. I mean she's hot. Like *hot* hot." She sighs. "It just sucks because I got an IUD for him and everything. What a waste."

That gets my attention. "Enlighten me, how is getting on birth control a waste?"

She sips her drink. "It's not. I meant that I switched my birth control to an IUD for him. You know," she leans in and whispers loudly, "so we could have raw sex."

No, I didn't know.

Two days ago, I was cleaning my apartment and found a folded piece of paper under my couch with aftercare instructions for an IUD placement. I figured it was from someone I'd slept with or maybe Tiana or Vicky... But right now Marrin is staring hard at the beer she's pouring. So hard *I know* she's actively trying not to look at me.

She did knock over her purse at my apartment the other night, and an IUD would explain her cramps a few weeks back...

Chelsea continues. "Don't get me wrong, you can totally have sex without condoms when you're on the pill. But, like, an IUD is always there, sitting in your uterus. There's no waking up at three in the morning and running out to get Plan B because you realize you forgot to take your birth control pill and—*fuck*—you do *not* want kids and abortions have so much stigma attached to them."

I try not to laugh. "Personal experience?"

"My roommate. I had to drive her to the drug store in the middle of the night because she doesn't have a car."

"You're a good friend."

"I'm a great friend."

"So is that why most women switch?" I glance at Marrin, she's stone faced and obviously eavesdropping.

"In my experience, yeah. But not always." Chelsea looks over the crowd, then turns to me. "What are you doing tonight?"

"Having a beer." I sip said beer for emphasis.

She grabs my arm. "No, I mean what are you *doing* tonight."

I finally catch Mar's eye. Her face is a mixture of amusement and sympathy. I look back at Chelsea. She's leaning to the side, tits practically spilling out of the too-small shells meant to contain them.

I say, "I'm driving my friends home. I'm the DD."

"Girl," Chelsea says to Marrin. "What am I doing wrong here?"

Mar shakes her head, holding in a laugh. "I think you need to be more direct," she says. "He might be one of those guys who's not as experienced with the ladies."

"Ooh."

I shoot Mar a, *What are you doing?* look. She shoots back a, *Living my best life,* look.

Chelsea grazes her leg against mine. "Sexy detective, do you want to sleep with me tonight?"

I choke on my beer.

I'm no stranger to being hit on. But never in my life can I recall a moment where a woman I'm sleeping with actively encouraged a woman I wasn't sleeping with to hit on me.

I wipe beer off my chin. "If I weren't seeing someone, I'd probably take you up on that offer."

Mermaid's face falls. "Damn. All the cute ones have girl-friends."

I don't correct her.

"Damn is right," Priya says, jumping in. "Whomever Sexy Detective over here is dating must be pretty fuckin' amazing if he's turning you down." Marrin's face heats. "Mermaid, you're a ten outta ten, babe. Don't sweat it. Men are a dime a dozen, and you don't need one to be happy or fulfilled in life. But if you're looking to go trick-or-treating tonight," she winks, "I'm sure a suitable participant will find you. The night is young."

With renewed confidence, Chelsea finishes her drink and melts back into the crowd.

I turn to Marrin. "Well that was uncomfortable."

She grins like a kid in a candy store. I open my mouth to say something, but she flashes me a warning look, reminding me we're in a crowded bar.

I pull out my phone.

Damian: *Was that some kind of test or something?*
Marrin: *Why would I test you?*
Damian: *I don't know. Maybe to see if I'm serious about being exclusive?*

There's a clatter as Marrin tosses her phone onto the back counter. She faces me, arms crossed. A long red nail taps her bicep.

I run through the texts, wondering what I said to piss her off.

I got nothing.

"Can I talk to you outside a moment?" She leaves before I can answer.

I count to five before following her out the back door and into the alley behind the arcade. She stands a few yards from the dumpster.

"Why on earth would you think I'd test you?" she snaps, clearly angrier than I'd thought.

"I don't know. You acted like you wanted that woman to hit on me, maybe even take me home."

"And you think that makes it some kind of test on my part?"

"I..." I step closer. "Why do I feel like there's no right answer?"

She makes a frustrated sound. "I'm not some jealous girlfriend, Damian. If I, for one second, thought I needed to test your fidelity, then we wouldn't be sleeping together."

I take another step, nearly backing her into the side of the building. "What are you saying?" I rasp, glancing at her mouth.

She notices. "I'm not going to hate on other women for no reason. Mermaid was a few drinks deep and had no idea you were seeing anyone. It's not like you're wearing a sign advertising you're in a rela—" Her lips smash together.

Now I do back her into the wall, confidence pouring over of me in a way it only does when I'm with her. "A what?"

Her jaw clenches. "That you're exclusively sleeping with someone. Why the hell would I hold that against her or anyone who hit on you? I have more dignity and under-standing than that, *thank-you-very-much*."

I cage her in and lean down so our faces are level. "You trust me."

"*Pffft*." She turns her head and crosses her arms over her chest, making no move to pull away.

"Say it."

When she doesn't respond, I grab her wrists and pin them above her head. She looks at me, pupils dilating with lust. I brush my lips along her cheek and she angles her head to let me ghost them over her jaw and down the delicate column of her neck.

"Say it." I force a knee between her legs.

Her throat bobs.

I chuckle darkly. Her breathing is fast, each exhale a puff of white on the air. Pinning her wrists with one hand, I reach into my back pocket. Between two fingers I hold up the folded piece of paper I found under my couch.

Her eyes flare with recognition.

Marrin

Fuckity-fuck-fuck.

I knew I should've thrown out the IUD aftercare instructions. But no, instead I'd thought it'd be a good idea to hold onto them just in case.

Damian waves the paper in my face. It must've fallen out of my purse in his apartment.

I don't know what's worse, the fact that he's smug as fuck right now or the fact that I'm so turned on my feet refuse to move. Every nerve in my body is alive with anticipation. Every cell on edge, waiting for what he might do next.

"At first," Damian drawls, "I wasn't sure this was yours. But after Mermaid's little talk at the bar, and the way you're looking at me right now, I think we both know the answer."

There's no good way to have this conversation, so I dive in. "Fine. I got an IUD. Big deal."

His erection presses against my thigh. I stifle a noise.

He smirks. "That's not the question though, is it? The question is, did you lie to me about being on birth control to begin with?"

"Jesus, are you serious? I was on the pill and switched. Sue me."

The arrogant look on his face morphs into something territorial and masculine. My pussy clenches, reminding me just how empty she is.

Suddenly, I feel defenseless, weak. Too exposed. I struggle against his hold on my wrists and he lets go, stepping back but not away. I cross my arms over my chest and stare at my feet, wanting nothing more than to run away.

I'm angry at myself for ever thinking this would be a good idea. Angry at the stupid look on Damian's stupid face. At the fact he probably thinks this means he's more to me than a fuck buddy—because he's not.

Liar.

"You want me to take you raw?" His voice an octave too deep.

I ignore the pounding between my legs and the overwhelming urge to submit to his dominant side. "Okay, we're done. You can leave now." I head for the door.

"No, really." He blocks my path, standing too close and holding my shoulders in his large, hot hands. Uncertainty mars his face. "I've never—" He cuts himself off and something gutters in his eyes, a memory maybe. He blinks it away and when it's gone so is the confidence boost he was riding. It's just us. Me and Damian. "I've always used a condom with my partners. You?"

I stare and stare and—

"Yes."

His forehead touches mine. I still. Heart pounding.

Thumbs knead my shoulders and the moment feels intimate. Feels like everything I'd wanted to avoid. So I add, "It's not a big deal. Just something I figured I'd try. No pressure."

I say the last part sarcastically while patting his shoulder as awkwardly as possible.

He claims my mouth with a blistering kiss, and whatever wall I'd just tried to erect between us comes crashing down. Lips move over mine, hands move over my body, mine over his. It's too much and not enough. It's more than I've let myself want from him, but I'm powerless to stop it because I *do* want it. Want him—*us*.

I'm addicted to him. I can't remember a time when I wasn't addicted to him.

There's something desperate in his kiss, something confident, too. I know right then I want to feel him move inside me, skin to skin. Want him to claim me, mark me, come inside me. I want to share my body with him in that way, to know him in that way because...

I trust him.

Even though I know I shouldn't.

"It is a big deal," he whispers, breath fanning my face. "Maybe not to you, but it is to me."

There's no mistaking the shred of pain in his voice.

"Okay."

"You're mine, Mar. That's the only way this ends."

I inhale sharply.

Damian kisses me once more then steps back, grabbing my hand and leading me to the door. We separate before it opens. He walks in first and when all the warmth in my body goes with him, I know I'm completely and utterly fucked.

10

Damian

"Christ on a cracker, it's cold outside," Vicky complains as she sits across the table from me, her white cheeks red from the nippy autumn air.

We're in a private study room on campus I reserved a few weeks back. Midterms are over, but finals are right around the corner at the beginning of December. It's early November, but still, professors are already handing out instructions for final papers, and I'd rather start early and get it done right than wait until the last minute and get it done wrong. I need a good GPA if I'm going to get into med school.

I move my backpack off the table so she has more room. "It *is* almost winter."

"I hate winter. Why can't it be summer year round?"

"It is in some places. Just not here."

She frowns and settles in.

I wait a solid thirty seconds before diving into the real reason I asked her here. "I have a personal question."

She stares at her notes. "Shoot."

I tap my book with a pen. I don't know why I'm nervous, Vicky and I have been friends since high school. She knows everything about my life, including the fact that I was abused. "You take birth control, right?"

"Oh, wow." She looks up. "It's one of those questions. Okay, yeah, I take birth control. Why?"

"So, like, outside of all the other benefits of birth control, have you ever used it so you could have sex without a condom?"

"Uh, duh. Not when I was younger. Back then it was to keep acne off my face and manage the amount of blood in my pants each month. Periods in middle school are the worst." She shivers. "Those were dark days."

"When did you finally have sex without a condom?" If anyone will call me out for an inappropriate question, it's Vicky.

"Not until Jayce."

That's the answer I was hoping for. "Okay, so what was it like?"

She leans forward, looking at me like I'm the most adorable thing she's ever seen. "Damian, are you asking because you're about to punch your v-card?"

"Ha. Ha." I chuck my pen cap at her. "That's not what I meant and you know it."

"No, I don't." She tosses the cap back. "Do you want me to describe what sex feels like with a vagina? Because I'm gonna be straight with you, that's going to go about as well as you explaining what sex feels like with a penis."

"No. I mean what was it like for you emotionally. Society puts all this pressure on women when it comes to sex. I just wanna know if sex without a condom was, like, different to you."

She considers. And for a moment, I wonder if she thinks this has to do with the incident at that house party in high school I told Marrin about where I nearly had a panic attack. Vicky was there that night. She knows why I was so freaked out.

"Yeah, I mean… any time anyone has sex, there's potentially a moment where we brush up against everything society has told us to think about sex and our bodies," Vicky says. "Like, we call first-time sex a loss of virginity when really it's the gaining of an experience, you know? And when guys have sex, society applauds. When women have sex, everyone has a fucking opinion. It's bullshit. Men also don't assume as much of the risk when it comes to sex. So yeah, sex without a condom could be a big deal for some women I guess."

"What do you mean about risk?"

"Pregnancy, for starters. Also, the lining of the vagina is thinner than the skin surrounding the penis, so women are more susceptible to getting infections. Sex is like…" She props her elbows on the table. "If I stuck my finger in your mouth right now, you'd have to trust that I wasn't lying when I said I'd washed my hands, right? It's flu season, you don't know where I've been." She wiggles her fingers like a mad scientist. "Now if I put a glove on and then ask to stick my finger in your mouth, it somehow *maybe* lessens the risk you incur. Right?"

"Right."

"But it's still intrusive. You're still letting me inside your body. I could be wrong, but I think any time someone lets another person inside them, there's the possibility for power to shift, or be taken, from the person being penetrated to the person doing the penetrating. Couple that with thousands of years of patriarchal rule telling women our bodies are sexual objects to be dominated by men, and yeah, that can mess with your head a bit." She tilts her chair back. "The first time I had sex without a condom, I had to actively remind myself that it wasn't a big deal."

"How so?"

"I told myself it didn't mean Jayce and I were going to get married, or that he'd always love me, or that I was somehow ruined for any penis that might come after his. I wasn't going to let that narrative taint my experience. I told myself that I was Carrie fuckin' Bradshaw and that this was my body, my experience, and what *I* wanted. Jayce was a total doll about it, too. We'd talked about what it'd mean for us both and our relationship beforehand. I hope that answers your question."

"It does, actually," I say. "Thanks."

"No problemo. Now can you please tell me you have bio notes I can copy because I have no clue what's even happening in that class anymore."

"Sure." I hand her my notebook. "One more question. I didn't bring up the whole sex without a condom thing, my partner did. We already kinda talked about it, but do I need to bring it up again?"

Vicky looks up like a bloodhound on a scent trail. "That's up to you. If you feel everything's been squared away and you're both on the same page, then you're probably fine. But if *you're* having doubts, especially ones related to what happened to you," she says carefully, "then you might need to bring it up again."

"No, I'm good," I say. "Thanks though."

"No problem. So, who is this mystery woman? I know you. You're not unwrapping the mummy for just any Egyptologist—"

"If you're about to make a Brendan Fraser reference, please stop."

"Why? *The Mummy* is a great movie and Fraser is a national treasure."

Before I can voice my rebuttal, my phone vibrates. I tilt the screen, hoping it's Marrin. It's not.

It's my brother.

Declan: *You're meeting us for Thanksgiving this year, right? Mom's bringing her new bf. If I have to suffer them alone, I'll kill myself.*

I groan.

Damian: *Where's dinner?*
Declan: *The lake house. It's 2 hours from you. You've got no excuse. Don't ditch me. I'll never forgive you.*
Damian: *I'll see what I can do.*
Declan: *I'm telling Mom you said yes.*
Damian: *Do NOT.*
Declan: *Too late. See you in a few weeks.*

I drop the phone on the table. "I hate Thanksgiving."

"Come home with me like you always do."

"Declan's guilting me. They're having dinner at the lake house and apparently Nadia's bringing her new boyfriend."

"I didn't know your mom was back in the dating pool."

"Neither did I."

"Good for her." She slouches. "Damn. I wanna go to your T-Day. My family is so boring, nothing exciting ever happens."

"I'd give up a kidney for boring any day. I already know how it'll play out. Nadia will start the day with a glass of wine and a side of Xanax, and Declan will take the opportunity to drink everything not locked in the liquor cabinet. I'll spend the holiday making sure Dec doesn't drown in his own vomit, while Nadia and I dance around the topic of my abuse because God forbid we acknowledge we're not the perfect family."

"I'm sorry," Vicky says quietly. "You can always have Thanksgiving with me and my family. My parents love you, plus Jayce will be there. Come on, I'll even let you pick my mom's brain about gross OB-GYN stuff at the dinner table."

"You drive a hard bargain, but I don't think I can abandon Declan."

"Then invite Jayce and me to your Thanksgiving. We can help run interference."

"Tempting. But I don't think Jayce would forgive you for subjecting him to my mother."

"I don't know," she muses. "They say shared trauma really brings people together."

I laugh.

Marrin

I get home sometime after eleven o'clock at night and go straight to the kitchen. I've spent the last five hours waitressing at the 13th Floor and my feet are killing me. I haul open the fridge and begin rummaging through its contents but... Something is off.

Abruptly I straighten.

And find myself face-to-face with a magnet I did not put on my freezer door. It's small and pictures a retro housewife holding a cucumber and a cocktail wiener with the caption "Size does matter."

I chuckle.

Read it again.

Then laugh so hard I cry.

There is no question who put this magnet on my fridge. The question is when. It's the middle of the week and the last time Damian was in my apartment was Monday night when we ran to my place because he needed more olive oil (which, for the record, I didn't have). He must've put it up then.

Have I really been so busy that I didn't notice a magnet?

My apartment is minimalist at best, empty at worst. There are no personal touches anywhere outside my bedroom. Partly because when I moved in, I wasn't sure when I'd be moving out. And also because in the off chance I ever let anyone into my apartment, I don't want to encourage them to stay. It's inhospitable on purpose.

Wiping my eyes, I pull out my phone.

Marrin: *It's hardly fair comparing a cucumber to a mini sausage.*

I've eaten dinner and am stepping into the shower by the time he replies.

Damian: *Not when you're the cucumber and all other guys are the mini sausage.*
Marrin: *Who says you're the cucumber?*
Damian: *I think we all know I'm the cucumber, babe.*
Marrin: *...*
Marrin: *I don't know. My jury's still out.*
Damian: *Would your jury like a demonstration?*
Marrin: *Always. But, sadly, this jury is in the shower and on its way to bed.*

Damian: *Shower pic? You know, for science.*
Marrin: *LOL. Not a chance.*

I put down my phone and get serious about washing. I hear it vibrate several times, but I don't look at it until I'm clean and dry and climbing into bed.

Damian: *:(But I've been a really good boy.*
Damian: *Wait. Did you just now notice the magnet?*
Damian: *Hellooo? Where are you?*
Damian: *Hope you're in the shower thinking of me.*
Damian: *It occurs to me that I've never seen you in the shower.*
Damian: *I think we should rectify this situation. Say... right now. Or tomorrow. Or sometime in the near future. I'm flexible.*
Damian: *What do you say?*

I'm laughing as I text back.

Marrin: *Goodnight, Damian.*
Damian: *You're alive! How was your shower? I bet it was lonely...*
Marrin: *Fantastically orgasmic.*
Damian: *You were thinking about me weren't you?*
Marrin: *Nope.*
Damian: *Wait. You're lying. You don't like masturbating in the shower.*
Marrin: *You remember that?*
Damian: *I remember everything we talk about :)*
Marrin: *I'm not sure if I should be creeped out or not.*
Damian: *Not creepy. You're just that unforgettable. Soooo rain check on that shower date?*

Marrin: *Goodnight, Damian.*
Damian: *Night, Mar. Dream of me :)*
Marrin: *I'd like to keep things nightmare free tonight.*
Damian: *Pffft. We both know this cucumber occupies a starring role in your best dreams, babe.*

I fall asleep with a smile on my face.

11

————

Damian

The next few weeks are some of the best of my life. Marrin and I spend as much time together as possible. She's slowly letting me in, and I'm finding that I like opening up to her about my life.

I haven't told her the heavy stuff because I don't want to freak her out, but I *want* to tell her. I think my old therapist would be proud of me. I used to get incredibly anxious about people finding out I'd been abused, to the point that I needed medication for a short time. I still keep an emergency bottle around just in case. But over time, and with a lot of therapy, I've learned to accept what happened and move on.

I do think my need to tell Marrin is motivated by a bit of self-doubt. A part of me thinks that if I don't tell her what happened to me, and she were to find out, she'd feel betrayed. Or as though I'd sold her on a version of me that doesn't exist.

I know that's the wrong way to think about it.

I don't need her to validate me, but knowing she understands that part of me and still accepts me... there is value in that.

Marrin's keeping secrets, too. For as much as she's opened up, she's also made it clear just how closed off she is. We've had to talk about boundaries once or twice in the last few weeks. Once when I asked about her family, and once when I asked about her waitressing job in the city. Both times she got overly defensive and I had to remind her that I'm not familiar with her triggers and that she has to let me know where her boundaries are.

Overall, November has been fantastic. On Saturdays we have breakfast in her apartment before I go to work. During the week when she's working, I'll show up on her break and try to beat her at *Realm Quest*. When she's not working, we have dinner at my place or hers, and usually watch a movie. She is slowly educating me on film noir, which I've gathered holds a special place in her heart. We've even driven to campus together a few times.

We haven't had sex. Call me a romantic, but I want her to know there's more between us than sex. I like hanging out with her. Sometimes that seems more intimate, too. We still make out and fool around, though. I'm not a saint and we both have needs.

She still refuses to stay the night at my place, and I don't push about staying at hers. I also haven't seen her bedroom, and I'm fine with that. She did let me take her out to coffee once, but made a big deal about how we needed to keep a safe distance from one another and bring textbooks so that, if needed, we could make the excuse that we were studying together.

So it's a surprise when she asks me out on a real date.

It's the Saturday before Thanksgiving and we're having breakfast in her apartment. She's sipping her coffee, toying with the small air plant I bought for her (which I snuck onto her countertop this morning when she went to the bathroom). "Have you ever been to a bar called Back Cellar in the city?"

I shake my head. "No. Why?"

"No reason. They have live music on Saturdays but you need a membership to get in. My cousin Alice has one and reserved two spots for her and her husband, but they're going out of town and won't make it. She said I could go in her place."

"Marrin Braxton, are you asking me out?"

She rolls her eyes. "You ruin everything."

"Wait. You're serious."

"Why are you so surprised?"

"Babe, we've been sleeping together for almost three months and every time you agree to be seen with me in public, you make sure to have a litany of excuses ready to give people as to why it's perfectly platonic for us to be out together."

"I do n—" Her face scrunches as she considers the facts. "Okay, that might be true."

"Might be? Mar, you keep a three-foot radius around us at all times in public. I'm the red-headed stepchild of this relationship."

The last word hangs between us for a moment.

She pokes at the air plant. "If you don't want to go, I understand."

I sip my coffee. "Oh, I'm going. You're going to take me out on a hot date and let people see us in public. You can pick me up at seven."

At seven fifteen, I open the door to my Jeep for Marrin. Beneath her leather jacket, she's wearing a flirty black dress with dark nylons and an old pair of black Keds. Her hair is curled and swept over one shoulder. I'm dressed just as casually in dark jeans and Nikes, a white shirt and an edgy jacket. Apparently the place we're going is low key.

We get on the highway and spend most of the ride in silence. The radio is on, but we're not talking. I don't know why, but I feel nervous. I get the impression Mar does, too.

This feels like a date. It looks like one, too. I reach over and lace my fingers in hers. I don't need to look over to know she's staring at our hands.

I rub her skin with my thumb, willing her to calm. When she starts humming along to the radio, I know it worked.

A thousand words threaten to spill from my mouth. Each and every one of them I know will scare her away. She doesn't do public emotions—at least not the intimate ones, the ones that make her feel vulnerable, exposed. I know she feels that way right now. This is a big step. Being seen in public together, going on a date. And I know we're in a city almost an hour's drive from where we live and go to school, and that because it's the weekend before Thanksgiving, half the student population has already left to start break early, so there's even less of a chance we'll be seen together...

But still.

This is one of her boundaries. A wall. And she's letting it down, letting me in. I'm not going to waste it.

I park on the street and we cross the road, my hand on her lower back. We reach the sign for the bar and walk down a steep set of stairs in a narrow alley before we get to the door. A bouncer checks our IDs and makes sure we're on the list.

The door opens and a rush of moist heat and live music

hit me. We step inside, and maybe it's the darkness, but Mar reaches back to grab my hand. I let her, resisting the urge to bring hers to my mouth for a kiss.

She leads me through the crowd, clearly having been here before, and to a small roped-off section. A man checks our names before letting us through and leading us to a small, intimate booth against the wall. It's secluded and dark and hidden—like a secret. A waitress takes our order. I get a beer and a water and Mar gets a whiskey on the rocks.

The place is little more than a dive bar on the east side of the city. It's classy and run down, the kind of place where any night of the week both Mos Def and Dita Von Teese might stop in for a drink or an impromptu performance.

When the waitress returns, we order some appetizers and settle in to listen to the music.

I'm not sure how much time passes, but eventually the band ends and a DJ takes over. Marrin's hand runs over my thigh and I look up to see her staring at me in a way she's never once done.

Her eyes glow like liquid gold in the dim light.

I lean in. "Whiskey eyes."

"What?"

"Your eyes," I say, letting my lips caress her ear as I speak. "They're the color of whiskey." I curl an arm around her waist and pull her in to me to kiss her gently. "If I looked my fill I'd be drunk off you."

She tilts her head, fully yielding her mouth to mine. I pull her closest leg into my lap and run my hand up her inner thigh, over the nylons that keep me from touching her in the ways in which I need to touch her. Her nails dig into my arm when I find the small bump of her clit.

"Everything about you intoxicates me," I say. "Hypnotizes me. I want to bury myself so deep inside you I won't know where I end and you begin. *You* won't know where you end and I begin."

Let me in, I think, willing the words into every gentle movement of my lips over hers. *Let me in and I swear I'll give you everything and take only what you offer.*

She pulls back. Hot, panting breaths that smell of whiskey warm my face. "Dance with me," she says.

I don't hesitate.

I take her hand and lead us to the darkened dance floor where a pop star croons about not being able to make promises to her new lover beyond the evening. I press Marrin to me until we touch from thigh to chest, and kiss her quickly before moving back. The song is sultry, delicate, but up-tempo enough to merit some space between us.

Marrin is mesmerizing. She moves the way an orchestra sounds—beautifully and perfectly in sync. She's definitely a trained dancer, she's too good for it to be an accident.

I watch for a moment more, before showing off my own skills. My mother refused to have sons who couldn't dance, so she insisted my brother and I take lessons. I'm proficient in almost everything from the foxtrot to break dancing. I mix a dash of upper body isolations with some footwork, and Marrin's face lights up so brightly I'm momentarily blinded.

We dance for what feels like hours, but it's probably closer to one because when the first slow song ends and we can't pull away from one another, we decide it's time to leave. Surprisingly, Marrin lets me pay the bill and I walk her to my car with a hand on her lower back.

As soon as we're on the road, her lips are on me. We're barely to the highway before her hot mouth is on my cock and I'm coming into her throat. All the while, I stroke her hair, rub her back, whisper encouraging words. I'd like to return the favor, but I'm driving, so I settle for stroking between her legs, over her nylons. She writhes and tries to take off the hose, but I tell her no.

She loves it when I give her orders.

I tease her all the way home.

Then we're in my apartment. My hands on her. My mouth. I pick her up and carry her into my bedroom.

I lay her out on my bed, hovering with one foot on the floor, a knee between her legs. She's panting, drunk off my kiss, wrists laid delicately by her head. I want to grab them and hold her down just how I know she likes—

But I don't.

My conquest is slow. My assault careful, deliberate.

I peel the straps of her dress from her shoulders and to her waist, freeing her arms. I kiss down her throat, drinking in her breathy moans as she arcs up, begging me to release her breasts.

I do.

Cupping one in my hand, I stare down into those whiskey eyes I love so much. I study the pleasure unfurling within them. Commit it to memory. Her eyelids are heavy with want. Her chest rises and falls with each short, shallow breath passed between parted lips.

I roll her nipple between my fingers—her eyes close, mouth opens. The sound that escapes her is one I'll forever hold sacred and never forget.

I take her nipple in my mouth. It's swollen and puckered and she mewls, bowing beneath me. I settle between her legs and look up at her in between my ministrations. I suck and kiss and touch—feeling her, worshipping her. Her skin is petal soft and glowing in the moonlight. Her body warm and welcoming. She's mine, this woman. *Mine.*

Slowly, I slide my hands over her hips and under her

dress, pushing it up until it rests high enough for me to see everything between her legs, but not so high that she'll push it down. She likes to keep her dresses and skirts around her waist, who am I to judge?

I hook my hands in her nylons and panties and then she's bare before me.

Her breathing turns heavy and thick, she's drowning in euphoria beneath my gaze, my touch. I slide my hands from her ankles to her knees, up her thighs to her hips. Then back to her knees.

"Please," she murmurs.

I press her knees apart—*slowly.* Wider and wider until the outsides of her thighs are flush with the bed.

The only light is from the moon, it spills in from the windows casting a ghostly glow over everything. It's enough to see the desire glistening between her legs. I run my fingers over her, catching that warm need and moving it around until every part of her is coated. Wet.

Tonight she's going to let me inside her with nothing between us.

Tonight she's going to let me be the first to claim her, mark her, come inside her.

I'd be lying if I said my inner alpha male wasn't roaring in triumph—foaming at the goddamn mouth.

I circle her clit with a thumb. "You like that, baby?"

She nods, teeth buried in her bottom lip.

I lean forward and suck her swollen bundle of nerves into my mouth. Her hips rock up and I have to pin her down with two hands. "Soon," I whisper into her skin. I lick once, twice. "Soon, baby."

She whimpers and I hear, more than see, her nodding.

The smell of her envelops me. Like citrus and honey and woman. I drink her in, teasing and coaxing and tasting until she's right on the edge. Until she's so drunk off my touch she'd start a war for me if I asked.

Never mind the exact opposite is true.

In this moment, I realize what real power is and why men claim to have started wars over women. Right now, I know for a fact I'd do whatever she asked of me. That'd I'd kill, maim, or brutalize anyone she told me to, or anyone who dared take her from me.

I bring my wet lips to her mouth and kiss her possessively, thoroughly. She drinks me in, tasting herself.

I stand and make quick work of my clothing. I'm fully erect and aching to be inside her. A warm hand finds my cock and Marrin strokes me then pulls me, shifting on the bed to bring me closer to where she wants me. I climb on top of her, lowering myself to my elbows.

She's moaning and moving, rolling her hips and guiding my cock to her entrance.

"Are you sure?" I whisper, peppering her jawline with kisses filled with words I can't speak.

Her legs widen and she rubs the blunt head of my cock against her clit. Pleasuring herself with me.

"Marrin..." I rasp. "*Christ.*"

"I trust you," she whispers. "I want you like this. Want you to be my first." Then she slides me lower, through her labia and past her entrance, coating me in her need. Preparing us both.

And if she keeps it up, I'm going to come all over us.

"Grab my shoulders," I say. She does. I reach between us and circle the head of my cock around the tightest, wettest part of her. The heat and sensation in the tip is maddening. "I'm going to take you raw, Marrin. I'm going to come inside you. I'm going to make it so good, I'll ruin you. You'll never want anyone else inside you."

"God, you have the filthiest mouth."

"I know."

I take her slowly. Pressing inside little by little, inch by inch. I learn what she feels like—*she* learns what *I* feel like —when there's nothing between us.

Raw. I'm taking her raw. Letting her take me raw.

I fill her with my bare cock.

We both tremble, pant.

"That's it, baby. Let me in." My voice is hoarse, guttural, my forehead pressed to hers.

She wraps her legs around my hips and rolls her body. And that's all it takes for me to be fully, utterly concealed inside her.

Then there's truly nothing between us. No secret arrangement. No Red, no Sir—no nicknames that mediate who and what we are to one another. There's nothing. It's just me and Marrin.

Her pussy is warm and wet, pressing against—*holding*— the entire length of my cock. She's everywhere, all around me. The most intensely exquisite pleasure surges through me, traveling like pockets of lightning from my cock to my balls, down to my feet and up to my neck.

I look down at Marrin and know she feels it, too.

Marrin

My eyes go wide when I feel Damian pressed to the hilt. I'm full of him, I've yielded to him, yielded everything. I've let him in.

Oh God, oh God, oh God.

I want to panic, know I should, but I can't. I'm fully

committed to the moment and—*God he feels so good inside me. So thick and full.*

So I let go. Completely.

"You okay?" he asks, voice like gravel. He's holding himself back.

I can only nod and kiss him. I cocoon myself around him, my hands in his hair, his in mine. He pulls back and we both groan when he sinks himself deep once again. I want him to go hard and fast, want to really feel him moving inside me.

But he doesn't.

He takes me slowly, carefully. We feel everything. Every roll of his hips, every slide of his cock, every clench of my sex around him. We feel each other's breath on our faces, each other's sweat on our bodies, every sound the other makes as it vibrates through us both.

Deep inside me, he moves. In a place we can't touch because it's not a place at all, it's a concept, an idea, an emotion.

I know he feels it, too, because there's a look in his eyes. A reverence. He's never looked at me this way, not directly anyway. It's a look I've only seen in the subtle glances he gives me when he thinks I'm not looking. It's the glow he gets when I smile or laugh. It's the satisfaction that flickers in him when I eat the food he cooks or when he knows I'm content because of him.

It's a look you feel as much as one you see. And right now it's radiating off him like heat from the sun. *He's mine*, is what the look tells me. *I'm his.*

My pleasure rises to a fever pitch. I'm panting and moving, listening to the sound of our bodies meeting, further proof of our joining.

Damian's inside me. He's inside me.

My nails dig into his shoulders.

"I'm…" I pant, "gonna come."

He tilts his pelvis to hit my clit with each deep roll of his hips. I'm painfully aware that his sole focus is me. That this is about my pleasure, my needs—he strokes my cheek, lips hovering just above my mouth. "Come, baby. I wanna know what this sweet pussy feels like when you come for me."

Release slams into me like a wrecking ball. Every muscle in my body clenches around him. I hold onto him as if my life depends on it. His name leaves my mouth. Words like *"harder," "deeper," "faster,"* leave my mouth, too, but I can't remember saying them, can't remember thinking them. The world is ecstasy, rapture. I'm nothing but this feeling.

Somewhere in the maelstrom, Damian curses into my mouth. His body tightens, jerks. His movements become less careful, he fights to maintain control. He sucks on my bottom lip, and I look up, stroking his cheeks as I come down from my high.

"Come inside me."

His eyes lock on mine and I swallow his grunts as he finds his release. His eyes close, muscles flex, and just before his head falls to my shoulder, I swear I feel a rush of warmth as he spills himself inside me.

Sometime later, I'm still wrapped around him. His body has softened, but he's still inside me. I trace lazy patterns over his muscular back, finger every divot of his spine. Every now and then I feel the gentle press of his lips to my neck and swear he's whispering words too faint to hear.

I don't want to move.

I'm terrified by what I saw in his face. By what I know he saw in mine.

We didn't have sex. Didn't *just* have sex. What we just did was more. A lot more. It was something I've never done. Something I told myself I'd never do.

Damian made love to me.

And I, fool that I am, let him.

Once he looks at me, once we break apart, the moment will shatter and reality will come crashing back.

He'll ask me to stay the night. I'll give the answer I always do because I can't sleep here. Vulnerable. I'm too vulnerable. What we did left us both too vulnerable and now we have to live with it.

"You're mine now, Marrin," he whispers into my neck.

I know, I want to say. But don't.

I close my eyes against the things that threaten. Close my mouth against the words and feelings and truths I'm too scared to speak.

Instead I'm silent, listening. I memorize the moment. Him.

Damian shifts. Shifts again. His heart is racing against my chest and now I shift to look at him.

"What's wrong?"

"Nothing," he croaks. Then he's off me, moving away to sit on the edge of the bed.

I slip my arms back into my dress and move to sit beside him.

I place a hand on his shoulder and he flinches.

Damian

Jesus Christ, this cannot be happening.

One second I'm thinking about Marrin, thinking about telling her how I feel, then the next thing I know, my chest tightens, my heart races, and my fucking brain starts telling me she'll never want me because I'm dirty, scarred.

I move away to sit on the edge of the bed. I inhale deeply, slowly through my nose and exhale slowly through my mouth. I recognize the bad thoughts. Recognize that it's the anxiety talking and nothing more. I work through them one at a time, placing each in an imaginary box then closing the top. Then I rethink each in a positive, rational way, just as my therapists have taught me.

I am *not* going to ruin everything. My brain is just latching onto insecurities from a long time ago.

I am not a child anymore.

I'm a grown-ass man.

There is nothing wrong with me, and I won't let the past ruin this moment. I can do this. I'm fine. I deserve to be happy. I deserve to be loved.

Still, anxiety crawls up my spine like ants over a dead bird.

Marrin touches my shoulder. I flinch—

Stop, Damian. Calm down.

I grab her hand. "Give me a second." I can't look at her. Not right now.

"What can I do?" There's no judgment in her voice, no hint that she's freaked out or that she sees me as weak or pathetic. All I hear is profound understanding.

I squeeze her hand.

I think about the prescription I keep in the nightstand. About the bottle of whiskey sitting in my kitchen. I don't need the medication, that's for emergencies and this is not an emergency. I don't need the booze because I am not my mother. This will pass, it always does. My therapists have all told me this could happen, that sometimes old trauma can resurface. It's normal. It happens to people like me. People who've survived.

I take another deep inhale. "Nothing. Just sit with me."

She does.

The anxiety starts to ebb a moment later.

Another few minutes pass, and I feel normal. A little shaky, a little sweaty, but mercifully normal. I wipe a clammy hand down my face and lay back, pulling Mar down so that her head is on my shoulder.

"Sorry." I hold her close, twirling a strand of her hair.

"What was that?"

"Something that hasn't happened in a long time," I admit. I don't know what it is about the dark, but I feel hidden—like I can say things I can't when the lights are on. "Remember when I told you that when I was younger, I wasn't sure if I wanted to be intimate with other people?"

"Yes."

"That right there, what you just saw, is part of it."

She's silent for a moment. Then, as if she knows exactly what I need to kill the embarrassment sloshing around my gut, she shifts and kisses the spot over my heart. Another kiss to my collarbone. She kisses up my neck to my jaw and then to my mouth.

She crawls over me, straddling my waist and I'm suddenly aware that I'm completely naked and that the only thing she's wearing is a dress. Her wet center presses against my stomach. She cradles my face in her hands.

"Let me take care of you, Sir."

My cock stiffens and I run my hands up and down the tops of her thighs. She's not submitting to put our kink back between us, she's submitting to hand me back my power, my confidence.

"Okay."

Her dress pours over my stomach as she slides back. Her hand finds my erection and she sits up—lowering herself down on me. Her body widens to accommodate my girth, and I lift the hem of her dress a little so I can watch.

She winces and pulls up before sinking down again to swallow a bit more of me.

"I've got lube, baby. Let me get it."

She shakes her head. She bobs up and down on me a few more times before I'm fully inside her. She slips her dress off her shoulders and arms. It pools black around her waist.

She holds my hands to her breasts. She's fucking beautiful. Blindingly so.

Rolling her hips, she moves on me, worships me. Her kiss is gentle and filled with unspoken understanding. She cradles me with her body, makes love to me. She means to erase the past if only for the moment. Means to show me that she still desires me, that what she saw doesn't scare her, nor does it make her see me any differently.

I must be a Neanderthal because it's exactly what I need.

I lose myself in her, rolling us over and pinning her beneath me, her wrists trapped above her head in my hands.

When we come, we come together. And when it's over I bring her a glass of water and we clean ourselves up. Then she kisses me until I nearly fall asleep. She leaves with my spare key, locking the door behind her and promising she'll return it in the morning.

I don't tell her I won't ask for it back.

Because I don't tell her I had the key made for her.

PART II

THE MINIBOSS

In gaming, a miniboss is a computer-controlled enemy that a player must fight, usually in the middle of a level, in order to advance. They are weaker than end-level bosses but more formidable than any of the opponents to player has encountered up until that point.

12

Marrin

Thanksgiving day at the arcade isn't as dead as I'd thought it'd be.

I'm working from noon to close with Elle and Conor. Conor's hanging out by the bar because it's early afternoon and we allow kids during the day. There are several families that have come in to play.

Elle and I are dusting the display case behind the bar when the phone rings. My stomach lurches. I jump off the ladder to grab it, but Elle gets there first.

"Braxton Arcade. How can I help—" Her brow furrows. She hangs up. "Weird. We just got a collect call from a state prison."

"Must've been a wrong number," Conor says, pulling Elle's attention away from me.

I run my hand over my lower stomach, swallowing back the bile in my throat. It wasn't a wrong number. It was my mother. She called last Thanksgiving. I didn't accept the call.

A kid in a Goonies T-shirt asks Elle for help with one of

the games and she leaves the bar. Conor catches my eye. "You okay?"

"Yeah. I'm going to get some air." I grab my jacket and head out into the alley. It's freezing, but I stand there for a few seconds, letting the cold seep into my bones.

Two years ago on Thanksgiving, Alice went out of town to visit Gavin's family. She'd invited me to come along, but I didn't want to spend the holiday feeling like an outsider. My mom had also invited me to dinner at her house in the city. I hadn't lived with my mom in years. She'd struggled with alcohol and addiction and eventually lost custody when Alice had enough money to take her to court.

It's a long story, but when I was younger, I used to dance at this studio in the city. Alice paid for my classes because my mom couldn't afford it. I loved dancing and spent as much time at the studio as I could. My ballet instructor at the time, Ms. Marie, knew enough about my home life to know I was unhappy. She kept an eye on me for Alice.

When I was sixteen, my mom's new boyfriend insisted I was too old to not have a boyfriend of my own. The whole idea was fucked up for a lot of reasons but made worse by the fact that my mother agreed with him.

She always picked her boyfriends over me.

Next thing I knew, a middle-aged man, a friend of my mom's boyfriend, came to pick me up from dance class. Ms. Marie took one look at the guy and flat out refused to let me leave with him. He blew up, but she didn't care. She called Alice, and Alice called the cops and Child Protective Services. I don't think I've ever seen Alice so mad. She was twenty-three at the time and that was the day she decided to fight for full custody of me. My mom eventually went to rehab and we didn't hear anything from her for a few years.

Then, fall of my freshman year of college, she started

calling. She told me everything I wanted to hear. Said she was sorry for what happened, for being a bad mother, sorry for putting her boyfriends before me. She asked Alice and me to come over for Thanksgiving. Alice couldn't go, but I said yes.

I spent the night at her house, met her new boyfriend, a creep named Frank whose biggest accomplishment in life was his stupid red truck. I spent Thanksgiving Day alone in my old house, waiting for my mom and Frank to get off work. I'd started making some food, but got all sweaty in the tiny kitchen, so I'd decided to shower. I'd brought a robe and a change of clothes into the bathroom with me because I wasn't about to walk around a house I didn't live in half naked. When I got out of the shower, I dressed and left the bathroom.

I was halfway to my old room when Frank grabbed me. He was home early and thought me wearing pajama shorts was my way of coming onto him. That's about when the screaming and fighting started, and it only got worse when my mother walked in the door.

November air fills my lungs and I rub at phantom pains in my lower abdomen. I hate Thanksgiving. I pull out my phone and text Damian.

Marrin: *Have you left yet?*
Damian: *Getting in my car now. Pray for me.*
Marrin: *LOL. Text me when you're back?*
Damian: *Of course.*

I turn to go inside and glimpse a red truck driving past the far end of the alley. I stop.

Frank went to jail for attacking me two years ago and my mom went to prison. But when Frank got out, and my mom was sentenced, he started following me around in his red truck. Bastard is the reason I've moved three times in two years.

I swallow my paranoia and go inside.

By six o'clock, the Arcade is dead. I play and watch *Sorry, Wrong Number* on the projector (it might be Thanksgiving but it's still Film Noir Thursday), while Elle and Conor have an intense *Tetris* battle. They're hunched over the controls staring at the screen. The most noise either makes is the occasional angry curse.

The movie ends around nine and I make the decision to close early.

I lock the front door and start closing out the register. Elle and Conor finish their battle and help with the rest of the closing procedures.

The phone rings. This time I get to it first.

"Braxton Arcade. How can I help you?" There's a muffled noise, but no answer. I hang up.

"Who was it?" Elle asks.

"Our mystery butt dialer I think."

We finish what we need to do then grab our jackets and head to the back door. I punch the alarm and grab the garbage before we exit. We say goodbye and I head to the dumpster to toss the bag. Walking to my car, I press my hands to my pockets, finding my keys and...

"Shit." I forgot my phone. I swivel around and head to the front door because the back door is an emergency exit and locks from the inside.

Conor pulls up beside me and rolls down his window, Elle's in his passenger seat. He must be driving her home. "What's up?" he says.

"Forgot my phone. You can go. I'll be fine."

Conor hesitates but eventually drives off. I unlock the

front door and disarm the alarm. I flip on the bar lights and find my cell next to the register. I grab it and jump when the shrill ring of the arcade's phone barges through the silence.

Something uneasy settles in my stomach. I blame it on having watched *Sorry, Wrong Number*. That film will make anyone wary of phones.

I head to the back door. In the corner of my eye, a flash of red passes the Braxton. My head snaps to the front of the arcade. It's almost entirely ceiling to floor windows. I see nothing.

Get it together. You're freaking yourself out.

I flip off the lights and head to the back door. I punch in the code then head out.

I'm three steps from the building when an old red truck pulls into the alley.

My heart starts racing.

The high beams kick on, sharp and blinding. The engine revs. Exhaust clouds the air. Stinks like diesel fuel.

Fear clamps down on me like the jaws of a great white. Adrenaline commands my feet to move. My car is too far away.

I scramble backward, flinging my arms out to grab the door handle. It's inches from latching closed. I haul it open. Rush inside.

But it's an emergency exit door—it's made to open easily and close slowly.

It also doesn't have a handle on the inside, only one of those locking push bars. I grab it and yank it toward me.

A truck door creaks open. Slams shut.

I throw my weight back, foot braced on the wall. Sweat makes the push bar hard to grip, it slips through my fingers.

Footsteps sound.

The door is inches from latching closed.

A dark, unmistakably male figure is backlit by the truck's high beams.

A scream rises in my throat—

The door clicks shut and I crash backward into the wall.

The door rattles and shakes as someone pulls from the other side.

I cower on the floor. Tears blur my vision. Panic clogs my throat. Each breath too shallow. Too short. I put my head between my knees feeling my blood pressure drop.

Frank pounds on the door. I know it's him. I know it. He's come after me—*again.*

Oh God, oh God, oh God.

Silence permeates the air. Everything stills. I wait.

My heart is a bass drum in my chest. Each beat reverberates through my body. Pounds in my ears. I hug my knees to my chest as the room shifts between the Arcade and the living room of my old house. It smells like alcohol and my mother's perfume. My stomach churns, bowels liquefy.

You're not there. It's in your mind.

The pain in my stomach is excruciating, I'm going to vomit.

Don't do this. Don't let this in.

My hands are numb, cold. Fingers tingle, pricked by a thousand invisible needles. All my

war

mth

lea

ks onto the floor in a dark red puddle...

Shrill beeping pulls me to the surface. I'm in the Braxton Arcade. The alarm is about to set. I find my feet and edge toward the security system, arming it to stay.

I'm not sure if I should call the cops. I could call Alice, but she's hours away having dinner with Gavin's family—

Phantom pain stabs my abdomen. I need to calm down. Catch my breath. Stop crying.

With a hand on the wall to steady myself, I walk back into the main room. I grab a bottle of water and slide to the floor behind the bar. I call Alice. It goes straight to voicemail. I call twice more and get the same result. I think I leave a message, I'm not sure.

I text her. I text her again. No response. I text Gavin. No response. Everyone I trust enough to call is either out of town or isn't someone I can have pick me up because if Frank is waiting outside, what the fuck are Priya and I going to do?

Frank is too big and too strong. He's like the boss in a video game, and I don't have the skills to face him. Hell, I don't have the *courage* to face him. Every time he comes around I run. It's what I'm good at. Oh God, I should just call the cops—but what if I'm overreacting and it's not Frank?

Why the fuck is my phone dying?

My chest rises and falls sharply. Tears spill down my face. I call Alice a few more times and leave a message. I have no idea what I say.

The Braxton's phone rings again and a new wave of fear rises in my chest. Maybe Frank is the mystery butt dialer?

Stop it. Stop it right now.

Thinking like that isn't going to help me. I need a plan.

I could call Conor. I should. But I don't want Conor. I want Damian.

I wish Damian were here.

I don't give my brain a second to talk me out of it.

Marrin: *I need help. I'm scared.*
Damian: *Where are you?*

Marrin: *The Braxton.*
Damian: *On my way.*

A strange calm settles over me. I don't let myself think about how needy and pathetic I must be. And I don't give myself a second to think about what a gargantuanly bad idea it is to bring Damian into this. I hug my knees to my chest and wait.

Damian is coming for me.

He'll be here soon and everything will be all right.

13

Damian

The drive to the lake house takes about two hours. Somehow, I manage to squeeze an extra thirty minutes out of it. I pull into the driveway and sit in my Jeep. I recognize my brother's BMW but I've never seen the black Rolls-Royce parked next to it. Unless my mom got a new car, it must belong to her new boyfriend.

Or is it manfriend?

At what point does a guy become too old to be called a boyfriend?

I'll have to save the deep thoughts for the drive home. Begrudgingly, I get out of my Jeep and walk up the ridiculous staircase to the front door. It swings open and Declan appears. A rocks glass in hand.

Great, it's going to be one of those Thanksgivings.

"Thank fuck," he declares, pulling me into the foyer and slamming the door.

The mansion is just like all my parents' houses. Expensive, shiny, and cold. It reminds me of a museum or a house you see in an architecture magazine. It's made to be looked at and admired, not lived in. It's a place that contains things used to make the act of living look prettier, but nothing about it can actually sustain life.

It's a façade.

"How much have you had to drink?" I ask.

"No more than what dad would've let me have."

I suppress a groan. Declan's barely eighteen. My parents are the kind of people who think it's fine to drink with their kids on special occasions.

Before I can say anything, heels peck across the floor, growing louder with each quick step. My mother comes into view. She's wearing a severe dress, the color of which compliments her flawless light brown skin, and her dark hair is pulled into a bun as tight as her smile. She's the definition of polish and poise. She could give Victoria Beckham a run for her money.

She stops at the opposite end of the foyer. "Damian."

"Nadia." I've been calling her by her first name for years.

Her face tightens imperceptibly. A blond man wearing a spray tan and a designer suit steps into view. "I'd like to introduce Richard."

"The guy she's bangin'," Declan whispers loud enough for the neighbors to hear.

Richard walks forward. He's tall and stately with an air of self-importance—just like my father. "Nice to meet you, Damian. Your mother has told me so much about you."

I shake his hand. "You don't have to lie to impress me, Richard. The mere fact you're dating Nadia is impressive enough."

He smiles uncomfortably.

Declan claps Richard's shoulder. "Dick here is the Pres and CEO of Gainnes. As in Gainnes Hotels." A global brand of full-service hotels and resorts. "He was just telling me about a string of tropical islands they purchased to build resorts on. I think we should plan a trip."

"I think you should switch to water," I say, taking his glass and emptying it into a nearby plant. He frowns when I hand it back. "You're in high school, remember?"

Nadia clears her throat. "Damian, why don't you put your jacket in the coat closet and join us in the sitting room."

It's not a question, but I do what she wants. I'm not looking to start a fight. The sooner we get through this dinner, the sooner I'll be gone.

The moment I sit down she turns to me. "Would you like something to drink?"

She's perched on a white leather sofa next to Richard. Declan and I sit across from them in matching armchairs. The fireplace is going and the piano in the far corner is playing classical music.

"No thanks."

"How is school?"

"Fine."

"How are your classes?"

"Fine."

She smoothes the hem of her dress. "I'm glad you could find time to come home for the holiday."

She pauses like she's waiting for me to agree. I say, "Declan made a compelling argument."

"Oh? And what was that?"

I don't need to look at my brother to know he's enjoying this.

"He threatened bodily harm. Naturally, wanting to preserve the *reputation* of this family, I decided to acquiesce to his request."

She smiles at Richard. "Boys. Always such a handful,

what with their jokes and stories and all."

Anger spikes my blood at her use of the word *stories*. Maybe I'm overreacting, but I think that was a jab at me. At *my* story. The one she and my father minimized by pushing it under the rug.

"Would *you* like a drink, Nadia?" I ask. "Your hands are noticeably empty."

She looks down her nose at me. "I'm not drinking anymore."

I snort—an automatic response to bullshit.

"I'm serious, Damian. Not drinking today is a big step for me."

Richard puts his hand on her knee. "Your mother has dealt with a lot since your father's passing. I'm very proud of her sobriety."

Declan chuckles. "Hate to break it to you, Dick, but the drinking didn't start with our old man's death."

"I'm aware," Richard says. "We've spent a great deal of time talking about the whys of her illness."

"Addiction," Declan spits.

"Dec," I warn.

He glares at me. "No. She doesn't get to rebrand her addiction just because she's finally acknowledged it."

"Alcoholism *is* an illness," Nadia snipes. "It's a disease."

"Disease it may be," Declan says, "but last I checked, Type 1 Diabetes didn't cause anyone to mentally check out of their parenting duties, did it?"

I must be an asshole because I see his point. Plus, he's angry. He's allowed to be angry. I'm angry too, but years of therapy have helped me accept that either of my parents acknowledging their faults or apologizing is not something I should expect. And while it would be nice to hear, it's not something I need to hear. Not anymore.

Also, if my mother were serious about her sobriety, then I think she'd be a little more receptive to hearing about how her substance abuse played a role in ruining our family.

"If you don't want to support me, that's fine," Nadia says. Then, to my utter horror, both my mother and her shiny new manfriend look at me.

I stare. And stare. And finally say, "What?"

Nadia bristles. "Wouldn't you like to set the example for your brother?"

I blink. Narrow my eyes. Put on a good show of acting like I have no clue what she's talking about. I open my mouth. Close it. "Are you... asking for my support?"

"Yes."

"*You're* asking *me* to support *you*?" And because I am a grade-A douchebag, I squint at the ceiling like I can't comprehend. And really I can't because support is the one thing she's never given me.

"Yes. Damian."

Declan pantomimes sipping tea.

I sit back, crossing an ankle over a knee, smug as fuck. "*If anyone finds out what happened,*" I say, "*it will embarrass this family and ruin your reputation.*"

Those words—her words—taste like acid on my tongue, rake like hot coals over my skin. I sit murderously still, willing her to see every ounce of hate I've ever wasted on her and my father. I'm not even sure she remembers saying those words to me. Not sure she remembers making me, *her own son*, feel like it was my fault when my father's friend touched me inappropriately. When he forced me to touch him inappropriately.

When she doesn't move, I know she remembers.

A sick, vindictive sort of satisfaction settles into my stomach. The part of me that needs control, needs to be heard and obeyed and *believed*, flares in triumph at the gigantic *Fuck You* I just served.

"Excuse me." I get up and leave the room, overwhelmed with the urge to call Marrin and share my victory with her. But I can't. Not yet.

Instead I find the kitchen and help my family's chef make dinner.

Just like old times.

Eventually, I have a mostly silent, tense dinner with Nadia, Declan, and Richard, which ends when I decide someone needs to put Declan to bed. Why anyone thought he should be allowed to drink is beyond me.

When Dec is safely tucked in next to a bucket and a bottle of water, I head for the door. I'm halfway into my jacket when Nadia walks into the foyer.

"Are you leaving?"

No, I'm going outside to take a piss.

"Yep."

"Well... Goodbye. Drive safely." She sounds like a robot.

I adjust the collar of my jacket. "Have fun with Dick."

When I open the door, she says, "I'm sorry."

Cold air assaults my face but that's not why I freeze.

I stare at my Jeep.

I don't need to stay here, I'm free to go. I've performed my proverbial son duties for the year. But the thirteen-year-old in me wants more.

"For...?" It comes out angrier than I intended.

"You know."

The urge to punch a fucking hole in the wall plows into me like an eighteen-wheeler on the interstate, right along with the need to scream at her to say what happened to me out loud. To fucking *acknowledge* what happened and to admit that she and my father were more concerned with reputation and image than with actually helping me.

"Later, Nadia." I slam the door behind me like a fucking child and proceed to stomp across the porch.

Behind me, the door opens and shuts lightly.

I don't turn around, taking the stairs two at a time.

"For what happened." Her voice is so quiet I almost don't hear it.

Emotion clogs my throat and I find myself rooted in place. My breath is hot, forming heavy white clouds on the air. For a moment, that's all that moves.

"I wasn't... I should have protected you."

She doesn't continue and I don't have anything to say. She's speaking for her benefit, not mine. If this is what she needs to say to maintain her sobriety, fine. Thanks for inviting me to Thanksgiving so you could use me to feel better about yourself.

I don't remember getting in my Jeep and driving away.

I do remember leaving a message about needing an appointment with a therapist I've used a few times while at school, and turning on a playlist that helps keep me calm.

A little over an hour later, I'm filling up my tank at some random station when my phone vibrates.

Marrin: *I need help. I'm scared.*

An acute sense of dread pools like oil in my belly. Marrin never asks for help or admits to being scared.

Damian: *Where are you?*

Seconds later, I'm in the Jeep, speeding down the highway.

14

Damian

I turn down the street where the Braxton is located. It's just after ten o'clock but because it's Thanksgiving, the streets are deserted. I crudely park in front of the bar and call Marrin. She answers on the first ring.

"Damian?" Her voice is hoarse, ragged.

"I'm here. I'm at the door."

"Okay." She hangs up.

Inside the bar is dark, but enough light creeps in from the streetlamps to catch silver-white hair when Marrin pops up behind the bar. She walks to the front and I can tell she's been crying. Those whiskey eyes I love so much are red and puffy and mascara has left murky trails down her cheeks.

She sets the alarm then unlocks the door.

Her eyes are frantic, wild, darting back and forth as she steps outside. I fight the urge to pull her into my arms. I hold back only because I can tell she's trying to hide that she's on edge.

Something's spooked her, and I worry that if I touch her, she'll shut me out.

She fumbles with the key, hands shaking so badly.

"Let me," I offer. I take the keys and lock the door.

Finally she faces me, and I'm gutted by the look in her eyes. She reminds me of a fawn caught in a clearing—terrified, alone, *powerless*. And that's the look that has me deciding to touch her because of all the times she's been utterly bare and prone before me, she has never once looked powerless. Not. Once.

The alpha male in me erupts like a demon from hell, ready to slaughter whomever did this to her, ready to do whatever it takes to fix this, to ease her.

It's an effort to keep him contained.

"Hey," I cup her face. "What happened? Are you okay?"

Emotion bubbles in her eyes and I swear I can see the wall she's trying and failing to erect between us. "I'm fine."

"You don't have to tell me what happened, but I want to know you're okay. Did someone hurt you?" I'm stroking her face, her hair, her arms.

She sags a bit, seeming to ease, and shakes her head.

I wrap a protective arm around her. "Do you want me to take you to your car—"

"*No*," she yells, eyes wide. "Let's go to your place."

I ignore the odd phrasing and lead her to the Jeep. I've seen this kind of behavior before. Like she's expecting someone to jump out at her. I see it sometimes in the people I meet at work. People who've been mugged or attacked. I probably acted like this once, too.

I help her into the vehicle and lock the door before shutting it. I jog around to the driver's side, scanning every inch of the dark street. I see nothing. I unlock the door and jump in. For her benefit, I hit the automatic lock button twice, wordlessly letting her know we're safe. Then I blast the heat and lace my fingers in hers.

Fuck. She's shaking.

I kiss the back of her hand. "You're safe, baby. I'm here."

A strangled noise leaves her throat. "Can we take the long way?"

"Of course."

We drive through the neighboring town, making a big circle before heading toward our complex. Mar glances in the side mirrors and looks behind us every now and then. It's obvious she's checking to see if we're being followed. I wish she'd tell me what the hell happened.

I decide to try and get her mind off things. "Have you had dinner?"

"No."

"How come you're working on Thanksgiving?"

She's silent for a moment. "I hate Thanksgiving."

"That makes two of us. I spent the evening running interference between my mom and brother. Nadia brought her new boyfriend—or manfriend—I'm really not sure it's appropriate to call him a boy anymore. And calling him her lover makes it feel gross."

The shadow of a smile touches her lips. "Nadia is your mother?"

"Yeah. I refer to her by her first name."

"Why?"

"I like to think it reminds her of her place in our relationship. Just because you birth a human doesn't make you a mother. Mother is a title you earn and Nadia hasn't done that." An image of my mom standing on the porch after I got into my Jeep flashes through my mind. I push it away. "Why do you hate Thanksgiving?"

She's silent so long I'm pretty sure she's not going to answer. "My mother was arrested on Thanksgiving."

I kiss the back of her hand. "I'm sorry. That must've been hard."

She stares out the window. "Thank you. For coming to get me."

She says it as if she'd thought I might not.

I stop at a red light and squeeze her hand. "Look at me." She does. She looks tired. Lost. "I will *always* come for you, okay? We could be in the middle of a huge fight and I'd come if you needed me."

She nods.

When we get to our complex, I open her door and lead her to our floor. At the landing, she picks around for her key.

If she thinks I'm just going to drop her off at her door and leave, she's got another thing coming. I steer her toward my apartment. "Let me make you dinner."

"Can I stay with you?"

For a second, I'm so shocked I forget how to close my mouth. She's never stayed the night. The urge to ask her what the hell happened tonight surfaces so hard, the words almost leave my mouth.

Something bad happened. Something that scared her enough to make her not want to be alone.

That oily feeling slides into my stomach again and the words Jayce said at Vicky's birthday come back to me, "*She moves a lot... Vicky asked me to help move her into a new apartment in the middle of the night.*"

The puzzle that is Marrin Braxton is coming together.

"Of course, baby. Anything you want."

"I'll just grab a few things," she says.

We enter her apartment and she doesn't turn on any lights. I wait by the door while she slips inside her bedroom.

A few minutes later she's gathered everything she needs in a small bag.

When we get to my apartment, I do everything I can to make her comfortable. I close the blinds, turn on all the lights and insist we both put on our pajamas. I wrap her in a blanket and put her on the couch. Then I move to the kitchen to make her dinner. She's not hungry but I make her a grilled cheese with a side of steamed veggies anyway. By the time we go to bed, she's eaten half the sandwich and most of the veggies.

She slips into bed first, putting her back to me. I have to fight the urge to pull her into my arms when I climb in. It's a big bed. We don't have to touch if we don't want to.

I lay on my back in the dark, staring at the ceiling. "Goodnight."

"Night."

I close my eyes, painfully aware how close yet how far apart we are.

The sheets rustle as she rolls over.

Fabric slides.

Now I'm the deer in the clearing. Waiting, anticipating.

Warm fingertips find my bicep and slide down to my wrist. I flip my palm and let her lace her fingers in mine. I'm so still I'm not even sure I'm breathing.

But she is. Because I can hear it. Soft and easy and calm.

"Marrin," I say, so low it's barely audible.

"Yeah?"

"I really want to put my arms around you."

"Okay," she says like she's relieved.

I turn on my side and pull her to me. We settle together, her back to my chest, and it's the most natural thing in the world. I press my lips to her temple, her cheek. Her warmth and scent seep into me, and I fall asleep with her safe and sound and in my arms.

She's mine. I'll never let her go.

Someone's knocking on my door.

Correction, someone's pounding on my door.

I slip out of bed careful not to wake Marrin. I throw on a pair of pants and check my phone before slipping it into my pocket.

It's three in the morning.

I throw on a hoodie to hide myself. If there's one thing I've learned studying martial arts and teaching self-defense over the years, it's that being underestimated by an opponent is a gift. Whoever the hell is at my door does not need to be tipped off that I'm more than capable of defending Marrin and myself.

Before I slip out of my room, I grab a baton from inside the nightstand. I don't sling it out, just conceal it at my wrist. I lock the bedroom from the inside then leave.

The pounding stops momentarily, voices sound in the hallway.

Adrenaline stirs in my blood.

I put on a pair of sneakers and scan the living room, taking a mental picture of where everything is. I've no intention of opening the door and inviting in a threat, but it's good to be prepared.

The pounding begins again and I look through the peephole. A gorgeous blonde with ice-blue eyes and an intense look on her face is standing at my door, cellphone to her ear. I recognize her immediately as Alice Braxton,

Marrin's cousin. She hasn't bartended at the Arcade in a while, but she's beautiful in a way that's hard to forget.

I unlock the deadbolt but leave the chain in place. And I'm glad I do because as soon as I open the door, I see she's not alone. Her big, scary husband, who I recognize from the Arcade, is standing to the side, purposefully outside the range of the peephole.

He's holding a pair of bolt cutters, too.

Jesus Christ, who are these people?

"Where's Marrin?" Alice demands, hanging up her phone.

"Who are you?"

"I'm her cousin, you're Damian Wane and this is your apartment. Marrin texted me the address hours ago to let me know this is where she'd be."

"Who's the big guy?" I jerk my chin at her husband.

Her eyes narrow in surprise. She didn't expect me to interrogate anyone who came looking for Marrin.

Surprise, Blondie.

"My husband, Gavin. Mar also texted him your address. I can prove it if you want. Please," her voice cracks, "tell me she's here and that she's okay?"

I size them up, unsure what to do.

"Listen, kid. You're going to open this fucking door and let me in, or I'm going to break it down. Either way I'm coming in. It's your choice."

Blondie is dead serious.

I look from her to Mr. Tall, Dark, and Scary. "How do I know you're not the reason Marrin called me in the first place?"

She hesitates. "How much did she tell you?"

"Enough," I lie.

"But not enough to know I'm not a threat."

The words aren't meant to hurt, but they do.

Something must show on my face because she adds, "Let me in and I promise I'll tell you as much as I can."

I know they're not here to harm Marrin. The concern on Alice's face was enough to let me know the moment I looked her in the eyes. I shut the door and unhook the chain. Then I open it and step back, keeping myself between them and the hallway that leads to the bedroom.

Gavin closes the door before scanning every inch of my apartment.

"Where is she?" Alice demands.

"Sleeping. And I'd like to keep it that way." I point to the concrete floors and high industrial ceiling that allow everything to echo.

She lowers her voice. "Who are you to Marrin?"

"I'm her b—*friend*. I'm her friend. A good friend."

"Thank you for helping her. Did you see anything? A vehicle, a person, something out of place on the street when you picked her up?"

"No. It was deserted. But..." I drop the baton on the counter, a movement Gavin notes. I rake my fingers through my hair. "She was scared. Like, *scared* scared. She barely said anything and I... think she was hiding behind the bar. She didn't want to get her car either. When I suggested it, she kind of freaked out."

"Is she injured?"

I shake my head. "Not that I've seen. She'd obviously been crying when I picked her up, but I couldn't see any defensive wounds or signs of a struggle or anything. She was wearing a jacket, though. And when I got her back here, she changed in the bathroom."

Alice's white skin pales as her eyes widen in the most horrifying way.

I quickly add, "She hasn't acted as if she's been hurt like *that* or as if she has bruises where I can't see—and I've asked as many times as I politely can. She's just rattled."

Gavin and Alice exchange a look.

I want to ask if someone is stalking Marrin. It's the only conclusion I can think of that fits.

The bedroom door unlocks with a click.

I turn around. Marrin takes a few hesitant steps, recognition and relief flood her face, and then she's running to Alice. The two embrace and Marrin starts to sob.

And I mean *sob*.

The sound is horrible and gut wrenching and it breaks my fucking heart. I want to make it stop, I'd do anything to make it stop.

"Shh, it's okay," Alice coos. "It's okay. I'm so sorry my phone was off." The look on her face is fierce and protective, it reminds me of a mother bear.

Jealousy slithers up my chest that it's not my arms Marrin trusts to cry in.

I know it's a stupid, selfish way to feel, so I push it away.

Now I feel like an interloper. Like an intruder in a private family moment. It reminds me of what it was like growing up when I'd watch my friends interact with their parents. Vicky's mom and dad were always so loving and supportive. I was lucky if my parents offered a combined five words to me by the time I went to bed.

Gavin watches me. "Are her things in your room?"

It's then I realize Marrin isn't staying. Maybe I should protest or ask her to stay—but what would be the point? She clearly wants—needs—to be with her family. If I ask her to stay, I'll only be opening myself up to a humiliating rejection.

I nod and go get Marrin's stuff.

I don't realize Mr. SEAL Team Six has followed me until I turn to leave my bedroom and find him taking up the entire doorway.

Look, I'm a big buy—a tad over six foot, muscularly built but not overly bulky. But Gavin... Gavin is a beast. I'm surprised he even fits through the damn door. He's well over six foot with close-cropped dark hair and muscles every-where. Not to mention that this close, I can see a vicious scar that runs down the far edge of his face and down his neck where it disappears beneath the collar of his jacket. It cuts through his tanned skin like a lightning bolt across a cloudy sky.

I hand him Marrin's things.

"You did good, kid," he says.

I'm pretty sure he's not talking about my ability to pack a bag. I opt not to say anything and follow him into the living room. Alice and Marrin have already left.

He pauses. "One suggestion. The martial arts magnets on your fridge tipped me off that you're at least a good enough fighter to compete. You might consider taking those down next time you let in a couple of strangers."

"I knew who you were the entire time."

Approval flashes across Gavin's face, then he's gone.

I lock the door and stand in the middle of my empty apartment. I glance at the fridge where a magnet advertising I was a finalist in a karate competition sits next to a magnet advertising my first place win in a Muay Thai competition. They're both small and hard to read from this distance. I have no idea how he saw them.

The magnets hold up a picture of me standing between Vicky's parents holding a trophy I'd won at one of the events. They're beaming like I'm their son, but clearly they're not my parents.

I wonder if he noticed that, too.

I go to bed.

It smells like Marrin and now everything hurts. Okay, that was kind of dramatic, but it's how I feel. I know I'm throwing a pity party, I just really wanted her to stay the night. A voice in my head says Marrin doesn't think of me the same way I think of her.

Why does that thought hurt so much?

True, she *did* ask me to come get her tonight and that's a win. But I wonder who else she asked before she settled on me.

I turn over, feeling stupid for having wanted to call her earlier to tell her about my petty victory over my mother. I'm glad I didn't. If I had, this moment would only be more humiliating.

Wait, what am I doing? Marrin and I have come a long way. Plus, she's sleeping with me, not Alice. Blondie might be her family, but I'm her... What am I, her lover? I'm not her boyfriend. Not officially. But we did go on a real date, one she asked me to.

I close my eyes and decide I'm being a Negative Nancy. Mar texted me to come get her. She trusted me to keep her safe. She even admitted why she hates Thanksgiving. Two months ago, that never would've happened.

I'll see her tomorrow and we'll figure it out.

15

Marrin

I stay with Alice and Gavin for the rest of the holiday weekend and spend most of my time working at the 13th Floor. My dance numbers for the Femme Fatale show are done, but the whole production isn't quite finished. A few sneak peek performances for the show will premier in December, but the entire production won't debut until New Year's Eve.

It's not until Sunday night that I finally go back to my apartment. I take the stairs two at a time and make quick work of getting inside. I haven't spoken to Damian except to say I was fine and staying in the city.

I let myself get too close to him. If he knew I had a stalker and why, he'd never look at me the same.

He and I come from different worlds. He's from a world of luxury mansions and designer shoes, I'm from a world where people struggle to decide whether to pay the rent or feed their kids. It's a place that molded and made me, and I wouldn't trade it for the world. But what happened two years ago still haunts me, *mars* me—

God, the irony of my nickname is not lost on me.

Now I'm good at keeping my scars hidden, but that wasn't always the case. Sophomore year I accidentally put a guy in the hospital when he tried to dance with me at a party. I'm *still* mortified when I think about it. I overreacted to the nth degree. I'm lucky I only got mandatory therapy and not jail time.

The thought of Damian looking at me the way everyone at that party looked at me—the way the university disciplinary committee had looked at me when the head of the academic accessibility department explained my situation without violating my privacy...

Words like mortifying and humiliating aren't strong enough to describe it. What I saw in the disciplinary committee's eyes was worse than pity. In that moment, I fit every stereotype of the poor kid who gets a college scholarship. I almost wished they'd given me a harsher punishment because at least then I'd have felt as if I'd been treated like the rest of the student body. Like I was normal.

So yeah, if Damian looked at me that way, it would destroy me. I like the way he looks at me now. I love it actually.

Because I think I love him.

Which is so not where I wanted this whole friends-with-benefits thing to go. I'm a goddamn cliché.

Being able to depend on Damian to pick me up the other night makes my lady parts all tingly. But it's also simultaneously horrifying. If he knew who Frank was, what Frank had done, what had been done to me...

I suppress a shudder.

After I'd made it to Alice and Gavin's place in the city, Gavin had asked Kiley to log onto the security cameras at the Braxton. The place isn't wired up like Alice's other businesses, so all the camera at the back door caught was black and white footage of the corner of what appeared to be a truck and a hooded man banging on the door.

I have no doubt it was Frank. Even Alice said it looked like him. But the grainy footage isn't enough to prove he violated the restraining order.

Alice is having Kiley install better cameras (and more of them) at the Braxton before the end of the week. Cameras won't stop Frank, they'll just help provide evidence that he broke the law. It's better than nothing.

I lay in my bed, wrapping Damian's blanket around me. It still smells like him and something about that soothes me. Damian soothes me. I've never felt so safe as when I fell asleep in his arms.

I sound like a lovesick schoolgirl. But it's true.

Feeling safe is a privilege most people don't realize they have.

Seeing how close Frank was to me on the security footage scares me when I think about it. If I hadn't gotten the door shut when I did, he'd have gotten inside. I don't want to think about what might've happened then.

Phantom pain arcs across my lower abdomen and I curl into a ball.

Then, because I'm weak and pathetic and very likely a masochist, I grab my phone and text Damian.

Marrin: *Hey, I'm back. Just got into bed.*
Damian: *Glad you're back. Hope everything is okay.*
Marrin: *It is.*
Marrin: *Thanks for coming to get me the other night. I don't want to talk about it, but it means a lot.*

It takes him a moment to respond.

Damian: *You're welcome. I'll always come for you, Mar. I won't ask about what happened, but I want you to know you can trust me.*
Marrin: *Thanks. Night.*
Damian: *Goodnight.*

The first Wednesday in December is the last official day of class and I trudge up the stairs to my apartment completely exhausted. I handed in my last research paper today and cannot be more excited to have tomorrow off. The day after classes end is always reserved as a reading day before finals start.

The Monday after Thanksgiving, Damian and I had dinner. He came over around six and we made tacos. I'd thought it might be awkward or that he might bring up what happened, but he didn't. We didn't kiss or anything, but the evening was perfect nonetheless. He even gifted me a pillow for my couch. It's big and white and reads "I have standards" in cursive beneath a black silhouette of a standard poodle. I laughed when I saw it because, in true Damian fashion, he snuck it onto my couch when I was in the bathroom and didn't say anything until I noticed it.

The days after were filled with final papers and prep for exams. Both Damian and I were hella busy. We found time to meet at each other's apartments for coffee breaks, and a few stress relieving, kinky sexual encounters. But mostly we've just been texting.

When I get to my apartment, there are a few fliers and

notices from management clipped to my door. I grab them before heading inside. I drop my purse and the papers on the counter. I'm walking away when a flash of neon yellow catches my eye.

There's a letter hidden in the stack of notices.

It's alarmingly bright, alarmingly yellow.

A sickly kind of heat washes over me, prickling my skin with sweat, as I pull out the card.

"Welcome Home" is written across the front in big, bright letters. Inside it's signed with the letter F.

I don't remember stuffing it inside my purse.

I don't remember leaving my apartment or getting into my car.

All I know is that I've just parked in front of the 13th Floor's high-rise. I cross the street. It's freezing out. I know it's freezing out, but I'm too numb to feel it.

I stumble past the fake receptionist and head for the staff-only elevator. Once inside, I punch in my passcode then the button for the fourteenth floor where the offices are located.

I can't catch my breath. It's like all the air has been sucked out of the building. The motion of the elevator makes me dizzy. I rise through the floors, but it feels like my blood didn't get the memo and stays in the lobby. I grab the wall.

A bell dings and the doors open. A brightly lit hallway stretches before me.

I take one step then another. The building sways.

An attractive man, wearing an earpiece like an FBI agent, strides toward me. He's tall and muscular, a sleeve of Polynesian tattoos down one arm.

"Marrin?" He lurches for me, bronze-brown skin blurring into the blue of his shirt, as the hallway tilts like in the movie *Inception*.

The lights go out. Then turn back on. I'm on the floor, Kiley crouched over me, finger on his earpiece.

"*...fainted near the elevator...*"

His voice is rich and deep and so, so far away—

"*...find Alice... meet us in her office...*"

—which is weird because he's right next to me.

"*...bring the doc...*"

It's not until he lifts me into his arms that I realize the power didn't go out, *I* did.

"Ki, what happened?" I try to swallow, my mouth is so dry.

"Hey, kiddo." He smiles. "What do you remember?"

I close my eyes, too dizzy to answer.

A door clicks and then he's laying me down on the leather sofa in Alice's office. He moves away and comes back with a bottled water and the jar of chocolates Alice keeps on her desk. "Take a sip of this for me."

I don't argue as he helps me take a drink. I spill more than I swallow, but Kiley catches most of it with a paper towel.

"Eat this," he says. And again I don't fight when he feeds a few chocolates to me. My arms feel leaden and my fingers are numb.

Three chocolates in, I say, "I fainted, didn't I?"

"Yep."

I groan. I've been a situational fainter since childhood. It doesn't happen often, but it does happen. I try to sit up, but Kiley stops me. "It's not my blood sugar or hydra"—Alice bursts into the room—"tion."

"What happened?" Alice demands.

Kiley wisely moves out of the way so Alice can crouch

beside me. Gavin and Addison, the concierge doctor Alice keeps on staff, enter the room.

Alice helps me sit up. "I'm fine." I eye Addison. "I'm not sick." She ignores me because I'm not her boss. I frown at Alice. "I said I'm fine."

"You fainted in the damn hallway. That's not fine. The only reason you didn't bust your head open is because Kiley saw you stumble into the elevator on the security monitors."

I give Kiley a look that says, *Thanks for ratting on me*. He throws one back that says, *You're welcome, kiddo*.

Addison starts going through her doctor bag and I throw a look of last resort at Gavin.

His eyes dart to Alice. "Mar, you look like shit."

"You're not exactly a vision either, Frankenstein," I say.

He grins and I can tell he's trying not to laugh. I've been calling him Frankenstein since we met. It's not a joke about the scar that runs down the edge of his face. He's legit huge like the Frankenstein monster. It wasn't until our fourth or fifth meeting that I actually noticed his scar and spent fifteen minutes explaining how it had nothing to do with me calling him Frankenstein. When I was done begging for forgiveness, he laughed and told me his nickname in the military had been Frankenstein and that he'd gotten it long before the scar.

"What happened?" Gavin asks.

I pull the envelope from my purse and hand it to Alice.

She goes very still then rips out the card. "Fuck." She storms to her desk. "*FUCK.*"

Both Gavin and Kiley stand like they're expecting the Russian mafia to storm the building.

Alice punches a button on her desk phone, it rings on speaker until her secretary answers. "Get the owner of Marrin's apartment complex on the phone, tell him I want the security footage of her building for the last month sent to Kiley by the end of the hour or we're hacking the system. I want the employee work schedules and time cards, too, as well as the logs for the door codes. I want to know who was in the building and when. Then contact that private security firm we've used before, and get my lawyer on the phone, I want to see her immediately." She hangs up and leans over her desk, fuming.

Gavin moves toward her.

"Who the *fuck*," Alice growls, "do I have to pay off to get Frank thrown in prison?"

"Told you I wasn't sick," I gloat. Addison throws me a sympathetic look before exiting the room.

Gavin says, "Frank's escalating. He's never tried to get this close to Marrin before. What's changed?"

In the two years Frank has been stalking me, he's never tried to approach me. The closest he gets is sending letters through the mail or sitting in front of my apartment in his truck.

Kiley crosses his arms. "The anniversary of the attack could've triggered him. Maybe the fact that Mar's less accessible in this new apartment?"

I ask the obvious question. "Do you think he got into my building?" I hate how small my voice sounds.

Alice sits next to me and wraps an arm around my shoulders, and while I appreciate the sentiment, the only arms I want wrapped around me are Damian's.

Oh God—Damian.

A stalker at a distance I can make up a story for, an excuse spun from the pieces of the truth I'm ready to share. But if Frank is escalating, if he has access to my building, that changes the fucking equation, doesn't it? I can't keep myself *and* Damian safe.

I shove the thoughts out of my head. I'll worry about that later.

"We'll get the security firm to track him down and put a tail on him," Alice says. "In the meantime, I'll have Conor—"

"No," I say. "I don't want a bodyguard."

Her jaw clenches. "Fine. I'll get a team to watch your building and you—*at a distance*—until we get eyes on Frank."

Eventually Alice drives me home in my car because she doesn't want me passing out behind the wheel. Gavin follows in his SUV. Alice assures me she'll do everything she can to get proof Frank violated the restraining order so we can throw his ass in jail. She promises to let me know what the security footage shows and when they get a tail on Frank.

I don't ask about the security team likely already watching me and my apartment complex.

She drops me off and I go upstairs. It's late. I lock my door and change into comfortable clothes then sink into my couch.

I can't keep the truth from Damian, can't keep him safe, not if Frank is this close. Too many variables. Too many things I can't control—*I can't lose control.*

But... I pick up my phone because I can suspend reality for a little longer.

Damian answers on the first ring. "Hey, babe. What's up?"

Tears hit my face and voice at the same time. "Can you come over?"

"What's wrong?" There's a clatter and I think I hear something fall.

"Just a bad day."

His door slams and I hear it both out in the hallway and through the phone. "I'm here," he says.

I hang up and open my door.

"Baby," Damian rushes in, hands on my face, eye scanning me. "What happened?"

I shake my head. "Bad day."

He wipes my tears and leads me to the couch where he pulls me onto his lap. We sit there for a moment, wrapped in each other. Then he pulls back, brushing hair from my face. "What can I do?"

The worried strain in his voice, the love in his eyes, is enough to bring fresh tears to mine.

I kiss him.

Then I kiss him again.

"Touch me," I say.

An anguished kind of knowing crosses his face. I see words he promised not to ask form in his mouth—he swallows them. Instead he kisses me like I'm the only woman in the world and a little piece of my heart breaks.

We haven't been intimate like this since the night at Back Cellar when there was nothing between us. Every time we've fooled around since, he's called me Red and I've called him Sir. Our kink doesn't sit between us like it used to, it no longer mediates who we are to one another because our relationship is more than just sex. We share something deeper.

But still, neither of us has initiated this kind of intimacy yet.

Damian is a good guy. The best. I know it's killing him not knowing what's going on with me but he doesn't ask because he promised he wouldn't. I'm a monster. *No*—I'm Irena from *Cat People*. I'm haunted by the truth of who I am, where I come from. And he's Oliver, patient and honest and too good for me.

His hands run beneath my shirt to unclasp my bra. "Mar," he breathes into my neck. "There are things I want to tell you. Things I need you to know about me."

I silence him with a kiss. Whatever he feels he needs to tell me, I don't want to know. I know he's keeping secrets, and if he spills them, it'll only be worse when I don't spill mine. And I can't because the way he's looking at me right now is how I always want to remember him looking at me.

"Not tonight," I say. Then I kiss him again and again and again.

Damian's on his back when we finally come together.

We're both partly dressed because we couldn't wait and it doesn't matter.

There is a desperate kind of rhythm to our bodies when I sink myself down on him. His hands grip my hips and he moves me where he wants, guiding me up and down, a little forward then a little back. I graze my lips over his, willing him to see everything I feel for him in my eyes.

"I love you, Marrin," he says, lifting a hand to tuck a strand of hair behind my ear. He leans up to kiss me and I'm gutted.

I nod my head, close my eyes.

He moves deep inside me.

I don't want to say anything, but then he kisses me like he knows what's coming. Like he knows this is our last time and the words tumble from my mouth. "I love you, too."

I crush my mouth over his as I start to come. *I'm sorry*, I say without words. *Remember me this way. Remember us as we are now.*

He finds his release shortly after me and when it's over neither of us wants to move. He holds me like he'll never let me go, and I hold him like I don't ever want to. Because I don't.

But I know I have to.

"You need space, don't you?" he says into the darkness.

I close my eyes to keep in the tears as I nod my head against his chest.

16

Damian

I'm a miserable son of a bitch.

Exams are killing me and I haven't seen Marrin in almost two weeks. I know she's busy with exams and that she needs time to think about our relationship. I also know she thinks I won't understand about the things that have gone wrong in her life.

That hurts the most.

I'd thought the same thing about her at first. But in the last few weeks, I've realized that I can tell her about my abuse and she'll understand. I wish she trusted me enough to feel the same, but I understand if she can't. I'm not exactly sure what happened to her, but I know from my own experience how terrifying and paralyzing confessing your trauma can be. Especially to someone you care about.

I just wish I could talk to her.

I've sent her a few texts letting her know I understand she's not ready to tell me things. That I'm willing to listen if she wants to talk. I tell her I don't want to pressure her and that I'm still loyal to her until she tells me we're not exclusive anymore. I tell her I won't contact her until our exams are over.

I sound so desperate.

I take my last final on Thursday. It's the second week of December and tomorrow is the last day of exams. I know I shouldn't, but I decide to head to the Braxton to see if Mar's working. When I walk in, I am instantly disappointed when I see only Elle working the bar. *Cat People* is playing on the projector and a wave of sadness ripples through me.

"Hey, Elle," I say, taking a seat.

"Hey. Can I get you a drink?"

"I'll take an IPA. You done with exams?"

"I have one more tomorrow at noon. You?"

"Finished today."

"Lucky."

"Don't you normally work with Marrin Thursday nights?"

"Yeah, but it gets slow here once everyone leaves for winter break, so she picked up some hours at her other job when she finished with exams."

I can't keep the hurt off my face. I didn't know she was done with finals.

"Hey, handsome," Priya says, stepping out of the break room. "You look like someone killed your puppy."

Certainly feels that way.

"Just wiped from exams."

She gives me a look like she knows exactly why I'm here, and I immediately regret coming. A few minutes later, she sends Elle home for the night. Then it's just the two of us.

Priya wipes the bar in front of me. "She's not here."

"I've noticed." I gulp my beer. "I told her I loved her."

"What'd she say?"

"She said it back. Told me she needed space. And now I

think she's avoiding me."

"Damn," she exhales. "I thought it was odd she picked up so many hours at the 13th Floor, but I figured it was because her semester was over."

Marrin's never told me the name of the other place she works. I keep that knowledge to myself. "Any advice?"

"Have you tried talking to her?"

I deadpan. "No, that hadn't crossed my mind." I wipe a hand over my face. "I've sent a few texts but she hasn't responded. I did agree not to contact her until after our exams were over, so expecting her to text back wasn't exactly fair. But now... Showing up tonight was my attempt to catch her in person. Unless you can get me into the 13th Floor I'm out of options."

She gives me an apologetic look. "Sorry. Members only. I couldn't get you in if I tri—" Mischief colors her face. "*I* can't get you in, but if I happened to mention we sell trial memberships for the main lounge online and you happened to buy one and show up—*say this Wednesday night*—then I wouldn't technically be breaking any rules. The question is, how much are you willing to spend for a chance at talking with Mar?"

Marrin

Backstage is crazy. The club is giving a sneak peek of three dance numbers from the Femme Fatale show tonight and one of them is mine.

I'm supposed to be waitressing but one of the dancers in my routine came down with the flu. Elle just started waitressing here to get some extra money, so she's going to cover my section while I fill in.

I warm up then hit the hair and makeup room. When I'm done, I slip into costume. It's little more than a retro bikini—a glittering black halter with matching high-waisted briefs. A trench coat goes over top with black leather gloves and sunglasses.

It's been almost a week since the semester officially ended, and I haven't spoken to Damian.

Since the last time we slept together, I've been going nonstop. I threw myself into studying for finals, and when I wasn't doing that, I was driving to the city to waitress or work on the show. I haven't slept, I've barely eaten. I think every shadow, noise, and bump in the night is Frank. He's like a shark and I'm the bleeding seal struggling in open water. I know he's lurking out of sight, I just don't know when he'll attack.

A constant dose of adrenaline taints my blood, making me jumpy, anxious. I can't stop looking over my shoulder, can't stop thinking about what'll happen when he finds me, if he knows about Damian. So I hyperfocus on the things I can control. I obsess about school, work, the show—anything to avoid dealing with my problems.

Alice hasn't been able to locate Frank and there isn't enough evidence to pin the letter on him either. The only good news is that he didn't get into my building. One of the maintenance guys said a man paid him fifty bucks to put the card on my door.

But that doesn't mean anything.

Just because Frank hasn't gotten into the building yet, doesn't mean he hasn't tried or that he won't find a way in eventually. Frank's a bad man with bad friends. If he wants to get to me, he will. Escaping may not be as easy as me finding a new apartment this time. I live in the most secure complex in the area, there's nowhere left I can move.

It feels as if my life is spiraling out of control and I hate it.

Damian is the one thing I can control. So I am. He's always respected my boundaries and my privacy. He's fucking perfect and I know I'm a coward for not just telling him, but the less he knows the better. The less I'm with him, the better. If Frank's escalating, then who knows what he's going to do. I can't risk Damian getting caught up in this. I want to protect him from Frank as much as I want to protect him from finding out that the Marrin he thought he knew doesn't exist. She was just a shiny, unattainable ideal that drew him in. A projection of what he wanted and the result of him letting his emotions cloud his judgment.

I'm the goddamn femme fatale.

Someone yells a three-minute warning. I close my trench coat and slip on my stilettos.

Damian

Wednesday night, I park on the street and make my way to a fancy high rise in the city. I was instructed to go around the building and enter from the back. I'm wearing a designer suit and shoes. I look casually edgy, but classy. I push through an easily missed door and find myself in a strangely professional lobby with three elevators and a pleasant, but forgettable, looking receptionist.

It's almost eleven o'clock. There's no reason for a receptionist to be working.

"Hello, how may I help you?" she says.

I glance around the lobby. It's just us. I approach, giving her my best smile. "Good evening. I have an appointment on the 13th Floor."

"Do you have your confirmation number or card?"

Cards, I assume, are for official members. I got a trial membership. It cost about as much as my tuition does a semester.

I recite the number from memory. She fiddles on her computer then hands me a black key card and directs me to an elevator on the left side of the lobby. I swipe the card and the doors open, revealing a black leather interior and dim lighting. I step inside and again swipe the card before pressing the button with the number "13" on it. It's the only button available.

The doors close, and up I go.

I step out into a stylish black room similar to the elevator. It's modern and elegant, but there's an edge to it. A beautiful woman in a black dress stands behind a tall desk.

"Good evening, Mr. Wane."

I'm not surprised she knows my name. "Good evening miss...?"

"You may call me Clarissa." She holds out her palm and I pass her the key card. She scans it then types into her computer. "I see you've already agreed to our terms and conditions, passed the background check and signed the non-disclosure agreement. Is there anything you'd like to ask before going in, Mr. Wane?"

"No, thank you."

It took over an hour to print off, read, sign and then scan and upload all the trial membership paperwork. It was three days before I heard back about whether I was approved or not.

Clarissa pulls out a small black box. "Cell phone and any electronics, please."

I expected this. I hand over my phone and she locks it in

the box. She slides it into a slot on the wall behind her and it locks into place next to several others.

She hands me my key card. "Follow me, Mr. Wane."

Not gonna lie. At this point, I feel like Batman. Ever since I was a kid, I've gotten a kick out of being called Mr. Wane. But right now, in this weird, secret club, I actually *feel* like Bruce Wayne (who—*fun fact*—has a son named Damian Wayne. Who, sadly, I was not named after). I'm dressed to impress and a beautiful, mysterious woman is escorting me. My inner preteen is geeking the fuck out.

Clarissa walks me down an underlit hallway. We stop at the end and she knocks once on the door. "Enjoy your evening." She leaves.

The door opens and a beautiful blonde wearing blood-red lipstick and a classy, yet intimate black dress greets me. "Good evening, Mr. Wane. I'm Taylor. Do you have a section preference this evening?"

"A booth would be preferable," I answer smoothly. "In Marrin's section."

She smiles like we've shared an intimate secret. "They're all her sections tonight." She winks, and I'm not sure what exactly she means.

Her hand finds the crook of my elbow and we walk as if I'm the one escorting her. The hallway opens into a large lounge where every booth and table has a view of the stage. It's darkly elegant and dim, underlit by neon lights. The upholstery is all fine black leather and velvet. I know there are people in some of the booths lining the walls, but they're hidden in shadow—or by curtains, which all the booths seem to have.

Am I in a sex club? Does Marrin work in a sex club?

Unease heightens my awareness, but I give no outward hint I'm uncomfortable. I need to play it cool.

I'm Bruce fucking Wayne.

Taylor leads me to a booth near the side of the stage. I slide in and she passes me a drink menu, saying my waitress will be here shortly.

Red lights turn on, illuminating the stage. The air is slightly murky like maybe there's a fog machine or something somewhere. Seven poles rise out of the stage floor and I'm trying not to have a fucking heart attack. Jesus, I need a drink. The website said nothing about what actually happens in the club, and I have no goddamn clue what I expected.

But this? This was definitely not it.

The place goes dark and music starts. A single grey spotlight illuminates a retro-looking blonde sitting in a chair at center stage. Behind her, cast in shadow, six other glittering women sit in chairs. From what I can tell, they're all wearing trench coats and stilettos.

"Oh shit."

I peel my eyes from the stage and look at the waitress. It's not Marrin.

It's Elle.

She's staring at me—eyes wide, mouth slightly agape.

"You need to leave. Right now."

"I asked to sit in Marrin's section."

"She's..." her eyes dart to the stage, "off tonight."

I follow her line of sight.

The lighting is as much a part of the performance as the dancing. Lights and projections pop on and off, revealing and hiding the dancers on stage. They're all wearing wigs and similar outfits. They strip off their coats and gloves, tossing them to the floor. The woman in the center strips off her dress and shoes, too. They all remove their sunglasses at the same moment.

My heart stops.

In the back row, on the side nearest me, Marrin twirls around a pole. She's elegant and charming, yet deadly and cruel. She whips around, bending and arcing and turning upside down. Each motion is effortless, fluid as ribbon caught in the wind.

She's mesmerizing, ensnaring. The spider at the center of a web. She commands my gaze, my attention. The dance is a story, her body the words.

She slides down the pole, landing in a split.

Her gaze sweeps the crowd. Our eyes meet. The collision lasts forever but ends too soon. Her eyes keep moving, don't stop.

But it's enough.

Recognition and fear flicker through every line of her body.

I want to look away. I should. But I can't. She's alluring and haunting. A woman I've never seen before.

When the lights go out and the dance ends, the spell is broken. Something terrible coils in my stomach.

I've just violated Marrin's privacy.

The one boundary I've *always* respected. The one I promised to always respect. Fuck.

Fuck, fuck, fuck—

Elle reappears. "You need to come with me," is all she says.

I follow her through a side door out of the lounge. We enter a bright hallway that must be staff only because suddenly we're standing at an industrial looking elevator. I step on and Elle does so only long enough to push a button before jumping off.

She says nothing. The doors close and I descend.

I step off on a sub level and into a too-white hallway. It's stark and sterile. To my left, a pair of glass doors. I'm not surprised to see Gavin standing just beyond. He points past me and I look to my right.

Marrin stands at the end of the hallway next to a door marked with a glaring red exit sign.

I walk to her. She's wearing track pants and a thigh-length silk robe. She's lost the wig and her silver-white hair is pulled back. She's staring straight ahead, motionless.

I approach, palms up. "Marrin, I'm sorry I—" I'm close enough now to see how emaciated she looks. "Baby, are you okay?" I reach for her.

She swats my hand away, finally looking at me. "No, I'm not." The words like venom. "What the fuck, Damian? What the actual fuck?" She looks on the verge of hysterics.

"I'm sorry. I just wanted to talk—"

"So you show up at my work like some stalker? I trusted you."

Indignation flares in me. "I'm not stalking you—*Jesus*. I just wanted to talk."

"Then text me like a normal person."

"I tried," I half yell. "You didn't answer."

"Maybe I didn't want to talk to you." She paces, arms wrapped around her middle to hide how badly she's shaking.

"I'm sorry. I shouldn't have shown up here."

"*I trusted you*," she whispers more to herself than me.

The hurt in her voice is crushing. "I know. I'm sorry."

"I think you should leave." She pulls my phone out of her pocket and hands it to me.

"Okay, but can we please talk about this later when you're off?"

"No. This isn't going to work, Damian."

Everything grinds to a halt. "What...?"

"What you saw tonight... " She shakes her head, unable to look at me. "You and I are two different people from two different worlds."

"What are you saying?"

She finally looks up. "I think we need to stop seeing one another."

I blink. Try to breath. Blink again. "No." The word as broken as I feel.

"Why, Damian? You're not my boyfriend."

The statement hits me like a blow to the face.

"*Then what am I to you?*" A desperate kind of panic takes over. "Because we certainly act like we're together. Maybe not in front of our friends, but we go on dates—you *asked* me on a date, remember? We spend all of our free time together. You're my best friend. I won't let you go. Not over something like this."

"Why not?" she yells.

I'm not sure what answer she's looking for, but I get the feeling there is a wrong one.

And from the profound sadness limning her anger, one she wants to hear.

"*Because.*"

"Because why, Damian?"

"*I can't,*" I yell, arms wide. Words spill from my mouth. "You're like a siren, you call to me. It's like you're inside me. I love you so much it feels like I'm dying whenever you walk into a room. When I'm not with you, it-it's like someone stole the sun. Like I'm a patchwork of pieces that only come together when I'm with you. You're the fucking thread. I don't make sense without you." Tears rim my eyes. "Don't look at me like you don't know what I'm talking about—I *know* you feel it, too."

She closes her eyes. Her throat bobs, chin trembles.

"Love needs trust and you violated mine by coming here tonight."

"Trust? You want to talk about *trust*? You told me you were a waitress, Marrin. Not..." I struggle for the right word.

"Not what?" she challenges, matching my anger.

"A dancer."

"A stripper. I'm a stripper. *And* a waitress here."

"And I don't fucking care," I shout. "You could turn tricks behind a KFC and I wouldn't give a shit as long as you came home to me every night."

"Yes, you would—"

"*No. I. Wouldn't.* I don't give a flying fuck what you do to make money as long as you're mine."

She says nothing.

I rake my fingers through my hair. "Is this what you've been hiding from me? The big secret you're too scared to tell me? Is this where your stalker came from?"

Her eyes go wide, and for a second, I think she's going to pass out.

Against my better judgment, I push. "Come on, it wasn't hard to figure out. You move a lot, there are a million locks on your front door, one on your bedroom. You were scared as hell on Thanksgiving and freaked when I asked if you wanted to get your car. And there was this look you had when Jake mentioned some guy from your old neighborhood asking about you. I'm not an idiot, Marrin. I'm sick of being dicked around. Tell me the truth."

"This conversation is pointless. You'd never understand. Just go." She points to the exit.

"Never understand? Understand what? That you come from a shitty neighborhood, you get paid to dance, and you have a stalker? Baby, this is me understanding. I don't care."

"Bullshit," she spits. "You come from money. You've had

privileges people like me only dream of or see on TV. Privileges you never even realized you had because it was normal for you. Don't sit there and tell me that being a stripper is normal in your world, okay? You have no idea what it was like for me growing up."

"And whose fault is that? You don't tell me anything."

"Fine," she yells. "You want to know what my childhood was like? It fuckin' sucked. We lived in a shit neighborhood, had no money, and my mom was a drunk who cared more about her boyfriends than me."

It takes us both a moment to process her confession.

She says, "So don't stand there and preach about understanding. You have no idea what it's like for people like me to be around people like you." She wipes her hands over her face and I see nothing but exhausted resolve. "You're the kind of guy who pays to come to a place like this to watch a girl like me take off her clothes."

"Wow," I say incredulously. "I mean—*wow*. First of all, you continuing to think I'd care about you taking your clothes off for money is insulting. That's *your* insecurity, *not* mine. Don't put that on me. What I saw on that stage wasn't stripping—wasn't *just* stripping. And even if it was, why the hell would I care? Stripping is a legitimate profession and one that some people are damn good at. Why would I shame that skillset or think less of people who can make money that way? If you think I'm that shallow, then clearly you don't know me as well as I thought.

"Second, don't you dare try to tell me that I'm incapable of understanding or empathizing with a shit childhood, okay? You wanna know why I almost had a damn anxiety attack that night we went to Back Cellar? Why I thought I wasn't good enough for you?"

My ribs constrict, breathing shallows.

Shit, I'm really gonna do this aren't I?

"My dad's business partner, a trusted family friend, molested me for months when I was a kid. *Months*. I was thirteen years old and no one noticed. Not my mom, not my dad. They were too busy ignoring their kids. When I finally worked up the courage to tell my parents, you know what happened? Nothing." My voice cracks. "Not a fucking thing. They were more concerned with their public image than their own kid."

"Jesus," Mar breathes.

"The worst part is, the guy didn't deny it when they asked. He offered to buy their silence and my parents accepted to avoid a scandal. I signed off that I'd never speak about it again, and got a disgusting amount of money for it. When I asked my mom why we weren't going to the police, you know what she said? She said, '*What am I supposed to do? Your father says you'll be a man one day, and if anyone finds out what happened, it will embarrass this family and ruin your reputation.*' My dad golfed with the bastard at their country club every weekend until he died two years ago. He spoke at my dad's funeral."

I rake a hand through my hair.

"Just because my childhood was gilded and shiny doesn't mean it was any less abusive, or that I'm somehow unable to relate to you. Abusers are all the same, mine just wore designer clothes."

"Damian, I'm so sorry."

"Don't be. I don't want an apology from you. I want you to understand that if you can accept a truth like that and still love me, then there's nothing—*nothing*—you could confide in me that would change the way I feel about you." I walk to the exit. "I know someone hurt you and I'm not asking you to tell me what happened, I'm just asking you to trust that I won't throw away what we have because of it. Think about it. And if you want to be my girlfriend, you know where to find me. I don't want to be another one of your secrets. I'll have you as my girlfriend or I won't have you at all."

I push through the door and walk out.

Marrin

The door shuts and a wedge of tears clogs my throat.

I don't know what's wrong with me, why I can't just tell him what happened. Why I can't trust that he'll still love me when I do.

A door creaks, and I turn around to see Gavin at the other end of the hallway. He probably followed me down because he's overprotective and nosy. I fold my arms across my chest and walk toward him.

"Enjoy the show?" I say when I get to him.

Standing on his left, I can clearly see the scar that runs down the edge of his face and neck.

"Just keeping an eye on you. It's none of my business." He hits the button for the elevator then leans back on the wall next to me.

"No sage advice?" I push angrily.

He shakes his head.

"You're not gonna tell me what my problem is or how I can fix it?"

He side eyes me. "Do you want me to?"

I look away. "I don't know."

"That boy loves you, Marrin."

"I know." My voice cracks and the tears fall. I slide to the floor and hug my knees to my chest. The elevator dings and opens.

Gavin doesn't move. Instead he joins me on the floor. "This is about your scars isn't it, kid?"

"No. Yes. I don't know." I wipe my face.

"How long have you and Damian been seeing each other?"

I give him a flat look. "Like you don't know."

He and Alice know everything about the people who live in my building. And if Damian got a membership to the club, they probably did a background check.

"Knowing about him and prying into your personal life are two different things."

I watch the elevator close. "Almost four months."

He crosses his ankles and his arms. "Has he seen the scars?"

"No," I admit.

"Damn, kid."

"I know. Guess I'm really good at hiding my shit."

He nods, considering. "Did Alice ever tell you how I got this?" He taps his scar.

"No."

"She must've asked a thousand times how I got it, but it wasn't until right before I'd planned to ask her to marry me that I told her the truth."

"Why?"

He raises an eyebrow. "Why do you think?"

"You were ashamed."

"In my mind there was no way she could ever want me after she found out. What I did, how it happened... I hated myself for a long, *long* time. The kind of hate that drives people to drugs and alcohol, to take advantage of the people they love, to want to die slowly over years because that's what they think they deserve. I did horrible things, was a horrible person and all because I couldn't forgive myself. Because I didn't think I deserved to be forgiven."

I know it's tacky but I ask, "What happened?"

He weighs and measures me with a look. "I drove an armored vehicle into a kid. I was on deployment, out with my team, and we were on our way back to base when we got intel that enemy combatants were mobilizing in the area. It was late in the day, I was driving through a small village where we'd spent some time previously. We were almost through when this kid, who I recognized, ran into the street waving his arms at us. Our orders were not to stop because the ambush potential was too high. After I hit him, I drove over an IED."

I exhale sharply. "He'd been trying to warn you."

He nods. "The explosion knocked me out, I came to when Kiley pulled me into the back of the vehicle. We were stuck in a huge crater and under attack. It was chaos and I was useless from a concussion. We got hit with an RPG and Kiley managed to push me over so that instead of getting gutted like a fish from a flying chunk of metal, I came away with this." He points at his scar.

"But... even if you'd stopped the vehicle, you still would've been ambushed, right? So it wouldn't have mattered. The kid likely would've been caught in the crossfire."

"We could what-if that shit all day, but it doesn't change what I did or what happened. Nor does it change what I have to live with."

"I'm sorry that happened to you. That you were put in that position, asked to make that kind of sacrifice. That's awful."

He nods.

"How did Alice react when you told her?"

A smile lights his eyes. "She hugged me. She accepted it —me. Then she asked me to marry her." He grins. "Pulled out a fuckin' ring and everything."

Now I'm smiling. But Damian's words about my insecurity echo through my head. I know it's a stupid question, but I ask, "Did you worry she'd, like, pity you or see you differently?"

Gavin's face softens. "Is that what you think Damian will do if you tell him?"

I shrug. "He's not like me."

"I don't think you honestly believe that." He stands and pulls me to my feet before hitting the button for the elevator. "Look, there's no moral to this story. I can't tell you what to do, and I'd be lying if I said the truth will set you free because sometimes it doesn't. But I've been where you are, I know what it's like to be scarred by something from your past—physically and emotionally. If I'd never told Alice, it would've eaten away at me until either I confessed, or stayed silent and let it slowly destroy us. The things that scar us have power. If left to fester, that power grows until the weight becomes unbearable. But once it's revealed, once it's no longer a secret burden only you carry... I don't know, it loses its power I guess."

The elevator doors open and we get on.

"I will say," Gavin adds, "that Damian kid is crazy about you. To the point that he did the emotional equivalent of getting naked in public and prostrating himself at your feet."

"You heard?"

He nods. "For anyone to say what he did takes guts. But for a guy to say that to the woman he loves..." He shakes his head. "That took a kind of bravery even I don't think I possess."

17

Damian

Two days after Christmas, I'm back in town. It's been a week since Marrin and I broke up.

I exit my therapist's office and get into my Jeep. There's snow in the forecast, so I head to the store for supplies before going home.

I spent the holiday at my grandparents' house with my brother. My mom and her manfriend spent the holiday on some beach somewhere. Thank fuck. If I'd had to deal with Nadia, I don't think I'd have shown up at all.

I'm unloading groceries at my apartment when my phone rings to the tune of Darth Vader's theme song.

I stare at the screen.

Nadia's calling.

She called me on Christmas, too, but I didn't answer. I talked about her with my therapist today. We went over what she said on Thanksgiving and what I'd confessed to Marrin in our argument. I feel better about both things now. I know not to expect anything from Nadia and to be patient with Marrin. As my therapist is so fond of saying, "*We can't change other people, but we can change ourselves.*"

When I answer the call, I don't expect my mom to apologize or acknowledge her failings as a parent. I don't expect anything remotely motherly either.

"What's up, Nadia?"

"Damian. I'm surprised you answered."

That makes two of us.

"What's up?" I repeat, stuffing bottled water into the pantry.

"I was calling to see how your holiday went."

Uh...

"Fine." It comes out like a question. It kind of is. My mom never asks how I'm doing. If we'd ever had that kind of relationship, then I doubt it would've taken me a whole summer to confess I was being abused.

Ugh, this situation perfectly illustrates what I hate about small talk. Right now, social etiquette dictates I ask how her holiday went. Problem is, I don't care.

But when the silence drags, I cave. "How was yours?"

"It was very nice. Thank you for asking."

Did I just detect a hint of sincerity in her voice?

"I missed you boys," she adds.

I pause. "Have you been drinking?"

"No. I haven't had a drink in almost seven months."

Well, color me surprised, I almost say, but don't. "What's this about?"

She inhales sharply. "I'm attending a few conferences in your area soon, and I was hoping we could meet. For coffee. Or something. Whatever you want."

I check my phone screen to make sure it is indeed my mother on the line. This feels weird. Nadia was never manipulative, but how the hell else do I explain her calling me up to chat and ask about hanging out?

"You don't have to give me an answer now," she says. "I'll text you the dates I'll be in town and my availability."

"Okay." Again, it comes out like a question.

"I understand if you don't want to see me. I'd very much like to mend things between us. I recognize that I need to earn your trust and atone for my actions. I'd very much appreciate the opportunity to try, but I know you may not be ready and that's fine."

Listening to my mother try and edge into a conversation about feelings is like listening to someone read stereo instructions out loud. It's perforating and sterile, and so matter-of-fact you end up more confused by the end than you should be.

"Okay," I repeat because it's all I can think to say.

We hang up and I stare at my phone—*because what the fuck just happened?*

I finish putting away my groceries then make dinner and eat alone in front of my TV. I'm once again struck with the urge to call Marrin and tell her about what just happened with Nadia. But I can't.

On the coffee table sit two novelty coasters I bought Marrin for Christmas. I didn't wrap them, I'd just intended to leave them in her apartment when she wasn't looking.

I try not to think about the hole Marrin's left in my life. I wasn't joking when I said she was my best friend. It feels like I'm missing a limb or something. Fuck, I don't know.

Before I go to bed, I look out the window to see a light dusting of snow on the ground. I scan the parking lot, finding Marrin's car.

At least I know she's home safe.

Three days later, it's still snowing. The governor has officially declared a state of emergency. The interstate is basically useless and none of the roads in town have been cleared. There's too much snow and not enough plows. We never get weather like this, so it's no surprise that we're not equipped to handle it.

Too bad it didn't happen after spring semester started. I'd be down for a few snow days.

My friends have all been calling to see if I'm all right and if I have power. I do, thank God. The second night of the storm, the power flickered, but it never went out. I've ventured outside a few times just to get out of the apartment but that's it.

I'm sitting on the couch, watching national news coverage of the storm, when my phone rings. I don't recognize the number.

"Hello?"

"Damian Wane, it's Alice Braxton, Marrin's cousin."

"Hi. How did you get this number?" I realize it's a dumb question. I bought a trial membership to her club, she has access to all kinds of information about me.

"Not important. Listen, have you heard from Marrin lately?"

"No, sorry." A tendril of fear knots my stomach. I move to the window, checking that her car is still here. It is.

"I need you to go knock on her door for me."

"Sure. Is everything okay?" I slip on a pair of shoes.

"I hope so. She wasn't feeling well yesterday. I've been texting her all day and she hasn't answered. I'd check in myself but the weather is making that difficult."

I walk to Marrin's and knock.

When she doesn't answer, I knock again. "Hey, Mar. I've got your cousin on the phone, I swear that's the only reason I'm here. Can you just answer the door?"

"Anything?" Alice says.

"No. But she and I aren't exactly talking right now, so she might not be answering because of me." I knock one more time. "Mar, if you can hear me, call your cousin to check in." I walk back to my apartment. "Sorry I can't be more helpful."

"It's okay. Thanks Damian."

"No problem."

We hang up and I try to settle back onto my couch but can't.

I put on a pair of boots and a jacket and go downstairs to check Marrin's car. It's colder than Rudolph's balls, but I don't care. I push the snow off the driver's side window and look in to make sure she's not passed out inside or something.

She's not.

Feeling like an idiot, I trudge back inside.

Three minutes after I'm back on my couch, Alice calls.

"Did she call you?" I say by way of greeting.

"No. I need you to go inside her apartment."

This is gonna be awkward.

"I don't have a key to her place."

"Check your bedroom door frame. Top right."

Huh?

"Marrin never trusted me enough to give me a key to her place."

"I know. Now walk to your bedroom door and check the frame."

I'm so fucking confused I do what she says. I slide my hand across the door frame and—

My fingertips touch the cold metal of an unmarked key. It's ordinary, like it could go to anything.

"The *fuuuck...*"

I don't even know I've spoken out loud until Alice says, "Good. You found it."

"What the hell is going on? How did this key get here?"

"Nothing's going on. I had Gavin hide it the night we came over to get Marrin. She trusted you enough to pick her up, so I decided to leave a key just in case."

My mind is reeling. This is some CIA-level shit. "Who *are* you?"

"Not important. I need you to go check on Marrin."

I slip on shoes and head down the hall.

I knock on Mar's door and announce I'm coming in. When I hear nothing, I unlock and slowly open it.

"Marrin, it's Damian. I swear I'm not breaking in. Alice left me a key I had *no* knowledge of until two minutes ago. She's on the phone and willing to vouch for my innocence." Alice chuckles. "Mar?"

The apartment is dark. The only light comes from the bathroom. The door is slightly ajar and the fan is on. I knock before I look in. "Mar, it's me. I'm just making sure—"

Marrin's unconscious on the floor, wearing only a T-shirt and underwear.

"—*shit.*"

I rush in, phone forgotten as I drop to my knees.

There's a towel under her head like a pillow, so I don't think she fell and knocked herself out. But I still check, tilting her head carefully. She's burning with fever and slicked with sweat.

"Marrin? Can you hear me? Mar?"

She doesn't respond, just moans and mumbles like people do when their whole body is racked with fever. I wet a washcloth with cold water and gently dab her cheeks. She groans and turns into the touch.

"It's gonna be okay," I tell her. "I'll be right back." I grab my phone and don't bother checking any of Marrin's cabinets. I know they're empty. "Has Marrin had a flu shot?" I ask Alice.

"No idea. What the fuck's happening?"

I fill her in as I race back to my apartment. I grab a thermometer and every liquid cold and flu medication I have as well as a bottle of water and a straw. Then I ask the most obvious question. "How the hell do I get someone who's unconscious to drink medicine?"

Unsurprisingly, Alice has an answer.

Back in Marrin's apartment, Alice reminds me to lock the door. I don't bring up Marrin's stalker and neither does she. Marrin never confirmed she had one, but the look on her face when I brought it up during our fight was all the answer I needed.

I put the phone on speaker and leave it on the coffee table with everything else. In the bathroom, I gather Marrin into my arms as gently as possible.

She whimpers.

It can't feel good to be moved. I had the flu once and the worst part was the body aches. Her limbs twitch slightly like she can't lay still from the pain. It only gets worse as I pick her up. But I have no choice. I'm not leaving her on the damn floor.

"Sorry, baby. I'm sorry. I have to move you." God, her skin is on fire.

I lay her on the couch. She's ashen and thinner than usual. Her T-shirt has ridden up, so I go to pull it down—

And freeze.

Three scars mar the skin just barely above the top of her low-rise panties.

I've never seen them before. Ever.

Two are staggered and horizontal and almost perfectly parallel, but the third is sharply angled somewhere between ninety and forty-five degrees. My hand hovers above them.

How have I never seen these before?

The truth hits me like a Mack truck: I've never seen Marrin completely naked.

She's always kept something around her waist—right over these scars. This whole time, I thought it was a kink. It never once occurred to me that she might be hiding something she didn't want me to see...

Anxiety crawls up my spine as I pull her shirt down. Now is not the time for this.

The blanket I left at her place months ago is draped across the back of the couch. I pull it over her then follow Alice's instructions on how to slowly coax a dose of liquid medicine down her throat.

I talk to Marrin the whole time just in case she's aware of what's happening. I get some meds in her then grab the water.

Crouching next to the couch, I put the straw in her mouth. "I need you to drink some water, okay? It'll make you feel better. I promise." She groans. "Please, baby."

I brush a strand of hair off her forehead and her lips close around the straw. She only takes a few sips but it's better than nothing. I try a few more times to get her to drink more but nothing happens. She's slipped back into the fog of pain and fever.

For the next few hours, I just sit with her. Watching her breathe from my perch on the coffee table.

I pull her hair out from beneath her and drape it over

the arm of the couch in an attempt to cool her. I keep a damp cloth on her head and administer another round of medicine per the directions. Her fever comes down, but she doesn't wake up.

Christ, if she woke up and saw me, she'd probably be pissed.

It's nearly ten o'clock when the door opens and Alice, Gavin and a redheaded woman I've never seen before walk in.

I get up to give Alice room, but she doesn't come over, the redhead does. She opens a large kit of medical supplies and gets to work. I fill them in on how Marrin's been since I last spoke to Alice. Her pain seems to have eased, but she hasn't had more than a few sips of water.

The redhead, who introduces herself as Dr. Addison, applies a tourniquet to Marrin's arm, swabs a spot with alcohol then pulls out one of those catheter needle things. Mar doesn't react when Dr. Addison hooks her up to an IV right there in the living room. The bag hangs on a collapsible pole clamped to the edge of the coffee table.

No one but me bats an eyelash.

Who the hell are these people?

I don't stick around to find out. I head to the door. I shouldn't be here anyway. If Mar knew I'd entered her apartment without her permission, she'd never speak to me again.

Plus, I can't look at her lying on the couch like that. She looked sickly and emaciated before the IV, but after...

My chest constricts and I slip out the door.

I don't know what's worse, the fact that Marrin looks like stress has eaten her alive, or the fact that I may have caused it.

And then there are the scars. What kind of guy sleeps

with a woman for almost four months and fails to notice three horrible scars on her body? What the fuck does that say about me? I feel like I'm going to be sick.

I'm unlocking my apartment when Gavin catches up with me. "You forgot your key."

I shake my head. "I don't want it. If she knew I had a key to her place and used it to break in..."

"You didn't break in. We asked you to check on her and it was a good thing you did."

"I doubt she'd see it that way."

He nods and starts walking away.

I should go into my apartment and close the door behind me. I should but—

"The scars on her stomach," I say.

Gavin turns around slowly.

"They're not from surgery... are they?"

"No, kid. They're not."

18

Marrin

Everything hurts. My face, my hips, my skin. I open my eyes and find myself in my bed, Alice is sitting next to me.

"Am I dead?" I croak.

She smiles. "Almost. How are you feeling?"

"Like shit." I have no idea how I got here. The last thing I remember I was laying down in the bathroom because I felt like I might vomit. "What day is it?"

"January first. Happy New Year."

"I've been out for two days? How long have you been here?"

"Since late Saturday night after Damian found you unconscious in the bathroom."

"Oh my God. You didn't." Alice purses her lips and my voice raises several octaves. "You did."

"We hid a key and I'd do it again. You're lucky you're not in the hospital right now."

I try to glare, but it makes the pounding in my head worse.

"I could've asked someone from your security detail,"

Alice continues. "But they don't have a key and even if they did, would you've preferred a stranger walking into your apartment over Damian?"

Well you got me there.

She fills me in on everything I missed (including an epic snow storm the area is just now starting to recover from), then she helps me to the bathroom.

I catch a glimpse of myself in the mirror—I look like hell warmed over.

I pee, brush my teeth, then jump into the shower. Nothing like hot water and soap to make a girl feel alive again. I wash my hair then soap up my body, running a hand over my stomach.

A thought hits me: I woke up in a T-shirt and underwear.

Did Damian see my scars?

Dread knots in my gut. There's no way to know unless I ask him, and I am definitely not doing that.

I fret for a moment more before another thought eclipses the first: Damian came over to help me even after we broke up. I said some horrible things to him and he still came over to check on me. To take care of me...

I dress when I'm done showering then join Alice on the couch. "Thanks for braving the storm to help me... and for leaving a key with Damian."

She gives me a side hug. "You're welcome. I'll always take care of you, Mar."

"I know."

She's quiet a moment. "Do you want to tell me what's going on with you and Damian?"

I shrug, resting back to stare at the ceiling. "We're not seeing each other anymore."

"How come? I thought you liked him."

"I do. I just... It's safer this way."

"Safer for who?" When I don't answer, she adds, "Is this about Frank and your mom... or is this about you?"

"You talked to Gavin, didn't you?"

"Maybe."

"Frank's dangerous. I don't want Damian getting hurt."

She's quiet a moment. "It's natural to want to protect the people we care about. There's nothing I wouldn't do to protect you."

"But you think I should've told him about Frank and my mom, don't you?"

"Do you think you should've told him?" she says, voice calm, judgment free.

I shrug. Talking about feelings has never been easy for me.

"What's the worst that could happen if you told him?" she asks.

"He'd reject and pity me."

"Perhaps," she contemplates. "Or maybe he'd accept you."

I roll my head to face her. Her elbow is propped on the back of the couch, her head resting in her palm. "How would you react to finding out the person you're sleeping with has a past like mine?"

She gives me a wry smile. "I'd probably ask you to marry me."

I wince, remembering the story Gavin told me.

"When I met Gavin, I knew he carried scars I both could and couldn't see. It didn't stop me from loving him... or from seeing who he truly was."

"Damian isn't like you, he wouldn't understand."

"It sounds like you've already decided that for him."

I open my mouth to argue but... she's right.

I rub at the new headache building in my temples.

Alice moves away momentarily, coming back to hand me some meds and a glass of water. I take both.

"May I make another observation?" she says gently. I nod. "It sounds like the problem isn't with Damian, it's with you."

The truth of her words, the sadness I feel, spread through my chest like a firework in the sky. I curl up with my head in her lap. She starts stroking my hair and I'm reminded of all the times we used to sit like this after I started living with her. And after I came home from the hospital following everything that happened Thanksgiving of freshman year.

"Do you remember what your therapist said?" Alice asks, referring to the psychologist the university disciplinary committee made me see. "About how it's okay to be vulnerable?"

"I don't like being vulnerable. Letting people in is how you get hurt."

"It's not fun when the people we love hurt us."

Tears thicken my throat. "She said she'd changed," I whisper. And I know Alice knows I'm talking about my mother. "And I believed her. I trusted her and look what happened."

"I know," she soothes. "But Damian isn't your mother."

"I know. And I know it's not fair to decide for him, *I do*. But I love him and I don't want him to hurt me like she did. If I tell him, then it feels as if I'm handing him the power to hurt me, losing what little control I still have. And then there's Frank. I *don't* want Frank to hurt Damian because he's with me."

"Two thoughts," Alice says. "First, don't worry about Frank. Let me deal with him. It's a matter of time before we locate him, and I've got people watching you and the apartment. You don't have to worry about him coming around you or Damian—or anyone, okay?"

I nod.

"Second thought, if you tell Damian the truth and he rejects you, is that outcome really any different from where you are now? You might be slightly sadder, knowing it's officially over—*and that he's a complete douchebag for turning you down for such a lame, superficial reason.*" I smile. "But feeling sad isn't unusual or uncommon after a breakup, is it?"

I turn to face her. "I guess not."

"Wouldn't it be better to know?"

"I suppose."

She strokes my hair. "So think about it. You don't have to do anything now, or at all."

"I don't think I can tell him everything at once. Openly asking to be his girlfriend will be hard enough."

"So tell him that," Alice says. "Just be honest with him. Tell him you can give him one truth at a time. One vulnerability at a time. Start with the small stuff and work your way up."

I like her plan, but...

Anxiety over all the ways it could go wrong makes me jittery. "But what about Frank? I can't control Frank. He could show up at any time and ruin everything."

"Look at me," Alice says. I do. "Let me worry about Frank. I'll find him, and when I do, I'll let you know. You can decide what you want to do after that, but there is no use worrying about it now. Okay?"

I nod, her words easing me.

We spend the rest of the day watching movies and eating popcorn. Gavin arrives just before sundown to pick her up and drop off some much needed groceries.

Alone in my apartment, I spy two coasters on my coffee table I've never seen before. I pick one up. It depicts an old movie poster for *Cat People*. It shows Irena and says "She was marked with the curse of those who slink and court and kill by night!"

I smile. And then I cry because I know who left these for me.

Damian

The first weekend after spring semester starts, Vicky invites us all out for a night of fun at a local dive bar called Church. It has billiards and darts and good local beers.

At half past ten, I pick up Hayden and we head to the bar. When he got back in town a few days ago, I told him everything that went down between Marrin and I. I had to. I couldn't hold it in any longer. Besides, if he'd asked me what was wrong one more time, I'd have started throwing things. So I told him.

We park on the street and head inside.

I know Marrin was invited and that she's coming. Tonight will be my first time really seeing her since we broke up three weeks ago. She texted me to say thanks for helping her when she was sick, and I responded that it was no problem. Other than that, I've had no contact with her.

I told myself I was prepared to see her. That I'd act cool and give her space. However, the moment I enter the bar, I start searching for her.

I find her across the room looking as lovely as always in dark jeans and an old band T-shirt. Our eyes collide and a sad, hopeful smile touches her lips. I mouth the word, *Hi,* and she starts rapidly blinking like she's fighting tears. Pain slashes my heart like a whip.

Hayden steers me toward the bar. "Let's get you a drink."

"Let's get me a few drinks." I order two shots of whiskey and two beers. I take one shot and pass the second to Hayden along with a beer. "For you."

He declines the shot but accepts the beer.

"Come on," I say. "You're at Church. Take the sacrament, cleanse your sins."

"I'm not religious," Hayden says. "And one of us needs to be of sound mind to drive your drunk ass home later."

"True." I down the whiskey, trying not to think about how it's the same color as Marrin's eyes. It burns its way down my throat, warming my belly but not my heart.

Did I really just think that? I need a timeout.

I grab my beer and we make our way to the table where our friends sit.

We mingle and I make a normal amount of eye contact and conversation with everyone—except Marrin. Awkward doesn't even begin to describe the air between us. I try to act normal, but I'm not sure how long is too long to look at her and how much is too much to talk to her. Too many things hang between us. I know she feels it, too.

I'm beginning to understand why Vicky didn't want me dating any of her friends.

Marrin mostly talks to her girlfriends at the other end of the table and I mostly talk to the guys at my end of the table.

Well, until Devon arrives.

"What's up?" he greets. Devon is one of those guys who's friends with everyone. He's a tall white guy with a perpetual suntan and chin-length blond hair. "How was everyone's break? Heard the snow storm was insane."

"I wouldn't know," Vicky grumbles, "I wasn't here. Damian and Marrin were, though."

He looks at Marrin and does a double-take. "You okay?"

"I'm fine," she says, uncomfortable with the attention.

"Dude," Devon replies. "Not trying to be rude or give an unsolicited opinion about your appearance, but you look like you need a sandwich and a yearlong nap."

"I had the flu."

I know it's not a lie, but I can tell it's not the whole truth either because her smile doesn't reach her eyes.

"You get a flu shot?" Devon asks.

"Nope. I'll never make that mistake again. I now understand how people can die from the flu."

Dev still looks concerned. "Did you see a doctor?"

"Yeah. I'm fine. Just kind of stressed with school and life and all that. How was your break? Didn't you go on a surf trip?"

She changes the subject like a racecar driver shifts gears, and I'm pretty sure I'm the only one who notices. Devon launches into a story about his break and that's that.

Suddenly, I'm angry. How hard is it to confide in your friends about your life? This woman is keeping so many secrets I could break something.

Or maybe I want to break something because I was one of those secrets.

Pain and anger roil in me. Jayce shoots me a quizzical look. I ignore him and head to the bar for another drink. He follows.

"What happened with Marrin?"

"Nothing," I say.

"Bullshit," Jayce replies. "I can practically see the awkward air between you two."

"What happened is we're not sleeping together anymore," I say bitterly. "It wasn't my decision."

"Shit, dude. That sucks... I *did* tell you she was bad news, though."

"Yes, thank you for rubbing that in. You're a true friend." He chuckles as I pay for my beer.

"Lighten up, Dame. There are plenty of single women here tonight to help you forget about her."

"I don't want to forget about her." The words check my anger enough for me to explain that I'm not done chasing Marrin, and that even if she never wants to date me, I don't want to lose her as a friend.

"I understand that," Jayce says.

We start walking back to our table.

"*DAME.*"

I turn and see Holly from work walking over with a big smile on her face.

"What's up, Hollywood?" I say, as she hugs me. "What are you doing out? Didn't think I'd see you until next Saturday."

Marrin

Coming out tonight was the worst idea ever. Seeing Damian is more painful than I'd thought it'd be, and to make it worse, he's talking to some gorgeous brunette. She's pretty in all the ways I'm not. She's bubbly and personable and a heaping pile of cleavage protrudes from her shirt like two melons trying to escape a Ziploc bag.

Ugh. When did I start being jealous of other women? Who am I right now? I'm not mad at her. She's just living her life, talking to a hot guy at a bar—*who's clearly enjoying her company.*

I'm mad at Damian for talking to her. No, I'm mad at myself for being mad that he's talking to her. But mostly I'm mad that this beautiful woman seems so open and free, and I can't even tell the guy I love a stupid fact about my life that seems so lame and insignificant compared to the one he told me.

It's okay to be vulnerable, Marrin.

From the moment Damian walked in, I've been trying to work up the nerve to talk to him about how I feel. He's everything I want.

He's my best friend.

But it's that realization that makes everything so much harder because now I have so much more to lose. Before if I told him about my life and he rejected me, I'd only be losing a fuck buddy no one knew about. Now if I tell him and he rejects me, it's like I'm losing a piece of my soul.

Two days ago, Alice called to tell me she was able to put a tail on Frank. Which means I no longer need a security detail. The moment Frank tries to get close to me again, the team tracking him will notify us. Therefore, I can keep him away from Damian. And that means Damian is safe and that I have time to ease him into my baggage at my own pace. Frank won't be popping up to ruin everything.

All night I've been going back and forth in my head. To tell Damian I want to be his girlfriend or not to tell him. Five minutes ago, I was ready to just tell him. But the way he's talking to this woman like they're old friends has my stomach in knots because what if I'm too late? What if he's decided I'm more trouble than I'm worth?

Stop. You sound like some wishy-washy soap opera character.

Aw crap. I *am* a wishy-washy soap opera character.

Tiana nudges me with an elbow. "What's up? You've been weird all night."

"Nothing. Just stressed."

Vicky leans toward us from across the table. "This wouldn't have anything to do with," she lowers her voice, "*Damian,* would it?"

"Yeah," Tiana says, "because you two are acting suspect."

"What? No, I'm just stressed."

"Confess your sins," Vicky pushes. "You're at Church."

I glance at Damian and tears prickle my throat.

I stand. "I need to use the restroom and get another beer."

When I come back to the table, Devon is in my seat and the only spot left is between Vicky and Damian.

Great. Just great.

I sit next to Damian—who has no idea because he's turned in the other direction talking to the cute brunette. I take a too-long sip of beer, trying and failing to ignore the way Damian smells. It's fresh and masculine and reminds me of all the times we kissed and touched and—

I need to stop before my *ho*-varies get the better of me.

I focus on my friends. Jayce and Vicky are to my left, talking about spring break. In front of me, Devon orders a pitcher of beer for the table then goes back to talking to Tiana. Hayden sits next to Devon, talking with Damian and the cute brunette at the head of the table.

All around the room, people are talking and catching up with friends.

I look at the people around me. At my friends. They're laughing and sharing stories and having a good time with one another... but not with me.

I'm sitting at a table of friends and I don't think I've ever felt more alone.

I sip my beer. This is my fault.

I've kept them all at arm's length because I'm too embarrassed of who I really am.

I take another swig of beer. Then another. And then I don't put it down. I just keep chugging until I'm tilting my head back to empty the bottle.

"Damn, Marrin," Hayden blurts. "Show that beer who's boss."

I ignore him. I ignore everyone as they turn to watch me finish.

Only one person in this group really knows me.

It's okay to be vulnerable.

I pull out my phone because I don't trust myself not to burst into tears if I speak to him out loud.

Marrin: *Can we talk?*

The waitress delivers the pitcher of beer Devon ordered, and I don't say no when he pours me a glass. "You must be stressed, Mar. I've never seen you drink like this."

"Me either," Vicky says, shooting Tiana a wary look.

I take a healthy gulp of booze. I feel Damian's eyes on me like a touch.

I *wish* he were touching me.

He's so close I can feel his body heat. If he asked me to fuck him in the bathroom right now, I'd say yes. I'd let him have every part of me because really, he already does. Alice was right, he isn't the problem with us. I am.

Something happens in my brain and suddenly I can't even hold a smile or a conversation. Both feel forced, fake. Just like me.

Another swig of beer it is!

Someone produces a deck of cards and I narrowly avoid

getting roped into a game of poker. I pretend to follow along with Vicky, but even that's hard to fake.

A few minutes in, Damian pulls out his phone. My heart picks up and I take another sip of beer.

Damian: *Right now?*
Marrin: *Yes.*
Damian: *I'm not sure that's a good idea.*

A feeling runs over me like rain down a windowsill. It's a moment before I'm able to put a label on it. Crestfallen, dejected.

They play a few more rounds of poker and I'm just tipsy enough to send a few more texts.

Marrin: *I understand if you've moved on.*
Marrin: *I wouldn't blame you if you did.*
Marrin: *Just tell me.*

But Damian doesn't check his phone.

I chase the sinking feeling in my gut with beer. It's only my third drink, but I'm a lightweight, which means I'm well on my way to being white girl wasted. Hooray.

Damian

My phone has vibrated three times since I put it back into my pocket and I know each was a text from Marrin. She's sitting next to me chugging beers, and I'm not sure what to do. I want to talk to her, but if I've learned one thing from my mother, it's that you can't have a serious conversation with someone when they're drunk.

Tiana wins the round and I get up to get Holly and myself fresh beers. It's almost midnight and the place is fairly crowded. I find a spot at the bar and wait for the bartender to come over.

I'm about to grab my phone and check my texts when a flash of silver-white catches my eye.

"Hey," Marrin says, appearing at my side.

I startle. "Hey."

She opens her mouth but the bartender interrupts. I order two beers and when I turn back to Marrin, pain and disbelief twist her face. She looks away, blinking hard. I'm not sure if she's fighting tears, but if she is, then she's probably had too much to drink. The bartender brings my order and asks for hers. She doesn't hear him.

"Marrin. Bartender asked what you want."

She shakes her head. "N-Nothing. Can we talk?"

"Not right now, no." I don't mean to sound harsh, but I'm a little floored she's asking in person. She's probably drunker than I'd thought.

Her eyes dart around. "Later maybe?"

"I want nothing more than to talk to you, but tonight's not a good idea. We've both been drink—"

"What's taking so long?" Holly says, popping up at my side. Her eyes flit between Marrin and I. "My bad. Am I interrupting?"

I wait for Marrin to answer because it's her choice. But she only stares at me. So I say, "No," and hand Holly her beer.

"Thanks. Who's your friend?" she asks with a genuine smile.

"This is Vicky's friend, Marrin."

Holly extends her hand. "Nice to meet you, I'm Holly."

The next second is the longest of my life. Marrin looks at

me like I killed her puppy. Then politely introduces herself to Holly.

Once they shake hands, Marrin excuses herself and bolts.

I'm not sure what to do.

Holly grabs my beer. "I don't know what you did, but if you don't chase that girl, I will."

Shit.

Marrin's halfway to the exit before I grab her arm and spin her around. "Wait up. What's going on?"

"Nothing." She keeps her head down.

"Look at me—"

"No."

"Baby—"

Her head snaps up. "*Don't* call me that." Angry tears rim her eyes.

"What's this about?"

"You should've told me."

"Told you what?" I'm so fucking confused.

"That you were bringing a date." Her voice cracks and she wipes at a few tears. "I get it. I don't blame you, but you should've told me."

With gut wrenching clarity I understand. I reach out to touch her face, but stop when I remember we're in public. "Holly is a friend from work. I didn't invite her, we're not on a date and she has a serious girlfriend. Nothing is going on. I swear. Ask her."

"Then why are you ignoring me?"

"I'm not. I read your first few texts and figured you sent them because you'd had too much to drink. I didn't want to start a conversation you'd regret in the morning."

Her whole body seems to sag. "You're not mad at me?"

"Baby, why would I be mad at you?" The urge to touch her is unbearable.

"Because I'm a mess. Because I can't just tell you what's wrong with me."

She looks so pitiful it's almost funny. But the truth sobers me enough to focus. "A part of me is angry, but not at you. I'm angry that I didn't do enough to earn your trust. I'm angry that I showed up at the club without considering your feelings. I'm angry that I agreed to keep things between us private which put me in a position to feel like I was just another one of your secrets." I rake a hand through my hair and sigh. "I want to talk to you, but I love you too much to fuck this up again."

"You didn't fuck this up," she whispers. "I did. I broke up with you because that was easier than letting you in."

I can see her walls coming down, and I have to rein in the urge to shout from the fucking rooftops. When I do, I remember how much she hates public emotions.

"So you agree," I say teasingly. "We *were* dating."

The smile that curls her mouth is enough to stop my heart and vanquish any awkwardness between us.

She wipes her eyes. "I need to go before I embarrass myself. I'll talk to you tomorrow?"

"It's a date." I wink.

Tears of relief flood her eyes as she turns and walks away. I fight the need to run after her just so I can take her home and fuck her till she's begging to be my girlfriend.

My inner alpha male is a gross Neanderthal and I have zero fucks to give about it.

Holly comes over and holds out my beer. But before I grab it, two things happen.

The first is that Jake the Jackass steps in front of Marrin, looks right at me and practically yells, "Pretty Boy finally kicking your ass to the curb? I told you you're not good enough for these people."

The second is that he grabs her arm, preventing her from walking away.

Oh. Hell. No.

19

Marrin

When I got up from the table to follow Damian to the bar, I honestly thought this night couldn't get any worse.

Then he ordered two beers, one for himself and one for Holly. It felt like someone pushed me off a cliff and I was falling. I couldn't move or think.

Then he said he didn't want to talk to me, and I didn't know whether to cry right then and there or try and make it to the bathroom first.

Then Holly popped up. And she was lovely and nice and Damian introduced me as "*Vicky's friend, Marrin.*" The whole world just... hollowed out. All I could think was, *Vicky's friend. I'm Vicky's friend. Not his friend. Or just Marrin. I'm Vicky's friend, Marrin.*

It shouldn't have hurt as much as it did because I put myself in that position. I made Damian my secret, so what did I really expect?

But even after all that, after I ran away and he chased me and I confessed this whole mess was my fault, did I think— for a second—this night could get any worse.

Boy, oh boy, was I wrong.

I'm on my way to tell Tiana I'm getting a cab home, when Jake obstructs my path.

Misinterpreting my tears, he looks at Damian and shouts, "Pretty Boy finally kicking your ass to the curb? I told you you're not good enough for these people."

Mortification bleaches my face. Everyone around us quiets, stares.

"Out of my way." I shove past him, but he grabs my arm.

My rage skyrockets.

"Let go of me. Now." I'm seconds away from kicking him in the balls and making a scene. He might be my friend, but no one puts their hands on me without permission.

"Let her go," Damian orders. I turn around and he's right behind me, closing in fast.

Jake straightens. "And if I—"

"Stop it," I command, getting between them. "Please don't do this. Jake didn't mean it, he's just joking. Right, Jake?"

Why am I protecting this jackass?

Disbelief contorts Damian's face. I shoot him a wide-eyed, pleading look to back down. He blinks.

Jake yanks my arm and I crash into him.

Damian lurches forward.

I regain my footing and hold up a hand. "I don't need you to defend me, Damian," I shout, authority and fear twisting my voice. I know he hears both because he starts calculating, assessing the situation like it's a puzzle he's almost put together.

Jake chuckles. "Run along, Ivy League. She's not good enough for you any—"

Damian's fist stops an inch from Jake's jaw. Jake flinches back, letting me go.

"Wrong, Jackass," Damian says viciously, stepping between me and Jake. "She's better than all of us. *Especially* you."

I realize we're surrounded by a crowd of people.

My heart rate climbs.

"I get it now," Jake spits, embarrassed and livid. "Ivy League doesn't know why you're not good enough, does he?"

"Jake," I warn, coming around Damian. "Please, *please*."

"Outside. Now," Vicky growls, suddenly beside me.

Jake looks her up and down, before focusing on me. "She's the only one who knows—"

"Out. Side," Vicky demands.

Damian shoots me a look that says, *Knows what?*

Jake's smile drips with malice. "Marrin's old lady's in prison—"

"*JAKE*," I shriek.

"—for trying to kill her own kid."

No, no, no, no, no.

Deafening numbness slams into me like a meteorite hitting the planet. I swear I see the world crumble around me. Seconds pass, hours maybe.

Everyone knows.

I can't look at Damian. At Vicky. I think I'm looking at Jake, but I'm not sure because my brain has stopped registering colors and shapes and details—

Oh God, everyone knows.

From somewhere far away, I hear Jake say, "Don't worry. She makes ends meet by taking off her—"

Jake hits the ground.

Vicky snarls, "This is why we can't have nice things, jackass."

Then everything happens very quickly.

Chaos erupts in the bar. Vicky and Tiana grab my arms.

Cold air assaults me as they drag me outside. A car door opens, I'm stuffed into the backseat, then we're flying down the road.

I don't know when I start crying, all I know is tears are soaking through my jeans.

Then we're suddenly at my apartment. I'm on my couch next to Tiana and Vicky, and I just start talking. It begins with, "I've been sleeping with Damian," and ends when I've confessed the whole story.

And I mean the *whole* story.

Everything about Damian and I, and all the parts Tiana doesn't know about my life. For so long, Vicky has been the only one of my friends who knows everything because she happened to call my phone after Jake got me to a hospital. It's liberating and terrifying to confess because Tiana comes from the same slice of society as Damian.

When I finish, I wait. Hands shaking.

If Tiana looks at me like everyone did at that party sophomore year when I put a guy in the hospital, I don't know what I'll do.

Tiana slumps back, staring at the coffee table. "Shit. I mean... *Shit*. When I left my house tonight, the biggest problem in my life was deciding where to party for my birthday next weekend, but now..."

"I'm sorry," I say.

Her head whips to me. "For what?" She throws her arms around me. "I'm the one who should be sorry. I feel like the worst friend." She pulls back and I see nothing but love and compassion in her eyes. "I'm so sorry this happened to you. I have no idea how hard it must have been to carry that around and to feel like you couldn't tell anyone. I want you to know you can *always* tell me anything. I'll take your secrets to my grave, and as a policy, I'm a judgment-free zone."

"Thanks." We hug again and then Vicky joins in and we're all one big pile of hugging, teary-eyed humans. When we break apart, I take a deep breath. "What do I do now? The whole bar heard what Jake said. And Damian..."

How can I face him now? There is no way to undo this kind of damage. I should've just told him about my mom weeks ago.

"I don't think you have to worry about Damian," Tiana says. She jerks a thumb at Vicky. "While this one was running her mouth, his focus was only on you. Pretty sure he punched Jake to get him to shut up."

"Agreed," Vicky says. "And who cares? If he can't accept all of you, then he's a douchebag who ain't worth your time, babe."

I nod.

There's a knock on my door.

"Marrin?" Damian calls, from the other side. "You there, baby?"

Damian

Marrin's mother tried to kill her.

My mind is still reeling.

When she got between me and Jake, I was furious. I couldn't understand why she'd let him put his hands on her. But it was the look in her eyes and the tone of her voice that had me backing down. She was scared, but not for the obvious reasons.

It wasn't until Jake had spouted some shit about me not knowing why he thinks Marrin isn't good enough, that I figured out she wasn't protecting him or me. She was protecting herself.

Then he'd gone and done it. Told a room full of people Marrin's deepest, darkest secret.

Marrin's mother tried to kill her.

It still sounds fake in my head, like someone else's reality or the plot of a movie.

After he'd said it, all I could think about were the scars on her stomach. The scars she'd hidden from me for four months.

Everything about Marrin made sense in that moment. The scars she carries are as much physical as they are mental and emotional.

When Jake had started talking, the color drained from Marrin's face. I'd thought she might pass out. She'd screamed at him to stop and I swear I felt the pain in her voice like an icicle piercing my heart.

And the bastard had kept talking. Kept trying to bring her down and—

I fuckin' snapped.

I laid Jake out flat on the ground with a right hook to the face. Jackass never saw it coming. My only regret is not getting the opportunity to hit him again.

Half the bar stepped in to keep us apart. I remember running my mouth. Remember telling him he was the worst kind of person because he preys on people's insecurities and tries to bring them down with him. I remember Jayce getting up in my face and telling me to *"shut the fuck up"* because while I might've grown up rich and privileged, the cops were going to see me as just another college kid who hit a guy at a bar.

That was a sobering moment.

Luckily, most of the people in the place were on my side

and the cops were chill. It helped that Jake the Jackass had a history of fighting and run-ins with the law. No one wanted to press charges, so no one got a ticket or spent the night in jail.

We got lucky.

I grabbed Marrin's jacket from the table before we left. Devon went home, Hayden drove my Jeep, and Jayce followed us to my apartment.

I'm not sure how long we've been sitting in my living room, but I finally pull out my phone and see the texts Marrin sent at the bar. I feel like a total ass for not reading them earlier. I stare at the screen, wondering if I should text her an apology. But what the fuck do I even say?

Marrin's mother tried to kill her.

"Fuck," I growl. Jayce and Hayden go silent. I bury my head in my hands. "Jackass just shared her trauma with a room full of people. What the fuck am I supposed to do now? How do I make this all right?"

I jump up to pace because I can't sit still.

"She'll never speak to any of us ever again," I say.

"You don't know that," Jayce placates.

"Wanna bet?"

"Is she really a—"

"Finish that sentence," I growl, "and I'm not sure I'll be able to stop myself from hitting you, dude."

I know he was about to ask if Marrin is a stripper. Jake said enough for anyone with half a brain to put it together. When I told Jayce and Hayden about me showing up at Marrin's other job, I left out the part about her dancing. Not because I was ashamed or anything, but because it's not my secret to share.

"Okay children," Hayden says, holding up his hands. "Let's get back on track. Dame, you obviously know her better than the rest of us, so your judgment on what to do next will probably be better than anything we can suggest. But I'd go with either calling her or going over and seeing if she wants to talk. I'd advise against sending a text because that seems kinda douchey."

"Little bit," Jayce agrees. He pulls out his phone. "FYI she's home right now. Vicky's been texting me. Needed to let me know she wasn't bailing me out of jail. True love ladies and gentlemen."

Hayden chuckles, but I'm not paying attention. I grab Marrin's jacket and head to her door.

I knock. "Marrin? You there, baby? You don't have to answer. I have your jacket..." I rest my forehead on her door. "I'm sorry about tonight. About all of it. I need you to know I don't care what anyone said or claimed. I told you my secret and I'm still waiting for you to tell me yours. I'll wait however long you need, however long it takes. I don't care. I love you. Nothing's gonna change that."

I wait. And wait. And when I realize she's not coming out, I turn and leave.

Halfway to my apartment, I hear locks slide and the sweep of an opening door. My heart skips, thinking it's Marrin, but when I turn around, it's Vicky stepping into the hallway.

"Is she okay?" I ask.

She shrugs. "I think so. She just needs time."

I pass her the jacket and nod.

"She heard you, though."

I nod again and start retreating. "Sorry I broke your dating rule."

She snorts. "That rule was for your benefit more than anything." At the confused look on my face she adds, "You went down on my friend at that house party in high school and... you were traumatized." She shrugs. "I knew you were too freaked out to try being intimate with anyone for a while, so I set the rule so you'd have an excuse. It just worked out that my friend from the party wanted more from you, and I don't know, over time enforcing the rule just became a thing I did."

I blink. "Thanks."

"Don't mention it."

20

Marrin

The next night, I unlock the door to my apartment and slip inside.

I spent the entire day hiding at the 13th Floor, still too mortified by what happened. I texted Damian and told him I was too ashamed to face him and he respected that. He told me that when I'm ready to talk, he's ready to listen.

I'm not sure I'll ever be ready.

How do I explain what it feels like to be attacked by your own mother? To be so unwanted by the person who gave you life that she decided to take it away? Then add a crazy stalker on top of it all and it's gonna take a three part episode of *Dr. Phil* to explain how messed up and insecure I am.

I pause on the way to my bedroom, looking for the right key. There are five keys on the loop. One to my apartment, my car, my mailbox, my bedroom...

And one to Damian's apartment.

He never asked for it back and I never offered.

I've been carrying it around this whole time.

I toss my keys on the coffee table and sit on the couch, staring at Damian's key.

I lean back and my eyes fall on the opposite end of the sofa. A small dent is beginning to form in the cushion. The fabric showing the first signs of age.

I've never noticed.

Since I bought the couch, it's looked brand new because I'm the only one who ever uses it. I also always sit in the same spot.

This new weathering isn't from me.

It's from Damian.

There is a Damian-shaped indentation in my couch.

That was his spot. Where he'd sit when he came over. Where I'd let him sit when he came over.

The refrigerator magnet he gave me catches my eye.

The coasters on the coffee table.

The poodle pillow I'm holding in my arms and the air plant sitting on the countertop.

All around the room—my once empty, lonely apartment is filled with things. Imprints of Damian. Signs of his existence, that he was here. *Him.*

He's everywhere I look.

Yet nowhere to be found.

I curl up in Damian's spot. This is where he sat the night he brought me medicine and a heating pad and a blanket. The same night he became the first person ever to watch a movie with me in my apartment. He laughed in this spot, joked in this spot...

Told me he loved me in this spot.

I pick up one of the *Cat People* coasters he left me. It shows Irena and says, "She was marked with the curse of those who slink and court and kill by night!"

Clarity hits me like sunrise after a storm. I sit up.

I'm a fucking idiot.

This whole time, I'd thought I was the femme fatale. Thought I was Irena—doomed to suffer the consequences of a past I hadn't chosen, a past that would eventually catch up with me and cost me Oliver. Or in my case, Damian.

But I'm not Irena and Damian isn't Oliver.

I'm Oliver. I'm married to Irena—aka my emotional baggage—and if I don't divorce her, she'll turn into a blood-thirsty panther and destroy me. Or worse, she'll destroy Alice Moore. And I can't allow that because Damian is Alice Moore in this weird analogy and Oliver has to end up with her. They're best friends. They're perfect for one another.

Damian didn't just leave a mark of his presence on my couch or my apartment, he left one on me—*in* me.

It's okay to be vulnerable.

I grab my phone, find the right number, and hit send.

"Tiana? I have an idea about what we can do for your birthday."

21

Damian

"This place is hella fancy, Tia," Vicky says as we walk up to the bar.

Tiana theatrically flips her braided hair over a shoulder. "Thank you."

We're in the city at a new club called White Rabbit. It's high end but not stuffy. The interior is all dark, moody colors, and there's a bit of a lounge feel to the room. Comfortable seating and tables line the walls, centering on a low stage just a few feet off the ground. It juts out into the middle of the room and I think it's for dancing but I can't tell. My guess is the place turns into more of a dance club later in the evening. I guess we'll find out.

I order a whiskey on the rocks and tell the bartender to put Tiana's drinks on my tab. She is the birthday girl, after all. Once we all have a beverage we head over to a roped-off section at the end of the stage.

"VIP?" Hayden asks.

"It's no big deal," Tiana says, "I happen to know

someone who knows someone who was able to reserve the best seats in the house for us."

Jayce plops into a leather armchair. "This is some swanky shit."

"No joke." I move across the intimate seating area to a spot near Hayden. "Serious crème de la crème."

"Sit by me, Damian." Tiana pats the seat next to her. "We never talk, and since it's my birthday, I get what I want."

I roll my eyes sarcastically and sit next to her in the chair closest the stage.

Hayden lounges back. "Not gonna lie, I was a bit worried about the dress code."

"You're wearing jeans," Vicky says.

"Yeah, but they're *nice* jeans. And I had to borrow this shirt and jacket from Damian."

White Rabbit doesn't have a dress code, but it's the kind of place that attracts people who wear only the latest fashion. When Hayden met me at my apartment earlier, I told him there was no way in hell I was letting him walk into a club—*Jay-Z was rumored to have been at the opening of*—wearing a navy-blue button-up shirt with matching jeans. Nope. Sorry. I'm too good a friend and I have a reputation to uphold. I threw him a designer flannel and a dark jacket and told him to change.

When he came out of the bathroom, he complained that he looked like, "*Justin Timberlake or some shit.*"

I'd counted to ten before telling him that was the fucking point.

"Where's Marrin?" Devon asks.

Here we go.

I look at my lap to avoid everyone's eyes. I've talked to her enough to know that she is coming tonight and that she wants to talk to me after.

"On her way," Tiana says. "Said she'd be a bit late."

"Cool. Cool." Devon taps his foot. "So... how is she?"

Leave it to Devon to bring up the elephant in the room. The night of the fight was only a week ago. I imagine someone has told him about Marrin and I because it's technically no longer a secret. It is, however, not something we've all acknowledged out loud in a group yet.

I get the feeling they're all waiting on me to respond.

When I don't, Vicky says, "Good."

"So, like, is it gonna be weird when she shows up?" he asks.

My alpha male snaps. "Why would it be weird?"

Devon has the good sense to look slightly guilty and I have the basic decency to look ashamed.

"I only meant weird because this is the first time we'll all be together after everything went down. Correct me if I'm wrong, but was I the only one who left Church feeling like there's a lot about Mar we don't know? Not trying to be an ass, but we've been friends since freshman year and I had no idea about..."

Vicky and Tiana exchange a look I can't quite place.

A heavy moment passes.

I'm surprised to find that it's me who breaks the silence. "Don't bring it up. When Mar gets here, let her bring it up if she wants. Otherwise, it's off limits. I mean it." I look them all in the eyes. "Marrin is our friend and we're not going to talk behind her back about shit some jackass said to hurt her."

"Cheers to that," Vicky proclaims.

We all lift our glasses in silent agreement and take a drink. The music cuts off and the house lights dim.

"It's starting," Tiana squeals.

"What's starting?" Jayce and I say at the same time.

Vicky and Tia both *shush* us.

Every light in the place goes out. I can't see a damn thing. I hear something mechanical and a bit of shuffling from stage but can't make out anything but a few shadowy figures.

"This isn't one of those musical theater clubs is it?" Hayden whines.

"Please no," Jayce whispers. "I'm not—*ouch.*"

"Hush," Vicky says. "Tia wouldn't do that to you."

"You could've said that without elbowing me," he grumbles.

A low hum of music starts at the same time the floor of the stage lights up a deep purple, illuminating seven dancers sitting in chairs lined up in a V-shape. Each wears stilettos, briefs and an oversized cropped hoodie all in black. The dancer in the center is the only one who differs. Her bottoms are red and her hoodie is hiding her face.

A pop star begins singing about secret moments shared between two lovers in a crowded room and the dance begins.

Each movement is sharp and sexual, then soft and intimate. The dancers are mercilessly in sync with one another and as flexible as rubber bands. They bend and turn, and suddenly they're lying with their backs on the chairs. Hair whips, legs spread, spines arch—then they're upright with a heeled foot on the chair.

The music continues with a line about how everything stops when the singer's lover says her name, and the dancers begin unzipping their hoodies. Peeling them off slowly, sensually. Hips pop, bodies roll, and clothing hits the ground as the women sit back down.

The dancer in the center is the only one still hidden. But as the singer croons about wanting her best friend as a lover

—she begins unzipping her hoodie. The two dancers closest help pull it off slowly. They lean sharply to one side and then the other—the movements bordering on break dancing.

The top vanishes and silver-white hair whips from a high ponytail.

It's Marrin.

Marrin is the main dancer.

I sit bolt straight, completely shocked and unsure what's going on.

A spotlight hits her and the other dancers vanish into the darkness beyond. Her hands roam her body as she bends and rolls, twists and arcs.

I know I'm in a room full of people but I can't shake the feeling this whole performance is for me only.

The second verse starts and Marrin stands. Still the only point of illumination in the room, she walks to the end of the stage and descends the few stairs. Then she's right in front of me, grabbing my hand and pulling me up.

There's a line about how even if the singer gets burned by taking a chance with her new lover, it was worth it. I see it in Marrin's eyes as much as I hear it with my ears.

I let her pull me on stage and the other dancers surround us in a circle. I have no idea if they're dancing or not because suddenly Marrin is dancing before me, *against* me. She makes her way sensually to the floor, then slides up my body at a painfully slow pace. It's as intimate as sex and as public as exhibitionism. And I suppose that for Marrin, this *is* a form of exhibitionism. She's literally taking down her walls and letting me in.

I'm not surprised to see the corner of her mouth quirk up when she realizes I'm hard as a rock. I don't even care that there's a good chance all my friends, and a room full of strangers, can see, because I can't even remember what planet I'm on.

When the chorus begins again, Marrin faces me. Two dancers grab my arms and one whispers, "Walk backwards, we're going to lead you to a chair." I don't even blink when I realize it's Priya from the Braxton Arcade. I just nod and watch Marrin, trusting them to make sure I don't fall on my ass.

Marrin follows, hips rolling as she walks in the most seductive way I've ever seen in my life. My legs hit the edge of a chair and I sit.

The stage lights up again and Marrin begins dancing for me. Our eyes lock when she wants me to see her lip-syncing lines she means for me to understand. I gather she doesn't want me as a best friend and that she bought a dress for the sole purpose of having me take it off. She's not currently wearing a dress—*more like the sexiest bikini I've ever seen in my life*—but that's not the point.

She's showing me all the things she couldn't before. Showing me the side of her she was afraid I'd reject. Showing me, because for her, showing is easier than talking. She's physically and metaphorically laying herself bare to me and to her friends. There's meaning in her eyes and in every line of her body as she moves.

Yet her expression is hard to read. I know she's nervous, uncertain. I think I see resolve... And a bit of sorrow, too.

This is a secret she's lived with for a long time. A way of life she's honed and perfected. The Marrin who steps off this stage will not be the Marrin who stepped onto it. She'll be different. Altered. Exposed in a way she's always feared.

She backs up step by step—lips moving to lines about how I always saw the best in her, saw the truth in her lies. With someone else's words, she tells me that she's finally woken up and realized I'm the one she wants to be with. She turns suddenly and launches into the air—swinging around a pole.

Holy Mary, mother of fuck.

I have no idea where the pole came from but I'm pretty sure this is what miracles look like. The other dancers twirl around their own poles and—yes, this is exactly what miracles look like.

Halle-fucking-lujah. Praise be. Take my ass to church at the Temple of Marrin and I'll worship devoutly for the rest of my goddamn life.

The world is nothing but legs and arms and hair. I'm surrounded by acrobats. They curve and flex and swing around in amazing displays of athleticism. I'm not sure what my face is doing, but as they slide to the floor and into the splits, the phrase *kid in a candy store* comes to mind.

They whisk around, legs in the air, then kick up to land perfectly on their feet. Now I know I'm grinning because —*holy shit*—I can barely do that and I've been studying martial arts for years. Also, these ladies did it in stilettos.

They spin around the poles a bit more and end the last note of the song in a wicked backbend. The lights go out, people applaud, Marrin grabs my hand and I follow her backstage and down a hallway.

We don't stop until we're inside a private dressing room and the door is closed.

It's just us.

We say nothing.

With her back to me, we stare at one another through a light-bulb lined mirror.

Sweat glistens on her skin, she pants lightly through parted, red lips. She's wearing nothing but a modest red bikini and stilettos that make her almost as tall as me.

I'm torn between shoving her up against the door or bending her over the vanity counter and burying myself inside her.

Instead, I hold her gaze in the mirror while stepping closer. I wrap my arms around her from behind. Her eyes shut and her throat bobs like she's savoring the moment, the feel of me around her. Her head tilts and I kiss the sensitive spot just below her ear.

"Mine," I whisper. I kiss just beneath the first. "Mine." I splay a hand over her taut abdomen and run the other over the top of her thigh. I pepper kisses down her neck until I reach her collarbone. "Mine."

"Yours," she whispers.

My arms tighten around her possessively. I lean my head against the side of hers and close my eyes. She smells like fresh laundry and citrus and sweat.

Her arms cover mine and I've never felt so content, so whole. We stay that way for a long while.

"I missed you," she whispers.

I open my eyes and see her blinking away tears in the mirror. I turn her to face me. "I missed you, too. Don't cry, baby." I cup the back of her neck and press her against me.

She relaxes, threading her arms beneath my jacket to cradle me. "I'm sorry. About everything."

"I know, baby. It's okay. I'm sorry, too."

She kisses me. "I'd like to be your girlfriend. Officially. If you still want me."

"More than anything." I kiss her again, slipping my tongue into her mouth and that's all it takes. We devolve into a mess of kissing and touching. Her hands burrow beneath my shirt, ruffle my hair, brush over my erection. Mine pull her hair to angle her mouth just where I want it. One slides over the curve of her ass to dip between her legs.

I back her into the vanity, wrapping one of her legs around my waist before grinding myself against her. Her head tilts back, a moan slips out.

I slide a finger along the hem of her red briefs. "These were a nice touch."

"A secret for only you."

"A gesture I very much appreciate. However," I trace the seam along her inner thigh, "it's not the secret I want to know at the moment."

Anxiety tightens her body.

"Are you wet for me, Red?" I breathe into her mouth as I cup between her legs. She relaxes.

She thought I was going to ask about her mom, ask about all the things we still need to talk about. But right now she's too vulnerable, too exposed—her confidence balanced on a tightrope. So I do the one thing I can in this moment that will help. I slip into the role of her Sir and ask her to give me control so I can show her how much I still desire her, show her that what I saw doesn't scare me, nor does it make me see her any differently.

She presses her chest against mine and kisses me. "Not at all," she says coyly.

"Don't lie to me, Red."

"I'd never lie to you, Sir."

I bite her neck then drop to my knees in front of her. I hook her leg over my shoulder and watch her bite her lip as I pull the fabric between her legs aside. "You sure about that?"

She shakes her head, *no*.

I blow onto her exposed vulva, eyes never leaving her face.

She white knuckles the edge of the vanity.

Finally, I look between her legs. My mouth waters.

She's glistening. For me.

"Look at me." She does. I slide a finger through her warm center, her body jerks, breath hitches. I stroke her swollen labia from core to clit then clit to core. I pull my finger away and suck it into my mouth. "Fuck I missed this taste."

My inner alpha male breaks free of his leash. I yank the briefs roughly to the side then pull her pussy wide before shoving my tongue inside. Her hips buck as I fuck her with my mouth.

She's hot and aching and dripping. My tongue swirls.

"Oh God, D-Damian. What if s-someone hea—" She moans loudly, pulling my hair hard enough to rip.

I kiss and suck my way up, parting her flesh to give me better access. "Do you want me to stop?" I say with my lips around her clit.

She shakes her head.

Didn't think so.

I suckle her swollen bundle of nerves with my lips, tongue, and teeth. She goes off like a rocket, panting and grinding herself on my face. I work her until she's too sensitive to touch.

When I stand up, she's slumped against the mirror.

I take a moment to admire my handiwork before pulling her up and kissing her. "As much as I'd like to stay here and make up for lost time, it *is* Tiana's birthday."

That snaps her out of her lust haze. She runs around the room, grabbing her clothes before twisting up her hair and disappearing into the bathroom for a quick shower.

"You could've changed out here," I say, when she re-enters the room a few minutes later, wearing nice jeans and a sheer top that shows off the bra beneath. Her hair and makeup still intact. "Few appreciate the female form as I do."

She snorts. "I'm sure, but you need to get your penis under control before we leave this room."

"Not likely, babe. You should've just changed where I could watch."

"I didn't want to torture you."

"Too late. Thoughts of you shaking it in that skimpy outfit are going to torture me for the rest of my life. Only one thing is going to fix the tent I'm pitching for you and if we start that now, we're going to miss Tia's birthday."

She eyes my package as we move to the door. "To be continued then."

"Damn right."

Marrin

When we get to the door that leads into the club, I pause. My heart begins to race as fears flood my brain.

What if they judge me? What if they think less of me? What if they ask about my mother?

Damian puts a hand on my lower back and presses a kiss to my forehead. "Let's stop at the bar first." I nod. "I'll be there the whole time. No one is going to judge you. They're your friends, they love you. *I* love you." His lips find mine for a deep, thorough kiss. It swallows my fears and reminds me what this whole night is about.

I whine when he pulls away.

He smirks but lust glimmers in his eyes. "If we start this again, I'm going to drag you back to that dressing room and you'll have to explain to Tiana why we missed her birthday."

"I think she'd understand," I tease, wiping my lipstick off his face.

"Come on."

We get a drink then find our friends. I have no idea what I was worried about. They're all excited to see me and impressed with the show. I explain that Alice owns this club and that I thought to kill two birds with one stone by treating Tia to a great birthday and laying it all on the line for Damian—and my friends.

They ask about when we started seeing one another and we explain, working our way through the weeks until we get to last weekend. No one asks about what Jake said, and I don't offer any details. Vicky and Tia know everything, but no one else does. I want to tell Damian first and go from there.

When the night ends, Damian and I follow each other back to our complex. We enter the building together and take the stairs hand in hand. My heart pounds as we get to our floor.

I take a deep breath. "Do you want to spend the night at my place?"

His smile is blinding. "Hell yes."

I'm not sure when his mouth finds me, but it's definitely *before* I get the door unlocked. His lips press against mine—greedy and demanding. I submit and we damn near tumble into my apartment.

We don't bother with lights.

He kicks the door closed and fumbles for the locks. Metal scrapes as the deadbolts slide, shoes scuff as they come off. Two jackets are abandoned on the floor.

Clumsily, we make our way to my bedroom, my sex haze so thick, I have to actively think about *how* to unlock the door.

Insert key, turn.

Sounds easy, but when Damian's hands and mouth rove every inch of my body, basic tasks become mind-bendingly difficult.

The door opens and I pull him inside, absentmindedly flipping on the light.

His hands stop their perusal, his lips slow down. I open my eyes and see him taking in my room. Wonder crosses his face and he pulls back but not away.

My room is the one place in my apartment I do decorate. Framed all around are old movie posters, three wall hooks hold years of pink satin pointe shoes. There's a picture of Alice and me on the dresser next to a vintage perfume bottle and an old film camera. A bright, multi-colored bedspread sits like a cloud atop the bed, beneath a small mountain of pillows with clashing, uncoordinated prints.

Damian steps toward the dresser and I take the opportunity to close the door. The lock clicks as I turn it into place, but it's the sound of the chain sliding that pulls Damian from his survey of my room.

His eyes go straight to the chain then the deadbolt. A grim sort of comprehension crosses his face and his eyes find mine. His expression is calm, aware. We both know what's coming. It's not a conversation I want to have, but it's one he deserves to hear.

It's now or never.

My heart gallops in my chest as I grip the hem of my shirt and pull it off.

I know Damian's looking at me but I can't look at him. Not as I reach behind me to unhook my bra.

Maybe the sight of my breasts will distract him from the sight of my scars.

Black straps slide down my arms, satin whispers as it hits the floor.

I unbutton my jeans.

I pull down the zipper.

I grip the two pieces of fabric, holding them together. My hands shake.

It's okay to be vulnerable.

I close my eyes, inhaling deeply through my nose and exhaling slowly through my lips. Part of me wants to vomit and I know if I focus on that part, *I will* vomit. I inhale and exhale again. The third time I exhale, I do so while pushing my pants down.

Strong hands hold my wrists. "Let me."

My eyes open right into Damian's. Warm breath fans my face. Gently he pulls my hands away, guiding them to my sides—where he leaves them to slide his own lovingly up my arms to my shoulders. His lips brush mine.

His kiss is soft, delicate. Quiet in the ways of midnight whispers and shared sorrow. It's paper-thin but strong as steel. A kiss to calm, to reassure.

He does the same to the corner of my mouth,

the curve of my jaw,

the column of my neck,

hollow of my throat,

the valley between my breasts.

His lips move down my body. There's a reverence to his touch as his hands slide down my sides to my hips. His thumbs hook in my jeans, my heart skips, he guides them down, slow and attentive. They scrape my thighs my calves, then I'm stepping out of them.

"Look at me," he says, hot breath caressing the skin just below my belly button.

I open my eyes. He's kneeling before me, adoration in

his eyes. A slip of red silk is all that's between his eyes and me, but I'm already bare.

The panties sit too low on my hips.

His lips find my skin and he presses kisses beneath my belly button. Once, twice—

The first scar is numb—they all are. I feel only where his lips touch the skin around them, the rest is a dull, tingling awareness that's uncomfortable if I think about it too long.

"Beautiful," he whispers. He kisses the second scar and then the third.

An ache starts in the back of my throat, a wisp of moisture circles my eyes, my jaw trembles. Damian looks up at me and I have to close my eyes because what I see in his...

He stands and scoops me into his arms then lays me on the bed. I open my eyes when the covers come over me. He strips to his briefs then turns off the light. Bare, muscular flesh caresses my body as he slides in beside me. My breasts compress against his chest as he pulls me to him. He hooks a hand beneath my knee and pulls it over his waist. His warmth seeps into me like summer sun.

"Tell me," he whispers into the darkness.

22

Damian

"Let me."

Marrin's eyes open, she looks like a doe in a clearing. I know she's about to show me her scars. She doesn't know I've seen them and right now that's not the point. The point is she *wants* to show them to me. Even though it terrifies her.

I guide her arms to her sides and kiss my way down her body. I will my love into every touch, every caress. I worship her like a sinner after salvation.

I remove her pants, she stills. I look up to see her eyes wrinkled shut. I stroke her hips. "Look at me."

She does, and again I'm reminded of a scared animal. Only this time she isn't a doe, she's a wounded bird looking up from inside a shoe box. She's trusting me to care for her, trusting I won't hurt her.

And I won't. I wouldn't.

I resume my path of kisses. The third lands on the first scar. A part of me aches for her. For the trauma and memories she carries along with the scars. I know her mother stabbed her. It's not hard to guess.

"Beautiful," I declare before kissing the next two scars.

When I look up at her, it's with more love and understanding than I've ever shown her.

Relief and gratitude transform her face and she closes her eyes. It breaks my heart to think she worries people won't accept her after they learn the truth. Makes me sick to think she'd thought I would be one of those people. But I get it. Because I've been there.

Sometimes horrible things happen. And while some of the people they happen to can move on and thrive, other people cannot. When I told my parents I'd been abused, the look on my dad's face...

It was as if he didn't know who I was. As if when he looked at me, he only saw a victim, not a person. A failing, not a blessing. I wasn't his child anymore, I was the sum total of a collection of someone else's horrible actions. Only worse because he looked at me as if it was somehow *my* fault. I was a blemish on his perfect reputation. He wasn't worried about me, he was worried about himself. Worried what people would think about *him* if they knew about *me*.

It's a look that's burned into my brain. A look that drove me to feel ashamed and guilty for years. It was the look I didn't see two years later when I drunkenly confessed to Vicky's parents what'd happened to me. It was the first thing I spoke about when I sat down in a therapist's office after Vicky's parents made me go.

Something horrible happened to Marrin and I would never, ever judge her for that or see her differently.

I pick her up and tuck her into bed next to me. Her skin is soft and warm in all the places mine is not. She molds to

me like a key does a lock. She was made for me, this woman
—*Marrin*.

"Tell me."

She takes a deep breath. "For a long time, my mother has had boyfriends and a drinking problem."

She tells me she grew up alongside Alice and that her childhood was mostly happy. But as she got older, her mother started drinking more and bringing home her boyfriends. She tells me about a man who came to pick her up from dance class one day and how Alice got custody of her soon after.

She jumps to Thanksgiving two years ago, telling me her mom had reached out wanting to see her and how she'd hoped her mom had changed.

While her mom and her new boyfriend were at work, Marrin started making dinner but stopped to shower before anyone got home. She tells me she'd brought clothes with her into the bathroom because she didn't want to walk around a house she didn't live in half naked and because her mom's boyfriend gave her the creeps.

"I got out of the shower and dressed in my pajamas, closing my robe over top. It was one of those big, fluffy, knee-length ones. When I left the bathroom, I was fully clothed—*I swear*."

"I believe you." I have a sick feeling I know where this is going. "I wouldn't care if you weren't."

"*But I was.*"

"I know, baby. I believe you."

Her voice is quieter, shakier. "Halfway to my bedroom, Frank grabbed me from behind and, like," she swallows audibly, "pressed himself against me. He was home early and, like, started saying all this weird, fucked-up shit about how me wearing shorts meant I was coming onto him."

She pulls away, needing space. It's dark, but I can make out her silhouette as she sits against the headboard, knees to her bare chest.

I grab my T-shirt off the floor and hand it to her.

She mumbles, "Thanks," and tugs it on. "When I realized he wasn't going to stop, I got serious about fighting him. Not that I wasn't serious before. I'd made it explicitly clear I wanted nothing to do with him from the beginning—*I swear*."

"I believe you." Dread buzzes through my body like the hum of neon lights, building slowly with each word she speaks.

"I managed to get all the way to the living room before he tackled me. There was a lot of screaming and fighting and he, um..." Another audible swallow.

The buzzing in my body turns up and my fists clench, jaw grinds, every muscle contracting to the point of pain as I brace for what I think she's going to say next.

"My mom walked in right as he was pulling at my bottoms."

Her bottoms, not her shorts, not just her shorts.

A savage kind of fury erupts into me because I've been there. I know what that feels like—know the rage and humiliation and fear when someone overpowers you like that. I hope this fucker's in prison or dead because I am going to end him.

Stop, you fucking Neanderthal. Anger is only going to make this worse for her.

"I was so relieved to see her," Marrin continues. "Frank backed off immediately and my mom started yelling. I remember running to her because I wanted, like," her voice cracks, "a hug or something, I don't know. I remember not understanding why she was looking at me and yelling and not at Frank. And then I realized she wasn't yelling at Frank, she was yelling at me. Calling me names and accusing me of trying to steal her boyfriend. Frank just egged her on."

She sniffles and I can make out just enough in the moonlight to see her wipe her eyes. I scoot closer and wrap an arm around her. She leans into me.

"Then out of nowhere there was a knife in her hand and she was coming toward me and I didn't know what to do or think. She was my mother, *her* boyfriend attacked *me*. The whole thing wasn't registering in my brain, and then she grabbed my hair and I was on the ground and she brought the knife down. I was screaming and fighting and begging my almost rapist for help, and he just stood there like a fucking idiot."

I press my cheek into the top of her head.

"Then Jake charged in and got her off me. She ran off with Frank and Jake called 9-1-1. A policeman, Officer Lawson, was close by and showed up almost immediately. He had a medical kit and together with Jake, they packed the wounds and saved my life. I remember Jake holding my hand and telling me it was going to be okay. I made him promise not to leave me and he didn't. He rode with me in the ambulance."

"That's why you put up with him."

She nods. "No matter what he does, I know deep down he's still the guy who threw a chair at a window so I could go to the bathroom and change my tampon. It sounds so stupid—"

"It's not stupid at all."

"I know it all happened fast, but Jake was the only one who came to help me. Where I used to live, people screaming and yelling isn't out of the ordinary. But there's a difference—*you know?*—between someone screaming out of anger and someone screaming because something is wrong."

I nod.

"That's the night Jake and Vicky met. Why he remembers her. He grabbed my phone before we left the house but couldn't unlock it. I didn't have a wallet on me or anything, so he had no way of getting in touch with Alice. Vicky happened to call and he answered and told her what happened. Her family was having Thanksgiving at a relative's house about an hour away, so she and her mom drove to the hospital. Vicky unlocked my phone and called Alice, which is how they met."

"Not in your dorm?"

She shakes her head. "Alice and Gavin drove back that night. Vicky and her mom stayed at the hospital until they got there. Alice did go to my dorm to get my things when I had to withdraw from classes, but the story Vicky tells about how they met isn't what actually happened."

"I'm so sorry this happened to you." She nods and we settle back under the covers. "What happened next?"

"I had two surgeries, one that night and one early the next morning. One of the stab wounds punctured my uterus —hard to accomplish being that it's about the size of a lime and tucked behind the pubic bone. Vicky's mom, who I guess you know is an OB-GYN, was adamant about having a surgical specialist friend of hers take a look at me. The lady works at one of the university hospitals and came right over. I guess she decided they needed to go back in and make sure some stuff was done a specific way or something. I don't know, I was out of it. I remember waking up the next day and asking Alice why the walls were moving, I was so high on pain meds."

"Been there," I say. "Had my wisdom teeth surgically

removed senior year. Woke up and thought I was in a lava lamp."

"Same. It was trippy... The cops arrested my mom and Frank. Turns out my mom was high on some new synthetic drug. She got seven years in prison and Frank went to jail for, like, a month."

"*What?*"

"Yeah, I know. But violence against women is institutionalized. What're you gonna do..."

"Is Frank your stalker?" It's out of my mouth before I can stop it.

"Yes. He's not a stalker like in the movies. He doesn't have a collage of my face on his wall or try to sneak into my apartment to watch me sleep or anything. He just likes to let me know when he's around. It's like a scare tactic or something."

"That's stalking."

"I know. It's just more on the *Asshole* side of the spectrum than the *Psycho* side I guess. I'm not trying to make excuses, I just don't want you thinking he's planning to kidnap me or something. He's pissed I put my mom in prison and took away his meal ticket."

I tilt her chin to me. "You didn't put anyone in prison. She did that to herself." I kiss her forehead. "I'm sorry that happened to you. I can't imagine how hard it must've been. It took an incredible amount of courage to tell me."

"Thanks. It was pretty horrible. When I came back the following semester, I was still having trouble maneuvering stairs, and I wasn't allowed to lift anything heavy. Alice assigned Conor to be my bodyguard slash nanny. He carried my books and helped me get around campus while also keeping an eye out for Frank. I'm fine now, so I can't complain."

"Were there any... complications?"

"Not physically, no. Well, unless you count not being able to poop for a week."

I laugh. "Surgery will do that to a person."

"There's a chance I could have a hard time getting pregnant from adhesions and stuff, but I've honestly never wanted kids so..." She shrugs. "There are surgeries to fix that, but so far so good." She shifts onto her back, quiet for a moment. "Remember when you asked if the rumor about me putting someone in the hospital was true?"

I nod.

"Fall of sophomore year, I went to a party with Vicky. It was the first big social thing I'd done since everything happened. Conor had stopped playing bodyguard by then and I was anxious about being out at night and in a crowd... We started dancing and this guy came up behind me and put his hands on my hips. I totally freaked out. It felt like I was suddenly back in that hallway with Frank. The guy's hand grazed my scars and that was it. I panicked and kicked him in the balls. He passed out from the pain and spent the night in the emergency room with a severely swollen testicle."

I cringe, imagining the pain. "Ouch."

"I still feel bad about it." She turns back into me. "The school disciplinary committee got involved. Luckily, they were sympathetic and only sentenced me to mandatory therapy. Turns out it was exactly what I needed. I still go from time to time. It helped a lot. I was more affected by what happened than I'd thought."

"Therapy is funny like that."

"Did you go after...?"

"Yeah. It was a few years later in high school and only because I showed up drunk at Vicky's house in the middle of the night. I think I did it because I wanted someone to help me and didn't know how to ask. Her parents had always been kind to me. I think her mom always suspected but wanted to let me come to her. But, yeah, they sat me down, asked what was wrong, and I lost it. Ugly crying—all of it. I spent the night on their couch and the next day they made me an appointment with a therapist. It was the best thing that ever happened to me. That and martial arts. Vicky's dad enrolled me in classes. It helped me channel my anger and build my confidence."

"Wow."

"Yeah. Vicky's parents kind of adopted me. I owe them a lot."

"That's why you said you didn't know if you wanted to be intimate with other people, wasn't it?"

I nod. "I had a hard time being intimate with myself for a while. All the feelings and memories it brought back. Sometimes it was fine, but other times... The thought of someone else seeing me that way was enough to make me never want to try. It was like a miniboss in a game—a big ugly monster that suddenly appeared in the middle of a level and wouldn't let me pass. So I avoided it, resigned myself to never moving forward. But with therapy, I was able to face it. Knew that I could. It wasn't a battle I always won, but eventually, defeating it became second nature until it wasn't a problem anymore. Well, until that night you and I came together after Back Cellar."

When we didn't use a condom and I almost had an anxiety attack.

"What happened that night?" Mar asks quietly.

"Old insecurities," I say honestly. "One of the reasons I always use a condom is because a part of me thinks no one could ever want me like that if they knew what happened to me. That night, I knew I was in love with you and that you'd trusted me to share something no one ever had before. I felt like I didn't deserve it because I hadn't been entirely honest with you."

Her arms tighten around me. "I wish you'd told me beforehand."

"I could say the same about you." I kiss the top of her head.

She groans. "You promise you're not totally freaked out about how white trash I am?"

"You're not white tr—"

"My mom tried to kill me—"

"Marrin, stop." I level our eyes. "Is that why you didn't want to tell me? You thought I'd think less of you?"

She shrugs, nods.

"What your family members do and don't do is not a reflection of who you are. You aren't them and they aren't you. Only you can decide who you are and how you see yourself. What anyone else thinks is just an opinion, not a fact." I smirk. "And you know what they say about opinions...?"

She smiles. "They're like assholes. Everybody has one."

"Exactly. So you had a shitty upbringing. So did I. It's no big deal. It happens."

She nods. "I'm sorry about what happened to you."

"Thanks. It was a long time ago."

"I know, but... If you ever want to talk about it, I'm here to listen."

"Thank you. I feel the same. If you ever want to talk, I'm always here."

"Thanks. I actually think I need to start seeing a therapist again," she admits quietly.

"How come?"

She shrugs, tracing small circles on my chest with a finger. "All this stuff with you. How I acted. I guess you could say that's my miniboss. Running away, keeping secrets... It's how I've learned to protect myself. I'm clearly not as adjusted as I thought I was. And then..." She takes a deep breath. "Frank showed up on Thanksgiving. It's why I called you. He's never approached me before, usually just sits in his truck. But that night he got out and I almost didn't get the door shut in time."

I clamp down on my anger because it has no place in this conversation. "Did you ever call the cops? Or sic Gavin on his ass?"

She huffs a laugh. "The security camera didn't show enough to prove it was him so it wasn't worth getting the cops involved. Alice put a tail on him, though."

"I wanna know what he looks like."

She pulls away. "Please don't do that."

"Do what? I'm not going to go looking for him, but I want to know what he looks like in case he comes around."

"This is why I didn't want to tell you."

"You're mad I want to help protect you?"

"He's dangerous, Damian."

"Which is why I want to know what he looks like."

She turns her head away. When she won't let me pull her chin to me, I climb on top of her, straddling her waist and keeping my weight in my hands. "Hey, look at me."

Begrudgingly, she does.

"Protecting the people I care about is something I do. I trust you not to abuse the information I've shared with you, and I want you to trust me not to abuse the info you've shared with me."

"Are you going to punch him in the face like Jake?" she says dryly.

I grin. "I'll admit, hitting Jake wasn't my finest moment, but he was asking for it. He was trying to hurt you and it was the only way I could think to stop him. And trust me, if I hadn't hit him, Vicky would've." I nuzzle her face before pulling back. "I want to look out for you, Marrin. I want you to do the same for me."

She fights a smile, powerless to resist my charms. "Who might I need to protect you from?"

"My mother for starters—and clowns. Always hated clowns."

"Clowns?"

"Yeah. They're always smiling. It's creepy." I settle beside her and she lets me pull her until she's half on top of me. "I'm not going to see him and turn into a raging, territorial Neanderthal. But I can't promise that if he approaches you again, I won't have a few words with him."

"I don't need you to protect me," she whispers.

"I know you don't *need* it. You're a testicle-kicking badass. But wouldn't it be nice if I could help watch your back, share the burden of always looking over your shoulder?"

"I... never thought of it that way."

"You're welcome." She flicks my stomach and I chuckle. "And don't pretend like you're not into my territorial, alpha-male Neanderthal when he comes out to play, *Red*."

Her head pops up. "Is he coming to play right now?"

"Hmm..." I rub my chin. "I don't know."

She sits up, pulling off the shirt she's wearing. I can clearly see the silhouette of her breasts.

I chuckle. "So eager." Her tits press into my chest as she settles back into me. I tighten my hold on her and inhale deeply of her scent. "I think he just wants to hold you for now if that's okay?"

She yawns. "I'd like that."

"You don't have to show me what Frank looks like if you're not ready. But will you do something for me?"

"What?"

"Come with me to work tomorrow morning."

"Okay. What *do* you do for work? You've never told me."

"You'll see."

23

Marrin

I wake up in my bed pressed against a warm, muscular body. A heavy arm is wrapped around me and my breasts are exposed. My spine stacks in panic.

"Just me," Damian says.

My eyes land on his face and I remember how we got here. Heart still hammering, I settle back. "Sorry. It's been a while since I woke up next to someone."

"No worries." His fingertips stroke my arm.

"How long have you been up?"

"Long enough to have brushed my teeth."

My eyes narrow. "You weren't watching me sleep, were you?"

"No, that's creepy."

"So what *were* you doing?" I'm careful to cover my mouth to spare him from my morning breath.

He gives me a sly smile. "Trying to decide which drawer holds all your red panties and how mad you'd be if I went looking."

I bark a laugh and roll out of bed. I stretch, more than a

little satisfied with the way Damian devours the sight of me. I walk to the door, tapping one of my dresser drawers. "Knock yourself out."

I brush my teeth and see to my needs. When I return, Damian is elbows deep in my panty drawer.

"What's this?" I point to the pairs he's laid atop the dresser.

"This pile holds all the ones I've never seen you wear, and this one," he points to the other pile, "holds the ones I'd like to see you wear again."

I deliberate. "Okay." I hook my thumbs in my panties and shimmy out of them.

Damian sucks in a breath. "What's happening right now?"

Completely naked, I pick up a pair of red panties from the never-before-seen pile. "I thought you wanted to see."

A muscle twitches near his eye and he grabs my wrist. "This isn't going to work."

"Oh?"

"Nope. Drop the panties, Red."

"Yes, Sir."

A thrill twirls my spine as he yanks me forward and thrusts my hand down his briefs. Liquid heat pools between my legs as I grasp his growing erection. "Don't tease me, Red. Pull me out. Get me hard."

Hello again, Mr. Alpha-Male Neanderthal.

I drop to my knees, removing his briefs as I go. I stroke his cock until its thick and full. A bead of pre-cum pools at the tip and I rub it on my lips like lipstick before sucking him into my mouth.

"Fuck, baby," he hisses. "You don't know how much I've missed your hot mouth on me."

I work him in long pulls and sucks, swirling my tongue and humming around him.

He grabs my hair and pulls me off. "Did you miss me?"

I nod.

He cups my chin and strokes my cheek. "What did you miss?"

"Everything."

He hauls me to my feet and presses his mouth over mine. I welcome his tongue's intrusion and the two fingers he forces inside my pussy. I gasp, try to moan, but he devours the sound, stealing the breath from my lungs and the thoughts from my head. He pushes me onto the bed and mounts me. My hand finds his powerful cock and I point him to my entrance. I need to get him inside me.

He chuckles and slides down my body, pulling himself from my hand.

I whine in protest.

"Patience, Red." A hand to the chest forces me to lay back. He drinks in the sight of my breasts, groaning like a thirsty man in the desert. He palms me then works my nipples with his tongue.

It's not enough and all too much.

Waves of pleasure flash through me like lightning. They shoot straight to my core and I clamp down on the emptiness there. The need to be filled grows more and more demanding, consuming. It's been weeks since I've had Damian inside me and now that he's within reach, my desire for him is maddening.

"I need you inside me, Sir." I thread my fingers into his hair. "Please. I ache for you."

"Keep talking," he groans.

Filthy, dirty things come to my mind and I say and mean them all, drunk off my wanting. "I want you to fuck me with your cock, Sir. I want you to shove it inside me, stuff me with it until I'm forced to come for you. I want you to fill me with your hot cum as you use my body to pleasure yourself. I want you to dominate me, claim me in every way possible."

He rolls away and hauls me on top of him, propping himself against the headboard. "Ride me," he demands. "Hands on my thighs so I can watch that pretty little pussy swallow this big cock."

Jesus H. Christ.

I situate myself over him, leaning back to find his thighs—

It's broad daylight. This position puts me on display. My scars are completely exposed.

My mouth goes dry—*everything goes dry*—and I hesitate, a hand going to cover my lower abdomen.

Damian's expression softens and he sits forward, stroking my face with two hands. "Hey. It's okay. Do you want me on top?"

Yes.

"No." I shake my head. "I can do it." I grip his shoulders, holding him to me as I settle over his erection. His eyes never leave my face.

I sink down on him and don't make it farther than an inch. I lift up and force myself down harder. I maybe get another inch of him inside me before it becomes painful, abrasive.

"Marrin—"

"I forgot how big you are," I lie, trying to paint a trivial smile on my face.

I press down on him again and he grabs my hips. "Stop."

"It's fine I—"

"It's not fine." A finger presses into my core and I can't keep the discomfort off my face. "You're not wet anymore."

"That's not uncommon. Sometimes it happens—"

"Baby, stop." He cups my face. "It's okay."

His expression, the tone of his voice—tears prick my eyes. "I'm fine."

"Then why can't you look at me?"

Well, you got me there.

"Oh fuck, you're shaking." He wraps himself around me and I melt into him. "I'm sorry. I didn't know it would upset you."

"It doesn't," I say. "I mean it did, but it doesn't. I just had, like, a momentary freak out. I'm sorry."

"Do not apologize for the way you feel. This is my fault. I'm a greedy Neanderthal and I wanted to enjoy the sight of my woman impaling herself on me." I huff a laugh and pull back to look at him. "I didn't consider your feelings and I'm sorry." He brushes hair back from my face.

"You're forgiven. I *do* want to have sex like this, though." He opens his mouth, but I add, "I just don't know if I can start in that position. It felt like..." *Like my scars were on display.* "Like I was too exposed."

"Fuck. I don't ever want you to feel uncomfortable with me."

"I don't. That was a me thing, not a you thing. Normally, I really, *really* like it when you objectify me during sex." I lean to the side and pull a bottle of lube from my nightstand drawer. "I want you like this. I promise. Letting you see my scars is..." *Exposing in a different way.* "New."

He looks unsure but then I grab his hand and squirt lube on his fingers. I push him back into the headboard and guide his fingers to my vulva.

I close my eyes when he takes over—massaging the cool gel into my clit, coating my lips and the inside of my pussy. I put some on my hand and lather it over his cock, which comes back to life almost immediately.

He grabs my hip and adds another finger inside me. "Jesus, Marrin, this pussy is begging to be fed."

His words seduce me back to that place where only sex and pleasure exist. I tighten my muscles around his fingers. "Keep talking."

"You ready for me, baby? Ready for me to give you what you need?"

"Yes." I angle his erection to me and let him guide my hips. He presses me down and my pussy swallows him whole in one motion. "So good," I groan. Ecstasy races through me as I grind my hips to his.

"*Fuck*..." Damian curses. "Kiss me."

"You're so bossy."

"You like it."

I do.

Even after everything that's happened to me, I still find pleasure in being dominated and put on display. Some people might not get it, but no matter whether I'm dancing at the 13th Floor or in bed with Damian, I'm completely at ease because I'm in control. I have agency and nothing happens without my permission. The club has strict rules about consent, and anyone who knows anything about fetish and kink knows it's a world built on defining the boundaries so everyone feels safe. When Damian and I first decided to explore our kink with one another, establishing what consent meant to both of us was the first thing we did.

Damian squeezes my ass. "Give me your mouth. I want to fill you in two places."

My pussy clenches and I obey, opening my mouth for him.

Gripping my hips, he pulls us apart then pushes us back

together. He controls the pace, controls my body—controls the depth, force, and angle. I'm nothing but submission. Nothing but feeling, as his thick, powerful cock steadily plunges in and out of me in strong, full strokes.

"How do you want me?" I breathe into his mouth. He knows what I mean.

"Sit back. Hands on my thighs."

I reach behind me and settle in, letting my body and spine arch back and away. My scars, breasts, and pussy are on full display for his viewing pleasure.

"Christ, you're beautiful. A fucking gift for me and only me."

My head falls back, eyes closed as he feeds me his cock how he wants. Uses me how he wants. I give him complete and utter control and it's the most liberating thing in the world.

Everything slips away when we're like this. I trust him implicitly. He knows how to take care of me, knows what I want, knows that sex isn't just about getting off for me. I need more, need to get lost, to give over my sovereignty and let Damian be my king and conqueror. Here there are no decisions to be made, no anxiety over choice or fear or my past. There's no need to think because I'm not in control, he is. If I need to stop, all it will take is one word. One safe word that *technically* gives me all the power. But I push it away because I don't need it. I just need him.

"Look at me," he rasps. "I want to see what my cock is doing to you."

I lift my head and find his eyes heavy and lusty. He slows our pace to something reverent.

"Damian?" I whimper as he sinks full and deep.

"Yeah, baby?"

"I love you."

"I love you, too."

He slides me over himself purposefully. The whole world narrowing to his cock, to how thick and long it is, to the slick sound of our bodies meeting, to the thousands of nerves alive with pleasure at the feel of his rhythmic movement inside my body.

It's overwhelming. *He's* overwhelming.

He hasn't looked at me the same way since I told him about what happened. But it's not in the way I'd feared. He looks at me now like he sees all of me... or maybe he always has, only now I've let him see me up close. Like a painting by van Gogh. From far away it's lovely and complete, but it's not until you get up close that you see it's really a mess. An intricate, brilliant, purposefully chaotic mess.

I think that's the way I look at Damian now, too. There's something sacred about it, about the trust between us.

About the fact that his bare cock is inside me. That he's taking me raw, seeing me raw. He's going to come inside me, taint me with his cum, and I'm going to let him because I trust him. I'm going to enjoy letting him be the one to claim me like that. Going to enjoy walking around with the physical proof of him having been inside me—having fucked me to completion—all day.

"Dame, I want to come for you."

"What do you say, Red?"

"Please, Sir. Let me come."

He reaches between my legs and draws tight, firm circles over my clit.

I curse, head falling back just before I detonate. Pleasure like chaos surges through me, sweeping me away. I hear him gasp and curse and I know he's coming because his thrusts get harder, deeper. His hand clasps my hip hard enough to bruise and we're both too gone to care.

I start to go limp as his cock contracts and expands. Warmth hits me in a place I can't quite feel but am somehow aware of and I know he's just emptied himself inside me. The thought is erotic and taboo, and I collapse onto his chest enjoying the idea that he's somehow claimed me for himself. Marked his territory in such a way that all other men will somehow know and stay away.

Maybe I'm the Neanderthal in this relationship?

We lay in a pile on my bed. Panting and sweaty and smelling of sex.

After a time, Damian says, "I seem to remember a shower date we rain checked..."

I burst out laughing.

PART III

THE FINAL BOSS

In gaming, the final boss is the last computer-controlled enemy that a player must defeat at or near the end of the game in order to complete the game's storyline. The final boss is usually the most powerful opponent in the game and is often hard or impossible to defeat without knowing the correct fighting approach or without having first acquired specific items or skills.

24

Damian

After a thorough shower and breakfast with Marrin, we're out the door and off to my work.

I'm kind of nervous bringing her, which is weird because I doubt she'll care. The thing is, she knows why I got into martial arts and it's going to be pretty damn obvious why I volunteer teaching self-defense every semester.

I'm also nervous because it's the first day of class and you never know who will show up or what their story will be. I don't want to retraumatize anyone—especially Mar.

She opens the gym door for me, and I pretend to tip an invisible hat as I walk past.

"You still haven't told me what you do," she says, following me inside.

"You'll see."

I lead us into a small gymnasium where my coworkers Holly and Vinny are already setting up the mats. A few new students sit on the bleachers across the room.

Holly walks over when she sees us. "Hey-hey, what's up. You're Marrin, right?"

Marrin smiles. "Yeah. You're Holly."

"That's me. You here for class?"

I say, "She's not registered, but I brought her along to see if it's something she'd like to do. Vicky and Tiana are also coming." I invited them this morning, it worked out they were both free.

"The more the merrier. No worries about registering today," Holly says. "It's a free course, we really only need a headcount so we can get approved for the space each semester. You trying to learn how to take down dudes like that guy at the bar last weekend?"

Marrin looks confused. "Wait. What do you both teach?"

"The art of self-defense. Or Ball Kicking 101 as I like to call it." She leaves to help set up the room.

Marrin turns to me. "You teach self-defense?"

"Figured it was a nice way to spend my Saturday mornings."

"This is where you work? You volunteer?"

I mock a bow. "Damian Wane: panty-reading fortune teller, gifted sex god and devastatingly handsome man who enjoys giving back to the community, at your service."

She tilts her palm back and forth. "Sex god is a bit overblown."

"That's not what you said in the shower this morning when my face was between your—"

"Hey peeps," Vicky says, slapping me hard on the back. "Let's kick some balls, shall we?"

"Why did we invite her again?" I ask Marrin.

"I'm also trying to learn how to kick some pussies because you never know," Tiana interjects. "By pussies, I don't mean cats or a sexist slang term for cowards. Although," she muses, "anyone who'd attack another person is kind of a coward."

"Ooh. Sorry Damian." Marrin taps my chest with the back of her hand.

"Ha. Ha. Very funny. The thing with Jake was a bit different."

I show them where to sit, then I help my coworkers set up the room.

Once everyone arrives, class begins. Holly addresses the group and goes over introductions. Because it's the first day, we hand out pamphlets and fliers, and spend the first hour of class going over self-defense principles.

"A big part of self-defense is reducing the risk of attack," Holly says. "In the old days, someone teaching this class might've told you ladies that reducing risk meant"—she air quotes the following phrases—"dressing modestly, abstaining from alcohol, watching what you say—and all that blame-the-victim nonsense. This is the twenty-first century and the third wave of feminism. *Assailants* are the problem. Not the length of your mini skirt, the amount of cleavage you're sporting, or the fact that you're blackout drunk. Nope. That kind of blame-the-victim B.S. will not be tolerated or taught in this class."

That earns a "whoop-whoop" from Vicky.

"Let me also say that it is not lost on me that we teach women to protect themselves, while we do not teach men how to act appropriately. If I had my way, and I hope I will soon, this school would offer a mandatory class on consent and appropriate behavior to *all* students enrolled. Sadly, as of yet, it does not. Now, I'm going to get into some non-victim-blaming ways we can all do our best to stay safe.

"First rule of self-defense: always listen to your gut instinct. If you take one thing away from this course let it be that. Your gut will never let you down. Your brain will. The human brain is too rational for its own good. How many of you have ever met someone who immediately made you uncomfortable? Someone who didn't have to say or do anything for your gut instinct to warn you something was off about them?"

Almost everyone raises a hand, including me.

"And how many of you have ignored that feeling simply because you had no proof to support the claim?"

Again, almost everyone raises a hand. Myself included.

"That's because your brain convinced you that you needed proof. That you were overreacting. Gender norms perpetuate these ideas, too. Society tells women we should give people the benefit of the doubt, that it's not okay for us to be rude, assertive, set boundaries, or say no. Society makes us feel as if we owe men something for paying attention to us. People, I'm here to tell you that *those* are the voices you need to ignore—not your gut. Your gut instinct is your bottom bitch. She's been with you the longest and she's always reliable. She doesn't need proof to know someone's a creeper or that something's wrong. She calls it like it is. Number one takeaway here: listen to your gut."

A little over an hour in, we get to the ass kicking. Vinny and I let Holly use us as human dummies. We go through most of the moves the participants will learn in the course, then break into groups to practice escaping wrist and arm holds.

When class ends, Marrin and I get back into my Jeep.

"Did you like it?" I ask.

"I did. It was actually really fun."

"Good."

She taps the armrest. "Why did you bring me?"

"Why do you think I brought you?"

"Answering my question with a question, how deflective."

"Fine. I wanted you to see where I work and..." I shrug. "I think you should know how to defend yourself."

"Because of Frank?"

I lace our fingers together. "Does that make you uncomfortable?"

She thinks for a moment, relaxing back into the passenger seat. "No. It's kind of sweet. In a patronizing kind of way."

"Whoa. I am in *no way* trying to be pa—"

"Relax," she chuckles. "I was joking."

"You'd tell me if you thought I was being patronizing, right? Or if I wasn't validating your feelings or something?"

She smiles. "Of course. And I'd want you to tell me, too. Now, back to what you were saying."

"Learning self-defense helped me take back my power. Knowing I wasn't helpless made me feel safer, too. It might work for you."

We stop at an intersection behind a red truck. I look over to see Marrin's brows pinched with apprehension.

I squeeze her hand. "What's up?"

She blinks. Blinks again. "He drives a red truck. Frank." She jerks her chin at the one in front of us. "Same make as that one but older."

The vehicle in front of us looks like it was made in the 1990s.

"I don't have a picture of him. Alice probably does. I can ask her to send you one, but I don't want to see it. Or be near it."

The light turns green and I accelerate, my thumb sweeping along the back of her hand.

She's staring out the passenger window the next time I look over. "I can ask her. I kind of saved her number in my phone when she called me over break."

That gets her attention. "Oh my God. Thanks for not being totally freaked by the whole key thing."

I smile. "You're welcome. I'll admit that finding—"

Darth Vader's theme song blasts from my phone. I reach down to where it sits in the cup holder and silence the ringer.

"Answer it, I don't mind," Marrin says.

"I do."

"Why?" She glances at the phone's screen. "Oh."

I turn into our complex. "Out of the blue, Nadia's decided she wants to subject me to her presence. Something called *getting coffee* or *meeting up*. Not sure what it means, all very new age, you know?"

Marrin squeezes my hand. "Do you want to talk about it?"

"Not really."

"Okay."

Later when I'm alone, I check my voicemail. My mother left the dates she'll be in town and the times she'll be free. I write them down and don't know why. I have no idea if I want to see her. I'm not even sure it's smart for me to be alone with her.

Marrin

Work is insane. The bar is slammed and two of the games are malfunctioning. Elle is trying to fix one, which leaves only Priya and I working the bar. I've had no time to eat or pee, I'm sweaty and cranky, and if I did the math right, my stomach is cramping because I'm about to get my period. Control freak that I am, I stuck in a preemptive tampon in hopes of avoiding a potentially disastrous situation.

I'm on autopilot. Asking for orders, making drinks, running cards. I'm barely registering faces or small talk, but when I look up to ask for the next drink order, I'm shoved back into the present moment by a pair of soulful eyes and sinful lips.

"Hello, Red."

"Hello, Sir."

Damian gives me a panty-shredding smile and my lady parts burst into song. I'm still exquisitely, thoroughly satisfied from everything we did this morning, but, call me crazy, whenever I get my period I turn into one horny bitch.

I rest a hand on my hip. "How may I serve you?"

His eyes make a lazy perusal of my body. My breasts go tight, heavy. "What's on the menu?"

"Everything."

"Hmm." He rubs his chin. "I need some time to think over the entrées." Another lazy perusal. "While I do, I'll take that IPA you have on tap."

I get his beer and slink back over. "Don't forget about the dessert menu." I wink.

He pays for the rest of our friends' orders. I'm placing Tiana's on the bar for Damian to hand back when the phone rings. I grab it, not bothering to look at the caller ID. It's a new cordless phone Kiley installed when he redid the security system and I'm still not used to it.

"Braxton Arcade," I shout over the bar noise. "How can I help you?"

"Hello, Marrin. Nice of you to answer."

Indignation seeps into me at this asshole's entitled tone. I check it, plugging my other ear so I can hear more clearly. "Sorry, buddy. Loud bar. Can you repeat that?"

Priya shoots me a, *Who's that?* look. I shoot back, *No fucking clue.*

"Been a while since we talked," the man says.

With my other ear plugged, I can hear more clearly.

Blood ices in my veins. I know this voice.

"I heard you—"

I hang up. Echoes of Frank's voice slither through my head. I feel violated, my peace of mind desecrated. I can't keep it off my face.

Priya pauses. "Marrin, what's wro—"

The phone rings again, and I can't get it out of my hand fast enough. I fling it at the bar and back up.

Comprehension sours Priya's face. "*Motherfucker.*" She charges over and answers. "Call here again, you sick fuck, and I will personally end you." She hangs up and slams the phone on the charger.

A hush falls over the nearest patrons and I realize they're all watching. Priya pushes me out from behind the bar and into the break room. A warm, sturdy hand finds my lower back and Priya backs off.

"Mar?" Damian's deep voice vibrates through me, breaking me from the stupor I didn't realize I was in.

Priya closes the door. "Why don't you take a break? Or the rest of the night off?"

I plop into a chair and rub my face. "No way. We're too busy." Damian sits next to me, hand still on my back.

"Don't worry about it, we'll manage."

The door opens and Conor walks in looking mean as hell. Like one of those guard dogs with the sharply pointed ears and chain collars. "What happened?" His calm, even voice seems at odds with his expression.

"Asshole called," Priya snarls.

Conor's face is unreadable as he pulls out his phone.

"Frank?" Damian blurts.

I nod, waiting for him to leave so he can go outside and

look for a red truck. But he doesn't. He looks as though he's *considering* options that include flying into a caveman rage, but when his eyes find mine, all I see is a weird longing I can't place.

"Asshole called," Conor says into his phone.

"*Twice*," Priya interjects.

"Twice," Conor repeats. "About a minute ago... yeah... hold on." He hands me the phone.

"Hello?"

"Hey, kiddo," Kiley's bright voice answers. "You remember what Asshole said?"

My throat tightens, "He said 'Hello, Marrin. Nice of you to answer,' and then something about it being a while since we talked. 'I heard you' was the last thing he said before I hung up."

"I'm sorry he called," Kiley says.

"Me too. What are you gonna do?"

"See if we can tie the phone number to him and use it to have him arrested. Can you put Conor back on?"

"Sure." But then I add, "No, Ki. I won't tell you what Priya's wearing," before passing the phone to Conor.

A faint, but distinct, "Priya, I did *not* say that," comes through the phone.

"Perv," Priya calls, cupping her mouth.

After a bit more convincing and a phone call from Alice, I take the rest of the night off. Damian and I say goodbye to our friends before heading out. My stomach is full on cramping now, and it's reminding me too much of when I was stabbed.

Ugh. Thinking and saying that never gets less weird. Stabbed. I was stabbed.

Damian rode with Jayce, so I ask him to drive my car back to our complex. He does and decides to take the long way home, discreetly checking in the rearview for any sign we're being followed. Pretty sure my clit grows three sizes at that—but the hussy will have to wait because I can't have sex with cramps this bad or with Frank's voice in my head.

I feel like I need a shower to wash off the gross.

When we get inside my apartment, Damian speaks in his sexy voice. "I've decided what I'd like to order off the menu."

I ready myself to give him a *not tonight* answer, but he surprises me.

"I want you to change into your most comfortable pair of sweatpants and the dumpiest T-shirt you can find, then I want you on the couch with your feet in my lap."

I can't hide the smile that breaks over my face.

Three minutes later, I'm on the couch and Damian is massaging my feet. He set a bottle of ibuprofen and a glass of water on the table, and plugged in the heating pad I've officially stolen from him. It warms my lower abdomen.

"What gave me away?" I ask.

"Your boobs were wonderfully engorged this morning, I found a tampon wrapper in my bathroom trash, and the entire drive home you sat with your knees to your chest."

I close my eyes, relaxing beneath his touch. "I don't deserve you."

"Yes, you do. You're perfect for me."

I open my eyes and find him watching me. The look on his face is identical to the emotions flooding my body at his words. We are perfect for one another. I knew it the moment we met. It's why I couldn't stay away from him, and why I tried to push him away.

I nod in agreement.

He says, "Do me one favor?"

"Okay."

"Let me show you how to defend yourself."

"I'd like that." Another rush of emotions and hormones and all those wishy-washy chemicals flood my brain and body and... and I don't care. Loving someone and letting them take care of you isn't a weakness, it's a strength. Shouldering a burden alone—that's the real weakness. Accepting help is hard. *Allowing* someone to help you is hard. But it doesn't mean you're putting your problems on someone else or giving up control.

It's the opposite.

Accepting Damian's help is me owning my problems. Owning that I've tried and can no longer carry them alone. Owning that I need help and I trust him to help me. To be there when I need him and to be my strength when I have none of my own.

He makes us falafel for dinner and I turn on a movie. I eat way too much and fall asleep way too early. I wake up when I feel myself being lifted off the couch. My eyes flutter open as Damian carries me into my room.

"What time is it?" I mumble.

"Late. Go back to sleep."

I close my eyes as he lays me on my bed and tucks me in. He returns with the heating pad and ibuprofen. I smile through my grogginess. He moves toward the door.

"You're not leaving, right?" I mumble.

"Not a chance."

A minute later, the bed dips as he slides in next to me.

25

Damian

"Hook your foot, Mar."

"I'm trying. Your damn leg is too muscular. I can't get mine around it."

"Try hooking your foot around my calf from between my legs."

"I feel like I'm going to—*oh I got it*," she squeals.

I'm holding her tight to my chest in a bear hug. "Now what?"

"My other leg steadies me while I pry the fingers of your top hand to get free and elbow your creep ass in the face."

"My creep ass is waiting."

"You're so bossy."

I give her a squeeze. My arms are banded around her waist. She finds my top arm, the one I'm using to grip my other arm with, and wrenches my index finger back. My hold on her breaks and she gets free, taking the opportunity to pretend to elbow me in the face.

She prances around my living room like Rocky at the top

of the Philly Museum stairs. I admire her a moment before I attack again.

I hit her from behind like a bull, grabbing around her waist and hauling her up into the air.

"Come here, little girl," I say in my creepiest voice.

She kicks as I drag her back. Then, just as we practiced, she hooks one foot around my leg to anchor herself and pries my finger until I lose my grip. She gets free and twists around, pretending to ram her elbow into my face.

I fake stagger back and she turns on a heel to face me. "You know," she says, hands on her hips. "This would be kinda hot if it were dark, we were half naked and I didn't fight back."

Blood stiffens my cock. I give her a bedroom smile and walk right into her space. "You want me to pretend to chase you, Red?"

Unmistakable lust clouds her eyes. "Sure, but not in a consensual non-consensual sex kinda way. Nothing against people with that kink, it's just not for me."

"Same. I don't think I'm cut out to be fake mean to someone I love."

"Just bossy."

I knead her hips with my fingers. "You want me to manhandle you, Red?"

She shrugs. "Only if it's in a you-punishing-me-for-trying-to-deny-you kind of way. *Sir.*"

I give her another sultry once over and step back. "I'll think about it."

Her eyes go wide. "Oh shit—what time is it?"

I pull out my phone. "Half past noon."

"*Shit.* I'm supposed to be at work by one to cover for Priya. I totally forgot to set the alarm on my phone." She runs around, frantically gathering her things.

"Go get dressed, I'll drive you. I told Hayden I'd meet him for an afternoon of beer and games."

She runs back to her apartment to change, and fifteen minutes later, I'm driving her to work. It's the beginning of February and cold as hell outside. The roads have been icy from sleet for what feels like weeks, so I've been driving Marrin to work when I can. Her car doesn't have four-wheel drive, and frankly I just don't trust it to deploy the airbags let alone hot air when the heat's on. She can't afford a new car and refuses to borrow Alice's. And while I'd love nothing more than to offer to buy her a car, I know her well enough to know that would make her incredibly uncomfortable.

The Neanderthal in me likes the idea of buying her a car. A safe, reliable car. He likes the idea of providing for her. But he understands that part of providing for a woman like Marrin is letting her provide for herself. She needs that. So until such a day comes that we're either living together or married, I'll settle for driving her around in my safe, reliable vehicle.

I meet up with Hayden at the Braxton Arcade and decide to never again visit during the day on Sundays. The place is wild with children, parents too far gone in the nostalgia of an old game to care what their spawn is doing. It's a madhouse—sans the straight jackets.

Hayden and I are playing *Mr. Do!* It's not two-player, so we have to take turns. Hayden is currently two levels further than I've ever made it in the game and I'm trying to absorb as much info as I can, so when it's my turn, I can beat him. I'm also tuned into Marrin. I can't help it. I keep catching bits and pieces of her voice over the din of my concentration, the droves of unattended minors high on sugar, and the incessant ringing of the bar's phone that started a few minutes ago.

"You need to leave," I hear her say.

I pivot. And find Mar in the middle of the room near a table. She's posturing a bit, standing as tall and intimidating as she can. But she's rigid, too. The pasty-white dude standing in front of her is just shy of being tall, just shy of being muscular, just shy of being old, and just shy of looking like a contributing member of society.

I put down my drink.

The man says something I can't hear.

"Leave," Marrin hisses, voice hard and mean. A few patrons look in their direction.

I glance around for Conor. I don't see him but I see Elle. She's behind the bar, watching Marrin and the man. Her normally deep gold skin is white as a sheet and she's entirely too still. A rabbit that's spotted a cat. Everything about her reads like an open book. She clearly has experience being around someone who was prone to violent outbursts. It's a look I'm familiar with from the people I meet at work and it's a look I've seen in her once before when I got in Jake's face at the bar last semester.

I move to the side of the bar, keeping my eyes on Marrin.

"Where's Conor?" I ask. The bar phone is still ringing, the sound urgent like a warning.

"Outside," Elle breathes. "Grabbing something from his car."

"Do you know who that guy is?"

"No. He just walked in."

The hair on the back of my neck raises. "Walked in and what?"

"Went straight to Marrin."

"Elle," I say very calmly. "Go outside and get Conor."

She blinks, nods.

I'm already moving when the man steps forward. Marrin

lurches to the side, putting a table between them, and I get my first real look at her face. She's pissed as hell and scared.

"You can't be here," she growls.

"Says who?" the man replies, eyeing her up and down.

"Says me, Grandpa." I come up behind him, resisting the urge to get in his face. Instead I move to stand level with Marrin. I want to stand in front of her, want to put myself between her and this man, but I only *think* I know who he might be and I don't want to take Marrin's authority.

Grandpa gives me a dismissive once over. "Me and the lady have business, boy. Why don't you run along and play your little games?"

I ooze sarcasm. "Sorry, Gramps. Business is over. She told you to leave." Then I speak to Marrin like we're characters in a play having an aside. "Nothing worse than a man who doesn't hear 'no' amiright?"

He points between us. "So you're spreading for him, now are you?"

I snap—not from the words, but from what he implied.

Grandpa goes down like a domino. In two moves, he's on the ground, arms immobilized behind his back, pinned with my knee in his spine.

I growl into his ear, low enough for only Marrin to overhear. "Only in your wildest delusions would a woman like her ever lower herself for some sleazy, old ball sack like you. And forcing a woman ain't the same thing, Asshole."

He laughs. "That what she told you? That her cunt wasn't—"

I twist his arm and he yelps like a dog whose foot just got stomped on. I'm a hair's breadth away from dislocating his shoulder.

What was that, Grandpa? Didn't quite catch that last part.

Heavy footsteps sound and I ease up, aware of the crowd

now forming. Conor crouches beside us, a pit bull before the bait beast. Eerily calm, yet somehow viciously poised.

"Long time no see, Frank." His voice emotionless. He pulls out two pairs of handcuffs, slapping the first on Frank.

"I got questions," Frank snarls.

"So will the cops." Conor looks at me. "Let him go." I don't hesitate. He hauls Frank to his feet and locks the second pair of cuffs to the first.

"What are you doing? You can't arrest me."

"I just did." He zips Frank's jacket. "You violated a restraining order, I'm holding you until the cops—"

Frank twists toward Marrin. "This isn't over, you white-trash whore."

Marrin goes utterly vacant.

I'm in front of her in a second, blocking her from his view.

"You'll get what's coming to y—"

Conor jerks him toward the door and it's the only reason I don't break Frank's fucking jaw. Once outside, Conor cuffs him to a bike rack and makes him sit on cold concrete.

Marrin's breath is shallow and jagged when I turn around. She's ashen and trembling and I know better than to thoughtlessly touch someone who's just been retrauma-tized and who may or may not be experiencing PTSD. I read once that ninety-four percent of rape survivors experience PTSD in the first two weeks after their assault. For half of survivors, symptoms will continue for years or decades after. Symptoms can even lay dormant, or seemingly go away, for years before manifesting again in some way.

I know Marrin wasn't raped, but she was attacked. Frank has two hands. It's not hard to imagine what might've happened between the lines of what she told me. That coupled with what happened when her mother got home are enough for anyone to need a moment after what just went down.

I check my body language and rid myself of any lingering anger. "Marrin?" I say, voice calm, concerned.

She doesn't respond. Just stares as if lost in a memory.

"Marrin, it's Damian. Your boyfriend. I'm going to hold your hand, okay?"

"Okay," she exhales. A shred of presence flickers in her eyes and I know she recognizes me.

I slowly take her hand. She's ice cold. I see Hayden on the edge of the lingering crowd and jerk my head for him to stay back. Just in case.

Marrin squeezes my hand and when my eyes find hers again, I know she's fully in the present with me. "There you are."

"Can I sit down?" Her voice breaks along with a little piece of my heart. She's not asking for permission, she's asking me to take control. Letting me know she has no fucking clue what to do and she needs me to take care of her so she doesn't have to think.

"Of course." I wrap her in my arms and lead her to the break room.

When the door shuts, she starts sobbing. Borderline hysterical sobbing. Her breath chokes and hitches, and it's the worst sound I've ever heard. She's a puddle in my arms. I pull out a chair and settle her on my lap.

"Don't cry, baby. It breaks my fuckin' heart."

We sit like that for a while. Marrin latched to me, face buried in my shoulder. I try to console her. Say things like:

"You're safe."

"I'd never let anything happen to you."

"I'll always protect you."

Some of it works and some of it makes her cry harder.

Elle comes in and lets us know Alice is on her way. She also says the police are here and that a detective is waiting to take our statements. Marrin composes herself, but the evidence of tears linger on her face.

We walk out into the arcade, my arm wrapped protectively around her waist. The detective waits by one of the high tables. He's tall and lean with dark brown skin and short hair. When he turns around, recognition lights his face.

Marrin sways, fisting my shirt. "I'm gonna faint," she slurs, just before every muscle in her body shuts down and her knees give out.

"*Shit.*" I grab her as she loses consciousness.

She's completely limp as I lower her to the floor. Fear guts me like a fish. *What's wrong with her? Is she okay? I'm gonna murder Frank.*

"Marrin, baby, look at me. Wake up."

Her eyes flutter open.

I stroke her cheek, her head and shoulders in my arms. "Hey, you're okay. Just breathe."

"Sorry," she mumbles.

"Lean her back a bit," the detective says, taking a knee near Marrin's feet. I catch his last name on the ID clipped next to the badge on his belt, Lawson. There's something familiar about it that I can't place. "I'm going to elevate your feet, okay?"

I realize what he's doing and follow his lead. While he raises her feet to his thigh, I shift until Marrin's head is in my lap. We sit like that while she comes back to life.

She looks at me. "You're totally freaking out right now, aren't you?"

"Full honesty? Yeah, little bit."

"I faint sometimes. Not often, but it happens. I'm embarrassed."

"Don't be. As long as you're all right."

"I am. Promise."

A moment later, we sit her up.

"Do you recognize me?" she says to the detective.

He smiles. "I do. You're Marrin Braxton. Surprised to see me?"

"Clearly," she jokes, face reddening. "Damian, Detective Lawson was the officer who saved my life two years ago."

The one who showed up on Thanksgiving and kept her from bleeding out.

Emotion clogs my throat. This man saved her life. Had he not been there, she'd very likely have bled out before help arrived.

"Thank you." It's all I can manage to say.

He shakes my hand. "Just doing my job."

So many words about not downplaying his hero status flood my mouth. If I say even one, I know I'll lose it, so I keep my mouth shut. But I think he understands because he nods before looking away from me so he can't see the tears burning my eyes.

I get myself together and we help Marrin into a chair at one of the high tables. I stand next to her, caging her in from one side in case she faints again.

Lawson explains he's now the detective in charge of Marrin's case. We shoot the shit a bit more before giving our statements. I go first. Then Marrin.

While she's talking, Alice and Gavin show up, and the look on Alice's face, in every line of her body, could put any mother bear to shame. She's alive with rage and the instinct to protect. When she hugs Marrin, even I have to fight the urge to back up and give her the space she demands.

But I hold my ground—a move that does not go unnoticed.

When she releases her cousin, Marrin's crying again. But instead of crying in Alice's arms, she turns to me.

I can't lie, it's grossly satisfying that Marrin chooses me over Alice. My inner alpha male growls like King Kong, baring his teeth in threat at anyone stupid enough to try and take her from me.

She's mine, I want to roar. *Mine, mine, mine, mine, mine.*

Alice's face is like a PowerPoint presentation on emotion. First slide is full offense, next is suspicion, then pleasant surprise, acceptance, then finally ending in a combo of smug and impressed.

"Saw the video of you taking down Asshole," Alice says to me. "You'd make a decent bodyguard."

Marrin whips around. "Don't you dare."

"What?" Alice says, feigning innocence.

Gavin waves his phone. "Not bad, kid. Kiley sent the security footage." To Lawson he says, "We can send you a copy."

They square away the details and then Marrin continues giving her statement.

"He wanted to talk to me outside. I told him he had to leave."

"Did he say what he wanted to talk to you about?" Lawson asks.

She hesitates, grabbing my hand. "He asked if I liked the letter he left on my door about a month or so ago." I straighten. "He wanted to know if that was why people had been following him."

Lawson blinks. "Wait, wait. He approached your door?"

My thoughts exactly, dude.

"Not directly," Alice cuts in. "We believe he paid off a

maintenance guy who worked in her building to leave the letter. That man's since been fired, and no, we didn't call the police because there was no way to prove it. Until now."

"Still," Lawson says, "he's escalating."

Marrin

Damian's quiet on the ride home. Guilt sours my stomach. I should've told him about the letter. We talked a little bit about it before we left, but not much. He asked when I got it and I told him. All he said was, "That's why you pushed me away."

Before we left the arcade, Alice told us Frank slipped the team hired to watch him. He did such a good job, no one knew he was gone until over an hour later. They called Alice and she immediately started calling the bar. But by then, Frank was already in the building.

Damian and I spend the rest of the day at his place. At some point, I ask him to show me some self-defense moves and that seems to get his mind off things.

We run a few drills before he gets quiet again.

"I'm sorry I didn't tell you about the letter," I say. "I was going to. I swear. I just didn't want to give you all of my baggage at once. And I was scared it meant I might have to move."

He looks surprised. "Is that why you think I'm being quiet?" I nod. "I don't like the idea of him trying to get close to you. It's one thing to approach you at work, it's another thing to approach you at home. But I'm not mad you didn't tell me. I was just... wondering what it was he said that made you freeze up."

I know what he's talking about. I was handling Frank

fine, but then he said something that sort of... I don't know, triggered some bad memories or something.

"'*You white-trash whore.*' He said that on Thanksgiving, and when he said it today, I kinda got stuck in my head, replaying the moment."

Damian nods stoically and I wrap my arms around his waist. He cages me in his and I get the sense he's savoring the moment, like his eyes might be closed.

"Can I ask a favor?" I say, listening to his heartbeat.

"Anything."

"Can you show me how to get away from someone once you're pinned on the ground?"

26

———

Marrin

I lay on my back in the middle of Damian's living room, he kneels between my legs. We did this in reverse, me attacking him, so he could show me how it works. The move is called a triangle choke and it's basically going to allow me to strangle him with my legs.

He leans over me, planting his hands on either side of my head.

A shiver of anxiety runs through me.

Every time he's mounted me like this I've been more than willing, but this time feels different. We both know why I asked him to show me how to defend myself in this position. Where I'd normally feel aroused by his proximity, I feel vulnerable, aware of my physical disadvantage. I know he can sense it. He's done this a hundred times with people whose trauma is way fresher than mine.

He leans over me and I grip his shoulders. My breath shallows.

"Use whichever leg feels best," he says calmly, "but we'll try it enough that you're comfortable with both."

I nod and pull my left leg off the ground, snaking it between us until it's hooked over his right shoulder. I bring my legs together and hook my left foot beneath my right knee and squeeze. Then I "shrimp out" by turning to my right and pulling Damian's left arm. He falls to the side, choked between my legs and his arm. From this position, I can gouge out his eyes or simply choke him until he loses consciousness.

I do neither of course.

We run the drill a few more times on both sides. By the time we're doing it full speed, I feel like a fucking boss. Damian pins my arms above my head and all I do is get one of my legs between us, get him in a triangle choke and turn to the side. He goes down like a tree before Paul Bunyan. Hands free.

"When you get free, you run," he says. "Most assailants won't chase you. They want easy targets."

Damian

The next weekend, I'm still thinking about how Marrin didn't tell me about the letter. We talked about it some more and I totally get where she's coming from. I know the reason she didn't tell me wasn't because she doesn't trust me. But it still kinda bothers me.

Then again, maybe I'm just feeling guilty because right now I'm driving to go have dinner with Nadia.

It's early Saturday evening and Marrin has the night off. I'd much rather be hanging out with her, but instead I told her I had plans and that I'd see her after. I didn't tell her I was meeting my mom and she didn't ask.

I pull up to the restaurant and exit my vehicle.

A minute later, I'm sitting down across from Nadia.

Less than twenty minutes later, I get up and leave.

My chest is tight, my throat clogged. I'm sweaty with fury and a sadness I don't understand.

I didn't say goodbye—just peaced the fuck out.

I don't remember the drive back to my apartment. All I know is that at a quarter till eight, I'm knocking on Marrin's door.

She answers and I fucking crumble at the happy, surprised look on her face.

She pulls me inside and my forehead finds her shoulder.

"Dame, what's wrong? What happened?"

"Nadia," I choke. "Fucking. Nadia."

White-hot fury scores my back. For a second, I wish I'd never come here. I want to break something. Want to ram my fist into something to take the edge off my anger.

The concrete floor is looking pretty good. That won't break.

But my hand will.

"Fuck," I growl. "*Fuck.*" I back away from Marrin, wiping angry tears. I cover my face and retreat until I hit the wall. I knock my head against it once, twice—

"Stop," Marrin orders. She takes my head in her hands and forces me to look at her. "Baby, what happened?"

I don't think she's ever called me that before. I hate how much I like it. Hate how much it calms me down—how much *she* calms me down, the compassion in her eyes. I want to be angry... but I can't find the strength.

I slide to the floor, bringing her with me. I pull her onto my lap and hide my face in her shoulder. Thank fuck I've stopped crying.

She cradles my head. "What happened?"

"Nadia invited me to dinner. I've no clue why I went. I

got there and she was her usual robotic self. I asked why she'd invited me and she told me she wanted to talk about what happened to me. Said *she's* finally able to talk about it. *Like*—right there in the middle of a fucking restaurant for fuck's sake. Who the fuck does that?"

I feel the tears again and tilt my head up to the ceiling.

"I hate her. I *hate* her. She's a selfish fucking bitch who told me to keep my mouth shut because God forbid anyone know her son had been molested by a grown man. God forbid *he* have to suffer any consequences. Or my family. They acted like nothing happened—*nothing*. I was the only one who suffered. I kept my mouth shut because I was a kid and I was scared and my parents told me to stay quiet so I did. Parents are supposed to *protect* their kids, Mar. They're supposed to protect us."

"I know, baby. I know."

"My dad was a cold bastard, but my mom hadn't always been. She used to be warm and loving and—*I remember liking her*. I remember thinking she was a good mom when I was little. But then she changed. And now all of a sudden *she's* ready to talk about what happened to me? *Are you fucking kidding me*? She doesn't get to decide that. Right?"

"Right." Marrin holds my face, leveling our eyes. "Only you can decide when you're ready to talk to her. She doesn't get to dictate terms just because she's suddenly willing to acknowledge what happened or that she failed as a parent. She doesn't get to decide how you feel or when you're ready. She doesn't get to decide whether or not you forgive her. She doesn't get to decide any of it. The best she can do is own what she did and apologize."

"She hasn't even done that—apologize. She just started talking and I couldn't take it. It wasn't fair." Tears leave my eyes. "It felt unfair."

"It *was* unfair. And thoughtless and selfish and cruel. You deserve so much better than that. I'm so sorry this happened."

I pull her to me and inhale her scent. She cradles me and we stay that way until I'm able to get up.

Sometime later on the couch, she says, "This might sound shitty, but at least Nadia is trying to reconcile. She might be going about it the wrong way, but that's more than I got from my mom."

"She's never apologized?"

"In court, yeah, but not really. Not honestly. Her defense team tried to argue she'd been manipulated into taking drugs and that's why she attacked me. She calls the Arcade every year on Thanksgiving, but I've never accepted the call."

"How come?"

She shrugs. "It's easier. If I only let her be the villain then she can't disappoint me again. Frank got two months in jail, by the way."

I perk up immediately. "Did he now?"

She nods. "Yep. Alice called earlier to let me know. Judge said next time he violates the restraining order he's going to prison."

"Nice. Though, he should already be in prison."

"Agreed. But I'll take what I can get."

We hang out for a few more hours then I leave to go sleep and think at my place.

Problem is I can't sleep. And when I think, I feel angry and helpless. I hate feeling helpless. Hate feeling uncertain and weak. I need to be in control. Need to feel powerful and respected and confident.

Damian: *You up?*

It's past midnight, I doubt she is.

Marrin: *Yeah. Why?*
Damian: *I want you in a bad way.*
Marrin: *I'm listening.*
Damian: *Remember what you said about manhandling? I wanna do it. I wanna chase you, catch you, then fuck you. I wanna own you. Full submission, but I want you to play hard to get.*
Marrin: *(squeals) Right now?*
Damian: *Yes. That okay?*
Marrin: *Hell yes. Give me 10 minutes.*
Damian: *Safety word is still parakeet, right?*
Marrin: *Yes. And if I can't talk, I'll tap you or something three times.*
Damian: *Yep. Understood. Could you wear nylons?*

Marrin

Damian shuts the door to my apartment. It's dark. I'm wearing a simple black dress and black nylons. My hair is tied in a loose braid. He's in jeans and a black T-shirt. I back away as he takes off his shoes and socks.

"What's your safety word?" he says. His voice is vicious and low and laced with promises of punishment.

"Parakeet," I reply because I know he needs to hear it, needs to make sure I know I'm in control and that we can stop the scene at any time.

"Come here, Red."

A thrill twirls through me and my clit grows heavy. The game has begun.

I back away. "Why, Sir?"

"Because you belong to me. Your body belongs to me, your pleasure. Everything. Come here."

I keep the smile off my face as I take a step back. "*No.*"

Damian lunges for me. I get away only because I leap onto the coffee table and he has to go around. I hop over the couch and land on the floor behind. He rounds the opposite end and I back away.

He stops his hunt.

I stop my retreat.

"You wanna know what I thought when you fainted? Like I was a king and you were a foreign kingdom ripe for the taking. I wanted to conquer you right there. Fuck you for everyone to see just so they'd all know who you belong to."

My ovaries are going to explode. Blood is rushing to all the right places in my body and I can't remember why I'm supposed to run from him.

I remind myself it's about him tonight. He wants to feel in control, wants the conquest, the power. So I say, "I'm not a kingdom, Sir."

A savage kind of desire settles over his face.

"But you *are* mine," he croons. He removes his shirt, flashing the goods I'm ready to max out my credit card for a taste of. Hard, sculpted muscles—tense and heavy in the glow of the moonlight pouring in from the windows. Just the right amount of tattoos—

Kill. Me. Dead.

I lick my lips. I'm so turned on, it hurts.

He smiles like a predator. "You're wet aren't you, Red? You've been without me for too long. We both know it's true. Both know I have what you need." He cups the erection straining against his jeans. "What your slutty little pussy craves. Now come here—"

He lunges and the nylons make the concrete too slippery

to get away. He grabs me from behind, hands taking liberties as he does.

"Struggle all you want, but *this*," he gropes between my legs, "is mine."

But then he snakes his hands together in a bear hug and I know what he wants. I hook a leg around his and pry his top finger until I'm free.

"You'll have to catch me first," I tease, prancing across the room.

Then it's on. Damian hunts and I flee. He catches me and I get away a few more times before he catches me in such a way that I know we're past the foreplay.

His arms are like iron bands around my torso and he hauls me into the air.

"You done running?" he growls.

"Yes, Sir," I pant.

"Good."

He bends me over the back of the couch with the grace of one throwing a wet towel over a clothesline. A large hand forces my head down toward the cushions, my feet strain for purchase on the slippery floor. He shoves up my dress to my hips—*SMACK*.

Jesus fuck.

Damian doesn't just smack my ass, he smacks my pussy. It's painful and erotic and touches my clit just enough that I definitely want him to do it again —*SMACK*.

I throw out my arms to hold myself up as sensation goes through me like lightning.

Hands slither up my thighs and grab the fabric covering my sex. There's a distinct ripping sound and the thought of Damian tearing my nylons, how it must look, causes warmth to flood my core.

Cool air hits my vulva just before hot breath. My whole body tightens in anticipation.

"No panties today, Red?"

"No, Sir—"

SMACK.

There's no time to recover before Damian shoves his entire cock inside me. It's barbaric and obscene and border-line painful. The collision of our bodies so violent I gasp and squirm—unable to hold myself up.

He grips my hips and spears me with his cock over and over and over again. Greedy and cruel. No thought for my pleasure as he fucks me. Taking and taking and taking.

I love every goddamn second of it.

He pulls my hair hard and I arch back. He shoves up my dress as far as he can then leans forward long enough to unhook my bra with his teeth. The weight of his body is momentarily crushing, thoughtless. He releases my hair to grab the back of my neck and bend me just enough for his other hand to get a rough fistful of my breast.

I yelp in pleasure and pain.

"Fuck yeah," he grunts, cock still driving into me in brutal, gluttonous thrusts.

Everything about him is uncivilized and filthy. He's fucking to claim, to conquer. To force submission. I feel branded and used, and so incredibly turned on. I hear us meet every time he fucks into me. It's absolutely obscene and I'm doing this to him. I'm allowing him to take what he wants and it makes him so hard and happy. I grow wetter at the thought.

"What're you thinking about, Red?"

"How greedy you are," I gasp. "How you're fucking me like a Neanderthal. How much I want your hot cum inside me, all over me."

Grunting like a beast, he releases my neck. He hauls me up, pulls out of me, flips me around, shoves up my dress and bites each of my breasts *hard*.

I half yelp, half moan. He points to the ground. "Elbows and knees."

I consider not obeying, trying to gauge if that's what he wants.

But he's all business and cruelty. "You want me to get you off, Red?" He slaps between my legs. "Then get on your fucking elbows and knees and put this pussy in the air for me to take."

"Yes, Sir." I move faster than a bat outta hell. Then I wait, prone and ready, ass in the air. Jeans rustle but I can't see what he's doing.

"Christ..." He massages my ass cheeks. "If you could only see the view, Red. Best view in the whole world and it's just for me, isn't that right?"

SMACK.

"Yes, Sir."

He shoves two fingers into me and I moan at the unmistakable cooling sensation of lubricant. He grabs my hips. "Quiet."

He slathers me, then shoves his cock inside me to continue his barbaric intrusions.

I moan. The sound and feeling exquisite.

"Silence, Red. Not a peep."

But another moan escapes me as he varies his shallow strokes with a deep thrust.

He reaches around me and pulls one of my nipples. I whimper.

He pulls out. All sensation gone.

"What did I say? If you can't follow the rules, there are other ways I can shut you up, Red."

I clamp down on my bottom lip. I love bossy, caveman Damian.

He starts to fuck me again, grunting and groaning. Filthy, nasty things leave his mouth. He pushes me down so that I'm propped on my cheek and knees then he folds my arms behind my back, holding them with a hand. He pumps into me, balls slapping my clit. It's degrading and bestial and my climax grows and grows until it rushes over me.

"What do you say, Red?"

I'm nothing more than a twisted ball of moaning and groaning and panting. But I manage, "Thank you, Sir—*oh fuck*—Sir, thank you for your cock—*oh shit*—I love your cock, Sir."

"Jesus Christ. This pussy, baby," Damian pants, and I know his control is slipping. His orgasm barreling for him as mine starts to ebb.

I smile. "You gonna come for me, Damian?"

"*Yeah*," he grunts.

"Gonna feed my hungry cunt everything your big cock has to offer?"

"*Fuck yeah.*"

"Fuck me, Damian. Fill me with your hot cum. I wanna take it. All of it."

That does the trick. He grips my hips and shoves himself into me almost frantically.

Skin claps, fluids leak. It smells like sex, sounds like rutting, feels like fucking and so much more.

Damian collapses on top of me.

I slide forward until we're both lying flat. His weight is crushing, but I don't ask him to move. Instead I use one of the self-defense moves he showed me and slowly push him off.

He takes the hint and rolls over, bringing me with him

until I'm lying with my back across his chest. His softening erection slips free and I feel the evidence of our play drip from me and onto him.

"God," he finally says. "That was..."

"Filthy? Nasty? Neanderthal-esque?"

"Amazing." He cups my breast with a hand, dipping the other between my legs to feel the evidence of us. "I didn't hurt you, did I?"

"Hell, no. Quite the opposite."

"Yeah?" His fingers move to my clit and he begins drawing lazy circles. His other hand kneading my breast. "You sure?"

I bite my lip and spread my legs. "No. No, I'm not sure."

"Not too sensitive?"

"Not yet," I exhale, back arching, hips rocking. Damian growls with approval from deep in his throat, the sound spurring my pleasure.

He moves us until he's sitting with his back against the wall, mine still to his chest. He removes the rest of my clothes and hooks my feet over his shins to control the spread of my legs. He opens me up as far as his legs can go. I rest my head back on his shoulder and he looks over mine to see where he strokes my pussy and works my breasts.

He comments on my wetness all the while, on the sounds and motions of my body under his touch. On how next time we do this, we'll have a mirror so we can both watch me come. He explores my body like it's his first time learning what I like. He nibbles my ear, my throat and my lips until I come apart in his hands and all over the floor.

When his cock stiffens, I turn in his lap and we make love, slow and deep, in the dark.

27

Marrin

It's the second week of March and spring break is in full swing. The college town is a dead zone but the neighboring public school kids are trying to make up for it. They have the same spring break, so we open the Braxton Arcade at ten in the morning instead of noon. The place is loud with teens and kids. And while I'm happy we're busy, tips are lousy.

I'm working the morning shift with Elle who is currently out on the floor giving a group of kids a rundown on how to play *Marvel vs. Capcom*. I've spent the morning ringing up soda orders and finalizing details on a local band we've booked to play a show tomorrow night because if we don't get some locals in here buying alcohol and leaving tips, I'm going to have to sell a kidney to pay my rent.

The phone rings and I move to check the caller ID. It's a collect call but it's not from the state prison. It's not my mom.

When Damian said Nadia was trying to reconcile their failed relationship, I was horrified by the way she'd gone about it. But at least she was trying. A small part of me is envious and I don't know why. The thought of talking to my mother makes me queasy, but at the same time, I don't know, she's still my mom. It's stupid to think she'll ever be a good mom or the mom I deserve, but it'd be nice to know she was honestly sorry about what happened. I don't need her to love me or anything. At least that's what I tell myself. I just need something. Closure maybe. I don't know.

Answering the phone when she makes her once-a-year call to the Braxton on Thanksgiving would be one way to find out what she wants, and a way to facilitate whatever it is I think I might still need from her. But in order to do that, I'd have to be willing to open myself up to the potential for more disappointment. And I'm not there yet. I'm not sure I'll ever be.

I suppose I do have a while until next Thanksgiving, though.

Toward the end of my shift, I go out front to clean trash off one of the benches. It's unseasonably warm today and a few patrons have been sitting outside.

A well-dressed woman crosses the street but I pay little attention. I stack a couple of glasses, pick up some straws, and step on a cigarette butt someone tossed on the ground and didn't put out all the way. I make one more sweep of the area before turning to go back inside.

"Excuse me, miss?"

It's the well-dressed woman. She's in a fitted designer pants suit, a designer bag hangs at her side and I'm pretty sure she's wearing shoes worth more than my tuition. Her dark hair is pulled into a severe twist at the back of her head and there's something familiar in her features.

"Yes?" I say, glancing at the car she got out of—a black Rolls-Royce.

"Are you Marrin Braxton?"

My spine goes shotgun straight. I measure the distance to the door. "Who's asking?"

"My name is Nadia Wane. I'm Damian's mother."

That's why you look familiar.

"My apologies for intruding. I only wish for a moment of your time."

I eye the door. Damian's home writing a paper, but that doesn't mean he couldn't show up at any moment. "I don't know if that's a good idea."

"Please," she says.

And it's the look in her eyes that gets me. Like she knows she doesn't deserve to be asking but she's so desperate she's willing to grovel. "Let me put these inside. Hold on."

"Thank you."

I race inside and set the empties on the bar. Then I'm back outside. We don't sit and I keep an unfriendly distance between us. "I don't have a lot of time."

She inhales sharply. "I'm not sure what you know about my relationship with my son, but it's not good. I'd like to make it better, but I messed up recently. Now he isn't returning my phone calls or answering my texts."

My face is a mask of indifference, but inside I'm screaming at her full force.

"From looking at social media, I have reason to believe you're his girlfriend, or at the very least a close, personal friend of his. I was hoping I might persuade you to talk to him on my behalf—"

"Let me stop you right there. If you're about to pull out a checkbook, consider this conversation over."

She blinks, momentarily affronted. "No. No, I was just hoping you could let him know I understand that I approached things the wrong way and that I'm going to stop trying to contact him. Not because I don't want to speak with him, but because I realize that I need to wait for him to be ready. Please, if you could just tell him that I'm sorry and that whenever he wants to speak to me, I'm ready to listen."

I drag out my silence. Both to make her sweat and because I'm thinking about what to say.

"*Please.*" Tears cloud her eyes but don't fall. She looks like a broken woman. A woman who knows she fucked up and is willing to put in the work to make amends and prove she's changed.

"I'll see what I can do, but I can't make any promises. If he knew we spoke..." I shake my head.

"Thank you," she says. "*Thank you.*"

I nod and go back inside.

Damian

The beginning of April rolls around and Marrin and I go out for our first real date. It's not that we haven't been on real dates, it's just that it's been so cold we've mostly stayed at home or played games at the Braxton. (And by games, I mean *Realm Quest*, which I still haven't beaten her at.)

Tonight I take her to dinner at a rooftop restaurant in the city. It's nice, but casual and the weather is decently warm. I'm in jeans and a T-shirt and she's in a dress—*or maybe it's an oversized shirt?*—and sporty-looking leggings with slices of mesh fabric that show off her legs.

We sit outside and have a few drinks, watching the sun set and enjoying our dinner.

When we're done, and the check is paid, we linger and talk. The patio we're on is lit by dim, golden lights and it's early enough in spring that there aren't any bugs.

In a rare moment of silence, Marrin shifts in her seat just

enough that I can tell something's on her mind. The sun has completely disappeared now and the night air grows steadily colder. Almost uncomfortably so.

"What?" I ask.

She nails me with a look, with those whiskey eyes I love so much. "Nothing."

"That's not your 'nothing' face. Something's up."

She wrinkles her mouth to the side. "Okay," she sits forward, "but I don't want you to get mad."

I match her stance. "Why would I get mad?"

"Because... it's about Nadia."

"What about Nadia?"

She looks down, then back at me. "I met her. Last month at the Braxton."

Insecurity stacks my spine, the whole rooftop fades, blocked behind a wall of quiet so loud every muscle in my body strains to hear Marrin's next words.

"She came up to me when I was out front and asked me to talk to you on her behalf."

"To say what exactly?" The words come out harsher than intended.

"She wanted me to tell you she's sorry about how she handled things last time the two of you met. She's not going to contact you anymore, but she still wants to reconcile. She's just going to wait for you to be ready and initiate."

Anger hits me like a shovel to the face, so fast I can't stop it. "And you kept this a secret *because...*?"

Her brow furrows. "It's not a secret."

"Then why didn't you tell me when it happened?" I demand.

"Because I knew you'd be upset."

I take a deep breath, trying and failing to swallow my emotions.

"I shouldn't have brought it up. Let's just go."

We get up and head downstairs. My anger mounts with every step, multiplying like a virus in my body. Not just at my mother for having invaded my private life, but at Marrin for not telling me. What the hell else is she keeping from me?

I climb into my Jeep, slamming the door unintentionally. "I need you to tell me everything Nadia said to you."

She does.

I drive in a silent rage. Pouring over every detail Marrin gave me. Every syllable, word and sentence. We're nearly back at our complex before I speak again.

"That's *all* she said to you?"

"Yes."

"Are you sure?" I accuse.

Her head whips to me. "What's that supposed to mean?"

"I don't know, Marrin," I half yell. And I don't. My brain is alive with confusion about what she's just told me. It feels like I'm coming apart at the seams. "You tend to keep secrets, so I have to wonder."

I can feel anger building in her silence. Feel the heat and hurt coming off her in waves. When she speaks, her voice is far too quiet, far too calm.

"I've already apologized and explained my reasons for keeping things about *me* and *my life* from you. This is not one of those things. Don't you dare try to make it one. The only reason I'm telling you this now is because it's been a few weeks, and I thought you might be more receptive to hearing what she had to say."

"Unbelievable. So you're her agent now, is that it? You sure you didn't take her money?" I don't mean it. I believe what she said about her conversation with Nadia. I'm just so mad I can't stop myself from lashing out. And right now Marrin's the closest target.

"*Excuse me?*"

I pull into the parking lot of our complex. "Shit. I'm sorry, baby. I didn't mean—"

"Don't *baby* me. I kept this from you because I knew it would upset you. I made the call I thought would protect you the most. I had every intention of telling you eventually and *not* on her behalf. Not ever on her behalf. But the fact that you think that—I can't even look at you right now."

She gets out of the Jeep and slams the door.

I grab my jacket from the backseat and put it on as I jump out.

She's pissed to high hell, but her voice quakes with the calm she's trying to hold onto. "You're allowed to be angry, Damian. But you're not allowed to be an asshole."

"What am I supposed to think when you bring this up? You should've told me right when it happened."

"Well I didn't. You were clearly still upset about your dinner with her, and I didn't want to make it worse. I made the call I thought was right, and I regret that decision now. I'm sorry."

I run my hands through my hair. "What did you think would happen when you finally told me? That I'd break into song?"

"I don't know," she yells. "Not this. Obviously. I'd hoped you'd be more receptive to hearing her out. She wasn't faking it. She wants to make things right. The ball's in your court."

Jesus. Now *I* can't look at *her.*

I shake my head, rake my hair. "Are you trying to fix me? Is that what this is? Am I a Sunday School project to you?

This is my life, my *private* life, and you invaded it. Violated it. *You* of all people."

At the look on her face, I know I should stop. Should shut my damn mouth, get on my knees, and grovel for forgiveness. I'm screaming feelings at her because I can't scream them at myself and because I hate that I know she's right. But rage like gasoline floods my veins, fueling the pain that spews from my lips. The hurt look on her face is the mirror to what I feel inside and it strikes me like a match.

"She isn't *your* mother, Marrin." Hot tears hit my eyes the same time my words hit her ears. "She's mine. Fixing my relationship with her won't fix you. Or your relationship with your mother. Some people don't deserve a second chance."

It's dark, but the street lamp illuminating this part of the parking lot is bright enough that I see tears gleam in her eyes.

"You're right," she says, voice too quiet. "Some people don't deserve a second chance."

She's not talking about our mothers.

She starts walking away, but not in the direction of the complex.

"Where are you going?" I half yell.

Marrin doesn't turn around. "To get a textbook from my fucking car. Want me to send you a picture as proof I'm not lying?" she shouts, but I hear the crack in her voice.

It resonates like a crack in me and allows a drop of sanity to spread in my veins like ink in water. "Marrin, wait. I'm sorry."

"You should be," she fires back from somewhere in the darkness just beyond the street lamp. Her footsteps stop and when she speaks again, she sounds exhausted. "Go inside. Find me when you're less triggered."

Her tone implies I better be gone by the time she gets back because I'm the last asshole she wants to see. She's right, too. I can't talk about this until I'm calm enough to keep my anger from clouding my judgment. I've done enough damage already.

So much for being confident, calm, charming Damian.

I walk to the door and key in the code. Inside, I slouch on a couch in the lobby and bury my head in my hands.

Somewhere in my head, I hear my mother's voice, smell her perfume...

"What am I supposed to do? Your father says you'll be a man one day, and if anyone finds out what happened, it will embarrass this family and ruin your reputation."

A thirteen-year-old me stands in the hallway in front of my father's closed office. I stare at my mother's face. Her eyes are red and puffy, voice raspy from yelling at her husband. I couldn't hear what they'd been fighting about.

"W-What am I supposed to do now?" I say.

She wipes my tears, kisses my forehead. Then abruptly she stops, stands. "We'll sign the paperwork and put this behind us. Your father won't tolerate any more talk about it. What's done is done. You have to move forward, be a man." She starts walking away.

I don't know what else to do, so I follow.

She goes into the kitchen and pulls out a bottle of wine. She pours a glass. Her hands shake as she sips, then gulps, then pours another glass. And then another.

"Mom?" I say.

When she looks at me, it's like I'm the single greatest source of sorrow in the entire world. She bursts into tears.

"Mommy, don't cry." I half run to hug her. But she doesn't hug me back. She just blinks through her tears and keeps drinking.

At some point, I back away. Go to my room. Spend the whole evening telling myself my parents love me and that they're right. I need to put it behind me, man up. Be a man. If my father sees me cry again, it'll only make him more mad.

Declan comes into my room just past midnight. He crawls into my bed.

He says he knows. I tell him to leave. He says he loves me. I push him out of my bed.

He curls up on the floor of my room and whispers to me that I'll always be his big brother. He's ten years old.

I let myself cry one last time. Then I get out of bed and curl up with my brother on the floor.

Callus, bleaching sanity works its way through my body and I realize I'm a complete asshole. This has nothing to do with Marrin and everything to do with me and my issues with my parents. Jesus Christ, I said some horrible things to her.

What the fuck was I thinking?

I need to fix this. I *have* to fix this.

I stand. I have no idea how long I've been sitting and wallowing, but I'm pretty sure Marrin hasn't walked past me.

I turn to the security guard standing across the lobby. "Has anyone walked in after me?"

"No. Been just you and me for the last five or so minutes."

Something about that doesn't sound right. Marrin should've come inside by now.

I rush out the door and scan the darkness in the direction of her car. I see her vehicle but not her.

Maybe she's sitting inside.

I make my way to her car. The parking lot is dark. Only a few street lamps illuminate it. They do a shit job, too.

They're like spotlights, casting sharp circles of light directly beneath them. Marrin would call it low-key or chiaroscuro lighting, the kind they use in the noir films she loves so much.

At the other end of the lot, Marrin rushes into a pocket of light. She almost looks black and white with her silver-white hair and dark clothing. Her eyes are fixed on the complex door. She opens her too-red mouth, my name forming on her lips—

Frank grabs her from behind and yanks her to the ground.

Oh. Fuck. No.

28

_____

Marrin

Damian is allowed to be angry, but he's not allowed to act like a total jackass.

"Where are you going?" he shouts.

I keep walking. "To get a textbook from my fucking car. Want me to send you a picture as proof I'm not lying?" I yell every word, but I can't keep the hurt out of my voice.

"Marrin, wait. I'm sorry." His voice is honest and a little bit dejected.

I march into the darkness beyond a street lamp. "You should be. Go inside. Find me when you're less triggered."

I'm too exhausted to continue this conversation, and he's too angry to think rationally. He's said some things I know he didn't mean and likely already regrets, but I can't handle an apology from him right now. Triggered or not, he's a grown-ass human and grown-ass humans recognize when they're too triggered to talk about something and they own it. They explain what's happening and remove themselves as best they can from the situation. I'd have kept my mouth shut about it until he was ready to talk, but *nooo*. Dipshit had to keep running his mouth—

Something moves in my periphery.

I stop, glance around. I swore I heard footsteps that weren't mine. I'd assumed they were Damian's... but, as I turn in place, I don't see him.

I take two more steps before I realize I'm not uncomfortable because I'm mad at Damian. I'm uncomfortable

because

something's

not right.

Something's off.

I scan the darkness and Holly's words come back to me, "*Your gut instinct is your bottom bitch. She's been with you the longest and she's always reliable. She doesn't need proof to know someone's a creeper or that something's wrong. She calls it like it is.*"

Right now my bottom bitch is tingling like Peter Parker's spidey sense.

I abandon any idea of heading to my car and turn around. I haul up my anger at Damian and use it like a shield. Willing anyone who might be watching to see that anger and to know I'm not going to be an easy target. I pass through another sharp pocket of light and it's not lost on me how similar the situation is to a scene in *Cat People* where Irena stalks Alice Moore at night.

Really, Mar?

I'm hit from behind like a shark attack. Jerked back so violently my teeth slice into my bottom lip.

For a moment, I think it's Damian. We've practiced this so many times it must be him. But everything smells like cheap booze and cigarettes, tastes like blood in my mouth.

"Looky here. Cat finally caught the mouse."

Frank.

Blood drains from my body, pooling in my feet.

Frank.

My breath shallows, blood pressure plummets.

Frank.

I'm going to faint—*Oh God, I'm going to faint.*

"So you're good enough to give it up to that boy but not me? Well we'll see about that."

Each word is slimy and greasy, and it sets off a chain reaction inside me. Adrenaline trips the breaker on my fainting and my body comes back online like the power in *Jurassic Park*.

I'm a live wire of fear and blinding rage as Frank drags me into the darkness between two cars. Every self-defense move I've learned comes back to me and I don't think. Just react.

I hook my leg around his and wrench his top thumb back as violently as possible. He loses his hold around my torso and I hit the ground running—but not before I elbow him in the goddamn face. Something crunches, Frank screeches.

I take off at a dead run. Eyes fixed on the complex door.

Most assailants won't chase you, but Frank is in the slim percentage of predators that will give chase. I dart through the darkness, unable to spare breath enough to scream. Which is weird because I feel like the fucking Terminator. I'm powered up like Sailor Moon and as lethal as Michonne from *The Walking Dead*.

Halfway to the complex, Frank's footsteps pound up behind me. He grabs a fistful of my hair and dress then yanks. My body halts violently and I tumble backward off my feet. The collar of my dress tears and I hit the ground. *Hard.*

At once every ounce of air is forced from my lungs. My vision blurs, stars pop. I don't lose consciousness, but I'm momentarily stunned.

It's all the opportunity Frank needs.

He pins my legs with his weight. His forearm comes at my neck to cut off my air, but I manage to tuck my chin before he presses down—just as Damian taught me.

Backlit by the street lamp, Frank's nothing but an obscure, dark figure. He wipes blood from his broken nose onto the back of his shirt sleeve.

"This looks familiar. You know how hard it was to get you alone on Thanksgiving? Most I ever did to wet myself on a dumb whore like you."

"Get off me, Asshole."

"Keeping your mom away was easy, though. Just took the right amount of manipulation." He grabs my chin hard enough to bruise. "Now stay still and be quiet, I'll make sure you enjoy this, too."

I don't have space to process what he's saying because his knees slide between my legs. I move. Hooking my left leg around his neck and locking that foot behind my right knee. I pull on his arm and he crashes to the side. I crush my legs together, choking him. He beats and pulls at my thighs to no avail. I only crush harder.

I'm pretty sure I'm screaming for Damian, cursing, maybe growling—anything to burn off the adrenaline sizzling my veins. It's fight or flight and I'm fighting, strangling. I can't stop it.

It's a raw, primal kind of chemical surging through me, eating me alive from the inside out, commanding me to attack. I know it's just adrenaline but it feels older than the universe, older than time and light and matter. Feels like a million years of evolution bearing down on me. It's all-consuming and it's everything I can do not to claw out Frank's eyes, rip out his hair or pound my fists against his face.

One wrong move from him and I know I'll do it. Without a thought.

Suddenly Damian is there. He wrenches Frank from my grasp and launches him across the asphalt. I scramble backward.

Damian spares one second to scan me for injury. His eyes are cold as ice and hard as steel. His gaze darts over my body, landing for a moment too long on my shoulder. His eyes flash like living flames before he turns back to Frank.

Panting, I take stock of the situation. My body is numb to pain, but I can see the damage. My pants are ripped and my knee is cut. I know my lip is split because I can feel warm blood running down my chin and neck. And my dress is torn, a triangle of fabric hangs awkwardly from my shoulder.

I lean back against a car I didn't know was behind me and find Damian. He stands like a pillar—unmoving and steady. Balanced on a razor's edge to protect me.

Just past him, Frank stands.

Damian

I install myself between Marrin and Frank like a brick fucking wall. I scan her once. Blood coats her from mouth to chest, her dress is torn at the shoulder. Pure, unadulterated fury crashes into me like an avalanche. I turn back to Asshole.

Echoes of Marrin screaming my name reverberate through me.

I check my breathing, my defensive stance. I examine Frank for injuries, weakness I can exploit.

He gets to his feet way too fast.

"Oh-ho, come to defend your whore, boy? She ain't worth it."

His eyes are too alert, too wild. His lips stick to his teeth and he's twitchy. Asshole's high on something. Something that's making him energetic and over confident.

He circles wide and I match every step, keeping Marrin at my back. He's got to be high as fuck if he thinks I'm going to let him anywhere near her.

I sense her behind me like an extension of my being. An innate awareness that both adrenaline and the situation are allowing me to pick up on. I don't need to see her to know exactly where she is.

She's mine.

Mine to protect, mine to keep safe.

Frank postures like a UFC champ. Only he's not. He's just a middle-aged man whose drug-induced high has convinced him he's capable of mixed martial arts.

He rushes me, swinging at my face. I dodge easily, ramming my knee into his stomach. He staggers, recovers, then swings again. I sidestep the blow and use his forward momentum to send him careening to the asphalt with little more than a tug on his arm.

"Motherfucker," he roars. He shoots to his feet, pointing at Marrin. "You better run, you white-trash whore, because when I'm done with him, I'm gonna fuck you in every hole you got."

My jaw compresses to the point of pain as every threat and snarky remark imaginable wrestles for release. I hold them back, tracking Frank as he paces the edge of darkness cast by the street lamp above. I command my shoulders to ease, my body to react only to his movements and not his words. Losing your temper in a fight will make you sloppy. I am anything but a sloppy fighter. Frank on the other hand...

"You mean rape. Not fuck," I taunt. "Those are two different things. Honest mistake for a meathead like you, *Frankie.*"

"What'd you call me, boy?"

"You heard me, *Frankfurter.*"

With a roar, he comes at me again. A predictable jab followed by a pathetic excuse for a right hook. He may have put on a pair of boxing gloves once in a while, but his movements are artless and untrained. His stance is laughable and he's as out of shape as a wet sack of potatoes.

I block the hits and retaliate with a quick chop to his throat with the inside edge of my hand. He lists to the side and I grab his arm, chopping his exposed neck with the outside edge of my hand. I hit hard enough that he staggers back, dazed and holding his throat, but not hard enough to kill him.

He falls on his ass, choking.

But as any good stimulant drug can do, it's got him on his feet again a second later, barreling toward me.

He aims to hit me around the waist, but I grab his arm and twist it in an attempt to dislocate the shoulder. He turns before I can, so I tackle him.

We go down.

Frank uses some wannabe wrestling move to briefly get on top of me and take a few swings. I barely register Marrin screaming. He attempts to wrestle me into a chokehold but doesn't get far.

I excel at fighting on the ground because—*fun fact*— that's where most fights end up. In a matter of seconds, I'm on top of him. I hit him twice in the face in quick succession.

"You done?" I shout.

He smiles through bloody teeth made bright by the harsh light of the street lamp. "Should've seen the look on her face first time I fucked her," he says. "Priceless. Secret just between me and her."

"*LIAR*," Marrin screams.

"She was young, too. Fifteen or so. Completely untouched—"

The world slows down almost to the point of stopping. Frank is a pathetic, weak man, crafting ludicrous, disgusting fantasies at the expense of others because he has nothing better to do. I know he's lying. I do. My temper should remain on its leash. The fight is over. The threat neutralized...

But in the split second between the word *untouched* and whatever's coming next, several things flicker through my mind, snapping the tether on my control.

The terror in Marrin's voice when she'd screamed my name as she'd choked him.

The last thing Frank said to her before I pulled him off, "*Now stay still and be quiet, I'll make sure you enjoy this, too.*"

The face of my abuser when he'd said nearly the exact same thing to me almost nine years ago.

The fact that Frank just bragged about assaulting a minor.

My arm snaps back and my fist collides with his face.

Again

and again

and again

and again.

He's not Frank. He's my abuser. He's my dead father, my lousy mother. He's the physical manifestation of Marrin's pain as well as my own—

Footsteps pound down the road, echoing off the surrounding buildings.

—He's every sick fuck who's ever preyed on a child. Every sick fuck who's ever sexually assaulted or manipulated another human being for gratification or power or control. He's everything that's wrong with society. Every person who ever told me to keep quiet, to be a man, not to cry, not to *feel.*

He's the reason we tell women not to walk alone at night, not to get drunk, not to wear revealing clothing.

He's the reason society sees women's bodies as sexual objects too distracting to men not to be covered up in public.

He's the reason we shift blame from assailants and heap it on victims for being assaulted.

"Damian—"

He's the reason we teach women to defend themselves, teach children not to talk to strangers instead of teaching men not to rape, not to assault—*not to behave as if they're entitled to another person's body.*

"That's enough, kid."

He's the reason we should teach everyone about consent and boundaries and respecting other human beings.

Muscled arms lasso my torso and rip me off Frank.

29

Marrin

Sirens wail in the distance. A security guard runs toward us. An SUV speeds into the parking lot and suddenly Gavin is pulling Damian off Frank.

I'm not sure where to look or what to do. I'm not sure I can move. I'm not sure I want to move. If I stand, I have to face what happened. Have to face what *almost* happened to me. And I'm not sure I'm ready.

I stare at Damian.

He glares at Frank. Gavin's arms hold him back like a seatbelt in a head-on collision. His chest heaves and he's shaking so violently I'm not sure if he's standing on his own or if Gavin's holding him up. His teeth are bared and a jagged, raw kind of instinct screams from every line of his body.

Kiley crouches next to Frank. He's a swollen, bloody mess. But he's moving.

"She's safe, kid. You're both safe. You did good," Gavin says, eyes searching the darkness for me.

Damian's eyes snap to mine like he knows exactly where

I am. Because he does. My name forms on his lips but I can't tell if he speaks or not. He pushes forward and Gavin releases him, following closely.

Damian staggers into the darkness, eyes flickering over me. A strangled sob leaves my throat. He wipes bloody knuckles on his pants as he moves toward me.

Exhaustion hits and relief fills my eyes.

He's okay. I'm okay. We're okay.

Damian drops to his knees before me, body still trembling with adrenaline. He's at least an arm's length away.

"What are you doing?" I half sob.

A new kind of fear bleaches his face. He backs up. "I'm sorry, what you saw, I just lost it—"

"No." I shift forward, weakly grabbing a handful of his jacket.

Immediately he understands, closing the distance between us and pulling me into his lap. He blankets me in his arms and I can't stop the tears. Neither can he.

"Are you okay?" He kisses the side of my head. "Please be okay, tell me you're okay."

"I'm okay."

He pulls back to look at my face, my torn dress. Hysteria gutters in his eyes but he clamps down on it. He cups my chin like a wounded bird, but still I wince from pain. Immediately his hand retracts.

"No. Please," I sob, grabbing his wrist and pressing his palm to my cheek. "*Please* touch me."

That hand comes alive, threading into my hair and holding me to him. "I'm right here, baby. I'm right here. What happened? Did he hurt you?"

"No, j-just tackled me. I bit my lip when he grabbed me. I broke his nose. My n-neck hurts where he held me d-down." My thoughts are muddled. I'm barely making sense.

"I'm sorry it hurts. Can I see?"

I tilt my head and open my mouth. Gavin crouches next to us and clicks on a little flashlight to examine my busted lip.

"Not deep enough for stitches," he says. "But it's gonna swell."

"We'll ice it," Damian answers, smoothing my hair.

"Can I touch you?" Gavin asks. After I nod, he prods my neck. "Any of this hurt?"

"Not really. It's just sore."

"Any trouble breathing? Anything feel like it popped or shifted?"

"No. I tucked in my chin before he could really st-str-strangle me."

"That was smart." Gavin clicks off the flashlight just as blue police lights flood the parking lot. "Did he hurt you, Marrin?"

I cover the torn shoulder of my dress with a hand and shake my head. "No. I got away."

Damian's arms tighten around me and I sink into his chest, trying to hide. "Yeah you did. I'm so proud of you, Marrin. So fucking proud. When I saw him tackle you..." He buries his head in my hair. "Fuck, I was scared. But you got him. You stopped him without any help. You had him."

Gavin leaves to meet the police.

"He lied," I sob. "I didn't even know him when I was fifteen. He never touched me that way—"

"I know, baby. I know, I believe you. I'm sorry. *Jesus*—I'm so fuckin' sorry. I shouldn't have left you in the parking lot, shouldn't have accused you in the car. I didn't mean it, I was stupid and angry—"

"It's okay. I don't want to talk about it now. I just need you to hold me. Please, keep holding me."

"I've got you, baby. I've got you, you're safe, we're safe."

He rocks us back and forth, buried in each other's arms.

I ask if he's hurt and he says no. We agree to talk about what happened later when we're both calm. At some point he takes off his jacket and puts it around me.

An ambulance arrives and the EMTs get Frank on a stretcher. The cops ask for statements and I hear Gavin explain the restraining order I have on Frank and that he just got out of jail for violating it two months ago. He says that Damian is my boyfriend and that he's had to get Frank away from me before.

Then Kiley explains how he and Gavin were together when the private company hired to watch Frank called and said they'd lost track of him. They immediately came here to watch the apartment and check on me. When they pulled up, they saw Damian and Frank fighting.

Our apartment's security guard gives her statement next, saying she went to check on Damian when he didn't reappear in the lobby. She says something about pulling security footage from the parking lot then heads toward the building with an officer.

Gavin comes to get us when it's time for us to give our statements.

Damian and I huddle together when we explain what happened. It takes about twenty minutes but it feels like hours.

The female officer pulls me aside to take pictures of my injuries. Almost as soon as I slip off Damian's jacket, tears want to slip from my eyes.

I blink them away.

It's not the loss of the jacket, but what everyone can now see. The bruises rapidly blooming on my chest, neck and face—the rip in my dress. A piece of fabric hangs awkwardly down the front exposing a thin slice of shoulder. I'm still completely covered, but it's *the way* it looks that bothers me. The evidence of what Frank tried to do.

The officer photographs every inch of me. I feel exposed, on display, vulnerable. I want to hide in Damian's jacket and arms. I feel ashamed and I don't know why.

"Marrin," the officer says when she's done. "It wasn't your fault."

I almost burst into tears. But don't. Instead, I nod my head because that's *exactly* how I feel. Like this was all somehow my fault. Like I did something wrong. I feel like a non-person. A body to be exposed beneath a torn dress.

The unfairness of it claws at me. The knowledge that most men walking around are capable of overpowering me. It's humiliating and infuriating in a way I can't describe. To have that power taken. Stolen.

But Frank didn't take anything from me because I won't let him.

Two years ago after he attacked me, I lost my peace of mind and my sense of self. I was left broken and partial, damaged and scarred. I couldn't see myself outside the boxes I'd allowed his attack to put me in: *white trash, worthless, weak.* Coupled with what happened with my mom, those labels defined me, made me unwilling to trust, unable to move on.

But after tonight, I realize I am not a non-person. I'm not just a body. I am a whole person who just kicked a grown man's ass. I'm smart and strong. I am not the sum total of my body or what happens to it. I get to decide how I see myself and how I move on.

Tonight scared the hell out of me. I was once again confronted with the ugly truth about what it means to live in a patriarchal society without the privilege of having been born a cisgendered man. And as scary as that is, I also learned that I can take care of myself. I didn't need anyone to save me.

I saved myself.

But I'm grateful Damian was there. He knows I didn't need his help, but he offered it anyway. And I wanted it, I welcomed it. Letting Damian take care of me isn't me handing over my power to him or showing weakness, it's me choosing an ally. Choosing to trust someone enough to let them help me when I need it, and when I'm too broken or weary to do it myself.

30

Damian

After the cops and EMTs leave, we trudge up to my apartment.

I take Marrin into my bathroom and set her on the edge of the tub. I thoroughly wash my bloody hands before grabbing three washcloths and a bottle of rubbing alcohol. I strip her dress and bra, tossing them into the trash because both have likely come into contact with Frank's blood. He told the EMTs he didn't have any bloodborne illnesses, but we're not taking any chances. We've already agreed to get tested before we have unprotected sex again.

Adulting—amiright?

Marrin's only real cut is on her lip, and surprisingly, I didn't cut my knuckles on Asshole's face. But all it takes is a speck of blood, carrying the right pathogen, to come into contact with an open wound or a mucous membrane (such as the ones located in the nose, eyelids, or mouth) and that's it. Pathogens can spread. I was right up in Frank's face when I hit him, and when I hauled him off Marrin, he'd been way too close to hers.

I dampen a washcloth in rubbing alcohol, then wipe up the blood from Marrin's neck and chest. I trash the cloth when I'm done and use the second one to clean the abrasion on her knee. I save the last one for the blood on her face.

"It smells horrible," she says.

"I know. I'm sorry."

When all the blood is gone from her skin, I stand her up and strip us both. Everything we're wearing goes into the trash. I turn on the shower and help her in.

Her elbows are scraped, her limbs are bruised, and her body is stiff. Still, I know she doesn't need my help, doesn't need me to tend her wounds or wash her body. *I* need to do these things for her. It's like a program I can't turn off. I think she knows it too because she lets me.

I put her under the hot water and start soaping her up. There's nothing sexual about it, just an uncontrollable need to care for her, to provide comfort, to make sure she's all right.

The Neanderthal in me fussing over his woman.

Maybe I'm overcompensating for the fact that she didn't need me to save her. Maybe I still feel guilty about our fight. Or maybe it's because I can't stop my brain from replaying the look on her face when I got to her and all the horrible things that could've gone wrong.

When I was abused, there was no one there to help me. No one to make me feel safe or comforted, or to tell me it wasn't my fault. I won't do that to Marrin. I won't let her feel isolated or ashamed or unsafe. She hates being out of control, so I take that burden away. I control the situation so she doesn't have to. And in doing that, I'm giving her what she needs and she's giving me what I need. Yes, that's part of our kink but it's also more than that. It's part of who we are and why we balance one another so well.

I soothe soapy hands over the bruises darkening her neck and shoulders. I move across her body carefully, watching her face for any sign of discomfort. Aware of each touch, each pang of anger I feel at the sight of a new bruise or scratch marring her skin.

I kiss each one.

She does the same for me. Washes me, cherishes me.

When we're done, I shampoo and condition her hair.

"I like washing your hair," I say.

"I think you just like touching my hair." She looks over a shoulder, a smile turning her lips.

An intense wave of satisfaction fills me because I helped put that smile there. Helped call it back to the surface.

"I do." I rinse her then pull her into my arms. We stay that way for a while. Feeling one another, safe in one another.

Eventually we get out. I dry and braid her hair, then dress her in one of my T-shirts and a pair of pajama pants that are way too big. I get an ice pack for her chin, then lay her on my bed and tuck her into my arms beneath the blankets.

I speak first. "I think I got mad because I knew you were right about my mom and I didn't want to face it. I'd accepted that I'd never get an apology from her, that she'd never acknowledge what she and my dad did, and what it did to me. But then Thanksgiving happened and then she called me and... I don't know. I'm sorry I yelled. I took my anger and confusion about this whole situation out on you and I shouldn't have. I'm so sorry. I'll work to do better next time."

"It's okay. I understand. I'm sorry, too. I should've told you about Nadia as soon as it happened and I didn't. I thought I was protecting you, but I see now why it was the wrong decision. I'm gonna work on that, too. Can I tell you a secret?"

"Always." I sweep my thumb across her cheekbone. We're lying on our sides, facing one another with our foreheads nearly touching.

"I still care about my mom. I try to deny it because I know it's stupid after everything that's happened—"

"It's not stupid."

"—but I can't. Two years ago when she called and said she'd changed, I believed her. I *wanted* to believe her. She calls the bar every year on Thanksgiving. I never answer because it's too public and what am I going to say to her? She gave birth to me and then she tried to get rid of me. And I still love her."

I hold her close. "I want you, Marrin. I'll keep you. I promise. I'll keep you forever or until you say when."

She wipes at a few tears. "I think when your mom approached me, I thought if you could reconcile with her, then maybe I could reconcile with my mom one day. Again, really stupid way to see—"

"That's not stupid. Not stupid at all. Being angry is easy. But forgiveness, letting go, letting people back in... that's hard. And after what Frank said tonight..."

Frank told her he'd manipulated her mother somehow. It falls in line with what her mom's defense team argued when the case went to trial. I can't imagine how confusing and painful Frank's admission must be for Marrin. To know that her mom might have actually changed and that Frank's actions ruined it for both of them.

"You know what I was thinking?" Marrin says. "I was thinking that maybe when my mom gets out in a few years, if I'm ready, I could talk to her in a controlled setting. Like a therapist's office or something. That way someone trained in mediating these things is present. Maybe you and Nadia could try that. Not today or soon, but if you ever want to talk to her. That way she won't blindside you like she did at dinner."

I smile. "That's a brilliant idea. What did I ever do to deserve you?"

Her phone vibrates on the nightstand and she wiggles away to check it.

"Alice again?" I ask.

"No, it's Kiley. He says Frank's lab work came back negative. We don't need to worry about getting tested."

"Thank fuck," I groan in relief. She curls back up next to me. I pause on a thought. "Question. What exactly does Kiley do that he'd have access to that kind of information? What does Alice do that she'd employ someone like him?" The question has been nagging me for months.

"Honestly? I have no idea. I don't ask. I know what you mean, though. Alice is weird about cops, she runs several businesses that cater to rich clientele, she retains a concierge doctor and a driving service that will pick you up whenever and wherever, no questions asked."

"Not to mention she had a tail on Frank and hired a bodyguard for you."

"That too."

"She isn't, like, in the mafia or something is she?" I remember when Alice and Gavin showed up at my door ready to break it down if I didn't let them in.

"I don't know. I figure the less I know, the better."

"Seems reasonable."

"Damian?" she says, propping herself up on an elbow.

"Yeah, baby?"

She traces my jaw with her fingers. "Thank you. For not

running away after you learned how messed up my life is. And for not giving up on me. For saving me."

She's not talking about Frank.

"You're welcome." I brush a thumb along her bottom lip. "Thank you for putting up with me. For trusting me with your secrets and for letting me trust you with mine."

I push up and kiss her quietly. Her fingers weave into my hair and her mouth follows mine back down to the pillow. I pull her to me, cording my arms around her waist. She mewls into my mouth and I answer by sliding a hand beneath her shirt and palming a bare breast.

She's warm and soft.

My thumb traces circles over her skin, smaller and smaller until the pad rolls over her peaked nipple. Another small noise escapes her mouth.

"What do you want, Mar?" I whisper between kisses.

She presses my hand to her chest, feeling where I cup her. "I want you to touch me. To make love to me. *Please*."

It's the last breathy word that gets me. I move over her body, caging it with my own.

I love the sight of her in my clothes. My T-shirt hangs loosely around her, rippling with each soft jiggle of her breasts—I toss it to the floor. My pajama pants rumple around her hips, there's something endearing in the way the drawstring keeps them from falling—they find the floor, too.

I sit back, pulling the covers with me. She's gloriously bare before me. Skin marred by scars and bruises but no less lovely.

I strip my shirt, my pants, my briefs. A small, warm hand strokes my erection, tugging me toward the bed. I follow it down to Marrin. Easing myself over her and holding my weight in my elbows. She smells like citrus and soap. I trace her body with a hand. Her full, warm breasts. Her tight, soft stomach. The bank of curls that lead to her sex. I cup her there with a hand as I kiss her mouth, careful of her lip.

She angles my cock toward her entrance, legs spreading wide, giving me access and entry. Inviting me to share her body.

"Not yet," I whisper, kissing a path down to the sensitive skin below and around her ear.

I ghost my hand over her inner lips, feeling how swollen her clit has become. The touch is slight, but enough to make her hips rock. Enough to make her hum a moan deep in her throat. Her body is an instrument I alone have the privilege of playing. The privilege of plucking and strumming, of using to compose a song for only my ears to hear.

She swirls her thumb around the wetness at the tip of my cock. I swirl a finger around the wetness at the center of her. I moan into her neck at both the feel of her hand on me and the wetness that calls from between her legs.

"This is for me," I murmur with a kiss. "This is mine. You're mine. Always. I'll never let you go, Marrin." I sink myself deep inside her, pressing her thighs open with my hips. "I want you for a lifetime."

Her eyes grow wide at my words and my intrusion—the exquisite pleasure of us. Her mouth falls open in time with mine and words are lost to her. She nods her agreement as she welcomes me inside her, cradling me with her body.

I hold her beneath me. Rocking into her, disappearing into her, descending into her. Over and over and over again.

Our rhythm is slow, languid. Our kisses deep and savoring.

"I love you," I whisper.

"You're mine," I whisper.

"I'll marry you someday," I whisper.

"Yes," she breathes. "Yes, yes, *yes.*"

We come apart at the same time. Her body tightening around mine, mine around hers. Her name leaves my lips —*over and over and over again*—as I empty myself inside her —*over and over and over again*. And when it's all over I know she's taken a hell of a lot more from me than my release. Know I've given a hell of a lot more than that, too.

She's taken everything from me. I've *given* everything to her. My heart, my soul, my future. She can have it all because I don't want any of it without her.

31

Marrin

I lean back onto the hot hood of Damian's Jeep, soaking in the sun. It's the third week of May and classes are over. We're officially seniors. The thought is mind-boggling. The fact that I'm going to graduate on time next year is mind-boggling. I've been busting my ass taking extra classes and summer school ever since I had to throw away my first semester of college because of everything that happened on Thanksgiving.

Everything is falling into place.

I pull my phone from my shorts and check the time. Not quite three in the afternoon. I go back to soaking up the sun.

Frank is going to prison. Stupid bastard. The charges were upped when the cops found a roll of duct tape, a hunting knife, and a brick of cocaine in his car. I don't think about what the tape and knife might have been used for and the cops are convinced he'd intended to distribute the drugs. Doesn't matter now, though. I won't be running into him for a while. The case hasn't gone to court yet, but Alice says the FBI is getting involved because of the cocaine. As it stands, he's facing at least twenty years, but if they can link him to big drug traffickers, then he's looking at life.

Fine by me.

My phone vibrates.

Damian: *Coming down now. Really need you.*
Marrin: *I'm out front with the Jeep.*

I sit up and hop off the vehicle's hood. I drove Damian to his appointment today then ran some errands. I've been happily waiting in the sunshine for about fifteen minutes.

The door to the office building opens and Damian walks out. I wave an arm as he scans the parking lot. He spots me and makes a beeline.

I can tell how upset he is before he even gets close. His head is down, his shoulders stiff. I stand on the sidewalk, arms open.

"What happened?" I say.

He doesn't answer, just pulls me into a massive hug, burying his face in my neck.

I hold him, rubbing a hand over his back.

"Today was hard," he finally says.

"I'm sorry, baby. Do you want to talk about it?"

He inhales deeply, squeezing me once. The tension in him seems to ease. "Not right now."

"Okay."

"Mmm. You're nice and hot."

"I've been laying on the Jeep's hood."

He huffs a laugh, but doesn't release me. "I have another appointment tomorrow. Just me this time."

"To talk about what happened today?"

He nods into my neck.

"That bad?"

He nods again.

When he speaks next, I can hear the anguish in his voice. "She said... she said my father abused her. Not physically, but emotionally. Says that's why she didn't do more, why she drank so much."

"How did that make you feel?"

He shrugs. "I don't know. *I don't know.*" His breath shudders. "Confused. Pissed. Angry."

"Did you feel like she meant it as an excuse?"

"No. Not at the time. It was just an explanation she gave for her behavior. She didn't say it like I was supposed to feel bad for her or give her a free pass. But... I don't know what to think."

"It's okay." I lean back to look at him. "You don't have to decide right now. You don't have to decide at all. You're allowed to be confused." I kiss his cheek. He nods. "Let's go to the Braxton, I'll let you try and beat me at *Realm Quest.*"

A smile crashes over his face. "Oh, you will, will you?"

"Mhmm." I squeal as he hauls me off my feet into another hug.

Before he puts me down, I notice Nadia walking out of the office building. Her eyes land on us for a second and she briefly holds my gaze. Then she turns away, heading for her car.

Damian and I get into his Jeep and drive away.

He's been seeing a therapist with his mother for a few weeks now. Things are rocky, but at least they're both trying. I'm not sure where it will go or if a reconciliation is even possible, but I'm here to support him regardless.

Just as he's here to support me.

My mom won't be released for another five years, but I've been talking to a therapist about her, about everything. I think if Damian can sit in a room with his mother, and try to heal the wounds between them, then maybe I can try and do the same. Maybe I can work on my confidence and insecurities... and one day pick up the phone when my mom calls.

Damian and I are both scarred, both marred by things from our pasts. But just because we couldn't control the things that happened to us, doesn't mean we can't control the way we survive. How we move on.

The scars we carry don't devalue us, or make us less than, or *other*. Not if we don't allow them to. They are proof of the battles we've fought and won, and of the battles we've fought and lost. We carry the victories as well as the defeats. Show them equally, proudly.

Our scars are proof of our strengths.

The wounds that lay between my mother and I may never fully heal, might always leave a scar. But I don't mind the scars.

My scars led me to Damian, and his led him to me.

YOU'VE JUST FINISHED ADORE'S FIRST BOOK!

You've just finished my first EVER published novel (screams!). *Would you please leave a review for this book?* Any and all are greatly appreciated. You can leave one on Goodreads or the place where you purchased this title—or both if you're feeling generous!

SEXUAL ASSAULT RESOURCES

"Every 98 seconds, an American is sexually assaulted. And every 8 minutes, that victim is a child." —RAINN

Sexual assault knows no boundaries or limitations. It does not discriminate against sex, gender, age, race, ethnicity, religion, socioeconomic status—*anything*. There are no lines of which it does not cross. It is not always violent, for sometimes it is quiet. It is not always overt, for sometimes it is manipulative, subtle. It is not always committed by a stranger, for most often it's a family member, a friend—someone we trust. It can happen to anyone, can be committed by anyone...

And no matter the circumstances, if you are a survivor, **I believe you.** You deserve compassion. You deserve to be heard. And you deserve help.

If you or someone you know is a survivor of sexual assault, please know that when you are ready, there are people waiting to listen and help you.

RAINN - Rape, Abuse and Incest National Network

www.rainn.org
www.rainn.org/es

National Sexual Assault Hotline (Free. Confidential. 24/7.)
    Call: 800-656-HOPE
    Chat Online: https://hotline.rainn.org/online/

Loveisrespect - Love is respect
    https://www.loveisrespect.org/
    http://espanol.loveisrespect.org/
    Call: 1-866-331-9474
    TTY: 1-866-331-8453
    Text: LOVEIS TO 22522

READY FOR ELLE AND CONOR'S STORY?

She moved into his house... then into his heart.

Coming July 16, 2019

Elle Lee is on the run—hiding from her ex and his family. After secretly moving to the other side of the country, she wants nothing more than to stay shielded behind the carefully constructed armor that's kept her, and her secrets, safe all these years.

But when she befriends Conor—the strong, quiet guard who works security for the mysterious Alice Braxton—she finds herself wanting to step out from behind her armor and experience life again.

Conor Kahele is a protector—always has been, always will be. So when timid Elle gets a job at the Braxton Arcade, he can't help but watch out for her. They become fast friends and when Elle finds herself with little money and no place to live, Conor is unable to stop himself from asking her to move in.

Platonically, of course.

But friendship goes out the window the more they learn about one another, and soon Conor finds himself agreeing to take Elle's virginity. What neither agreed to was giving the other their heart.

While people from Elle's past hunt her, demons from Conor's past haunt him. If he can guard her heart, Conor just might save them both. But if he fails, if he goes too far, he might become the very thing that stalks them.

<u>Buy Guarding Her Heart (Braxton Arcade Book Two</u>)

ACKNOWLEDGMENTS

Here goes my attempt at thanking all the kick ass people who helped me get this book into your hands.

To my manfriend, thank you for supporting my dreams, for being weird with me, and for being the only person who can say, "*I don't think we should eat pizza four nights in a row,*" to my face and live to tell about it. You are my person for life and I love you.

To Tatyana W., you are the best fucking writing friend I could've asked for. You are The Reason I finally got my shit together and started writing down the stories that were haunting me. We survived Paola, we survived that creepy misogynist in our creative writing class, and one day we'll survive book tours and people knowing our names.

To Rachel D., you were the first person to read this book and your enthusiasm, feedback, and knowledge of kink and fetish has been invaluable. You are, and will always remain, one of the best things that has ever happened to me.

To Abigail A. (aka The Ultimate Lesbian), we met in a prop shop when we were just two nerds trying to survive college, gender norms and fandoms. You approached this book thoughtfully, objectively, and with the mindset that not all characters are perfect and that it's okay. Your advice about feminism, inclusion, and Damian (LOL) have been invaluable and I could never thank you enough.

To Rachael and April, for getting drunk with me that cold November day when we had to confront the truth about our place in the world, in history, and that sometimes the bad guys win. Thank you for keeping my secret and for giving me the chance to chase it.

To my parents, for pretending they didn't know my secret, and for everything. You deserve a bigger mention than this, but I'm saving it for a different page in a different book.

To my friends. There are too many of you to name, but I'd like to highlight: Shannon O., for quality texts, conversations, and for keeping me sane. Rubi, for Russian adventures, being thoughtful, and for that elaborate "Black Tip" headcanon I still think should be a comic book. Caity and Meg-o, for all the years of quality friendship, for being there when I needed you, and for every angsty song you introduced me to in high school. My love of angst owes you both a life debt. Navid, Chelsea G. and Vinny, for quality friendship and conversations, for always lending me an artist's eye when I need a second opinion, (and Navid for helping save me from my lack of Photoshop skills!). Ashley O., for being the first person to introduce me as a writer. Ced Linus, for random chats about chasing dreams and getting it done— no excuses. Sunny, for being floofally and sweet, and Sophie, for being a loaf.

To Dr. Hillis, for film noir talks in a basement room with a checkered floor in an old, crumbling building. I remember everything you taught me. I SWEAR. This book (and how it engages with film noir) is 100% me picking and choosing what I wanted to use because it served the plot. It is in no way meant to be an overview of the movement. I just wanted to hint at those things and use a little of what you taught me because your class was/is one of my forever favorites, and I could never thank you enough for all that you've taught me.

To Braxton, you're a goddamn badass and I could never

thank you enough for all that you shared with me—including that Taylor Swift album I wanted to hate, but ended up loving. You are an inspiration and I will take what you've shared with me to the grave. (P.S. Remember when you said I couldn't work in references to Swift songs? Eat your goddamn heart out. P.S.S. Yes, I named the arcade after you.)

To Kareem, Micki, and everyone I ever met or shared a game with at the Baxter Arcade. Thank you for welcoming me into your lives, for getting nerdy with me, and for showing me all those combinations I never would've figured out on my own. This book was born from every late night and drunk day we shared, and every high score we chased. (Oh and shoutout to Jeff for letting me pick your brain about arcade guts!)

To Nikki L., for teaching me self defense in the middle of a crowded living room at an apartment party I wasn't invited to.

A huge thank you to my Tumblr family. There are too many of you to name, but this book is a direct result of the confidence you gave me, the community you welcomed me into, and the amazing things you shared with me and let me share with you. You loved this story long before it was finished and when it was trying to be something it was not. Thank you for reading the first two chapters and for understanding and supporting me when I confessed I couldn't finish it as it was because the characters were all wrong and the story I wanted to tell just wasn't working. This is not the story that has lived with me the longest, but it is one that has haunted me since I spent my days in a prop shop and my nights at an arcade. It deserved a better life than what I was prepared to give it and each and every one of you helped me see that. To honor you, I may have left a few hints here and there if you know where to look (wink-wink).

To Mel, for being fuckin' brilliant, for hooking me up (you know what I'm talking about!), and for letting me vent to you about life and books and whatever the hell else I have on my mind.

To Erika, for being a peach and sharing smutty head-canons with me, and for letting me bombard you with ideas while I was trying to flesh out this book.

To Tess and Irelis, for being complete and utter trash with me. Your nudes are in the mail.

To Brittanie Smith, Diane Rinella and Lexxie Couper, for all your help and advice and for messaging me back. You have no idea how nervous I was showing up or hitting send, nor do you have any idea how many people I'd reached out to looking for help and who never reached back. Thank you both for your kindness and for sharing your time and knowledge with me.

To all the authors I met on FB who showed me kindness, helped answer my questions or let me rubberneck off theirs.

To Natasha Snow, for designing a kick ass cover and for not murdering me when I emailed you a billion times asking for separate files. I promise to have my shit together next time.

To Nancy Smay, Lisa LaPaglia and Becca Mysoor, you were the fairy godparents of this book and I could never thank you enough for all your edits and feedback.

To Dani at Studio Dodge (aka my preferred vagina artist), you brought my ridiculous idea for a logo to life and I could not be more happy!

To all the bloggers, the readers and reviewers, for taking a chance on me. Thank you for letting me share this book with you. You may have loved it, you may have hated it, but you set aside your time to read it and for that I will be forever grateful.

To my nosy neighbors, I will never ever tell you what I do for a living or why you never see me outside (Hint: I'm avoiding you).

LET'S STAY IN TOUCH

Facebook: @AdoreIan
Instagram: @Adore_Ian
Twitter: @Adore_Ian

For more news, updates, and for newsletter and ARC team
sign up, please visit: www.AdoreIan.com

ABOUT THE AUTHOR

Adore Ian grew up in a mixed race family in Hawaii and has loved steamy romance novels ever since finding a Harper paperback discarded on the sidewalk when she was a kid. She's a proud dyslexic, an intersectional feminist-in-progress, and a lover of standard poodles. She lives with her manfriend on the east coast where she spends too much time bunny watching and not enough time writing. She believes the ingredients to good romance are too much smut, quality fluff and angst, and a dash of guerrilla sex ed. Her novels are best enjoyed with a slice of pizza and an ice cold beer.

Join her in the trash can. #iAdoreRomance

For more books and updates:
www.AdoreIan.com

COPYRIGHT